PT BOATS

Terrors of the Pacific

PT BOATS

Terrors of the Pacific

GERRY FELD

OTHER TITLES BY GERRY FELD

A Journey into War, Published 2017
A Soldier's Final Journey, Published 2019
Vietnam; Honor and Sacrifice, Published *2020*
Sarah Rosenbaum's Dachau Redemption, Published 2021

CONTENTS

Preface...9

Acknowledgments 11

Information on PT Boats and Their Areas of Operation.........12

Chapter 1: Air Raid Pearl Harbor.....................................15

Chapter 2: A New Beginning 36

Chapter 3: Panama Canal...58

Chapter 4: Noumea, New Caledonia.................................65

Chapter 5: Tulagi..75

Chapter 6:Everything Goes Wrong...................................94

Chapter 7: Fire on the Water..114

Chapter 8: The Pilot Returns...121

Chapter 9: The 120 Boat...131

Chapter 10: Traitor 151

Chapter 11: Swenson Bellington 156

Chapter 12: Convoy's and Targets..................................164

Chapter 13: Fleeing from Manila 185

Chapter 14: Goodbye Rendova 198

Chapter 15: A Golden Find..223

Chapter 16: The Enemy isn'T Dead................................244

Chapter 17: The Philippines...255

Chapter 18: Island Fever 269

Chapter 19: Moving Closer to Tokyo 293

Chapter 20: Lingayan Gulf...310

Chapter 21: The Chase..322

Chapter 22: Luzon 334

Chapter 23: As Good As New 348

Chapter 24: Endings and Beginnings 387

Epilogue..403

Notes: Filipino Rebels 407

Diagrams and Maps 409

PREFACE

I was eleven years old when I read the book, PT-109, by Robert J. Donovan for the first time. The story documenting the exploits of President John F. Kennedy as a PT Boat Commander in the Pacific War absolutely enthralled me.

However, when the movie arrived on the big screen in 1963, my love affair with PT Boats really began in earnest. I started searching for any information I could find, and purchased several more books on PT operations during World War Two.

For Christmas of 1963, the only thing I asked for was a plastic model of PT-109. I spent countless hours carefully assembling it. It became the pride of my World War Two ship fleet.

Several years ago, JoAnn and I visited the PT Boat Museum at Battleship Cove in Fall River Massachusetts. Along with many wonderful displays and artifacts, they have PT Boats 796 and 617 on display, in a temperature and humidity-controlled building. It was a wonderful experience and well worth visiting. Of course the main feature of Battleship Cove is the U.S.S. Massachusetts, BB59. If you should get to Battleship Cove, make sure you have at least four to six hours if you want to tour everything they have on display.

However, through my research, I have sadly found that only about half of the baby boomers I have spoken with still remember the story of PT-109, and most of them don't even remember what the boat looked like. Needless to say, very few people I speak with under the age of fifty have any idea what a PT boat is, or what valuable service they performed during World War Two.

So, to enlighten people as to what these marvelous vessels added to the war, I decided to put together a story of PT Boat action in the South Pacific during World War Two. All the bases I use are factual, as are some of the raids the boats actually went on. Of course I have used literary license to enhance the story, while creating characters and incidents that will keep readers interested right up to the very end. I hope you enjoy, "PT BOATS; TERRORS OF THE PACIFIC."

ACKNOWLEDGMENTS

Of course my interest in PT boats could never have taken root if my parents had not taken me to the PT-109 movie, and purchased my model for Christmas. Although they have both since passed, I think they would be shocked to see how my studying every facet of World War Two has turned into a life-long passion.

I would like to thank my wife JoAnn for supporting my desire to spend the hours at my computer writing and researching material for my books. Although she knew very little about PT boats, it was fun running ideas by her to get her reaction. It was no surprise that many times she came up with interesting questions I then realized had to be answered in my story.

Of course I need to thank all of the World War Two Veterans I spoke with over the years that have now since passed. The stories and experiences they shared with me, provide a wealth of information to draw from. May God Bless them all!

INFORMATION ON PT BOATS AND THEIR AREAS OF OPERATION

The biggest myth about PT Boats is that they were made from plywood. Although plywood was used in many internal spaces of the boats, it was not used in the hull. The hulls were constructed of two layers of mahogany planking, separated by a sheet of water proof canvas. The planking was screwed into the large wooden skeletal frame with brass screws to prevent corrosion. The larger Elco class boat was built by Elco electric boat works in Bayonne, New Jersey. The Higgins class boats were built by the Higgins boat works in New Orleans, Louisiana.

PT boats were powered by three Packard V-12 engines that were converted from aircraft usage. They gave the boats an awesome 4,500 shaft horsepower, allowing them to reach a top speed of 43 knots. Each boat had three fuel tanks holding 3,000 gallons of highly explosive 100 octane aviation fuel. Running at their top speed of 43 knots with the engines turning 3000 rpm, a PT boat consumed 500 gallons per hour and covered just 120 miles in just a six-hour period of time. At their cruising speed of 23 knots, with the engines turning 2000 rpm, the boats were more economical. The three engines would burn just 198 gallons per hour, or 66 gallons an hour per engine, and could cover roughly 520 miles over a 12-hour period. The boats weighed 121,000 pounds or more, depending on what weapon configurations were adapted to the boats throughout the war. Pound for pound, PT boats were the most heavily armed vessels afloat during World War Two. Each boat had six mufflers, two for each engine. They could be adjusted with a switch, allowing the exhaust to flow freely, or they could be turned on, allowing the exhaust to flow down a pipe into the water a short distance for quiet operations at night near islands. It gave the boats a mellow bubbly sound when they were idling.

During my story I refer to the slot on many occasions during the fighting in the Solomon Islands. The slot is a narrow band of water 217 miles long, officially named New Georgia Sound. Guadalcanal is on the extreme southeast end, with Bougainville on the northwest. Six major islands and over nine hundred smaller islands dot the sides of the channels open water, thus giving it the unofficial name of the slot. There are many channels, straits, and gulfs that separate islands in the Solomon Chain. Most of them have shallow sand bars, large coral reefs and rock piles that were not charted up until World War Two. There are also several smaller groups of islands in the chain such as the Russell Islands, The Florida Islands and New Georgia Islands.

PT boats primarily operated out of two islands early in the war. The smaller base was on the Island of Tulagi, which was located in the Florida Islands just northwest of Guadalcanal.

The larger and more modern base was located on the Island of Rendova in the New Georgia Islands. There was also a base on Rennell Island southeast of Guadalcanal, that contained heavy repair shops for PT boats and other small landing craft. Rennell also had a PT base for conducting patrols in the southern approaches to the Solomon Islands. Crew members varied on the boats depending on what weapon systems were deployed, but the average crew was thirteen to seventeen men.

Prior to the war, many of the islands were basically owned by large American, British and Dutch fruit companies, where they had large plantations for pineapples, coconuts and other fruits. Some plantations had factories for producing oils and other fruit by-products. Companies that owned these plantations were driven out by the Japanese as they invaded the islands, and most never returned.

Christian missionaries operated on islands throughout the Solomon's, trying to convert the natives to Christianity, and stop plantation owners from abusing the local tribes. Most missionaries were known to have powerful shortwave radios that were used many times to call in downed planes and damaged allied boats. Incredibly, during World War Two, many tribes were still cannibalistic, and known to be head hunters, much to the dismay of many Japanese soldiers.

Reading my story, you will also hear me talk about Coast Watchers. Australia and New Zealand had set up a well-organized group of coast watchers, throughout the South Pacific islands. They worked well with the local natives and had powerful radios that were used to transmit information on Japanese ship movements, supply convoys and aircraft operations. They also worked incredibly well with the PT bases, giving information as to where they could retrieve damaged boats or pick up stranded crew members. Australian coast watchers nicknamed the boats Peter Tare's, and used that call sign when referring to them. As the war moved, so did the coast watchers. They moved from island to island, or from one side of the island to another, depending on Japanese troop movements. If a coast watcher was captured, it meant certain torture and death.

Many naval men referred to the sleek, fast, and highly maneuverable PT boats as Mosquito Boats, the Japanese referred to them simply as Devil Boats.

Diagrams of PT boats and island drawings are available in the Note section, in the back of the book.

CHAPTER 1
AIR RAID PEARL HARBOR

The western sky over the dark blue waters of the Pacific Ocean was painted brilliantly with pastel shades of yellow, oranges and red, as the sun dipped behind the low hanging puffy cumulus clouds. The banyan trees on Ford Island, just fifty yards away from battleship row, rustled gently as the moderate trade winds created a perfect tropical evening at Pearl Harbor.

Across the main channel of the harbor, the lights of Honolulu glimmered like diamonds in the gathering darkness. From time to time, the winds allowed sounds from the battle of the bands taking place at Block Arena, to drift out over the harbor. Tonight, bands from each of the eight battleships berthed in the harbor, were vying for bragging rights in front of hundreds of sailors, each hoping to be judged best band in the fleet.

Along Kapiolani and Ala Moana Boulevards, sailors and marines ducked in and out of bars enjoying the night life and the soothing Polynesian music. The beaches at Waikiki were filled with tourists staying in the high-class hotels, and the families of men stationed at the many military bases around Oahu. It appeared as if no one had a care in the world. What could possibly go wrong in a paradise like Hawaii?

At Opana Point on the north side of the island, soldiers manned the new radar system that should give ample warning if any aircraft attempted to fly into Hawaiian airspace. To the east of Oahu, the destroyer U.S.S. Ward was patrolling the restricted waters of the Pacific Ocean leading into Pearl Harbor. The only other ship in the vicinity was the naval tug U.S.S. Antares.

All was quiet at 2345hrs on December 6, 1941, and that was just the way Lt. jg Brian (Buzz) Maddox liked it, as he strolled slowly along the aft deck of the U.S.S. Oklahoma with a hot cup of coffee in his hand. He had drawn duty tonight but really didn't care, as the ship had been mostly quiet since1600hrs when passes were handed out. True, it would get a bit rowdy in the next few hours as way too many drunken sailors arrived back to the ship, but many of them would just find a place on deck to lay down and sleep it off, without causing problems in the berthing compartments. Buzz had come to know many of the men aboard the Oklahoma, and found most of them to be fun loving kids that never caused serious problems. Many of them had joined the navy out of desperation during the depression, simply because finding a job back on main street just wasn't possible.

Buzz had been assigned to the Oklahoma as a gunnery officer just six months ago, after graduating from Annapolis. The men in his division were first rate gunners and scored high in every training program set up by the Captain.

It could be said that Maddox was worlds apart from the enlisted crews he would command in the navy. He grew up in a family of great wealth in Kennebunkport, Maine, sheltering him from the true experiences of the depression years.

His mother, Mary Drumond Maddox, grew up in Portland, Maine, in a family that derived their fortune from timber, railroads, and shipping. They were a rather stoic family, preferring to live the life of quiet high society. The family made no excuses when they traveled to Boston or New York City to attend social functions in their private rail cars.

Buzz's father Alfred, and his grandfather Ephraim, had built one of the largest fishing fleets, and cannery operations on the east coast. Although the Maddox family had amassed a rather large fortune, they continued as a somewhat humble family, always helping out employees and friends that fell upon hard times.

It was a complete shock to the Drumond family when Mary decided to marry a fisherman, and move to Kennebunkport to raise a family. The only really good thing they saw about her move south, was that it was on the rail line heading for Boston.

Alfred and Mary had three sons and a daughter. Josh the oldest, was totally invested in the fishing fleet, and loved every minute of his work. Carl, the second oldest, had attended Princeton, but kept his nose in the family business until he decided what he really wanted to do with his life, and was known to be a bit of a playboy with the girls. Brian the youngest, loved nothing better than being out at sea. He loved the challenges of the open ocean, the creatures that lived in it, and became a first rate boat handler in all types of weather. He earned his nickname Buzz, when he was two years old. He decided to knock down a beehive from a tree with a stick, and had been stung over fifty times. Every time someone inquired as to what had happened, he would wave his little arms as if he were swatting bees and yell out, "Buzz, buzz, buzz." His older brothers began calling him Buzz as a joke, but it wasn't long before he started to tell people his name was Buzz Maddox.

The last child in the family was a petite, pretty blonde girl named Jolene. Her brothers made her life a pure hell, as they drove off any boy who showed interest in her they disliked, which turned out to be pretty much every boy in Kennebunkport. Although she loved her brothers very much, she was very happy when she finally went off to college at Rutgers.

Tensions began to build among the family as neither Josh or Carl wanted to get their hands dirty doing the heavy maintenance required to keep the fleet operating. They preferred handling office work, sales contracts, or simply skippering the boats. On a Friday afternoon in February of 1937, Buzz walked into the office of Griffin Fisheries, heading straight for his father's office. Seeing his father on the phone, he quietly walked into the office and sat down.

Hanging up the phone, Alfred smiled at his youngest son, realizing that something was not right. Leaning back in his chair he asked, "Well, did you figure out what was wrong with the hoist on the San Maria?"

Buzz nodded his head. "Yes, I did. The large pulley up in the rigging got bent somehow. The crew and I put in a new pulley assembly and it works like a charm. We also put a new rope on it while we were at it."

Alfred looked pleased as he studied his son's face. "Tell me, Brian, what's going on in that mind of yours. I've noticed something has been bothering you for a while now."

Buzz sat forward in the chair. "Dad, I love you very much, so I don't want to upset you. But I really can't do this anymore. I'm tired of all the long nights and little to no help from Josh and Carl. Last year I put in to attend Annapolis, and I just received my acceptance paperwork today."

After handing the letter to his father, Buzz continued. "I know this won't go over well with you and mother, but this is what I want to do."

Without saying a word, Alfred handed back the papers before walking out of the office. From there, everything within the family went downhill for Buzz. By April, he was so upset with the way he was being treated, he quit the business, moved out of the house, and found a cramped apartment just a few blocks from Annapolis, where he spent the summer working on a wharf, rebuilding engines on fishing boats.

Annapolis appealed to Buzz in a big way. He loved the pageantry and history of the school, and all the rules and regulations that made young men into Naval officers.

Upon graduation, Buzz was assigned to the Fleet Gunnery School in San Diego California. He loved learning how to operate everything from a standard machine gun to the massive sixteen-inch guns on battleships that were just beginning to join the fleet. Buzz had learned so quickly, the school kept him on board for several more months as an instructor.

Along with his promotion to Lt. jg, (junior grade), Buzz was handed orders to fill a gunnery officer job aboard the U.S.S. Oklahoma, stationed at Pearl Harbor, Hawaii. As tensions rose with Japan, it was clear that if a shooting war broke out, it was going to be somewhere in the Pacific, and Buzz wanted to be part of it.

But tonight as Buzz walked across the well-groomed teak deck of the Oklahoma, war really did not appear to be just over the horizon as many politicians predicted. At Pearl, most officers had not heard a word about the Japanese ship movements that would affect the fleet in just under twelve hours, and there had been no submarine sightings in any of the approaches to the Hawaiian Islands, or around Midway Island nearly twelve hundred miles to the west. Nevertheless, Admiral Kimmel and his staff at Pacific Headquarters still believed the Japanese would need to be dealt with sooner than later, so serious training went on, week after week.

As Buzz reached the fantail of the ship, Ensign Lew Mancroft walked up to him. "Sir, I thought you would be going ashore tonight. I was surprised to see you stayed on board."

Buzz smiled as he looked up at the stars overhead. "Well, apparently Mr. Mancroft, you did not see the changes our blessed Commander made to the duty detail for the weekend. He gave me the late watch tonight, even though I had already volunteered for the morning watch tomorrow. But it's no big deal. If I would have had the night off, I just would have gone into the city and had a few beers, then rushed back to catch some sleep in order to be ready to go by 0730."

The Ensign laughed as he nodded his head. "Yeah, first watch can be a bitch if you're still hung over, especially if the bugler is missing the notes during reveille."

Buzz laughed as he shook his head. "Yeah Lew, I've done that a few times and learned my lesson. First watch for me means staying home the night before and staying sober. Staggering across the deck to morning flag raising just isn't a good thing to have on your fitness record."

Lew looked across the channel toward Honolulu. "Buzz, do you think there's going to be a war with Japan? It scares the hell out of me because we'll be right in the middle of it. Then all those men over there drinking and having a good time will be asked to lay their lives on the line and many of them will not live to understand what the hell is even happening."

Buzz turned to walk back toward the superstructure of the ship. "Some days I wish I knew, other days I'm glad I don't. I guess all we can do is take it one day at a time and train the men as best we can. The more prepared we are, the better our chances to survive. And with that my friend, I'm going to make my rounds and keep an eye out for rowdy drunks."

After making his rounds, Buzz stopped in his cabin for a few minutes to set out his uniform for the following morning. Although they were in port, most ship captains required watch officers on Sunday morning duty to be attired in their dress whites at least until noon.

Although the thought of war, and all his responsibilities of morning watch circled around inside his head, Buzz felt he was mentally prepared for whatever happened. He was sure he had learned enough and trained the men in his division well enough, that they could give the Japanese a good fight if it came down to that.

Despite Ensign Mancroft's worries, and all the problems that would be staring him in the face first thing in the morning, he knew that as of 1800hrs Sunday night, he was off until 0800 Tuesday morning. The crews that had torn up Honolulu all weekend would be confined to their ships for training, and the Oklahoma was not going out to sea until Wednesday, so Honolulu would be all his on a silver platter for a great time, minus several thousand men.

By dawn, after dealing with a few too many drunks returning from a long night out, Buzz returned to his cabin at 0635 to prepare for Sunday duty. After a quick shower and getting dressed, Buzz ducked into the officers mess for a breakfast of pancakes and sausage. Walking into the watch office at 0730, Buzz filled out the log book, signing off for December 6, 1941. After reading over messages from fleet headquarters, Buzz reached into a cabinet, removing the huge American flag that was raised over the stern of the ship during reveille. Walking out on deck he was happy to see the parade team, bugler and Ensign Mancroft standing by to hoist the flag at 0800hrs.

"Beautiful morning, Lieutenant," Chief Petty Officer Warrens stated with a smile.

"That it is Chief, let's make it a quiet day. Why spoil perfection," Buzz replied, as he handed over the flag.

As the Chief arranged the top hole on the flag, Buzz looked around the harbor. Light clouds drifted toward the south in front of a deep dark blue sky. The wind had picked up a bit during the night, allowing him to hear the light slap of the waves against the hull. Around the placid harbor, teams were assembling on the decks of every ship, preparing to raise their flags, as a small barge glided across the tranquil waters of the harbor.

After snapping the rope onto the top of the flag, Chief Warrens smiled. "Did you hear the band from the Arizona won the big battle of the bands last night at Block Arena? Except for the morning watch crew, the rest of the ship gets to sleep in this morning, the lucky bastards. What time is it Lieutenant? My watch is in my pocket."

Buzz smiled as he looked down at his watch, "It's 0748, we have twelve minutes left chief, make sure that flag unfurls smartly this morning, we don't need an ass chewing from the skipper again."

As the chief loosened up the flag, Buzz looked strangely to the north as the sound of aircraft engines broke the morning calm. "Chief, who the hell would have planes in the air this early on a Sunday morning before reveille. Must be the damn Army trying to make points again with Gen. Short."

A moment later Chief Warrens pulled the rope lose from the flag as he watched the first planes begin their dive on battleship row. Once his brain understood what was happening, he yelled, "Those aren't our planes, sir. Those are Japs!"

Before Buzz could react, he was knocked to the deck as the first of eight torpedoes slammed into the hull of the Oklahoma. Within minutes the tranquil harbor was alive with diving aircraft, massive explosions, flying shrapnel and deadly machine gun bullets, all along battleship row. The Oklahoma shuddered once, then twice, as another torpedo slammed into her exposed hull. Since they were not at war when the ships were tied up on battleship row, it had become a custom not to drop anti torpedo nets along their exposed hulls. Now the Japanese were taking full advantage of the careless practice.

Members of the band scrambled for safety, as Buzz ran for the communication shack, with the chief right behind him. Grabbing the microphone from the stunned radioman, Buzz called out, "General quarters, general quarters, all hands man your battle stations. This is no drill, repeat, this is no drill. Man your battle stations!" After making the announcement a second time, Buzz turned to run back out on deck but never made it, as a wall of flame and debris threw him back into the room. Within seconds a third torpedo ripped open a huge section of the big ship's hull, causing the monstrous vessel to begin listing out into the harbor. Dazed by the explosion, Buzz struggled to his feet as he yelled for the chief. But Chief Warrens would never respond. A huge metal plate flying through the air had struck the chief about waist high. All that was left of his senior non-commissioned officer was the lower half of his body.

After realizing the chief was gone and Ensign Mancroft was nowhere to be seen, Buzz prepared once again to step out the door onto the main deck, but stopped abruptly. Searing flames, nearly thirty feet high from the ruptured fuel bunks, created an impenetrable wall of flames. Quickly, Buzz backed into the office, pulling the heavy water tight door closed behind him, to keep flames from spreading to the interior of the ship. As he turned to run toward the main companion way, another massive explosion sent him tumbling across the deck, slamming him hard into a steel bulkhead. After standing up and recomposing his thought process, Buzz charged up the stairway around the corner, making his way toward an anti-aircraft battery that was part of his normal responsibilities. He saw two enlisted men standing by the 20mm gun but not firing the weapon

"What the hell is the matter with you guys, get that thing going!" Buzz screamed in anger.

"We would have sir, but a commander came by and told us if we broke the locks of the ready boxes, we would be court martialed, so we weren't sure what to do," one of the gunners replied.

Removing the axe from the wall near the fire hose, Buzz knocked off the locks on the ready boxes. Immediately, the men slammed ammunition into the waiting weapon as Buzz grabbed the controls.

Turning to his left, he watched a Japanese pilot aiming his aircraft skyward after dropping his torpedo. Buzz took quick aim and began firing as the plane flew up past the Oklahoma. The aircraft was so close, Buzz could see the smiling face of the pilot. However, the 20mm shells Buzz fired tore open the engine cowling. In seconds, the aircraft began to sputter as it rolled over, crashing into the harbor.

As it exploded, Buzz stopped firing and yelled. "Smile about that, asshole!"

Immediately, Buzz attempted to aim at a plane that was flying about ten feet off the water, but he couldn't get the gun to come up far enough to fire at it.

Looking at the two men, Buzz yelled, "We're going over, the ship is rolling onto its side. We need to get out of here or we'll be crushed. Get across the ship and hold onto the railing! Without hesitation, the men disappeared inside the ship with Buzz directly behind them. They followed the short companion way that exited out onto a platform on the starboard side of the ship.

As the Oklahoma began to roll faster, Buzz yelled at the men to crawl over the railing and begin climbing onto the side of the ship as it rose out of the water. All along the starboard side of the ship, men were attempting to do the same thing in order to save their lives.

The Oklahoma groaned and shuddered as water rushed in through her torn hull, allowing bulk heads to snap under pressure and collapse, trapping men throughout the stricken ship. Suddenly, what had been the ceiling was now the floor, stairways that led up, now led down to decks filled with water and floating bodies. Confused and wounded sailors struggled through the interior of the sinking ship, trying to find a way out of the pitch-black darkness. Watertight doors that had been dogged shut at the beginning of the attack no longer opened at all, as twisted bulk heads refused to allow the doors to operate, and still the water flowed higher, from deck to deck, filling compartment after compartment, trapping more helpless sailors.

Buzz and his two men were now scrambling up the side of the ship as the Oklahoma began to complete its deadly roll. Just as they reached the bottom of the ship, which was now facing skyward, a Japanese Zero strafed the deck where a large number of men were gathered.

Buzz screamed out in pain as a bullet ricocheted off the hull striking his left shoulder, causing him to lose his footing. With nothing to hold onto, and unable to keep his balance on the slimy hull, he slid back down off the ship, slamming against part of the mast which sent him spinning nearly sixty feet into the oil covered water below. Dazed and under water, Buzz struggled relentlessly to get away from all the ships rigging, radio cables, and large radar equipment that could very easily trap a man, ensuring that he would never regain the surface.

Making matters worse, Buzz was now covered with thick black oil, making it difficult for him to see what he was trying to do, and the tremendous impact upon entering the water had forced a sizable amount of oxygen from his lungs. Without getting a breath of fresh air soon, he knew full well his life was over. Seeing something above him, Buzz reached out with his right arm, grabbing onto a large wooden plank, finally allowing him to get his head above water.

His lungs burned as he attempted to suck in copious amounts of air that was filled with thick black smoke. There was no doubt in his mind that if he did not find refuge soon, he would quickly be overtaken and trapped by the swiftly moving burning oil. Scanning the surface of the water around him once more, all he could see were walls of raging orange flame and thick black smoke. He knew his best move would be to swim under the water and make his way out into the open channel of the harbor.

After taking several huge gulps of air, Buzz let go of the piece of wood dropping down below the surface of the harbor. The water around him was very hot as the burning oil above him on the surface created a deadly roar, that sounded as if he were trapped inside a volcano. With his lungs once again ready to explode, Buzz looked up to see clear water above him.

Surfacing well out into the harbor, he turned back toward battleship row to see men still scrambling across the bottom of the Oklahoma. Tremendous walls of orange flames cascaded across the harbor, fueled by thousands of gallons of black oil seeping from the damaged ships.

Hearing the sound of rushing water, Buzz turned toward his right to see the destroyer U.S.S. Monaghan charging down the channel, trying to make for the open ocean and escape the carnage. He knew if he did not get out of the channel quickly, he would be sucked into the propellers and be torn to shreds.

However, as Buzz swam back toward the flames, he watched the ship turn toward the north shore, firing its forward five-inch battery. Buzz watched in amazement as the shell struck a derrick moored at Beckoning point. Unaware of what was taking place in front of him, Buzz continued to tread water. Moments later he was totally amazed to see the wake of a torpedo racing wide past the starboard side of the Monaghan and crashing harmlessly into the shore line.

After watching the torpedo explode against some rocks, Buzz spun back toward the Monaghan. He watched in total shock as the bow of the destroyer bounced off the hull of a Japanese midget submarine. As the skipper of the Japanese vessel began to submerge, the well-trained crew of the Monaghan dropped several depth charges off the stern of the destroyer. With Pearl Harbor at only forty-seven feet deep, the shock of the explosion was dispersed over the top of the waves. The blast was so intense, it actually raised the stern of the Monaghan completely out of the water, allowing Buzz to see the spinning props. Feeling confident the depth charges had completed the job, the skipper of the Monaghan poured on the power to complete his escape from the Japanese aerial attack.

The blast of the depth charges had also taken a toll on Buzz. After being hit directly in the face with the blast, it tossed him back toward battleship row like a rag doll. After gaining his composure, he realized blood was running out of his nose and ears, and his chest hurt as if someone had hit him with an iron anvil.

Turning once again toward battleship row and the burning oil, Buzz began swimming toward a break in the fire near the bow of the U.S.S. West Virginia, which was berthed directly behind the Oklahoma. Before he began to swim, he looked over to the west just in time to see a Japanese Zero skimming low above the water. Instantly, Buzz knew exactly what was on the mind of the pilot. Taking a large gulp of air, Buzz swam toward the bottom of the harbor as machine gun bullets ripped into the water all around him.

As the plane disappeared off to the east, Buzz swam as hard as he could toward the West Virginia where a clear path of water still was available.

With the badly damaged battleship already settling into the muddy bottom of the harbor, Buzz was sure he could grab onto the anchor that was now at water lever and hoist himself up out of the water toward the main deck. Thankfully, two sailors standing on the bow helped pull him up onto the fore deck and away from the burning oil as it began gathering near the ship. Choking and wheezing from the thick acrid smoke, Buzz thankfully knelt on a solid deck trying to regain his strength.

Looking up at the two men, Buzz inquired. "Where are you supposed to be during general quarters?"

"Forward 40mm bofors gun tub, sir, but it has been blown to bits along with every man that was in the tub when it was hit. Everything aft of that is on fire, and you can't get down the main deck without being burned alive."

Buzz nodded his head. "Well, let's get the fire hoses going, we can knock down some of those flames. Let's get with it!"

One sailor shook his head. "Sir, we tried that, there's no electrical power to run the pumps and I think the primary water main was severed when the torpedoes hit. We just don't know what to do!"

Buzz nodded his head. "Follow me, we need to help where we can."

Standing up, Buzz ran toward the starboard side of the ship that was tied up against the U.S.S. Tennessee. Coming up to an open water tight door that led into the superstructure of the ship, Buzz charged forward through the smoke-filled passageway, directing wounded men back toward the open door and fresh air. Climbing up several flights of stairs, he exited the super structure right by a 20mm gun tub. It was loaded but silent, as the bodies of two dead crew members were sprawled on the deck.

Looking at the two men that had followed him he yelled. "Pull their bodies out of the way! Get me more ammunition from the ready box, we're getting back into this damn war." Buzz shouted as he tossed several hot pieces of debris overboard.

Seconds later, Buzz was firing at several dive bombers, although the pounding from the weapon against his wounded shoulder sent shock waves of pain throughout his body. After taking a deep breath, he swung the weapon to his left, attempting to take on a Japanese bomber that had just completed its run and was dropping down towards the water to escape the anti-aircraft fire. He was sure he damaged the diving plane but he did not care, as a 40mm bofors gun up on the next deck blew the engine out of the aircraft. The plane appeared to stop in mid-air for a split second before exploding into a ball of flame.

One of the sailors loading ammunition into the 20mm screamed before tumbling to the deck as part of the propeller flew back toward the ship, ripping his chest wide open. The second sailor rolled him off to the side as he continued slamming drums of ammunition into the 20mm cannon for Buzz.

Suddenly, a tremendous blast shook the harbor sending a massive cloud of flame and debris hundreds of feet skyward. It was as if the devil had thrown open the gates of hell. The Arizona had erupted into an inferno like nothing Buzz had ever witnessed before. White hot flames shot up from every section of the doomed ship as nearly a million pounds of gun powder and its full fuel bunkers all detonated at one time. Additional explosions tossed huge sections of the ship across battleship row, killing and injuring men that were attempting to save their ships.

Buzz and his last helper were knocked from their feet by the monstrous blast. Attempting to stand back up, Buzz grabbed hold of a nearby railing as he grasped his left side. Instantly, his hand was covered in sticky warm blood. Looking down at his side, Buzz could see a large piece of metal sticking out of his rib cage. Shaking his head in disbelief, Buzz looked around for the sailor that had been feeding him ammunition. There was no doubt his loader was finished. His head had been sheared off by a large piece of metal from the Arizona that had embedded itself into the wall of the gun tub.

As the heat from the raging fire on the Arizona became unbearable in the open gun tub, Buzz backed inside the ship, pulling the water tight door shut and dogging it tightly. Not sure what to do next, Buzz leaned against the wall but found it intensely hot.

Fearing fire from the Arizona was spreading into the interior of the West Virginia, Buzz forced himself to work his way back down the stairs he had climbed earlier. He exited onto the main deck, just in time to get caught up in another explosion from the Arizona. The shock wave picked him up, throwing him off the ship, as a large piece of shrapnel ripped into his upper right thigh. He landed solidly in the water, directly between the Tennessee and the West Virginia. Buzz laid in the water for several minutes as he attempted to suck in air, but it was apparent that his hard landing into the water had forced either a broken rib or a piece of the shrapnel into his left lung.

Although being in the water kept Buzz safe from all the flying debris above, he was instantly horrified when he looked up. He was in a canyon with two massive damaged battleships on each side of his body.

It was a fearful site looking up to see the dark gray hulls of the ships rocking back and forth. The West Virginia creaked and moaned, as she continued settling into the muddy bottom of Pearl Harbor. He began to fear if he stayed where he was much longer, he could be crushed between the massive hulls.

Using his one good arm and leg, Buzz began paddling himself forward passed several torn bodies that were floating in the dark canyon. Rounding the bow of the Tennessee, Buzz looked for safety on Ford Island, but it was a long distance away and planes were still strafing anything they saw that was moving.

Finally nearing Ford Island, Buzz observed a large group of sailors from the battleships that had made their way to the island when the abandon ship calls went out. Waving his good arm, he attracted the attention of several men that came running to his rescue, hauling him up on shore.

A captain from the West Virginia looked down at Buzz as he removed his tee shirt, tearing it into strips. "Lieutenant, you look like hell. We don't have any medical supplies, but I'll wrap you up best I can until we can get some help over here. Try and relax, you've lost a lot of blood."

After the captain finished wrapping his wounds, he walked off to see who else he could help. Buzz rested quietly under the banyan trees, trying to control his breathing, when he noticed something dripping on his face. Opening his eyes, Buzz looked up into the trees, only to discover it was blood dripping off intestines and other body parts that had been blown up into the trees when the Arizona exploded. Looking left to right, he noticed other body parts entwined in the branches all along the edge of Ford Island. Feeling completely nauseous, Buzz used all the strength he could muster to slide himself along the ground, away from the dripping body parts.

When the second wave of Japanese planes attacked, Buzz saw all the men disappear and run for cover, as several of the attacking planes were going after installations on Ford Island. All Buzz could do was close his eyes and protect his face with his good arm as rocks, chunks of concrete and other deadly debris rained down all around him. The ground shook and ricocheting machine gun bullets screamed over his body, slamming into the armor plating on the hull of the Tennessee. In the distance Buzz could hear the screams of men that were being struck by the deadly projectiles.

As the attack intensified, Buzz realized he had to move or he was sure to be killed by the strafing aircraft. He had barely made it up to his knees when a blast from across the harbor sent him rolling painfully across the ground. Looking toward the dry docks, he could see the destroyer U.S.S. Shaw, had nearly disintegrated when a bomb ignited fuel and ammunition. Large sections of the ship dropped from the sky all over the harbor, including Ford Island. Unable to move quickly, Buzz decided to lay where he was, covering his head and hoping nothing large crashed into his already damaged body. When the rain of debris ended, Buzz sat up once more, watching the massive flames rolling skyward, blocking out the morning sun. He watched painfully as men on the pier attempted to attack the flames with large fire hoses, only to be cut to ribbons by exploding ordinance. Buzz screamed in anger as he watched an arriving fire truck tipped over after another massive explosion rocked what was left of the Shaw. Seconds later, the fuel tank on the truck exploded, killing the crew in the cab. Tears ran down his face as he watched his beloved navy being destroyed, ship by ship. He wanted to fight, but he had lost too much blood and was too weak to do anything. Reaching over to his holster, Buzz pulled out his .45 pistol and cocked it. As the next plane swooped low over battleship row, Buzz fired at the plane in vain as he attempted to yell.

"Die, you son of a bitch!" Out of ammunition and in tremendous pain, Buzz finally passed out.

It was impossible to say how long Buzz laid on the shore near the burning battleships before he awakened in a makeshift hospital, located in a battered aircraft hangar on Ford Island. Navy corpsmen ran from patient to patient, attempting to save the lives of the severely wounded men, although they realized that without specialized medical care, most would die.

As one of the corpsmen stopped to check on the battle dressings he had applied earlier, Buzz grabbed him by the arm. "Where am I, and what the hell is going on?"

The bloody corpsman looked down at Buzz. "We are at war, Lieutenant, the Japanese destroyed Pearl. We've got nothing left to fight with."

"Buzz nodded his aching head. "Yeah, that much I knew. Where the hell am I?"

"You are in one of the only hangars left standing on Ford Island. As soon as the next barge arrives back from Pearl, we'll load you up for a trip to the hospital. That's if the Japs don't come back again and attack us. There are rumors they landed several thousand troops on the north side of the island and are headed this way. God only knows how long we can hold out. We may all be POW's by nightfall," the anxious, overworked corpsman replied, with a look of fear in his eyes.

Buzz shook his head. "Do you really believe that story? I think this was a massive air raid to take us out of the war, since Roosevelt refused to pull the fleet back to San Diego. I don't believe they have landed a major ground force."

The corpsman stared at Buzz in disbelief. "Seriously sir, they have landed and are coming this way. There are rumors of dogs barking in code, to inform the local Japanese as to what is going on so they can rise up at the right time and take control of Honolulu. Radio station KGMB has been sending out warnings all morning that the water has been poisoned, and Japanese have been seen near diamond point, sir. This is the real thing!"

Before Buzz could respond, the corpsman took off across the hangar, as several more sailors arrived to pick up the wounded for the trip across the harbor.

The main hospital was in total bedlam when Buzz was carried in. Never had they planned to deal with that many casualties in such bad shape all at one time. Dead sailors that were burned beyond recognition lined the hallways, as men with radically amputated limbs screamed for morphine. Nurses attempted to triage patients for the doctors, but too often the men that were next in line for help had already passed on when the doctors arrived. The hospital reeked of thick black oil, vomit and burned flesh.

Buzz had no idea how long he laid in the hallway of the surgical ward as he continually drifted in and out of consciousness, but he remembered a nurse checking on the bandage a corpsman had changed on his thigh when he arrived at the pier, and telling him to hold on.

Finally, a man in his fifties looked down at Buzz, "Lieutenant, you are my next patient and the boys are going to wheel you into my operating room. We're going to clean you up a bit, then stitch up that thigh and calf muscle, and remove the bullet from your shoulder. Then, I'm going to open up your side to remove the shrapnel, and see what can be done there, as I'm sure you have a punctured lung. Be patient and just let me do my job, and we'll get you put back together." Putting a hand on his one good shoulder, the doctor chuckled. "You may be told later that I'm a dandy obstetrician and that is totally true. But since there are no births today, I was pressed into service as a surgeon. Too bad you don't need a c-section here today, Lieutenant. Rumor has it I'm the best in Honolulu."

Buzz smiled as he looked up at the doctor. Struggling to speak, he replied, "Doc, I can barely hear, I had blood coming out of my ears after a depth charge exploded, can you help me?

After looking into his ears with a flashlight the doctor frowned. "Were you in the water when the charge exploded?"

Nodding his head, Buzz replied, "Yes sir, and not that damn far away. My chest still hurts from the concussion."

"Well, you're probably lucky to be alive. Had you been under the water you surely would be dead. It appears that both your ear drums have been punctured, but they will heal on their own. In about two weeks your hearing should be close to what it was. Sorry to say you may always have some ringing in your ears, just from that blast. I think we'll x-ray your chest to see if your sternum is cracked or you have any other damage. We don't want to miss anything." The doctor stated before motioning for a corpsman to wheel Buzz into the operating room.

Feeling relived that he was finally going to get treatment, he looked up at the doctor. "Just give me what you got. You and my uncle the doctor can compare notes someday. He's an obstetrician at Boston General."

"Splendid! I'll hold you to that, Lieutenant," the doctor replied with a laugh as Buzz was rolled into the operating room.

Opening his eyes hours later, Buzz was able to see the sun just beginning to set behind the mountains to the west of Pearl Harbor. He tried to lay still on the bed, as every bit of his body appeared to be begging for peace and quiet.

At some point, a young nurse walked up to the bed. "Ah, Lieutenant, you are finally awake. I'm glad to see that. How is your breathing?"

Buzz nodded his head. "Not too bad, was the doctor able to repair my lung?"

After checking the IV flow, she responded. "Yes. Dr. Freman is a wonderful surgeon and you should be alright. We'll keep you here for a week or so to see how your lung holds up before sending you back stateside."

"Did I have any more damage to my chest from the explosion? The doctor was concerned that my sternum may have been damaged," Buzz inquired, as he watched every move the nurse made.

Picking up the chart from the end of the bed, the nurse read for several minutes before responding. "No, everything was intact, and he wrote that the pain was most likely caused by the force of the blast. That should subside in a few days." The nurse replied in a very business-like tone.

Buzz couldn't help but love her slight southern accent and deep green eyes. "You know my name and rank nurse, could you tell me your name?"

Smiling, the nurse placed her hands on her hips. "Oh, are we playing prisoner of war now? Well, if you must, it's Russell, Constance, Lieutenant, United States Navy, 17 163 085, and that's all I'm required to tell you according to the Geneva Convention. Now get some sleep."

Buzz smiled at the pretty nurse. "Understood ma'am! Thanks Connie."

Throughout the next ten days Buzz continued to improve, as did his desire to get to know nurse Russell a whole lot better. However, his transfer papers arrived, ending any real hope of establishing a relationship.

The evening before he was going to leave, he stopped Connie as she made her rounds.

"Well, it looks like I'm out of here tomorrow and headed back to the states. Would it be possible for me to get your address so we can write to one another? I would really like to stay in touch."

Sitting down in a chair beside his bed, Connie took a deep breath. "Lt. Maddox, I think you are a very special guy that I would like to get to know better. I have never allowed myself to get attached to a patient before, and this scares me. I know when you get back on your feet, the navy is going to send you back into combat, and the next thing I know, I'll hear that you're dead or missing. I'm sorry but I can't afford to take that risk. Please understand that if things were different, I would have no problem handing my heart over to you, I think you are a really great guy. But I can't with this war on. I hope you can understand."

As she stood up to leave, Buzz took hold of her hand. "We will see each other again, I promise. I am not going to let you get away this easily. Remember me, Connie."

As a tear ran down her cheek, she smiled slightly. "I will definitely remember you, I can promise you that. It's kind of hard to forget a guy named Buzz. And I'm keeping you to your promise that we will find each other when this damn war is over. We're both in the navy, find me!"

The following day, after Buzz was wheeled up onto the hospital ship, he sat along the railing taking in the destruction around the harbor. He stared at the overturned Oklahoma, where the war had started for him. Crews were still attempting to recover bodies from the interior of the ship. He pounded his fist on the arm rest of the wheelchair.

"I will be back, and I'm coming for you, Tojo. There's no place on this damn earth you can hide, not even in hell! God as my witness, I will avenge the deaths of every one of my men that never had a chance."

CHAPTER 2
A NEW BEGINNING

If there was one thing Buzz had not been looking forward to, it was recuperating back at home. However, he was sure that by now his family had overcome the anger they felt for him when he left for Annapolis. Arriving at the train station, his father and mother were waiting for him aside their 1941 Cadillac. Other than a few niceties, and slightly stiff 'glad you are doing well' type comments, the ride back to the house was very quiet and cold.

That evening after a comfortable dinner, Buzz and his father sat in the den having a glass of brandy. After taking a puff on one of his favorite cigars, Alfred looked intently at his son. "It was not right running out on Angeline as you did. Have you spoken to her at all? Since she heard you were wounded and coming home to recuperate, there is little doubt she still has marriage on her mind."

Setting down his glass, Buzz walked over to the large windows overlooking the back yard pond.

"I never even hinted at the possibility of Angeline and I ever getting married. That appeared to be a rather bad business deal you and mother worked out with the Stevensons. Yes, I liked her, and yes, she is beautiful, and yes, we dated a few times a long time ago, but getting away from her was the best thing that ever happened to me. I wrote her a long letter from Annapolis, telling her I wasn't coming back here, and that she should move on. I actually told her that Stan Winslow, that pompous ass dentist, would be a great catch for her. After all, with that huge smile, what could be better than to have a dentist in the family to keep those teeth looking great for the gossip magazines."

Upset by his son's remarks, Alfred bit down on his cigar. "You could do one hell of a lot worse you know. The Stevensons are a wealthy family with a long lineage in New England. She would be a great wife to have waiting for you when you come home on leave, and to build a family with."

Buzz shook his head as he walked back to his glass of brandy. "You know, Dad, I should have guessed this had all been worked out long before I left Pearl Harbor. But I should tell you I met a nurse, a woman by the name of Connie Russell, a southern gal with gorgeous green eyes." Laughing, Buzz continued, "And to tell you the truth, sir, I think I'm really in love with her."

"Love? What the hell does love have to do with marriage today. What matters are the connections you can make, and how it will affect your bottom line. Any two-bit idiot can settle down with a woman, screw the whore to hell, have kids with buck teeth, and wind up with a mortgage you will never pay off. But finding a woman like Angeline Stevenson can have advantages that you are not even aware of. You best think of that, son," Alfred remarked as he glared at his youngest son.

"Oh, does that include screwing the hell out of Angeline and having a dozen little tax write offs wandering around the yard?" Buzz replied angrily.

Before Alfred could say another word, Buzz finished his brandy and walked to the door. "I think I'll go for a walk around the yard to get some fresh air before retiring for the night. I still have the smell of fuel oil in my head at times, you know?"

Buzz sat on a bench in the flower garden for several minutes before Jolene came and sat down next to him.

"You scared me, Buzz. I thought for sure you were one of the men that was killed. I don't want you going back to the war. I heard you could get a teaching job at the gunnery school at Annapolis or the new school the navy opened at Melville in Rhode Island," Jolene explained, as a tear rolled down her cheek.

"Melville? That was a dump during World War One, I can't imagine what it must be like now. No, little sister. I hope to return to the Oklahoma once she is righted and overhauled. I want to fight the war from her decks," Buzz replied, as he gave his little sister a reassuring smile.

Angered by Buzz's last comment, Jolene stood up. "And what about Angeline, do you think she will want to marry a battleship sailor? Get real, Buzz, it's time to grow up!"

After a moment of silence, Buzz stood up as he watched several ducks take off from the pond. Kissing his sister on the forehead, he replied, "No Sis, I have grown up. More than you know, and I need to do what's right for me, whether or not the family accepts it." With that said, Buzz walked off to his bedroom.

Laying down on his bed, Buzz wondered about Melville and what the navy might have going on there. Slowly, he began putting a plan together that would get him back to the navy as quickly as possible. But first, the situation with Angeline Stevenson had to be settled once and for all, and he would take care of that first thing in the morning.

Around eleven o'clock, Buzz drove his father's burgundy 1938 Oldsmobile up into the Stevensons long circular driveway, stopping under the east portico. As he approached the front door, Angeline came out, walking toward him wearing a very expensive powder blue skirt and matching jacket.

"Buzz, I have been waiting for you all morning. I figured you would have been here hours ago. Let's go to the sitting room, we have so much to discuss and make plans for."

Although Buzz had been taught all his life to be honorable, this morning he was not in the mood for graciousness and delicacy. Holding up his hand he looked seriously at Angeline.

"I'm not coming in the house." After taking a moment to gather his thoughts, he continued. "Look, I figured when I left for Annapolis and sent you that letter, you would have understood that we were through.

Angeline, we have no future, and I'm not marrying you now or ever. I'm going back to fight the war until we kick Japan to hell, no matter how long it takes. Whatever schemes my family and yours have connived, you can kiss it all good bye. My family is the navy now, and this, all this, all the trappings of wealth and society is not what I want for my life. Please just move on and find someone else."

The color drained from Angeline's face as her jaw dropped open. "Buzz Maddox, that was the most rude and cruel thing I have ever heard. The navy has changed you, and I want no part of that. I would prefer that you just leave now!"

Without saying a word, Buzz climbed back into the Oldsmobile and drove south toward Rhode Island. Stopping along the coastline just a few miles from Melville, Buzz was intrigued by the small green naval boats that were screaming up and down the coast. He could see that they were armed with torpedo tubes, fifty caliber machine guns and twenty-millimeter cannons, and they flew like the wind.

Getting back into the car, Buzz drove to a gas station a few miles away. Walking up to the attendant he asked, "What do you know about those speedy green naval boats that are running up and down the coast line?"

"They are the newest secret weapon of the navy, or so they tell us. They are called PT boats. It stands for patrol and torpedo. They are training special crews over at Melville. That's about all I know," the man replied, after filling up the gas tank.

Since it was late in the day, Buzz checked into a motel for the night. First thing in the morning with his uniform on, Buzz drove down to the base, parking near a small office building. He loved the sign that hung over the entrance, '*Through these doors pass the best Motor Torpedo Boat Crews in the world.*'

Walking inside the office, a petty officer jumped to attention. "Good morning, Lieutenant. What can I do for you."

Smiling, Buzz replied, "At ease Petty Officer, is your commander in this morning?"

"Yes sir, wait just one moment." As the Petty Officer walked into a back office, Buzz stared at the photos of PT Boats on the wall. The more he looked at them, the more his interest grew.

Several minutes later, the Petty Officer returned, "Commander Sneider will see you now."

Buzz spoke with Commander Sneider for well over an hour, explaining his weapons qualifications and all that had happened to him while on the Oklahoma. When he was finished, Commander Sneider stood up and looked out the window.

"You come off a bit arrogant, Maddox. All too often that can lead to problems when it comes to taking orders. Are you an arrogant SOB, Maddox?"

Buzz had to laugh. "No sir! If I ever came across arrogant in front of my mother, she would have me cleaning silver for the next month. I'm not arrogant, sir, I'm just damn confident in my skills."

Sitting back down in his chair, the commander looked seriously at Buzz. "You understand these are wooden boats, and you'll be going up against destroyers, cruisers, or whatever the Japanese fleet throws at you. Your boat may get damaged, hell, it may even be shot out from under you. How are you

going to react, what are you going to do?"

Buzz took no time to consider his response. "My responsibility will always be to get my crew to safety, and search for anyone missing. When I worked for my father's company, I had a man fall overboard on a fishing trip. The seas were rough, and we were carrying a lot of weight. It took me three attempts to get the boat close enough, so the crew could snag him with a pike and haul him back on deck. He was damn cold, so we got him downstairs, covered him with blankets and headed for home. The man is still working on my dad's boats today."

"Fair enough, Maddox, fair enough. You sound like the type of sailor we need and want on our boats. It will not be an easy life, and hot meals and a warm cot may not be nearby every day. You'll operate for long hours in harsh conditions, shark infested waters, nearby islands that could be inhabited by the Japs, and sometimes hostile natives, that will turn your ass over to the enemy in a heartbeat for a moldy bag of rice. You'll need to train your crew to watch for patrolling aircraft that may try sinking your ass. Son, you'll wear a target on your back every time you leave the base. Does that sound workable to you?" the commander inquired, as he once more looked at Buzz, studying his face.

"We're at war, sir. I saw a lot of good men die on the Oklahoma. I want to fight the enemy, and take the battle to them one way or another. This sounds like the way I would like to do it. Give me a shot, Commander, I won't let you down," Buzz replied, dead serious.

Leaning forward, Commander Sneider smiled, "Maddox, I truly believe you won't let us down. So, here's what we're going to do. We'll put you up in the officer's quarters as an unassigned officer until I can get your orders cut. Once all the paper work is in place, the training starts, and you should know that it will not be easy."

After Buzz unloaded his sea bag from the Oldsmobile, he called his brother Carl to tell him where he could pick up the car. After Buzz gave his brother directions, Carl called him every name in the book for taking the car, since now he would have to drive all the way to Melville to pick it up. Plus, he told Buzz that the Stevensons had called and were highly upset with the way he had spoken to Angeline, and wanted a formal conference this coming weekend. After Carl finished his rant, Buzz made it clear that was never going to happen as he had training to attend. Before Carl could say another word, Buzz hung up the phone. Carl stood in his father's den shaking with anger realizing that Buzz had hung up on him, and had achieved the ultimate last word.

Hanging up the phone, Buzz laughed all the way back to the Quonset hut he had been assigned to. He knew Carl was not so much angry about the car and the Stevensons, as he was at having to pick up the slack with the fishing fleet.

Buzz had his first close up encounter with a PT Boat the following day, when he was allowed to go out on a landing barge to watch the crews train. He loved the sound of the powerful deep throbbing engines that drove those sleek boats across the water. He was enthralled as he watched skillful skippers zigzag their shallow drafted, light weight boats through maneuvers that nearly set the boats on their sides.

At nights there was not much to do at Melville but attend movies, read or get involved in athletic games. The PT school was actually a small part of the Portsmouth, Rhode Island Naval Base, located on Narragansett Bay. It was an old base that had performed many naval missions throughout her long existence. The base consisted of fifty-nine standard old naval buildings containing a small hospital, engine repair shops, wood working shops, weapons repair and storage facilities, and many other various normal naval functions. There were also 150 newer steel Quonset huts, used as barracks to house the trainees and the base staff. During World War Two, over 14,000 officers and men would be trained at this small but important base.

Three days later, Buzz received orders assigning him to a training unit. At 0700hrs. the first day, a big burly Chief Petty Officer named Pritchard called the officers together for roll call.

"Alright gentlemen, let's see who we got here, and who can follow directions. Sound off when I call your name. Ensign Sterling, Ensign Douglas, Ensign May, Ensign Albrecht, Ensign Walklee and Lieutenant jg Maddox." After every one responded, the chief smiled, "Fantastic, we have all the right people and it appears all you college boys can follow directions. A damn good start. So, now you'll walk down to Quonset hut five, where you'll find your name on a bunk, and directions as to how your gear needs to be stored. Get it done quickly, as Commander Wilson will be looking for you shortly. Remember one thing, gentlemen. Commander Sneider operates this school, but Commander Wilson will be your lord and master when it comes to these boats"

Hut five was clean and well taken care of. Every bunk was set up the same, with blankets pulled as tight as humanly possible. The men went right to work storing their gear and hanging their uniforms as directed, then finally changing into blue naval dungarees. As they were finishing, Commander Wilson walked in the door. He walked past the six men without saying a word. Immediately, he began opening their lockers and mumbling to himself. Reaching the far end of the hut, he returned toward the front door, looking over their beds and shaking his head. "I would expect crap like this from a marine who lives in a damn dirty fox hole, but never from officers wanting to be the best PT skippers in the world."

Immediately, he tipped over several bunks, before tossing clothing from lockers until he had a large pile on the floor. "Now gentlemen, see if you can do it right the second time. I'll meet you in hut ten in twenty minutes, and you best be on time!"

As he left the hut, the men scrambled to sort out the clothing on the floor, remake their bunks, and get everything reorganized for a second time.

Nearly out of breath, the men arrived in hut ten with one minute to spare. Commander Wilson smiled. "Gentlemen, now that I have your complete attention, let me tell you how this is all going to work."

After nearly a two-hour briefing conducted by several training officers, the men were allowed to have chow. Buzz looked across the table at Jack Sterling. "Well Jack, what do you think of Melville so far. Does it meet your expectations?"

Everyone at the table laughed, including several men that were sitting behind them. Jack smiled as he sliced up the hunk of beef the cook had placed on his tray.

"I figured it would be tough, they have just eight weeks to get us up to speed, so we either learn or we're gone. And I have a feeling the navy will not look honorably on anyone that washes out of the program."

Chuck May nodded his head. "I think Jack just said it all. We're all here because we volunteered, and we all have experience with small boats. We just need to pick up tactics, learn how the boats respond, help train our crews and then we should be good to go."

One of the men from the other table came over. "I'm Ensign Short, everyone calls me Shorty, go figure. But what your man just said is pretty much it. I've been here for two weeks now, so I can tell all of you that it don't come real easy."

"Pull up a seat Shorty, and tell us what you've learned," Buzz said with a big smile on his face. "Those boats are powerful, and can get away from you if you're not thinking. Getting your crew to work as a team can be a bitch. If you get a wise acre, send him packing right off the bat, or he'll mess up discipline in a hurry. Also, torpedo training can be tough, you need to learn how to be gentle, you need to make love to your boat, so she responds the way you want her to when you fire, otherwise your fish will be all over the place. So, welcome aboard men, enjoy the ride!" Shorty explained before returning to his meal.

Later that evening, Buzz was called to Commander Sneider's office.

"Maddox, your father and brother are here to pick up the car. Your father wants a few words with you, so take care of business and get back to your hut."

As Buzz approached the Cadillac, Alfred stepped out. "Son, you have some balls telling Angeline off the way you did. Not for one second did you take her feelings into consideration. What do you have to say for yourself."

"Just this, and I told you before. I never intended to marry Angeline, and I never gave her one single reason to think I would. In fact, the opposite is true. I don't know what part of that you and everyone else doesn't understand. Your high society crap and proper breeding is something I have always disliked. Take the car and leave, I have homework to do before I turn in tonight. Take care of yourself, and tell Mom I love her. And Carl, grow the hell up and take some responsibility. There's a damn war on!"

Before another word could be said, Buzz turned and walked back onto the base.

The following morning, Buzz could barely eat breakfast he was so excited. He could not wait to set foot on a PT boat for the first time.

Lt. Spriggs explained the control panel in the cockpit, the firing mechanisms for the torpedoes, and the importance of listening to their motor machinist, when he had problems or felt you were abusing the equipment.

The lieutenant smiled as Machinist Mate Crowder came on board. "Gentlemen, the boat you'll be assigned is in fact your boat, you are the skipper. But your motor mac. is your boss in every respect. When he yells back off, you back off. At times, he may be the only thing that stands between being stranded out in the ocean, or sleeping in a warm bunk back at base."

With that being said, Machinist Mate Crowder walked to the back of the boat, descending down into the engine room. Lt. Spriggs walked up to the controls in the cockpit, grabbing hold of the voice tube, he called out, "

Are we ready down there?"

"Go ahead sir, roll them over," Crowder responded.

Seconds later, the big Packard engines were throbbing nicely, as Crowder walked back up to the Lieutenant. "This boat has a full tanks of fuel sir, we can let everyone have a turn at her."

Buzz's heart almost jumped out of his chest when he heard those words. He quickly manned the front mooring lines, as Lt. Spriggs prepared to move the boat away from the pier.

Clearing the harbor, Buzz was excited to see five other PT Boats involved in training exercises. This is what he had been waiting for, he knew without a single doubt that this is what he was born for.

All the men took turns operating the boat, while being critiqued by Lt. Spriggs. When the Lieutenant called for Buzz to take the helm, his hands began to sweat, and his heart was throbbing like the huge engines below the deck. Taking the wheel in his left hand, he pushed the throttles open wider with his right. In seconds, the boat was skimming across the water like a greyhound. He threw the wheel hard to port, to see if the boat responded like his father's yacht, the Emma Jean. He was surprised how quickly this Elco eighty-foot, 121,000-pound boat turned with ease. Then he spun the wheel hard to starboard while pushing the throttles open a bit more. The boat responded instantly, sending up a wall of water and spray that blew back over the men.

Lt. Spriggs leaned close to Buzz, "Impressive, Lieutenant. Head her out toward that red buoy, swing around it without letting off the power and head her back home. Let's see what you got!"

Smiling, Buzz gave the throttles one more push forward as he raced toward his destination in open water. Just as the boat passed the buoy, Buzz cranked the wheel hard to port. The wooden vessel creaked and moaned as it skidded across the water, raising the starboard side. With the boat now headed back toward the base, Lt. Spriggs patted Buzz on the back. "Well done, Lieutenant, you proved a lot to me today. After running the Elco boat, the men took turns operating the Higgins and Huckins seventy-eight-foot boats. They all operated a bit differently, and they all had different centers of gravity a skipper had to contend with when maneuvering at full throttle or making high speed turns.

At the end of the day, Lt. Spriggs walked up to Buzz. "I saw six good boat handlers out there today, but you were clearly the most in command, regardless of which boat you were operating. If you had your choice, Maddox, which of the boats would you like to command."

Buzz smiled as he looked over at an Elco boat tied up nearby. "Sir, they are all nice boats, but I would really like to have an Elco. They ride a bit lower in the water, and respond in turns like you're on a roller coaster."

Lt. Spriggs smiled, "I know there are three Elco's unassigned right now, one of them is a bad luck boat. I'll keep you away from that one."

Buzz looked intently at the lieutenant. "Bad luck boat, sir? What do you mean?"

"It's the 113 boat. During construction, she slipped off a trestle and had a hole punched in her bottom. Then during trials, one engine broke lose, damaging the prop shaft and filling the engine room with water. After repairs, she arrived here ready to go. The first skipper that took her out had the throttles jam. He wound up striking a landing craft near shore, tearing a hole in the side of the boat. I would stay away from her if I were you," Lt. Spriggs explained as he made a sign of the cross.

Buzz busted out laughing. "The 113 boat sounds like a horse that just didn't want to be broke, sir. But I feel like she should just about be ready to settle down and be ridden. I'll take the 113 boat if I can have her, sir."

Lt Spriggs shook hands with Buzz. "Sounds like a plan to me. God help you, Maddox. I'll tell the commander you're all set so you can begin building your crew. Choose wisely because now the work really begins."

The following two days, the officers spent time in classrooms working out complicated navigational problems, studying tide charts of the southwest Pacific, and getting a rundown of every island in the Solomon Island group the navy knew about. However, much of the information was sketchy. They had obtained most of their intel from former tramp steamer captains that supplied the islands back in the thirties, along with missionaries and plantation owners that had been removed from the islands by the Japanese military, and transported to Australia directly after the Pearl Harbor attack. The navy was well aware that the Japanese were continuing to move their, 'Greater East Asia Co-Prosperity Sphere,' east across the Pacific, and it had to be stopped. So with little time, everyone estimated much of the information they were studying was well out dated.

The following morning Commander Wilson met the new skippers down on the pier. After a strong lecture on safety, each man was assigned a boat. Looking at Buzz he had to smile.

"So Maddox, I hear you're willing to take on our problem boat. She's not the first bad boat we've had, and probably won't be the last. However, she's been repaired, inspected and totally gone over from stem to stern, so she's all yours. Since you feel so brave to volunteer, I have assigned you the 113 boat, and wish you the best of luck."

Around 1000hrs, a truck pulled up beside the 113, dropping off the crew that had just finished seamanship school. Gunners Mate Dick

Wickman looked at the other men. "I'm not working this boat, I've heard all about her, she's jinxed. I'm asking the skipper for a transfer."

Torpedoman Ralph Ordman spoke up. "There's no such thing as a jinxed ship or boat. I've worked around boats all my life, sometimes crap just happens."

Before another word could be said, a jeep pulled up by the 113. Buzz stepped from the jeep, throwing his sea bag onto the boat. Jumping up on deck, he removed a sheet of paper from his shirt pocket. Looking down at the crew that was standing at attention, Buzz began.

"Before we get to know one another lets have roll call. Just give me a shout out when I call your name."

Quickly, he went through the list, Torpedoman Ordman, Ralph; Gunners Mate Warner, James; Radioman Yamry Thomas; 20mm Gunners Mate Johnson, Sidney; Gunners Mate Wickman, Richard; Gunners Mate Portland, James; Machinist Mate Crowder, Darwin; Cook Sims, Elmer; Torpedoman Anderson, Jeffrey; Gunners Mate Hollerman, Jerome; Torpedoman Greenman, Daniel." After he finished the list, he looked down at Machinist Mate Crowder.

"How the hell did I get you assigned to my boat, did you and Lt. Spriggs have a falling out?"

Crowder shook his head. "No sir. I watched you handle the boats every time you took one out. You know what the hell you're doing, and I want to get into the war and away from this damn base."

Buzz nodded his head in approval, "Welcome aboard, Crowder, you and I need to talk engines over the next few days. Make sure the engine room is up to speed."

Buzz smiled as he pointed toward Ensign Commers who was still standing by the jeep "This is Ensign Todd Commers, he'll be our executive officer. We do not have a chief as of yet, but we will before the day is finished. Does anyone have anything to say before we bring you aboard?"

Dick Wickman stepped forward, "Sir, I have heard how this boat is jinxed, and I would like a transfer to another crew."

Buzz nodded his head. "That can be arranged. I'll have your orders cut so you can transfer to the garbage detail over at Portsmith, I hear they need a few good men. Everyone else grab your sea bags and get situated on board. Wickman, just have a seat on the edge of the boat until the next truck comes along."

Wickman sat down on the boat angrily without saying another word. Just as a truck arrived heading back to the base, Buzz jumped off the boat with a slip of paper. He handed it to the driver saying, make sure Commander Wilson gets the paperwork along with this man."

Wickman jumped off the boat, jogging over to Buzz. "Wait a minute sir, are you serious about the garbage detail? I mean, all I want is another boat, I'm not trying to get out of anything. I'll do my duty, sir," Wickman stated as his knees shook.

Buzz walked up close to the Gunners Mate. "Wickman, I have a crew on board right now ready to go to work. I don't need a man that's superstitious and will cause moral problems. Superstitions can screw up a crew, and I need men that want to fight the Japs, not ghost stories."

Hanging his head, Wickman was not sure what to say. After a moment he looked up at Buzz. "Sir, can I have the twin mount on the port side."

"It's yours, Wickman, all you need to do is the job you volunteered to do when you enlisted. If you want to stay, grab your sea bag and get your gear stored," Buzz replied with a reassuring smile.

"Thank you, thank you very much, sir. I'll never let you down. You can count on me for anything, I'll prove it to you, sir," Wickman stated, as he shook hands with his new skipper.

Buzz took Ensign Commers aside in the chart room as the men were storing their gear.

"Todd, I need to drive up to headquarters to talk to a couple of chiefs. Why don't you walk the men through the boat and give them a good run down as to how we want things done. I should be back shortly."

As Buzz stepped out onto the deck from the chart house, he observed a Chief Petty Officer standing next to the boat with his sea bag. As Buzz stepped down from the boat he called out, "Is there anything I can do for you, Chief?"

After saluting, the forlorn looking man looked down at the ground for a moment before looking at Buzz.

"Well sir, I sure hope you can, otherwise I'm not sure where I'm headed."

Leaning back against the jeep, Buzz folded his arms across his chest. "I think you need to explain yourself, Chief. What's going on?"

"Sir, my name is Chief Petty Officer Walter Petrovski. I've worked every type of vessel this man's navy has to offer. I've been on tugs, barges, destroyers, battle-wagons and even a short stint on a carrier. Before that, I worked lobster boats out of Boston. When my wife got tired of my drinking, carousing, and bad manners, she divorced me, took my daughter and moved off to New York City, where she eventually married some high buck doctor. Well, that was in 1923 and I had nothing left, so I joined the navy. I did real well at first, although I had a big chip on my shoulder. I got pretty drunk in Singapore one night in 1937 and smacked a cop. No one was too happy about the incident, so the navy sent me to San Diego to work in the Supply Depot.

My chip got a little bit bigger and I drank a whole lot more. On New Year's Day 1938, I once again smacked a cop that was trying to arrest one of my buddies. This time the navy court martialed me, broke me in rank, and sent me to Norfolk, where I've been working on a damn supply ship. Well sir, I quit drinking some time back, I go to church when I can, and worked my way back up to Chief. When I heard the navy was looking for Chief Petty Officers for these boats, I came running. The problem is I had to go in front of Commander Sneider. Sorry to say, he remembered me from San Diego. He told me to hit the road, and that he wanted me nowhere near any of his crews. Sir, I nearly got down on my knees and begged him for a shot at a boat, any boat. Finally, Lt. Spriggs told the Commander he should at least give me a try. So he threw a list in front of me containing the six boats needing a chief. I saw your name, and inquired as to whether or not you were related to the Maddox family that ran Griffin Fisheries up in Kennebunkport, and they said you were. Back in the day, I heard your grandpa and your pa were pretty square shooters, I thought maybe you might give an old salt one more try at respectability."

Buzz was moved by the man's story and his humble approach. After a moment of silence, Buzz walked up to the chief. "Let me tell you how it is on the 113 boat. Every man does his job, no one will ever step foot on my boat drunk, and that includes officers. I'll accept good hearted ribbing, but I will not accept any one being abused, and there will be no blanket parties. It will be your job to maintain order, train these men to a razors edge, and lend a hand whenever and where ever necessary. You will always assure me the crew and boat will be ready to roll when we're called upon to fight. And lastly, I'm going to depend on you to give me every bit of your knowledge of the sea or problems on the boat, and I expect you to be my number one scrounge. Do you think you can comply with my demands?"

As a tear rolled down the Chief's weathered face, he nodded.

"Loud and clear, sir, loud and clear. Just point me in the right direction, I've never been on a PT Boat before."

As the men shook hands, Buzz added. "Chief, I have a small job for you already. Gunners Mate Wickman was bent out of shape that the 113 was jinxed. I gave him a chance to leave, but he said he wanted to stay. Keep an eye on him during training. If you see a problem or if he's messing with the crew, let me know and he'll be gone in a heartbeat. Also, I am thinking of adding either a .50 cal or a 20mm on the forward deck. Think about it and let me know what you come up with. Look the deck

over and see what needs to be strengthened. When we figure it out, your job as scrounge will be to start getting us what we need, without going through channels."

As soon as the Chief was settled, Buzz and Ensign Commers called the crew up on deck. They went through several dry run enemy aircraft drills, and torpedo firing procedures. Ensign Commers timed the men to see how quickly they could be ready when the General Quarters alarm was given. Buzz was very impressed with the spirit of the men, and the way everyone pitched in to help when he pointed out that someone was hit by enemy fire.

About 1500 hrs., Buzz had the mooring lines lifted, as he idled the 113 boat clear of the pier for the first time. Stepping aside, he turned the controls over to Ensign Commers. Like a true professional, he guided the boat from the harbor, while steering the 113 toward open waters. Buzz looked back over the boat and saw that every man was busy doing something, as Chief Petrovski kept a wary eye on them.

As they cleared the harbor, Buzz told Ensign Commers to crank up some speed into the rougher water. As soon as the boat was crashing through rough waves, he called out General Quarters. The men ran and skidded along the wet deck, heading to their combat positions. In just under twenty seconds, every weapon was manned and the gunners were scanning the sky as they had been trained back in gunnery school. The torpedo men had the firing mechanisms uncovered and were standing by tubes one and two, with tools in their hands to shut down a faulty torpedo. Nodding his head, Buzz looked out to sea at a tanker that was slowly underway up the coast.

"XO, make a torpedo run on that tanker, try to take her amidships."

Ensign Commers rolled the 113 hard to port in the deep swells and threw the throttles forward. The sturdy boat charged forward as the 4,500 shaft horsepower Packard Engines throbbed below.

"Range?" Buzz called out, as he watched the tanker with his binoculars.

"Seventeen thousand yards and closing sir!" Commers yelled out as he fought the waves and studied the gyro to keep the boat running on course.

"Very well XO, we'll fire at thirteen and break hard to starboard!"

"Thirteen thousand and break starboard, aye, sir," Commers called back with a smile on his face.

Buzz had to smile as the crew of the Turkish tanker were standing on the deck furiously waving their hands and yelling, thinking the PT Boat was either going to ram them, or fire a torpedo.

"Thirteen thousand yards, fire one, fire two, Ensign Commers called out, as he slammed his hand on the buttons. Both torpedo men struck the firing triggers that would normally send torpedoes toward their targets. As the boat screamed past the tanker Buzz kept a look at his watch.

"Boom, Boom," Buzz called out, as he watched Johnson on the aft 20mm, and Wickman on the port twin .50 caliber machine guns pretending to fire at the enemy vessel.

As they cleared the tanker, Buzz pointed out another ship a bit farther out to sea. He went through the entire scenario again, but this time he added that torpedo number three was stuck in the tube and running hot. He watched Torpedoman Ordman take the proper actions to stop the torpedo, as other men on the rear of the boat headed forward as they were supposed to do. A torpedoman has roughly four to five seconds to shut down a hot misfired torpedo, before the turbines on the torpedo break off and pierce the tube, sending high speed deadly shrapnel in every direction.

After shutting down the defective torpedo, the rest of the crew once again took up their positions for combat. Buzz was more than happy with the first drill for his crew. Taking over the helm, Buzz turned north, allowing his boat to break through some rather large swells as she cruised along at thirty-five knots.

Over the next few days, all the skippers at Melville ran their boats through many simulated drills and coordinated attacks set up by Lt. Spriggs, who was becoming increasingly happy with the progress of the new crews. There were a few accidents, but not one boat had been severely damaged or sunk, as had happened with some training groups.

The following Monday, all the boats were sent over to the navy's Newport Torpedo Station on Goat Island, which is located in Narragansett Bay. The tubes were to be loaded with torpedoes carrying dud war heads. They would then head out into the bay, and practice firing their torpedoes on the range that ran seven miles to the north toward Prudence Island.

Buzz was excited to see how the crew would perform firing actual torpedoes. Although he really

hated turning the boat over to Ensign Commers, Buzz wanted to be able to watch his men perform.

Approaching their first target, Ensign Commers began his run at sixteen thousand yards. At twelve thousand yard he pressed buttons to launch his first two torpedoes. Number one jumped from the tube slicing through the water, but nothing happened with number two. Sadly, they watched their first fish miss the target going wide to the left. Swinging wide around the first target, Ensign Commers re-positioned the boat, bringing it on course for his next run, firing again at twelve thousand yards. Both torpedoes three and four launched properly, and ran hot on course impacting the target barge. After making several dry runs, Buzz took the boat back to Goat Island. After removing the unfired torpedo, several technicians from the base examined everything pertaining to tube number two, finding a faulty electrical switch. Buzz was happy that the incident happened, because now his crew knew how to diagnose the problem and repair it themselves under combat conditions.

The following day dawned cold and windy but that was not going to deter Buzz or several other skippers. After loading up at Goat Island, Buzz charged the 113 north at high speed toward their first target. Keeping a close eye on the gyro he yelled, "Launch one and two!"

Both torpedoes leapt from their tubes at twelve thousand yards and found their targets right on the money. Several minutes later, the excited crew of PT113 had success with their last two fish.

After their fourth run during the week, technicians on Goat Island loaded two experimental torpedoes into tubes three and four, while explaining to Buzz they were to fire them at sixteen thousand yards. The entire crew was excited to be launching real torpedoes for the first time. After launching his duds at the first target, Buzz made a practice run on his secondary target that they were to attack with live weapons, as it was in a different location than they were used to. After completing the dry run, Buzz turned the boat back to the southeast to get the 113 lined up for his live attack. Closing on the target at twenty-one thousand yards, Buzz and Ensign Commers watched the gyro closely. Exactly at sixteen thousand yards, the torpedoes were launched. Buzz looked at his watch, counting off time to impact but was interrupted by a torpedo technician that had come along to observe the operation.

"Skipper, number four turned off course! It's headed for the shipping channel!"

According to the ensigns watch, number three exploded on time, sending a huge geyser of water up against the side of an old freighter anchored near Prudence Island, but number four was still running dangerously hot somewhere in the shipping channel. Needless to say its destination quickly became obvious as an explosion ripped apart an empty barge being towed north by a small tug boat. Without wasting time, the tug boat crew chopped the tow lines with fire axes, lest they be pulled down with the heavy barge.

In just minutes the barge disappeared from the surface while a stunned crew stood on the aft of the tug boat yelling profanities at the 113 crew.

Everyone at Melville from Commander Sneider on down was getting used to problems with the experimental torpedoes, as this was not the first such accident. Luckily no one was killed or injured, and the navy would handsomely reimburse the owner of the barge. Much to the chagrin of the navy, many local newspapers followed the ongoing incidents with PT Boat skippers, keeping residents that lived on the water front glued to their deck chairs, hoping to be the next person to report a story.

Live fire antiaircraft practice was completed out at sea away from shipping lanes and far from the prying eyes of reporters. The gunners on the 113 boat were proving to be worth their weight in gold, as they scored the highest amount of hits in the squadron. Buzz gave a large part of the credit to Chief Petrovski who stood near the front of the boat pointing our targets with a yard stick. Both Wickman and Portland paid close attention to his signaling and verbal directions.

Elmer Sims, their cook, hated every time the crew would go on a depth charge run over a target. The sound of the detonating can was deafening in the confined galley. More than once he would climb up to the cockpit giving Buzz or Ensign Commers a piece of his mind.

With training drawing to a close, Buzz felt confident the 113 boat and his crew were ready to take their place in the island fighting in the Pacific. By now Wickman no longer considered the boat jinxed, and felt like an integral part of the crew. Chief Petrovski finally acquired a nice single fifty caliber machine gun with armor plating to protect the gunner. He went to work with machinist mate Crowder, reinforcing the deck for the weapon, and mounted several water tight cases nearby to hold

cans of ammunition. Buzz was able to get an eighteen-year-old gunners mate named Kowalski from Brooklyn, New York to handle the weapon. He was a Jewish kid that just never seemed to know when to quit, and was always looking for a good tussle to get into. He had been tossed off two other boats for arguing that the skippers lacked real determination or imagination. Buzz had a feeling he was just the type of man he could use on the crew when things went bad. Since Chief Petrovski knew about him and made a positive recommendation, Buzz and Ensign Commers liked their odds.

During the last week of training, Buzz received a letter from his mother. She explained that Carl had attempted to enlist in the navy, but was turned down because of a heart murmur. So after a long discussion, he decided to work full time with the fishing business, allowing Josh to enlist in the Army Air Corp as a pilot. She blamed Buzz for losing another son to the war effort, because of his comments to Carl when they picked up the car. Buzz had to laugh at the letter, he knew somehow, some way, Josh would get his ass shot down trying to prove what kind of a real stud he was.

Commander Sneider held a small graduation party for the crews on Saturday night that was attended by trainers, shop workers, and office staff. It was a ritual the commander very much enjoyed, as this was when he was allowed to promote Ensigns to the rank of Lieutenant jg. Since Buzz already held the rank, his promotion to full Lieutenant would need to wait a while longer.

Sunday morning Commander Wilson and Commander Sneider stood on the pier shaking hands with each man wishing them, "Fair Seas and Following Winds," as they departed for Jacksonville, Florida, and the war beyond the west coast. They knew many of these men would never return home, and many more may very well end up listed as missing in action, but it was a job that needed to be done to win the war, and these were the best men for the job.

Since the refueling tanker was the only vessel in the convoy that had radar, the twelve PT Boats kept in close proximity to her like pups around their mother throughout the voyage. Entering the harbor at Jacksonville, the men spotted three LST's (Landing Ship Tank), tied up to the piers. The following morning, huge cranes lifted four, sixty-one-ton Elko PT boats onto LST - 1125, and four more on to LST - 1088. The four, forty-eight-ton Higgins PT Boats were loaded onto LST - 1114. As the yard crews had completed this job many times before, they made it look quite easy.

At 1700hrs. the LST's, a fuel tanker and two destroyers exited Jacksonville Harbor for the Panama Canal. After a meal with his crew, Buzz reminded everyone what was expected of them during the voyage to the canal and beyond. He made it quite clear that a trip to the brig for any offense meant you were off the crew, and there would not be any negotiations.

CHAPTER 3
PANAMA CANAL

The first night, Buzz slept rather well in the tight hot quarters he was assigned to on LST - 1125. However, every loud noise awakened him with a start, knowing German submarines made routine patrols throughout the Caribbean, looking for slow fat targets like these over loaded transports. The thought of running up the ladder to the main deck, releasing the harnesses that held his boat in place, so it could settle into the water and get away from the sinking LST boggled his mind. So, this would be the last night he would sleep on the ship, even though the captain of the transport requested no one sleep on their individual boats.

The following morning when Buzz moved his gear back to the 113, he realized that over half of his crew were already there. Lt. Jack Sterling's 110 boat was situated directly in front of the 113 on the port side of the ship. As the two skippers had become great friends during training at Melville, they enjoyed working out battle scenarios for their crews, attempting to keep everyone's mind sharp during this long voyage to the Pacific.

The second day at sea, a fast destroyer escort that had joined the convoy near Cuba, sighted a periscope as it was searching the seas off to the northwest. As one of the original destroyers raced forward to assist in locating the periscope, it disappeared. For an hour everyone stayed at their battle stations in case the submarine attacked. All three destroyers went sonar active as they searched the waters around the convoy but they were unable to pick up any trace of the vessel.

Due to the fact that a submarine was spotted, the convoy began sailing a zigzag course which slowed the progress toward the canal. During the next several days, United States patrol planes stationed at many islands and countries ringing the Caribbean, flew overhead in search of the elusive sub. On the third day, one PBY float plane notified the convoy they had spotted a submarine about three miles out. Two destroyers raced to the location, making several depth charge attacks, but once again the submarine skipper was able to slip away to fight another day.

Arriving within a hundred miles of Panama, the men on board the transports were happy to see a flotilla of American, British and Canadian destroyers slowly patrolling the approaches to the canal. It would now be suicide for any submarine attempting to sail into those waters, hence the ships no longer zigzagged. Everyone stood on the decks of their PT boats as they approached the canal, trying to get their first glimpse of the big ditch they had learned about in school. There were six cargo ships riding at anchor in Limon Bay, waiting to get permission to enter the canal. However the three LST's were considered a priority and were allowed to transit first.

Moving through the locks was a true experience for all the men, as they rode the ship up and down 85 feet as they passed from the Gatun locks on the east to the CoColi locks on the west. Search planes flew overhead as several PT boats patrolled the waters between the locks. There was no way the Allies were going to allow any enemy saboteurs to damage or destroy this vital waterway.

Arriving in the Pacific, once again a large armada of ships patrolled the waters in search of Japanese submarines, or aircraft carriers that might attempt another surprise attack. Exiting the canal, the three LST's docked at the U.S. Naval Support Facility near Panama City. All twelve boats were unloaded overnight.

The following morning the crews began training around the hundreds of small islands west of Panama. As some islands were uninhabited, they practiced landing Marine Marauders at night and removing them from beaches using live fire methods. Several older tug boats or barges were set up to look like Japanese vessels that would be plying the waters of the Solomon Islands where they would begin their combat. The PT crews played cat and mouse games with the enemy boats, while attempting to hide from American destroyers trying to hunt them down.

However, training became reality around 0200hrs. the third week in Panama. The skipper of the 102 boat made a perfect torpedo attack on one of the large tugs pulling barges through the islands. Completing his attack, the skipper threw his throttles forward at full speed to evade an old luxury cabin cruiser playing the part of a Japanese patrol boat that was in hot pursuit. In the dark and his haste to escape, he failed to see a destroyer that was sailing between two larger islands. The commander of the destroyer saw the boat coming toward him at flank speed, but knew there was nothing he could do to avoid impact, so he turned on his large search light to give warning. In an instant the skipper of the 102 spun his wheel hard to starboard in an attempt to avoid a collision. The port side of the PT Boat slammed against the side of the destroyer, ripping torpedo tube three off its mounting brackets, throwing it back over the roof of the crew compartment where it struck and killed the sailor manning the aft 20mm gun. Bouncing off the ship, the wooden boat skidded sideways across the water, slamming into a rocky reef about twenty yards from an island. As it was solid against the rocks with it props seriously bent, there was no way to get the boat moving again until high tide re-floated the boat the following morning.

Hearing the distress call, Buzz turned on his search light and rushed the 113 boat to the accident scene. Arriving at the stranded boat, he added his powerful light to that of the destroyer that had backed up to assist. Within minutes, it was evident there was a second casualty. One of the torpedo men was lying on the port side of the deck with massive head and chest injuries from the dislodged torpedo tube. It was evident he had been killed immediately when the tube tore lose. Once the crew of the 113 boat picked up the bodies of the dead and laid them on their fore-deck, they helped several more injured men on board. The skipper of the 102 and the balance of the crew chose to stay with their boat until morning.

As the sun was still rising in the east the following morning, a large ocean tug gave a quick pull dislodging the 102, allowing it to float free from its rocky grip. As the props and shafts were badly bent, the tug pulled them back to the base where the boat went into dry dock to be repaired. After a thorough inspection, it was determined the boat had not sustained any major damage to the hull. As it was estimated the repair work could take up to two weeks to complete, the 102 was pulled from the squadron and replaced with PT 84, an older Higgins class boat that had been used to guard the canal. She was in good shape and had just finished an engine overhaul, so the crew was happy to adopt her.

Midway through the following week, the boats were once more placed back on the LST's for the trip to the island of French New Caledonia. The men had learned a lot about night fighting in the blackness of the Panamanian Islands, that would become very useful when they arrived in the Solomon Islands. The crews were now very aware that every island or atoll could be filled with hostile enemy, hidden shore batteries, and large patrolling ships that could slice through their wooden vessels like a hot knife in butter.

At midnight, exactly one month after arriving in Panama, a convoy containing the LST's, six oil tankers, four cargo ships, a light cruiser, seven destroyers and three destroyer escorts, sailed west across the Pacific. It was a slow voyage as the convoy was required to zigzag the entire way, and those older heavy ships could only make about twenty-two knots at full speed, so estimated time of arrival in the harbor of Noumea was seventeen days away. Every PT crew was required to stand submarine watch on their ships, so that meant every fourth night, the men of the 113 boat would enjoy the tropical southern breezes under the constant watch of the southern cross constellation.

Buzz took up his position in the cockpit by the radio with a set of binoculars, so he could send out any alerts that were called out by his crew. On a clear night the moon and stars bathed the ocean and the fleet in a bluish light that almost took your breath away. But that also meant any lurking submarine would be able to see the convoy silhouetted against the dark sky, and see the phosphorescent wake each ship left behind upon the surface. All submarine skippers were well trained in following these wakes right back to their source. However on a completely overcast night, you could barely make out your hand in front of your face. On nights like that, men's nerves were strained to the maximum, hoping every ship was on station where it belonged in the convoy to avoid any collisions. Colliding with a tanker loaded with oil could easily create a massive chain reaction explosion that would wipe out both ships in minutes, and damage other nearby vessels. Since leaving Panama, a tanker filled with oil sailed to port of LST-1125. When the wind blew from the south, the over powering smell of the thick black fuel was enough to make most men nauseous. But what bothered most men, was the tanker behind them that carried thousands of gallons of high-grade aviation fuel and diesel fuel. That ship was just a tinder box ready to explode with the slightest spark. They were in a precarious position, but they all knew that the precious fuel those ships were carrying, powered the massive strength of the allied forces that were being thrown against the Japanese Empire.

Throughout the long voyage, the entire crew of the 113 slept on their boat. Most men just tossed a blanket on the deck and slept where they found room. However, waking from a deep sleep and getting up to walk was dangerous, as you could easily fall overboard on the port side and land in the ocean, never to be seen again; or, you could fall off the starboard side down into the well of the LST and land on trucks or artillery and be killed. But the men chose those risks over being down inside the hot stinking ship.

Keeping the men in shape was tough as there was little room for calisthenics or running. Buzz attempted to exercise the crew twice a day on the deck of the boat as best he could. He knew full well a crew could easily lose their edge after seventeen long days at sea. The other problem every boat skipper had, was to require their men to wear shirts as much as possible. The blazing hot southern sun not only gave you a dark tan quickly, but it burned and destroyed layers of the epidermis requiring medical attention, and rendering them unfit for combat duty for two to three days, or longer. It was essential to have every man ready for combat when the ships sailed into Noumea, or they would be removed from the boat and be court-martialed.

Two days out of Noumea, a Japanese midget submarine was sighted on the north side of the convoy. Two destroyer escorts bolted from the formation, preparing to attack the small submarine before it could crash into one of the ships in the convoy. Without firing a shot, the lead ship slammed its bow into the side of the sub just aft of the small conning tower, breaking it in half. As the destroyer sailed on past, the sub disappeared from the surface, but no one in the convoy relaxed. Everyone understood that a midget submarine had not traveled this far out into the Pacific without having a mother ship close by.

Every eye in the convoy scanned the dark blue waters looking for any sign of the lurking sub. Several hours later, a sailor on watch aboard LST-1110 sighted a Japanese submarine attempting to work its way into the confines of the convoy. Once again, several destroyer escorts charged forward to deal with the threat, but they were a bit too late. The Japanese skipper fired two torpedoes at a fat oil tanker in the middle of the flotilla. The explosion sent out a shock wave that blew off antennas, shattered windows, and tore gun mounts lose from their mountings on ships over two hundred yards away. The crews of the PT boats threw themselves to their decks, hoping they would be missed by all the flying debris.

As the submarine exited the convoy on the north side, the skipper of a British destroyer pummeled the boat with a barrage of hedgehogs, a British type of depth charge, that landed all around the fleeing boat. Explosion after explosion from the hedgehogs detonated nearly right on top of the sub. At the same time, American destroyer escorts were beginning to drop their depth charges. Geysers of dark green water raced skyward as the depth charges exploded with a massive roar.

Moments later, the bow of the submarine began to break the surface of the ocean as the destroyers circled with their deck guns preparing to fire. As the sub continued rising, it was clear the conning tower had probably taken a direct hit from a hedgehog as it was twisted and caved in on one side. The sub was listing hard to starboard as oil poured from a damaged fuel bunker. An officer covered in blood, carrying a white flag exited the hull from a torpedo loading hatch. As he walked back toward the conning tower, several more wounded men dragged themselves out of the hatch, falling prone onto the hull.

There was no doubt they understood no ship in the convoy was allowed to stop to offer them assistance. All they could hope for was that a skipper from one of destroyers would have his crew toss life rafts into the water for them.

Before anything like that could happen, there was an explosion from the rear of the submarine that was still partially under water. The sailor with the white flag was tossed into the air landing several feet from the submarine as it began slipping back under the waves. The men that had laid down on the deck, were now rolling toward the conning tower as the bow of the dying ship rose sharply up into the air before sliding back under the waves. As the convoy continued sailing forward toward Noumea, what was left of the burning tanker, rolled hard to starboard and began to sink, leaving a thick heavy oil slick on the surface of the south Pacific.

CHAPTER 4
NOUMEA, NEW CALEDONIA

Like all the crew members of the 113 boat, Buzz was over taken by the site of lush palm trees swaying with the moderate tropical winds all along the coast line of New Caledonia. With his binoculars, he could see children running up and down the beach, or throwing coconuts at one another in a sort of dodge ball game. Off duty sailors and marines were swimming in the warm waters or relaxing on the beach. It appeared to be a great place to be stationed.

Security near the entrance to the harbor was extremely heavy, as PT boats and destroyer escorts constantly patrolled the deeper water searching for submarines. Antiaircraft gun emplacements had been constructed all around the harbor, just in case a Japanese carrier slipped through the allied patrols.

The Island of New Caledonia was vital to sea operations in the South Pacific, and was to be protected at all costs. Besides the large harbor, the allies had worked incredibly hard building a command center that housed naval officers from the United States, England, New Zealand, Australia, and Indonesia, plus Free French naval officers, and those from several other smaller navies that were at war with Japan.

A tremendous amount of war equipment and supplies were stored on the island that supported bases all around the South Pacific. Aircraft from the many new airfields built on the island, scoured the shipping lanes west toward Australia and east toward the Panama Canal, searching for and attacking Japanese submarines threatening the vital supply line.

By the time this convoy arrived, there was not much left of the casual island life men had read about in books. The business of war had totally overtaken the island, and the high-ranking officers representing countries from all over the world had little time for anyone not involved in winning the war, or for anyone that caused problems or got drunk once too often.

Although there were a tremendous number of cranes available to help unload the supply ships, the navy had not delivered cranes like they had in Panama to unload PT boats. Engineers had concocted lifts made from coconut logs, old wooden pulley assemblies, and ropes that had been repaired more than once. These make shift lifts were operated by navy Seabees and island natives, most that really did not understand the process of what they were doing. Without proper cranes the unloading process was dangerous and slow. After an LST was tied to the pier, the make shift cranes would unload the two boats facing the shore and place them on wooden bunks. Then, the LST would have to be pulled away from the pier so the cranes could remove the boats from the bunks, and set them down in the water to be sailed away. Then the LST would need to turn around so the other side could be unloaded. In Panama, the proper cranes could unload two ships in the time it took these men to unload two boats.

Buzz and Lt. Commers decided to stay close to the LST while the 113 was being unloaded. They were impressed with the way the men handled the homemade equipment, but they had to laugh at the amount of swearing and cursing that took place during the operation. It became clear to Buzz that although the native men did not know a lot of English, they had learned every swear word at least, and had discovered many creative ways of using them.

While observing his boat being unloaded, Buzz noticed a gunner's mate sitting on a stack of pallets watching the entire affair. The sailor quickly jumped up and saluted as Buzz approached. "Sir, Gunners Mate Albert Stockey, sir and I'm looking for a boat. Could you use a top gunner?"

Buzz smiled. "At ease, Seaman. What happened to your boat?"

"Well sir, I came down with malaria as soon as I got to this damn island and ended up in the hospital. Needless to say my skipper replaced me and left, so I've been trying to find a new family ever since. The idiots over in operations keep ignoring me. Sir, I want to get out of here and get into the war. Is there anything you can do for me?"

Shaking his head, Buzz replied. "I just took on a new gunner for the bow .50 we added, so I just don't have room for another man." Slapping Stockey on the shoulder, Buzz added. "Hang tough, son, someone is bound to get hurt or sick in the near future and you'll find a new home."

With the 113 in the water, Lt. Commers idled it over to an area in the harbor where the boats were being gathered. Buzz put the crew to work washing down the boat, as it was covered in a heavy layer of salt spray. All the weapons and torpedo tubes were torn down so they could be given a good layer of fresh oil.

Elmer Simms, the cook, went to work rounding up and storing all the food supplies they were supposed to have on hand as they sailed from New Caledonia. Fuel tanks were topped off and spare parts for the Packard engines were placed in the machinist compartment.

Buzz, Lt. Commers and Radioman Yamry, searched naval headquarters and talked to skippers of commerce ships, trying to collect all the latest maps and reef charts they could lay their hands on for the Solomon Islands. Ed Yamry took special care to find logs containing radio frequencies used by commerce ships, PT squadrons, air craft, submarines and Japanese patrol boats. Buzz made it clear to everyone that they were not going into the Solomon's unprepared.

Returning to the boat from Central Pacific Command, Buzz and Ensign Commers observed an ambulance backed up to the pier. They could see several stretcher bearers loading someone into the truck. After a brisk run, Buzz arrived just as the ambulance began to pull away. Grabbing on to Chief Petrovski's arm he called out. "What the hell is going on, Chief?"

"It's Gunners Mate Portland, sir. He was cleaning out the gun tub when he grabbed his midsection and let out a scream. Yamry looked him over and thinks it may be a ruptured appendix. The doctor that came with the ambulance has a tendency to agree. Sir, that kid was in some God-awful pain, and he was snow white. Looks like we will need to find a new man before we can sail."

Buzz shook his head. "Damn sorry to hear that. Portland was a good sailor, but I think I just might know a guy that should be able to fill his shoes, if he's still around here. I'll let you know what I find out, Chief."

As the loading continued, Chief Petrovski checked and double checked every list, to make sure the men were getting everything that was required loaded and stored. He made it quite clear to the crew that Lt. Maddox said there would be no drinking aboard his boat, but he had not said anything about bringing several cases of Bourbon along for trading purposes once they arrived in the islands, and no one argued the point. It was here the men saw the chief begin to wear his custom made .45 revolver for the first time. It was rumored that the weapon originally belonged to Wyatt Earp, and that the chief had won it in a poker game in Tombstone when he was on leave years back. No one doubted his ability to use the weapon, as they had seen him on the range cover all six shots with a silver dollar at forty feet. That afternoon, as Buzz was checking over all the loading manifests with the chief, he observed Stockey leaning up against one of the pier supports, with his sea bag at his side.

Jumping off the boat, Buzz walked up to the sailor that was already standing at attention. "Gunners Mate Stockey, Albert reporting for duty for the open spot you have on your crew, sir!"

"At ease, Stockey," Buzz called out. "How the hell did you know we have an opening on our crew already? I haven't even gone over to the Bureau of Personnel yet."

"Sir, word travels fast around here, just like which girls to stay away from at any given bar on this God forsaken Island. This ain't paradise, but that beautiful Elco would certainly be a heck of a place to lay my hat, sir."

"So you say you are a fantastic gunner, do you know how to swim, Stockey?" Buzz inquired.

"Yes sir, growing up in Minnesota you need to swim with all those lakes around. We would spend all summer swimming and playing in the water. Of course, we didn't need to worry about sharks up there."

Buzz smiled. "Yeah, sharks may have a tendency to keep you out of the water down here." After a moment of thought Buzz nodded his head. "Alright Stockey, go see the chief and tell him you're our new gunner. Stow your gear, check out the starboard duel .50 mount, and be ready to show us what you can do. When I come back from personnel, we'll head out and you can fire at a tow rack."

Stockey smiled. "Thank you, skipper, I guarantee you made the right damn decision."

As Buzz prepared to walk away, he slapped Stockey on the shoulder. "Welcome home, sailor!"

When Buzz returned, Ensign Commers was standing near the starboard gun tub talking with Stockey. After saluting he inquired. "The new man says we're going for a ride, is that a fact, sir?"

Buzz nodded his head, "Yup, he's officially ours now, so we need to see what he can do. Plus, it never hurts to give the other guys a bit more practice. Get 'em fired up, Todd!"

In just minutes the 113 was idling out of the harbor, headed west into a rough Pacific Ocean. As they reached the western edge of the is-land, Ensign Commers could see a tug pulling a target rack about a half mile away. "General quarters, general quarters, man all battle stations!" He called out.

Spinning the 113 hard to port, he pushed the throttles forward. The sharp bow of the charging boat ripped through the heavy waves, sending huge geysers of water nearly twenty feet into the air. Every part of the boat was dripping wet from the heavy spray that was washing back upon them. But no man complained as they realized this was exactly what they were in for as part of a PT boat crew in the Solomon's. Nearing the ocean tug, Ensign Commers steered to port, allowing the 113 to come parallel with the tug and the target rack. When he was in range, he yelled out, "Open fire!"

Kowalski on the bow .50 and Stockey on the dual .50 let loose. Buzz and Petrovski watched with binoculars to see how they were firing. It did not take long to see they had made a good decision on both men. After passing the tug, the boat spun around to attack again, allowing Wickman on the port duel .50 and Kowalski on the bow to take on the bouncing target rack. Once again Buzz and the chief were well satisfied with the men's efficiency.

After completing that training, Ensign Commers steered the boat on a southerly course. In several minutes they came across the wreck of an old steamer that sat partially out of the water on a rock pile. When he came into range, Buzz yelled at Johnson who was already gripping the 20mm cannon on the rear of the boat. "Let her have it, Johnson."

As the ensign pushed the throttles farther open, Johnson began rotating the gun with the speed of the boat as he fired. The rapid boom, boom, boom, of the automatic cannon was always a delight to Buzz. But what was even better, was to see the amount of hits Johnson scored against the wreckage as the 113 passed by at high speed. That was exactly what Johnson would need to do during the desperate night battles against destroyers or larger ships in the dark waters of the Solomon's. He was impressed how fast Gunners Mate Hollerman could replace the ammunition canister on the weapon. There was no doubt this was a well-tuned crew that was ready for whatever the Japanese threw at them.

Returning from the practice run, Ensign Commers stopped the boat about 150 yards from the mouth of the harbor, as Chief Petrovski arrived on deck with two M-1 rifles. After tossing one to Buzz, the chief called out.

"Stockey, Kowalski get over here!"

When the men had assembled, the chief continued. "Drop your combat gear and jump in. You're the only crew members that haven't proved their swimming abilities yet. You can swim from here to the entrance of the harbor, then we'll pick you up."

Looking down at the water, Stockey called out, "Chief, there could be sharks out there!"

"You're right about that sailor, that's why the skipper and I have rifles. Stay close to the boat and we'll have the crew keep an eye out for them. And quit taking off your boots, you need to swim with them on. If we get sunk, you might have to swim to the shore of some small island. What the hell are you going to do if you have to walk across ten yards of coral rock to get to the beach. Your feet will be cut to ribbons and infection would be close behind, you got that!"

Kowalski shook his head, "Sharks, sharp coral. Jesus, what a great place to fight a war."

Before he could say another word, the chief grabbed him by the arm, tossing him overboard.

"Welcome to the South Pacific, gentlemen. It's not quite the way Hemingway described it, but it's what we've got to deal with."

The men swam at a very good speed about five yards away from the side of the 113, with the crew keeping a close eye out for any wandering sharks. When they reached the entrance to the harbor, the crew pulled the men back on board, before Ensign Commers brought the boat back to its berth.

During the next week, all the skippers took their crews out to sea to practice group battle maneuvers and more weapons tests. The crew of the 113 quickly proved they were second to none for their speed, accuracy and efficiency. Buzz and Ensign Commers were damn proud of their crew.

Several days before departure for Rendova, Captain Garriman, the commandant of PT Operations in New Caledonia, inspected all the boats along with his aide, Ensign Wilder. As they walked along the deck of the 113 boat, the ensign looked down at torpedo tube number four. After shaking his head, he called out for Chief Petrovski. "See here Chief, that tube has a six-inch long scratch. After salt water has contact with it, rust will begin to form. It needs to be sanded and painted immediately, or you will not sail with the rest of the boats!"

Before the chief could explode on the young officer, Buzz called out, "No problem Ensign, we'll get at it right away, right Chief?"

"Aye, aye, Skipper, we'll get at it straight away," Chief Petrovski replied as he turned to get some of the crew members.

Making matters worse, the ensign called out. "Chief, that will be three coats of base primer and four coats of finish paint for a proper job."

Before Buzz could respond, the chief called out, "Would that need to be painted by a right or a left-handed sailor if we need to do it by the book, sir?"

Trying to keep from laughing, Captain Garriman grabbed his ensign by the arm. "Move along son, there are other boats to check over."

Buzz saluted the captain as he prepared to leave the boat. "Thanks for coming aboard sir, the 113 is in terrific condition and ready for battle."

Nodding his head in approval, the captain smiled.

"Maddox, I wish I were going with you. The boat and crew look ship shape and will give the Japs a good ass kicking. Plus, I wouldn't have to put up with the Admiral's piss ant nephew who is attempting to make a name for himself by antagonizing every Chief Petty Officer on New Caledonia."

Jumping off the boat beside the captain, Buzz stated, "Sir, some PT boat or LST must need an executive officer. Assign the man on an emergency basis and get rid of him."

Captain Garriman smiled. "Don't think that hasn't crossed my mind, Maddox. I'm just afraid he'll get someone killed out there, and then I'll have to live with that."

Patting Buzz on the shoulder, the captain walked down to the 99 boat where the ensign had already started an argument.

Friday evening, the night before they sailed for the Solomon's, Buzz went to the hospital to visit Portland. He found his gunner in a very poor state of mind and angry at the world. It took Buzz several minutes of back and forth before Buzz got down to the real problem.

"Skipper, they're sending me back state side to recuperate. I may never get another chance at a PT boat, and that just ain't fair. I completed the school at Melville just like everyone else, so I should get another boat. You got to do something for me, skipper!"

Buzz shook his head in disgust. "Portland, I wish there was something I could do, but there just isn't. Look, when you get to California and are able to get around, go to the Department of Personnel and be the biggest pest they have ever seen, day after day. Eventually, they're going to want to get rid of you, and bang, you'll be on your way back here with their blessings. Trust me, that will work."

Portland smiled at Buzz. "Skipper, I believe that just might do it. When I get back here, I would like to serve with you again. But if that's not possible, see if you can get me into your division at least."

Standing up, Buzz shook hands with Portland, "Now that's the attitude of a PT boat man!"

Walking out of the hospital, Buzz saw a very familiar face that made him smile. Sitting alone on a bench was Nurse Connie Russell. Walking over slowly, Buzz said, "What's a gorgeous girl like you doing in a dump like this?"

Immediately, Connie jumped up, giving Buzz a hug. "I figured you would be passing through here sooner or later, and I was hoping to see you. Buzz, I was wrong. I want you in my life, even if you are heading out to war and on some damn wooden boat. That scares the hell out of me, but I will pray for you every day and night. Write to me and I will write to you, and let's build on what we already have. I am yours for the long haul, just come back to me."

After a long kiss and a few moments to visit, Buzz looked at his watch. "I'm sorry Connie, but I need to get back to the 113, we shove off early in the morning. I'm so glad you were here today."

Smiling, Connie replied. "I understand, but at least we found each other in this crazy war. Go now and stay safe. I'll keep a candle burning for you every night."

Early Saturday morning, a navy oiler, an LST, and three destroyer escorts sailed quietly out of the Harbor of Noumea. About a half hour later, ten PT boats slipped from their mooring spots, sailing out to meet the small convoy. With the boats nestled inside the convoy, the skipper of the lead destroyer turned north toward Vanuatu, 392 miles away. The boats would need to refuel at sea from the oiler one time before making port, and that was always dangerous, especially with heavy seas. Once at Vanuatu, the boats would be given a thorough inspection, checking everything over. If there was any question at all, that particular vessel would be pulled from the flotilla for an overhaul. Everything had to be perfect once they entered a combat zone.

When all the inspections were completed, the PT boats and the LST would sail the last 139 miles to the north east on their own. Of the ten boats, four would pull out of the convoy near the island of Rennell, and the last six would continue on to the Island of Tulagi in the Florida Islands.

Buzz was happy to see the 113 was assigned to Tulagi, along with the 115, 123, 46 and the 111. Each of those boats was skippered by men Buzz felt were outstanding officers. As the boats neared the Florida Islands one afternoon, it was clear they had entered a combat zone. Fighter aircraft flew low patrols overhead, as many types of naval landing ships sailed between the islands. In the distance, several destroyers were working on anti-submarine patrols in the deep water of the straights. Looking over the men of the 113, Buzz knew he was exactly where he belonged. Because just over the horizon on countless islands, the enemy prepared to throw the Americans back out of the Pacific. Now that the 113 had arrived, Buzz was going to do whatever it took to send the enemy packing back to Japan.

CHAPTER 5
TULAGI

The base at Tulagi had been hacked out of the dense jungle by Sea-bees and was rather crude. Most of the buildings on the island were made from wood and palm trees the engineers had cut down. A couple of newer Quonset huts were under construction deeper into the jungle. All the piers were made from coconut logs that were tied together with ropes or heavy palm fronds. The base had a very tropical look about it, as steam rose from the mud puddles that dotted the area from the over-night rain. Everyone arriving at Tulagi soon learned that mud was the main export of the island.

Three PT boats under repair were tied to the piers as men drenched in sweat labored over the precious but damaged boats.

Buzz had just picked out a spot to berth the 113, when somewhere on the island an air raid siren began to scream. "Reverse engines, reverse engines," Buzz called through the voice tube to the engine room. As soon as the engines were reversed, Buzz slammed the throttles forward, propelling the 113 in reverse, right back out of the harbor.

Seconds later, three Japanese Zeros streaked in from the north with machine guns blazing. Every gunner on the replacement boats, along with the guns from the damaged boats, sprang to life. The roar in the harbor was like nothing Buzz had ever heard before. With nine 20mm cannons pounding boom, boom, boom, mingled with the sound of nearly 40 machine guns hammering away, it was as if the air around Buzz was actually vibrating. One thing was for sure, the raiding party had not realized six new boats would be there when they arrived. The lead plane attempted to break off its attack and climb, but was hit so many times it burst into flames before tumbling into the water. The second pilot broke hard to the south climbing directly above the 113 and 111 boats. Its right fuel tank ruptured, sending a sheet of flame down along the side of the aircraft. The stricken fighter rolled over several times before crashing into the jungle behind the island headquarters. The third pilot dropped down close to the water, snaking back and forth just above the waves heading back out to sea and safety.

When the firing stopped, Chief Petrovski walked up to Buzz. "Good job, sir. We survived our first encounter. Now let's get this thing into the harbor so we can get refueled.

Refueling at a forward base like Tulagi was not a pleasant operation. There was no electrical power on the island, and the few small generators scattered throughout the island were already over-taxed, between the hospital and the small warehouse where ice was kept to keep food from spoiling.

To refuel, boats had to line up along the refueling dock and wait their turn in line. A fork lift continually delivered fifty-five-gallon drums of 100 octane gasoline to the docks. Crew members would then insert hand pumps into the barrels, and crank on them to fill the boat. Each boat held 3,000 gallons of fuel in three tanks, enough for a twelve-hour mission. The three thirsty 4,500 horsepower Packard engines would consume 200 gallons per hour cruising at 23 knots, or 500 gallons per hour running full out at 41 knots. Skippers had to keep in mind that although running at high speed was exciting, it dropped your endurance time down to six hours. Running out of fuel on a dark night in the middle of the Solomon Islands was something no PT crew ever wanted to do. On many days, refueling of the boats went well into the late-night hours.

With the arrival of the six new boats, squadron two at Tulagi was now back to full strength of twelve boats, not including the three boats laid up for repairs. Squadron Commander Nate Reddings was overjoyed to have his fleet up to the full complement again. He had been working his six boats nearly to the limit just trying to keep the enemy at bay. Now it would be possible for Squadron Two to take the fight back to the Japanese.

Nothing moved for two days after the boats arrived. Heavy rain squalls, coupled with wind gusts up to forty miles an hour kept everything clamped down. It was even too dangerous for the enemy to try and spring a surprise attack on the base. Frustrating as it may have been, it provided some down time for the crews, allowing them to catch up on sleep and write letters home

However, the officers were kept busy listening to the skippers that had been there for a while discussing reefs, rock piles, shoals, sand bars and the many passages between islands. Chief Petrovski worked hard updating the charts they had brought with them from New Caledonia. They were also given identification sheets of the many different types of aircraft the Japanese used.

As the storm blew itself out, the following night the 113 boat was assigned a patrol mission, along with the 111, 116 and 118. They were to patrol north east along the south coast of Santa Isabel Island, cross the slot over to Kolombangara, passing Kula Gulf, and then back home along New Georgia and Vangunu Islands. Buzz understood it would be a long night, especially for a new crew with no combat experience on the open water.

At 2200hrs, the four boats rumbled out of the harbor with the 116 boat in the lead, and the 113 bringing up the rear. As the sky was still heavily overcast from the storm, the darkness of the Solomon Islands was unnerving. From the cockpit, Buzz could barely see the bow of his boat, but he was lucky enough to navigate by the phosphorescent wake washed up by the three props of the 118. Using binoculars, Ensign Commers could make out the rear of the 118 once in a while as he scanned the open sea. It was comforting to know they had not made a wrong turn and become lost in the darkness.

Chief Petrovski kept walking from station to station, making sure the men were awake and alert. As he walked into the cockpit he leaned over to Buzz. "The men are about as nerved up as they can be. I don't think any of them counted on this darkness. To be honest, it has me worried, Skipper."

Watching straight ahead Buzz responded, "Go below and get us each a cup of coffee, Chief. Look over the charts for Santa Isabel to see where any large reefs are."

"You got it, Skipper," the chief responded, before ducking down into the chart room below.

"Buzz, there are no reefs along this area, I checked it myself this afternoon." Ensign Commers stated as he looked strangely at his boss.

"I know that, Todd. I just wanted to give him a task to get his mind readjusted. I don't want him that nervous, especially around the men. Besides, this will give him a chance to criticize the coffee and forget where he's at for a few minutes while he argues about it with Sims," Buzz responded.

Todd had to laugh as he shook his head. "Good move, Skipper, good move!"

Just as the chief returned with the coffee, Stockey leaned over the gun tub railing, "Skipper, small craft just off the southeast side of San Jorge Island. Can't make it out, but it's moving pretty slow and not very big.

Immediately, Ensign Commers and Chief Petrovski scanned the area with their binoculars. After several minutes the chief responded. "Small sampan, sir. Heading to the northwest. Could be Japs, could be islanders."

Buzz nodded his head, "Tell Yamry to radio Lt. Kellerman on the 116 and tell him what we saw."

As the 113 passed by San Jorge Island, Lt. Kellerman told them to leave it alone as they had a long night ahead of them yet.

Reaching the far end of Santa Isabel Island, PT 116 began its westerly turn across the slot, heading for Kula Gulf. Now was the time to be on alert for the Japanese destroyers that escorted convoys of men and equipment to the occupied islands. American sailors and air crews operating in the area named it the Tokyo Express. Several PT boats had already been rammed during night operations by the charging ships that just appeared out of the darkness at tremendous rates of speed. Chief Petrovski walked back and forth along the boat, peering into the blackness with his binoculars. Just a one or two second warning could make all the difference between life and death. But tonight it appeared that the Tokyo Express had taken an evening off. Except for a slow flying float plane that had come out of Kula Gulf, everything appeared to be quiet. All eyes were on the float plane as it made a wide circle around the small flotilla, keeping just out of range. The plane followed the boats for about a half hour before turning back toward the west and disappearing into a cloud bank. Since the pilot had not dropped any flares, Lt. Kellerman felt comfortable there were no lurking Japanese ships or patrol craft in the area. As the flotilla began their turn back toward the southeast, they ran into intermittent rain squalls that made visibility worse than it was before. Even Mount Veve, the 5,800-foot extinct volcano on Kolombangara, could not be seen in the overwhelming blackness.

The crew of the 113 was tired and totally stressed out as Buzz sailed the boat back into the harbor at Tulagi. Although no enemy contact had been made by any of his night patrols, Commander Reddings was happy all the boats had returned safely, without any damage from reefs or rock piles.

Once the 113 was tied up, Buzz called the crew together. "Gentlemen, you all did a good job out there last night. Go get some sleep and we'll get in line to refuel around 1300. Chief, I have a mission for you, follow me."

After walking a short distance away, Buzz leaned up against a truck. "Chief, I'm well aware of the trading bourbon you have stashed on board the 113, and I have no problem with it. But I was thinking out there last night. Would it not be a great idea to have a bazooka on board, just in case we ran into a close target in the dark. You could make a bracket to mount it in the cockpit so we can get at it quickly. We could put one round into the engine room or fuel tank of some unsuspecting vessel, and then run like hell."

The chief had to laugh as he scratched his head. "We'll have one before we sail tonight. I love the way you think, Skipper, the more weaponry the better. Should I use one or two bottles, sir?"

Buzz thought for a moment. "One bottle for the bazooka, and one bottle for let's say… six rockets. That should be a fair trade."

Nodding his head, the chief patted Buzz on the shoulder, "It shall be done."

As the 113 was being fueled, Buzz watched the chief and Wickman working in the cockpit with a drill and some other tools. He knew their newest weapon was being installed and he loved it.

Around 1600hrs., Buzz and Ensign Commers, along with the skippers of the 111 and 46 boats met with Commander Reddings.

"Gentlemen, tonight you'll be sailing over toward the Russell Islands. We are looking for activity on Pavuvu or Mbanika. Take your time, circle the islands and keep a good lookout. Then run over to Mborokua to see what the Japs are up to. Leave at 2100hrs, and be back by 0700. Maddox, this is your show."

Quite nervous about being in charge of three boats, Buzz backed the 113 boat clear of the harbor at 2045. The sky was filled with broken clouds, allowing some star light to help with navigation, but that also made it easier for the Japanese to see them.

Three abreast, the boats skimmed across the rather calm water of the Solomon Sea at 25 knots. Looking over to the bulkhead, below the starboard machine gun tub rested the bazooka and two rounds in a very nice set of brackets.

"The other four rounds are in similar brackets on the wall in the chart room. They make Yamry a bit nervous, but he'll get over it," Ensign Commers explained with a laugh.

The trip to the Russell's went off perfectly without any sign of enemy activity. Before beginning to circle the islands, Buzz ordered all engines to be muffled. Now, all you could hear from the giant engines was a dull muffled throb that was actually a very soothing sound. Scanning Pavuvu with binoculars, it was clear to see that on the north side of the island, two Japanese landing crafts were unloading in a cove. They found the same process going on in a cove on the west side. Over at Mbanika, there was a medium size transport tied up to the large pier that was used before the war by the coconut plantation owners. There were also two Japanese patrol boats idling just a short distance out from the pier, but they did not appear to have seen the PT boats skimming past. After circling the island and checking on Tikopia, which was quiet, the flotilla made their way back to Mbanika.

Buzz stiffened, when he noticed one patrol boat had left the area, which meant it was somewhere out at sea, and the weapons on board the boat made it a lethal challenge. Moments later, Lt. Downing from the 46 reported the patrol boat astern and closing fast.

Grabbing the microphone, Buzz called, "Unmuffle and go to full power. You guys go after it, I'll attack the other boat."

In seconds, the PT boats were circling around at full speed, with the 113 boat racing toward the second Japanese patrol boat that was attempting to get underway. As Buzz closed on the patrol boat, Kowalski and Wickman began firing their machine guns. Johnson blasted away at the stern of the patrol boat with his 20mm. Moments later, an explosion from the engine room tore off a large section of the rear quarter deck. The boat began listing over hard toward the port side as crew members dove of the deck. With that mission completed, Buzz turned back out to sea to catch up with the rest of the flotilla. In the distance, he could see streaks of tracers from the .50 machine guns from the 111 and 46 boats ripping into the damaged patrol boat as it began to burn.

As Buzz circled the area, the 111 and 46 boats cut off their attacks following the 113 off toward the north. Arriving off the coast of Mborokua, Buzz could see a destroyer rounding the island from the east. There was little doubt that the skipper of the destroyer saw the PT boats at the same time, as his front five-inch gun mount opened fire.

Lieutenant Downing immediately called out that he was going to line up for a torpedo run. That allowed the 113 and 111 boats to race up close to the ship and strafe the decks with their weapons. Exploding shells from the five-inch battery sent up geysers of water around the scurrying PT boats as they closed in tight on the charging vessel. Stockey, Kowalski and Johnson fired up into the superstructure of the ship, as Buzz flew by at an incredible rate of speed on the port side. Off in the distance, Buzz could see two flashes of light as Lt. Downing let go two torpedoes. Buzz counted off the seconds until impact while looking behind him, but saw nothing but a splash of water near the side of the ship. Once again, the Mark 14 torpedoes being used by the navy failed to detonate.

Looking back at the destroyer, Buzz could see several small deck fires caused by strafing from the 111 and 113 boats. He knew his boats had been very lucky tonight, they had made their presence known, but he did not want to press their luck.

After gathering his boats together once more, they sailed over toward Vangunu Island before turning back toward home.

Approaching the harbor, the men of the 113 stood silently as they watched the battered remains of the 118 boat being towed into the harbor by the 64 boat. The 118 had been battered horribly in a running battle with two enemy destroyers north of Malaita. Thankfully, the skipper of the 64 boat had intervened, sending a torpedo into the engine room of one of the destroyers, allowing the 118 to slip away into a fog bank. It was purely a miracle that anyone survived the night aboard that boat. As soon as the 113 was tied up, the crew ran over to the 118 to offer any assistance they could. It was an ugly job pulling the charred remains of the crew from the engine and chart rooms, where they had taken direct hits from a three-inch naval gun. Of the fourteen-man crew, three survived and one was missing, presumed thrown overboard and lost during the running battle. With the 124 boat coming out of the repair docks and ready for combat, the 118 was backed in to begin a rebuild.

As new men arrived on Tulagi nearly every other day as replacements, it didn't take long for Commander Reddings to assemble a crew for the 124.

Buzz received high marks for the way he handled his mission, including making the decision to take on the destroyer and create some damage. However, Commander Reddings once again sent an angry memo to New Caledonia regarding the failure of the torpedoes.

After several quiet days and nights, an Australian coast watcher send word to Tulagi that the Tokyo Express was putting together a large column of barges and landing craft for a push down the slot for Guadalcanal. After putting together two attack groups, Lt. Dawson from the 125 boat was put in charge of Devil Blue Force, containing the 113,111, 64, 43, and 125 boats. At 1800hr's, the skippers of the boats met in the operations hut to go over plans for the nights sortie. The boats would hug the shorelines of nearby islands in Kula and Vella Gulf, then attack after the lead escort ships of the Tokyo express neared New Georgia Island. That would allow the PT boats to attack the center of the convoy containing most of the slower barges.

Low dark clouds drifted over the Solomon's as the boats from Squadron Two sailed east up the slot. Halfway to their staging points, Devil Red Force turned off toward the northern islands, as Devil Blue continued towards the deep waters of Kula Gulf. Buzz took the 113, 111 and 43 boat into Kula Gulf as Lt. Dawson took his 125 boat and the 64 further up the slot into Vella Gulf at 2100hrs.

Buzz was nervous as this was going to be his first fight with the Tokyo Express, and if anything could go wrong, it normally did. With everyone maintaining strict radio silence, all Yamry could listen to was the low static that flowed from his headphones. Chief Petrovski stood aside of Kowalski on the fore-deck, scanning the entrance to the slot with his binoculars. Ensign Commers was leaning against the bulkhead below gun tub one, talking quietly with Wickman. Sims, the cook and all-around helper, stood on the ladder leading down to the chart room, talking to Buzz as they grabbed a cup of coffee.

Stockey sat in gun tub two, keeping to himself as he watched the clouds overhead glide to the southeast, allowing the stars and quarter moon to make an appearance from time to time.

On the rear of the boat, Johnson knelt below his 20mm mount, talking to Crowder in the engine room. Everyone on the boat was nervous, and somewhat scared, and talking seemed to help calm their nerves a little.

At 2130, the radio crackled with Lt. Dawson's voice. "Blue Leader to Blue Boy, lead destroyers your area in 10. Let them respond to my attack before moving."

Buzz nodded his head, allowing Yamry to know he had the message. "Blue Leader, have message," Yamry responded.

Ensign Commers flashed the other two boats with the red signal lamp, telling them to line up three abreast and fire one torpedo when directed.

Two minutes later, the roar of battle erupted from Vella Gulf, as the 125 and the 64-boat attacked. Instantly, the destroyer closest to Kula Gulf began a wide turn toward the west to help with the attack. As soon as the destroyer was halfway through its turn, Buzz threw the throttles forward with the 111 and 43 boats. Moments later Buzz yelled back at his Ensign, "Now Todd, now!"

With a quick flash of the message lamp, each of the charging PT boats cut lose with one torpedo, before beginning evasive action as their gunners raked the destroyer from stem to stern. Two large explosions brought the destroyer nearly to a stop as raging fires erupted from ammunition lockers near the front of the ship.

Several more explosions rocked the ship as fuel bunkers exploded, lighting up the channel as if it were midday. By now, Buzz was charging full speed into the middle of the scurrying barges. Every gun on board the 113 was picking out targets of opportunity to fire at. Several barges were already burning furiously from Lt. Dawson's attack. As Buzz turned back toward the east to attack a barge loaded with fuel, a huge explosion sent a geyser of water crashing over the boat.

Buzz cut off his attack as he began zigzagging the 113 clear of the convoy. "What the hell was that? Where the hell did that come from?" Buzz yelled out.

"Light cruiser off the port beam and closing fast!" Chief Petrovski screamed as he watched the bow closing in on them. Spinning the wheel hard to port, Buzz threw the throttles forward. In seconds, the 113 was passing alongside the cruiser in the opposite direction. As the cruiser passed them by, Buzz was hoping to make a torpedo run against it, but instead, found a medium Japanese gun boat coming at them from a hundred yards away. Both boats dueled with machine guns for several minutes as each skipper struggled to get the advantage, but no patrol boat could turn as tight as a PT boat. Making a quick turn to the right, Buzz was charging directly at the starboard side of the enemy vessel. Chief Petrovski leaned against the bulkhead behind the cockpit with the bazooka in his hands, as Torpedoman Ordman slammed the rocket into the rear of the weapon. As Buzz began to turn away from the patrol boat, the chief fired the bazooka. The rocket exploded as it slammed into the side of the boat, creating a major hole in the hull. The Japanese skipper turned away, hoping to salvage his vessel, but Johnson on the 20mm had other ideas. He pounded the engine room with round after round until the boat came to a stop and began to burn.

No matter which way you looked, there were fires burning all over the water. Off in the distance, Buzz observed the cruiser turning back toward the west. It was a fat target that needed to be dealt with, but the sight of two destroyers following up close behind gave Buzz second thoughts about attempting an attack. That turned out to be a good decision, as the front gun mounts on the cruiser fired a salvo in his direction. The 113 scampered off to the north at high speed to avoid more incoming shells.

As Buzz raced by Vaglena Island, he sighted a small landing craft laying in close toward the shore. Spinning the boat around, Buzz closed in on the hapless little vessel. Stockey and Johnson opened fire as the Chief prepared another bazooka rocket that he laid into the thin skin of the vessel.

"Cease fire, cease fire," Ensign Commers yelled out, as he watched Japanese marines attempting to scramble over the sides of the sinking landing craft. Although the Japanese were known for shooting at Americans in the water, Commander Reddings had made it clear that he would bring any crew member up on charges that was guilty of shooting men in the water.

About half a mile off in the distance, Buzz noticed a raging fire. Flames roared across the narrow channel separating Vaghena and Ghagne Island, as hundreds of gallons of explosive 100 octane fuel consumed what was left of PT-43. Cautiously, Buzz idled his boat around the burning wreckage, as he and his crew scanned the water for survivors. Chief Petrovski stood aside the cockpit, slowly moving the large spotlight over the wreckage. After several minutes, Torpedoman Ralph Ordman yelled out.

"Skipper, there's a guy in a vest just off the port bow. I can't tell if he's alive or not."

Buzz turned slowly toward the position, as Kowalski reached for the long pike to grab hold of the man's vest. On the second attempt, Kowalski snagged the vest, and began pulling the sailor toward their boat.

As they began pulling the man up to the deck, he began moaning and asking for one of his friends.

"He's alive, Skipper, but he's pretty banged up," Ordman called out as they laid the man on the forward deck. Immediately, Ed Yamry, the radio man who doubled as the medic, began attending to him.

After taking one more look around, Ensign Commers looked over at Buzz. "Sir, I think we better get the hell out of here. The skipper of that cruiser knows were still out here, and if he's close by or sends one of those destroyers this way, they might see our search light or our silhouette against the flames and come back with a full head of steam."

Buzz nodded his head. "That makes sense. Take over the controls and get us the hell out of here, then circle back to the north of Vaghena and come back out into the passage in the shallow waters near Velaviru, then we'll head home up the slot. It's 0500 now, dawn is just an hour away. I'm sure everyone else has scattered and headed for Tulagi already. Let's be careful and get out of here in one piece."

Spinning the wheel hard to the left, Ensign Commers opened the throttles, sending power to his Packard engines. In seconds, the 113 was skimming slowly across the dark waters around Vaghena. Ensign Commers pulled back on the throttles as they idled through the shallow channel separating the two islands. Too much speed or any wrong turn here could send you into a reef that would rip the bottom out of a PT boat.

As they neared the entrance to the slot, Velaviru and the larger Island of Choiseul was on their right, with Vaghena to their left. Sid Johnson, the 20mm gunner on the stern yelled.

"Destroyers coming at us on our starboard rear quarter!"

Buzz spun around to see the shapes of two Japanese destroyers racing toward them at nearly flank speed.

"Damn, we can't fight them both, and we're low on fuel. Todd, swing hard in toward shore, then double back the way we came at full speed." Looking toward the bow he yelled, "Yamry, get that man back in the cabin, we've got to run!"

"Shoals! We can't see the shoals at full speed, Buzz!" Ensign Commers yelled out as he began the turn.

Buzz shook his head, "No time to worry about that Ensign, drive this thing like you're back at home in your Plymouth, or we're dead for sure. Those destroyers won't be able to follow us through that passage, they'll have to go completely around Vaghena. That should give us time to find some cover.

Halfway through the turn, the lead destroyer fired two five-inch guns at the twisting PT boat. One shell landed far behind, while the second struck about fifty yards off their port side.

Knowing the second ship would be firing shortly, Ensign Commers pushed the throttles as far forward as he could, as sweat poured down his face. The sturdy Packard engines roared, as the bow of the wooden boat lifted about two feet out of the water.

Seconds later, four shells straddled the charging boat, one of them close enough to send a column of water over the port side dual .50 caliber machine gun mount.

Gunners mate Dick Wickman yelled at his skipper, "Sir, are we going to fight those bastards or just run? We need to show them we're the boss!"

Buzz ignored his favorite gunner, who was never one to back down from a fight, whether it be with fists, or his machine guns. But right now, fuel levels were low, and taking on two destroyers was not a good idea ever. As Ensign Commers attempted to streak through the narrow channel, once again those thirsty Packard's were gulping fuel like a kid with a bottle of soda.

"How about that cove on the north side of Choiseul we saw last week, it's deep and we can get in under the palm trees to hide," yelled Ensign Commers as he began turning in that direction following the coastline.

"No, we can't risk it. All they would have to do is pull in close and lob shells into the cove, hoping for a lucky hit. Otherwise, come dawn, they'll see us and blow us all to hell. Enough of this Todd, I'm taking the helm!"

Ensign Commers stood aside, knowing full well what his commander was going to do.

Quickly Buzz spun the wheel hard to port without letting up on the throttles. The boat nearly laid flat on its side as he cranked hard on the wheel while making the sharp turn. In seconds, the screaming PT boat was headed back into the deeper water north of Vaghena where the destroyers were surely headed.

"Ensign, tell the torpedo guys to get one and two ready to go, we'll make these son-of-a- bitches pay for not letting us get home," Buzz yelled out in anger and desperation. He knew if he could hit one ship, the other would stop to help their wounded companion, allowing them a chance to escape.

Shells splashed in the water once more, as Buzz swung his wooden vessel from side to side at high speed before making a complete circle so he could get a bead on the bow of the lead destroyer.

However, it was clear the skipper of the destroyer knew what he was up to and turned with Buzz, just enough so the 113 couldn't line up for a shot. Turning back to port at high speed, Buzz shook his head in disgust as several more five-inch shells slammed into the ocean, mere yards from the scrambling 113. Torpedoman Greenman screamed in pain as a large piece of shrapnel tore his right leg apart just below the knee.

As the Chief and Torpedoman Anderson carried Greenman forward, Buzz made another desperate turn hard to starboard, as his machine gunners fired at the decks of the destroyers. Attempting to block their escape into the slot, the skipper of the second destroyer turned hard to port, opening up his entire side. Spinning his wheel back to port, Buzz straightened out the 113 as he yelled, "Fire three and four!"

After the torpedoes were gone, Buzz once again spun hard to starboard attempting to avoid the incoming shells from the lead destroyer. Moments later, one of the torpedoes struck the destroyer amidship, sending a plume of fire up the side.

Realizing there would be chaos on the destroyer, Buzz spun the wheel hard again, sending the 113 nearly in front of the bow of the slowing damaged ship. The 113 raced astern of the damaged destroyer as Stockey and Kowalski raked the deck of the ship with their machine guns.

Taking a deep breath, Buzz knew he had given himself enough time now to escape the deadly trap. He knew the skipper of the undamaged ship, would have to support the damaged vessel back toward the huge Japanese naval base at Rabaul on the island of New Britain, about 350 miles to the northwest.

With one torpedo left, Buzz contemplated another run to try and sink the damaged destroyer, but decided enough was enough. It had been a long night and they weren't safe yet.

With both ships disappearing from site, Buzz backed off on the engines, horrified to hear from Crowder how little fuel was left in the bunkers. Come daylight, this would not be the best place for a wooden boat to be afloat and out of fuel.

Contemplating what to do, he looked over at his ensign. "We should be able to find a cove on Barora Ite we can use for cover with the fuel we have left. We can camouflage the boat with palm branches, then see if we can raise an Australian coast watcher on the radio, letting them know what we need."

As Ensign Commers took over the wheel once more, he said, "Nash."

Buzz looked at his executive officer, rather bewildered, and said, "What?"

The ensign smiled. "Sir, a while back you told me to drive this like the Plymouth I had back home. It was a Nash, sir."

Buzz busted out laughing as he slapped his ensign on the back. "I stand corrected, and will look into one when we get home."

About ten minutes later, the engines began to cough, just as they slipped into a dark cove. As Ensign Commers turned the boat around to face the open sea and back up along the shoreline, the engines quit.

Crowder walked up to Buzz. "Sir, what have I told you about running those engines out of fuel. We're going to need to prime the entire system on each engine once we get fuel to them. That's going to take time, and we don't have an air compressor here if we get an air lock either."

Buzz nodded his head. "Yeah, I know Crowder, but we didn't have much choice this time around. We'll do what we need to do once we get fuel. If we only have two engines, we can still get back. You can just take one off line, or maybe we'll be lucky enough to get a tow."

Nodding his head, Crowder looked intently at his skipper. "Are we going to get out of here, or are the Japs going to get us, sir?"

Trying to give his mechanic a reassuring smile Buzz replied. "Ensign Commers and Yamry are searching frequencies right now. They'll find someone to help us, don't worry."

The nervous mechanic nodded his head. "But if the Japs find us sir, then what?"

"We toss the machine guns and 20mm into the water, set the boat afire, grab what we can to survive and head inland, then we wait. We can hope there might be missionaries on the island with a radio set we can use to call for help, or we signal an aircraft. But let's not get ahead of ourselves here. Why don't you help cut branches to cover the boat, that's the most important thing now."

Elmer Sims was tending to the survivor of the 43 boat along with Greenman, the Torpedoman. Buzz knelt down beside them.

"How are they doing, Sims?"

"Not so good, sir. Greenman is running a real high fever. He's lost lots of blood, but we have it stopped now. He needs to be in the hospital back in Rendova, sir. The guy from the 43 is burned really bad and I think he's in a coma. There's nothing we can do for him but get him out of here, sir," Sims said as he tended the two men as best he could.

Buzz nodded, "Yeah, we all need to be somewhere else, but here we are. Hang in there with them, Sims, and let me know if anything changes. I need to check with Ensign Commers."

Approaching his capable XO, he knew something good was happening.

"Sir, we reached a coast watcher over on Santa Isabel. He called a guy on San Jorge who contacted Tulagi. They're sending two boats to give us a tow. They should be here by around 1300.

Buzz smiled. "That's good work. Look Ensign, I'm going to take Yamry and Wickman to keep an eye on the mouth of the cove. If you hear us firing, get the guys on the guns, we still may need to fight. Everyone else stays on the boat."

After a short walk, the three men took cover behind a downed palm tree right at the entrance to the cove. Looking back, they couldn't make out the boat since the crew had done such a great job camouflaging it.

The men held their breath several times, as Japanese patrol boats sailed by, slowly scanning the coast. Around 1200, a landing barge filled with about thirty Japanese Marines sailed right up to the entrance of the cove. They were so close, Buzz could hear several officers having a discussion. Carefully, he pulled a hand grenade from inside his shirt and prepared to pull the pin. He knew he could easily toss it into the barge if they decided to enter the cove.

After a very tense few minutes, the barge backed away from the cove, sailing off to the west. Buzz finally felt like he could exhale, as he placed the grenade back inside his shirt.

At 1305hrs, PT-61 and PT-55 sailed cautiously up to the cove. Buzz ran out into the water waving his arms like a mad man. The skipper of the 55 boat backed part way into the cove so the crew could attach a tow line. With the rope secured, all the palm branches were tossed off the 113, and the mooring lines were released.

Several hours later, the 113 joined her fellow boats on a welcomed return to Tulagi harbor. The 113 was allowed to be first in line for refueling, as it was going to take some work to get the engines up and running again.

Greenman and the survivor of the 43 boat were loaded onto a sea plane that happened to be unloading supplies in the harbor. They would be heading to the hospital on Rendova.

After Buzz filed an after-action report with Commander Reddings, he headed over to the pier to see what kind of damage the 113 had sustained. The repair crews pointed out several bullet and shrapnel holes that required patching, along with the firing controls on number three torpedo tube. Other than the minor damage the repair crews pointed out, the 113 came through the battle in great shape.

The fuel lines and engines would need to be purged, and they would need one new crew member before they could resume operations, but the 113 and crew had shown the Japanese they were there for the long run and ready to take on any fight.

After a hot meal in the mess tent, Buzz walked along the pier to watch the repair crews in action. It was evident they would be out of action for a few days, but that allowed time for the crew to get some rest. Buzz was extremely happy that friendly coast watchers were able to get them a tow back to Tulagi where they were safe, and the boat could be repaired. But he also stared at the empty pier where the 43 had usually docked, knowing the bodies of those brave men would never be found. It was the risk every PT crew took when they sailed out to meet the enemy on these wooden boats. They all knew it was their job to hold the line until a more powerful fleet could emerge from the shipyards of America.

There was no doubt the valiant crews of the PT fleet would do it to the best of their ability. Surely there would be tougher days to come in this war, but Buzz was positive the 113 boat and its battle tested crew were up to anything the Japanese could throw at them.

CHAPTER 6
EVERYTHING GOES WRONG

With repairs to the 113 boat finished, Torpedoman Bill Kester was assigned to fill out the crew. He knew his job well, and had a great sense of humor. Ensign Todd Commers was promoted to Lieutenant jg, and was assigned as skipper of the 118 boat. There was still quite a bit of work to be completed, but now he could build a crew to help with the final repairs. Ensign Gary Speidel, a new man to the South Pacific, became the new XO on the 113. The biggest promotion on the 113 was for Buzz, who was now promoted to full Lieutenant.

After completing a long shake down run, Buzz and Ensign Speidel were called into Commander Reddings office. Standing beside the commander was Captain Knight, the Chief of Operations for all PT boats in the southwest Pacific area.

Commander Reddings pointed at a map on the wall. "Gentlemen, this is the island of Ranongga. Up until now, it has not played a big part in the Solomon campaign. But aerial reconnaissance photos show us that the Japs are building a large airstrip near the town of Pienuna. Headquarters on New Caledonia are working on a plan to hit the base with carrier-based bombers in the next few weeks. However, there is one problem that needs to be taken care of before we start bombing anything, and time is of the essence."

The men stepped closer to the map, intrigued by what they were hearing. There was a large mission at Pienuna that the Japanese have already destroyed, and they killed most of the locals that attempted to defend it. The British missionaries were able to escape into the jungle, but are being hunted down as we speak. Making matters worse, Sir Albert Beckwith from the English Royal Consulate and also second cousin to the Queen, had never been evacuated from the island. So he, along with his wife Heather, and their children, a six-year-old son, and three-month-old baby, are now hiding out with the missionaries. Their capture is imminent if someone does not move fast, and MacArthur has assigned that mission to our squadron."

Captain Knight stepped forward. "Lt. Maddox, you will take the 113 accompanied by the 111 boat, and land a small detachment of Royal Marines on the south coast here," the captain stated as he pointed to a spot on the map. "It's the only sandy area along that stretch of beach, allowing you to pull your boats in close, so the missionaries can wade out and get on board. Churchill has made it very clear, if the Beckwith's and their children are captured, the Japanese will have a major bargaining chip. You must get them out at all costs. Any questions?"

Buzz shook his head, then looked at his new XO, "Anything you want to ask, Gary?"

"No sir, it's pretty clear," Ensign Speidel replied as he studied the map.

"Fine," Captain Knight replied. "You'll leave at 2000hrs. Captain Kosel of the British Royal Marines will meet you at your boats at 1930hrs. Good luck, gentlemen, you're going to need it."

Lieutenant Rodney Jurgins, skipper of the 111 boat stood aside Buzz and Ensign Speidel as the fourteen Royal Marines walked up to the pier.

"I want seven men on each boat, that gives us an edge as I see it. We will load everything up on the bow so we can stay out of your way, and study our maps one more time," Captain Kosel explained, as he directed his men to load.

Buzz waved his hand, "Captain, we cannot have your men and equipment up on the bow of the boats. They need to find a spot below decks, or they can sit back by the torpedo tubes. There will be no argument about it, sir. Now move them back so we can get moving."

After giving Buzz an angry sneer, Captain Kosel directed his men to move below to the crew quarters. Once the men were resettled, the boats backed out clear of the piers, taking a southeasterly course. It was irritating to Buzz that Kosel insisted on being in the cockpit area the entire trip, so he could help direct the boats as he saw fit.

Before Ensign Speidel could confront the cantankerous British officer, Buzz spoke up.

"Captain, you can be here to observe and observe only. You will not countermand any of my orders or directions, and you will allow my men to perform their jobs without interference. If you should decide to do otherwise, I have directed my chief to throw your ass to the sharks, and he will do as directed. Before we go any farther, do we have an agreement!"

Realizing Buzz and his crew were not going to be intimidated by his rank or pressure to change their operating procedures, the captain nodded his head.

"Yes, I can agree with your decision Skipper, but would you mind if I light my pipe and have a smoke. It always soothes my mind before I go into combat."

"Damn it, Captain, the light from a match or the glow of a pipe can be seen out here farther than you can imagine. Go below and have Sims my cook make you a cup of tea, he likes that crap. Without another word the captain disappeared down into the crew quarters.

Buzz was well aware that the boats would be running through some of the most dangerous waters in the Solomon Islands, including Blackett Straights. This was Japan's back yard, and their ships patrolled it constantly. Making matters worse, the United States Navy had no current charts of this part of the Pacific. They were operating from charts that had been created in the late 1800's by Australian trading ships. Although those charts were helpful, they did not contain locations of hundreds of reefs, shoals and rock piles that were patiently waiting to rip the bottom out of a wooden boat.

At 2130hrs, Ensign Speidel took a reading with his sexton. After checking the yellowed chart that Yamry had handed him, he nodded his head. "That's Parara off our starboard side, Buzz. We're right on schedule."

Half smiling, Buzz nodded his head. "Where the hell are the Japs tonight? This is feeling almost too easy and that can't be good."

After checking the charts again and looking at the compass, Ensign Speidel called out, "Should be a large sand bar off to port, come right ten degrees, we're now in Blackett Straights."

The hair stood up on the back on his neck as a shiver ran down his spine. Pointing to the northwest, Buzz called out. "Two fires on the water, keep your eyes open!"

Chief Petrovski joined Kowalski by the fore-deck machine gun mount, scanning the deadly waters. As Buzz turned farther south toward Ranongga, a massive explosion erupted near Ghizo Island.

Staring through his binoculars, the chief called out. "I can see a mast, sir. That's a ship on fire."

Buzz nodded his head, wondering if a sub had attacked the ship or if it had run into a mine. Either way, these shark infested waters were no place to jump from a burning ship.

Twenty minutes later Speidel took another reading with his sexton. "Ranongga, starboard side sir. Keep the course you have through the passage then turn east on my call."

Every set of eyes on the boat scanned the islands on both sides, as they quietly sailed through the narrow channel with the engines muffled. There was no way of knowing what was in the cove, or what might come charging at them out of a dark. Several minutes later, Ensign Speidel looked at Buzz, "Due east right now, sir. Point Tango is ten minutes away."

As Buzz informed Captain Kosel to assemble his men on the fore-deck, Chief Petrovski sent a message with the red blinker light to the 111. Running on just one engine for silence and maneuverability in shallow water, the 113 and 111 idled side by side to within five yards of the shore, allowing the British Marines to jump off in knee deep water.

With the Marines unloaded, the boats backed away from shore, holding station about a quarter mile out to sea.

Ensign Speidel and the Chief continually scanned the shore with their binoculars, watching for any sign from the Marines. About ten minutes, later a large fire fight broke out about a hundred yards east of Point Tango. Buzz began idling a bit closer to shore waiting for the rescue signal, but nothing came. Slowly, the gun fire died down and eventually quit. Ten more minutes passed, then half an hour, and everything was way too quiet.

Finally, a faint signal came over the radio. "Tango One this is Tango Two. We are torn up, mostly dead, and need evacuation. Japs moving northwest."

Once again, the 113 and 111 moved in close to shore, with the torpedo men up on the fore-deck to help the survivors. Buzz stared toward the dark beach as a few slow moving figures came out of the underbrush. First there were five, then three more followed behind.

With everyone on board, Buzz backed out to sea. Kneeling aside of a severely wounded Captain Kosel, Buzz inquired. "I count you and three more marines, and the others are missionaries. Where are the Beckwith's?"

"They ran when the fighting started and I don't know where they went. The Japs might have them, I just can't be sure," the captain replied as he laid his head down.

Ensign Speidel looked at Buzz. "What do we do now, sir?"

Buzz shook his head and was quiet for a moment. "Alright, here's the plan. The marine corporal is in good shape. I'll take him, Stockey, Kowalski, and Anderson. We'll go in and take a good look around and see what we can see. If we don't come back by 0500, get the hell out of here."

Chief Petrovski took Buzz by the arm. "No one goes ashore without me, Skipper."

Smiling at the chief, Buzz nodded his head. "Alright Chief, that works, glad to have you and your cannon with us.!"

Looking over at Ensign Speidel, Buzz smiled. "The 113 is your boat now, Gary. I'll let Lt. Jurgins on the 111 know what we're up to. If you need to run, run like hell and get across Blackett Straights as fast as you can."

Stockey, Kowalski and Anderson took M-1 carbines and grenades from the weapons locker, while Buzz took the Thompson and the Petrovski armed himself with a shotgun and several boxes of shells.

Once more Ensign Speidel slowly brought the 113 back toward the beach. After everyone had jumped off, he moved the boat out next to the 111.

Heading west, the band of men quickly came upon the sight where the battle had taken place. The bodies of several missionaries laid near the dead marines. Moving toward the north they came across the bodies of seven dead Japanese soldiers, but still no sign of the Beckwith's.

Using a red flashlight, Buzz and the marine corporal studied the map Captain Kosel gave them.

"Here to the northeast is a small village the missionaries went to quite often. Mrs. Beckwith accompanied them from what I understand. I think it's possible that's where they might have headed," Corporal Dunning explained.

"Alright, that's where we'll go," Buzz replied as he folded up the map. "Corporal, you take the lead with Kowalski and Anderson. Stockey, the chief and I will stay back about ten yards, so if something goes wrong, we don't all get jumped at once," Buzz explained nervously.

Slowly, the corporal moved forward, keeping a keen eye on the trail ahead of him. The jungle appeared to be way too quiet from what the corporal had experienced on Guadalcanal, and he didn't like it one bit. After stopping for a moment to listen to his surroundings, Corporal Dunning once more moved forward through the steamy, dark, forbidding jungle.

The sudden scream of a cockatiel followed by a sudden rustle of the underbrush dropped everyone to their knees. In mere seconds, the six invaders were surrounded by fierce looking men wearing war paint or terrifying masks. They all carried weapons, spears or bows, and yelled as they bounced back and forth on their agile feet. No one knew what to do, but they all understood these men would kill them in a heartbeat if they made any type of movement to their weapons. These island warriors had fought the Japanese on many occasions, and were not happy that these new strangers had invaded their islands.

After several nervous minutes, a voice called out in English. "Whom do you seek?"

Slowly Buzz raised his hand, and nodded at the warrior in front of him before speaking. "We are American's. We are looking for the Beckwith's. We were sent here to get them off the island, but the Japanese intervened. We mean no one any harm."

"What is your name and what is the name of your fighting vessel?" The man inquired.

My name is Lt. Buzz Maddox, my vessel is the U.S. Navy PT-113, a wooden torpedo boat," Buzz replied in a low voice.

After what appeared to be a rather long period of silence, a native wearing a strange mask came down the trail toward Buzz. After removing his mask, the man reached out for the Thompson machine gun Buzz held tightly in his hand.

"Give, or my men will shoot darts that will kill you all in seconds," the native stated boldly as he glared sternly.

Unhappy about doing so, Buzz relinquished the weapon after applying the safety.

After yelling out in an island dialect, the natives pushed the six men forward into a rather large encampment. Standing near a fire in the middle of the encampment was a man wearing a business suit. The native that had taken the machine gun walked up to him, handing over the weapon.

Moments later, the man walked over to Buzz. "I am Mr. Depree, a former plantation owner, the last of our people on these islands. These natives will die for me if I ask them to. They remember the good days here before the Japanese came, and they want the good times back, and all of you gone!"

Smiling, Depree handed the Thompson back to Buzz. "You are the only one without a weapon, so I suppose this belongs to you. That must make you the leader, so tell me what is it you want?"

After clicking off the safety, Buzz looked around the circle at all the curious natives. "As I told your English-speaking native, we mean you or these natives no harm. We are here for the Beckwith's. Our orders are to deliver them to Rendova, so they can be sent back to England by the request of the Queen."

"The Queen you say! Well, we French do not have much time for the arrogant British Monarchy. You see back in the—"

Buzz cut the man off as he took another step toward him. "Look, I could care less about you and the Monarchy. Tell me where we can find the Beckwith's, and we'll be off this forsaken island. I'm in no mood for any more games. Between me and the chief here, I think we can cut down more of these natives then they can us, so I'm not scared or one bit nervous. Now, where the hell are the Beckwith's?"

Looking down at the ground for a moment, Mr. Depree smiled. "Well, an American officer with grit. I do say that sounds like a welcome change." Looking over his shoulder he called out to the lead native, "Bring them out."

About a minute later the native returned from a hut with a nervous Beckwith family. The man walked forward up to Buzz.

"Is it too late to get off the island?"

Buzz shook his head as he looked down at his watch. "There are two PT boats waiting off shore ready to pick us up, but we're running out of time. If we're not there by 0500hrs, they're going to head back to Tulagi and return tomorrow night, I hope."

Before the man could respond, a hail of machine gun bullets ripped through the village, as the sound of screaming Japanese echoed out of the jungle. Buzz was horrified when he observed the small Beckwith boy fall to the ground as a bullet tore off the top of his skull. Buzz raced forward pulling the baby from its mother's arms as he yelled, "Ma'am, we got to get the hell out of here, your son's dead, there's nothing anyone can do for him."

As Buzz pulled her toward the far end of the village, Mrs. Beckwith screamed and clawed at Buzz arms, trying to pull way. She screamed "Willie, Willie," over and over as she sobbed.

Chief Petrovski knelt on the ground near a hut, covering Buzz's retreat, firing round after round from his shotgun at the advancing enemy.

Corporal Dunning pulled Mr. Beckwith by the arm, moving past his dead son as they ran toward the east, followed by the rest of the team. Warriors from the village attacked the Japanese with spears and hatchets as their women and children fled deep into the jungle. Screams of pain and fear filled the air as Buzz led his men deeper into the jungle and away from the killing ground, and regrettably much farther away from Point Tango.

About 0400, Corporal Dunning led the rescue squad into an old abandoned pineapple factory. Buzz chose the second floor of the canning factory for their temporary hide out.

As Kowalski and Stockey took up watch, Mr. Depree looked at Buzz. "Look, we can get out of here easily if we just turn over the Beckwith's and their child to the Japs. I'm sure they'll even give you safe passage back to your boat for the prize they have been seeking."

Chief Petrovski pushed Depree backwards with a heavy shove. "You are one sick bastard, Depree. There is no way in hell that baby becomes a pawn in this war."

Looking down the barrel of the shotgun, Depree smiled. "Fine! Let's see what happens when you are looking down the barrel of a Japanese rifle."

Angered by the chief's attitude, Depree went over by a stairwell and sat down as he yelled, "We are not out of the woods yet, you know!"

As dawn began to break at 0600, the first Japanese were beginning to roam the grounds of the plantation, searching every building cautiously.

Buzz called out. "Depree, what is the best way out of this place?" There was no answer. Everyone looked around the top floor of the building, but he was nowhere to be found.

Anderson shook his head. "He must have made his way down the stairwell and took off. Sorry Skipper, I never saw him leave."

"No, he didn't take off, he went and found the Japs and tried to work out a deal for the baby and the Beckwith's. I guarantee you, we haven't seen the last of him yet, we better move!"

After getting everyone assembled, Mr. Beckwith led the men to a small concrete block warehouse near the shipping pier. From the pier, Buzz and the chief could see Depree standing below the factory as he yelled. "It's over Lieutenant, Commander Yowada has agreed to give me safe passage. You and your men will become POW's, so hand over the baby!" After repeating the message three times, Japanese soldiers threw smoke grenades into the building before sending a twenty-man contingent inside.

When the soldiers returned empty handed, the officer standing to the left of Depree pulled his pistol and shot him in the head.

The sound of the shot awakened the baby and she began to cry. Several Japanese soldiers heard the cries and pointed toward the shipping pier. Mr. Beckwith grabbed his daughter and he and his wife ran from the building, with Anderson and Kowalski right behind them. Buzz, Stockey and the chief fired at the approaching soldiers as Corporal Dunning tossed several grenades.

Buzz knew all they had accomplished was to delay the enemy for a few minutes before they could get reorganized. It appeared as if Japanese troops were all around them, as the sounds of officers calling orders came from every direction. Reaching a small stream, Buzz turned to look at Kowalski.

"Do you think you can find point Tango from here?"

"Yes sir, I have a good idea as to where it should be." Kowalski replied, as sweat ran down his dirty unshaven face.

"Good, that's good." Buzz replied, as he organized his thoughts.

"Take Anderson and Corporal Dunning and get the Beckwith's and the baby ready for rescue at 0500 tomorrow morning. If the rest of us don't make it, leave without us and just list us as missing in action. That's all we can do at this point."

Although unhappy with his orders, Kowalski nodded his head in agreement. "Consider it done, Skipper. We'll get them out of here."

They were just about to leave when several mortar rounds began dropping around their small perimeter. Scared out of his mind, Mr. Beckwith grabbed the baby and jumped up. Before anyone could yell at him, he flew back into the stream bed as blood gushed from a large wound in his abdomen. Corporal Dunning scooped up the baby so she would not fall into the water as her father withered in pain. Quickly, Stockey attempted to apply a battle dressing to the wound, but it was all for nothing, as Beckwith gasped one more time before closing his eyes.

The Corporal did everything he could do to silence the baby, but she continued to scream. Buzz spun around, grabbing the baby from Corporal Dunning. "Run like hell. We need to go, try and stay together. Stockey, keep those bastards off our ass!"

As the mortar barrage had ended, the men raced out of the stream bed, running northeast as fast as possible, but the baby continued to cry, allowing the Japanese to zero in on them where ever they went.

Dropping down behind some fallen logs, the chief looked at Buzz. "Sir, try giving her some water from your canteen. I'm guessing she's hungrier than me. We don't have a nipple, but she will suck some of it if you go slow."

Nodding his head in agreement, Buzz opened his canteen and began dribbling water on the tiny little mouth. Just as the chief said, she began to suck in some of the water. When she quit taking in the water, Buzz smiled at the very dirty but pretty baby with big blue eyes. "You got a rough start here kid, but we'll get you out of here. Mark my words, we'll get you out."

With the baby quiet, the men were able to elude the Japanese for most of the afternoon. Late in the day, the baby once again began to cry.

Looking down at the girl, Buzz shook his head. "She's hot, she's burning up, Chief. What the hell do we do?"

After a moment of thought, the chief removed a small towel from his pack. "She smells like hell, Lieutenant. We can make a diaper from this towel and get her cleaned up a bit. Try and get her to drink again while I get the diaper ready."

Once again, the baby sucked in the water as the chief washed her off and placed his homemade diaper on her. When she quit drinking, the chief placed his hand on her forehead.

"She's sick, really sick, sir. She needs medical attention soon or she won't make it. Let's put a wet compress on her forehead to try and cool her down."

Kowalski looked at the chief as he made a compress. "What's wrong with her, Chief?"

Shaking his head, the chief replied. "Malaria, dengue fever, could be nearly anything out here in the jungle. All we can do is keep her comfortable for now."

Commander Reddings stood on the pier as the 113 and 111 boats idled into the harbor. Looking up at Ensign Speidel, he called out, "Where's Maddox?"

As the crew secured the boat and the medical staff removed the marines and missionaries, Ensign Speidel jumped off the 113. "Lt. Maddox, along with Stockey, Kowalski, Anderson, Petrovski and one Marine are back on the island. They went ashore looking for the Beckwith's. I waited until 0500 as agreed upon, then headed back here."

"Damn!" Commander Reddings called out as he looked up toward the sky. "Did you guys make any plans for a rescue before he left the boat?"

Nodding his head, Ensign Speidel replied. "Tomorrow morning at 0500. That's the best we could do at the time."

Commander Reddings walked down the pier for a moment before turning to face the ensign. "Well, alright then. Go get some chow and some sleep. You, the 111 and the 64 will return to pick them up at 0200 hrs. Get the other skippers organized with the plan. I can scrounge up about five marines to take with you."

As the crews were preparing the boats to leave, Doctor Rabnick walked up to Ensign Speidel. "Ensign, I argued like hell to go with you, but was shot down no matter what I said. But those people may be wounded and the baby might need attention. I feel it's best I go along with you. If there is any flack over this when we return, I'll take the heat for it."

Smiling, Ensign Speidel nodded his head. "Works for me, Doc. No way in hell are you going ashore, but you're right, they may need your help. We shove off in fifteen minutes."

Just a few minutes before 0200, the three boats slid out of Tulagi Harbor with the island of Ranongga as their destination. The winds were blowing out of the southeast at a steady ten miles an hour, making for three to four-foot swells. Broken cloud cover allowed enough starlight for crews to identify islands or vessels that might be prowling the open waters. Nearing Ghizo Island, Wickman called over to the cockpit.

"Skipper, there's something burning on the water just east of Kolombangara, but the flames are dying out. I've seen tracers from a machine gun firing in towards the beach, but I've not been able to make out the boat that is doing the firing. It must be one of ours."

Ensign Speidel nodded his head, "Yeah, I saw the fire, keep an eye on it for me."

Yamry was watching the charts tonight, and taking sexton readings to keep everyone on course. As they exited Blackett Straights, Yamry took another reading. "Come fifteen degrees to port sir, that will line you up with the channel east of Ranongga."

After making the course correction, Ensign Speidel mumbled, "Come on, be there Buzz, just be there."

Looking down at his watch, Buzz looked at the chief. "Forty-five minutes we should be at Point Tango if all goes well. This kid is getting hotter all the time. I'm really scared for her."

They had barely walked another fifteen minutes when the baby started crying, even louder than it had before. Mrs. Beckwith took the baby back in her arms and began singing to her as she pleaded for her to stop crying. Suddenly, ten Japanese soldiers jumped from the jungle firing their weapons. Anderson screamed as he fell to the jungle floor, and Corporal Dunning flew back against a tree as a bullet tore into his shoulder. But no one had seen the chief drop to the ground and roll off into the jungle.

As the firing stopped, a young Japanese officer called out. "Lay down your weapons and hand over the baby. The war is over for you now, and you will become POW's. You have caused us great trouble over the last twenty-four hours, this is your last chance!"

Walking over to Buzz, the officer asked, "Where is the child? It sounds like she must be sick, she cries so much. We need to get her back to our hospital right away."

Buzz looked around the small clearing in surprise. Mrs. Beckwith was nowhere to be seen. Shaking his head, he looked at the officer. "Mrs. Beckwith must have run off into the jungle when the shooting started. I have no idea where she went to."

Looking at three of his men, the Japanese officer called out an order, sending them running into the jungle in search of Mrs. Beckwith.

The three men had barely walked five yards when a loud laugh echoed through the jungle. The young Japanese Lieutenant quickly spun back toward the Americans as a deep voice called out. "Let her rip, Wyatt."

Suddenly, the chief jumped up behind one of the Japanese soldiers, putting a round from his .45 pistol into his neck. Spinning to his left, he fired another round into the forehead of a soldier barely five yards away from him. The last Japanese soldier was spinning around looking in every direction, trying to see who was doing the shooting, but failed to see the chief standing behind a tree less than three yards away. The .45 coughed one more time, sending the soldier flying backwards as blood shot out from his chest.

Seeing the Japanese soldiers in disarray, Stockey and Kowalski scooped up their weapons as the Japanese Lieutenant and his escorts began to run.

The chief gave chase, clutching his pistol in his right hand. As the Lieutenant turned one more time to see who was chasing them, Petrovski placed a well-aimed shot into the officer's upper leg. As he crumbled to the ground, his two escorts ran past him deeper into the jungle.

Carefully, Buzz walked forward praying the baby was alright, but was taken back by the sound of a woman's cries several yards to his left. Walking through the underbrush, Buzz and Stockey looked down at Mrs. Beckwith as she sat on the ground clutching her baby.

As she rocked back and forth, she kept crying out, "I put my hand over her mouth so the Japanese would not hear her and take her away. But she wouldn't stop crying. I pressed my hand tighter over her mouth until she stopped. All I wanted to do was to keep her quiet so the Japanese would not get her from me. Oh my God, I killed my baby, I've killed my baby."

Buzz knelt down aside of Mrs. Beckwith and took the child from her arms. After a quick check, he looked up at Stockey and nodded his head. Handing the body of the baby to Stockey, he helped Mrs. Beckwith from the ground.

"Come on ma'am, we need to go," Buzz said calmly, as he held on to a woman that had watched her entire family perish right in front of her over the last twenty-four hours.

Kowalski walked up to Buzz, unsure of what was going on. After seeing the body of the Beckwith baby in Stockey hands he stated, "Anderson is gone, the corporal is in tough shape, but he's alive and willing to travel. I think we can get him to Point Tango alright."

As Buzz turned to speak with Chief Petrovski, Mrs. Beckwith grabbed on to his arm. "My baby, my baby, we can't leave her here, my God we can't leave her little body here!"

Buzz nodded in agreement. "We'll bring her back with us, don't worry about that."

Mrs. Beckwith smiled slightly. "That's good. My husband and son will want to see her one more time. They're waiting for me in New Cale-donia, you know. When I get there, we will be a family again. You'll see lieutenant, we will be a family again, and the Queen will be so happy."

Chief Petrovski looked at Buzz before whispering, "I got your ass sir. Get everyone moving, I'll be right behind you, we can't wait."

Nodding his head, Buzz looked over at the wounded Japanese offi-cer. "Chief, we need to take him back with us. He may have information on troop strengths that will be helpful with the invasion planners. You and Kowalski make sure he gets to the boat. That's an order."

Nodding his head in agreement, the chief walked over to the wound-ed Japanese officer Kowalski was helping up from the ground. Looking coldly at the wounded officer, the chief inquired, "I don't suppose you knew a Chief Mark Saminski that was stationed at Pearl Harbor on December 7, back in forty-one. He was a good friend of mine. He was wounded during the attack and thrown into the water by an explosion. Several men watched one of your pilots strafe him as he swam away from the U.S.S. Honolulu that was on fire."

The lieutenant half smiled. "It was a great victory and we are not through yet. We will kill many more Americans before we win this war, and you will never make it off this island."

"Well, I'm sorry to tell you lieutenant, you won't be there to see it come to an end." Suddenly, a single gunshot echoed through the jungle. Sliding the pistol back into the holster, Chief Petrovski looked at Kow-alski. I thought he was going for your bayonet, and I couldn't let that happen."

Without saying a word, Kowalski let the dead officer fall to the ground. After they had walked about ten yards, Kowalski placed his hand on the chief's shoulder.

"Thanks for saving my life back there, I really appreciate it."

Nodding, the chief kept walking for a short distance before looking up toward the sky. With a tear in his eye he stated, "Rest in peace, Mark. Rest is peace."

Ensign Speidel stared through his binoculars at Point Tango, as the small group of marines lay flat on the bow of the 113. With engines muffled, he guided the 113 carefully into shore past the sand bar. When they were about ten feet from shore, the marines jumped from the boat and raced ashore.

Seconds seemed like hours as everyone aboard the 113 held their breath. Moments later, several figures charged out of the jungle and began climbing aboard the 113 with help from the torpedo crew. Buzz helped pass Mrs. Beckwith up to the doctor saying, "Look after her, doc, she just lost her entire family."

Before the doctor could ask any questions, Buzz turned and jogged back toward the beach with his Thompson at the ready. As he counted heads and pushed everyone toward the 113, he heard heavy footsteps coming from the jungle. Turning to his right he prepared to fire, but held off until he was sure of his target. Smiling and relieved, he was happy to hear those thundering feet belonged to the chief and Kowalski, running as fast as they could.

Looking at Kowalski with a puzzled look on his face, Buzz called out, "Where the hell is the Jap, Lieutenant?"

Shaking his head in disgust, Kowalski replied, "As I pulled him up off the ground, he tried to grab my bayonet and I couldn't break free. The chief had no choice but to shoot him."

Buzz nodded his head and ran for the boat, although he was sure there was more to the story than he would ever know, or ever care to ask about. He would never judge either man for what happened after what they had just endured. If there was any judging to do, he would leave it to God.

After Yamry finished pulling the last men on board, Buzz waved at Ensign Speidel yelling, "Get her out of here."

Turning toward the heavily breathing chief, Buzz smiled. "I wasn't sure if you were alive back there or not. I heard gunshots, but didn't have time to turn back to see what happened. It's damn good to see you, chief, but next mission be on time, or the train will pull out without you."

The chief laughed. "Naw, you would never do that to me. You know it was me and Wyatt that got your scrawny rich boy ass back to the boat tonight."

As Buzz walked over toward Doctor Rabnick, he slapped the chief on the back. "Yeah, I'm well aware of that, my friend. I never question your decisions, always remember that."

Jumping down into the crew quarters, Buzz saw Mrs. Beckwith on one of the bunks as she mumbled incoherently. Dr. Rabnick was sitting beside her, taking her blood pressure. When he was finished, he stood up.

"What the hell happened out there, Skipper? We were told it was essential that you guys bring that baby off the island in good shape. How did she die?"

After looking down at the floor for a minute, Buzz inquired. "Will she make it, Doc? Will she ever come back from the trauma she went through tonight?"

"Hard to say, Lieutenant. The mind can be a fragile thing."

Taking a deep breath, Buzz stepped away from the bunk and whispered to Dr. Rabnick. "She killed the baby by accident. The little thing wouldn't quit crying and the Japanese were all around us. Mrs. Beckwith covered her little face, attempting to keep her quiet, and you can guess what happened from there."

Turning to look back at Mrs. Beckwith, the doctor shook his head. "Such a shame, such a damn shame. I'll try and get her back to Hawaii as soon as I can. There's nothing anyone out here can do for her."

Arriving back up in the cockpit, Buzz looked to his right to see the 111 and 64 boats in perfect echelon formation as they continued on their easterly journey. Picking up the binoculars, Buzz scanned the ocean from left to right and back again, before looking at his executive officer.

"She's all yours, Skipper," Ensign Speidel stated as the men shook hands.

"No, she's all yours tonight. I'm tired, dirty, hungry and not mentally ready to operate the old gal tonight. Take us home, Gary. Take us home."

Buzz went below to the crew quarters, where the doctor was still monitoring Mrs. Beckwith.

"How is she, Doc? I don't want to lose the entire family, if you know what I mean."

"I'm guessing that physically she'll be alright. There's a good chance she has a mild case of malaria, by the way she is sweating. I'll give her some quinine when we get back to Tulagi. However, your British Marine didn't make it. The corporal had lost a lot of blood and there was nothing I could do for him. At least his body will be buried among friends."

About an hour later, Buzz watched Mrs. Beckwith drink some warm tea the doctor had made for her. But the look in her eyes was pretty much equal to the thousand-mile stare that soldiers have after seeing too much combat. He knew she would be in good hands when she arrived in Hawaii, and eventually back home in England. But he felt bad that she would never know where her husband and boy were buried, if they were buried at all.

Sitting down at the mess table, he looked at the chief who was munching on a hunk of bread he had taken from the kitchen.

"I guess rescuing one out of four isn't the worst," Buzz said.

"Odds were against anyone being rescued, Skipper. Everything was wrong before we ever got there, because the Japs wanted them as bad as we did. I wish we could have brought Anderson back with us, but I know it wasn't possible. Still, he was a damn good man," the chief replied, looking sad.

Arriving back at Tulagi, Commander Reddings congratulated the crew on what they had accomplished, although the results were not exactly what the British Monarchy had hoped for. He was glad to hear Mrs. Beckwith was going to be alright, although he was sure the royal family would hide her out until her mental condition improved. The following morning medical staff arrived on a PBY Catalina float plane from New Caledonia. They wasted little time getting Mrs. Beckwith prepared for the long flight, although it did not appear she had any idea where she even was. Before the air crew climbed back on board, the co-pilot carried a small box containing the remains of the Beckwith child to be buried in Noumea. Commander Reddings and Buzz watched the PBY skim across the water before taking back to the skies. They both knew there would be blow-back from the British on the loss of three members of the Beckwith family, but that was something President Roosevelt would need to discuss with Prime Minister Churchill. Here in the southwest Pacific, the war would continue and good men would die, regardless of the politics back home.

CHAPTER 7
FIRE ON THE WATER

There was little doubt that PT boat operations out of Rendova and Tulagi were starting to take a toll on the Japanese supply lines. More often than not, the convoys were now escorted by several large destroyers, and light cruisers. The range of the large guns on these ships had also taken a toll on the PT boat fleets. Many boats were returning so battered, they were stripped of armaments and then set on fire and sunk. Thankfully new boats were arriving in a timely fashion to replace the losses.

Torpedoman Marvin Olean was assigned to the 113 to replace Jeff Anderson, bringing the crew up to complement. He was a tough, smart kid that grew up on the streets of Milwaukee. True to form he liked his beer and could put down more than most men on the crew.

The first few missions the 113 made after the rescue mission were rather easy without much combat, and the crew was getting restless with the powder puff missions.

With the squadron being short three boats, the 113 was being included on an eight-boat mission that was to clash head first with the Tokyo Express off the Island of New Georgia. Coast watchers reported three destroyers and one light cruiser as escorts. Buzz was teamed up with the 118 boat, still under command of Lt. Commers. He had racked up a good record in a short time, and had proved his crew was not afraid of a good fight.

At 2200hrs, the flotilla sailed from Tulagi, headed east up the slot. With a crescent moon and plenty of starlight, it was rather easy for Buzz to keep the 118 in sight as they passed by the dark islands on their port side. As they passed by the small port of Hovoro on New Georgia, they ran into a small rain squall that was crossing the slot south to north. Knowing they were approaching the deeper waters of Kula Gulf, Buzz had the crew on full alert, as this was a primary hunting ground for enemy subs. Ensign Speidel and the chief scanned the dark waters watching for a periscope, or a half-submerged sub cruising near the coastline.

Quickly, Yamry popped his head up from the radio room. "Coast watcher on Kolombangara reports Tokyo Express passing Kula Gulf, headed our direction at fifteen knots. A destroyer is leading the column with two light cruisers on the port side in deeper waters.

Before Buzz could think of what he wanted to do, the lead boats sprang into action, charging the convoy. Buzz slammed the throttles forward and opened up the mufflers, giving the engines full power. The 118 stayed right with Buzz as they raced past the destroyer with their weapons blazing.

Making a quick cut into Kula Gulf and reversing course, Buzz raced directly toward a heavy barge sitting low in the water. "Fire one!" he yelled, as he punched the button on the control panel. Instantly, the large fish jumped from its tube, racing toward the barge. Spinning the wheel hard to port, Buzz was looking head on at a Japanese tug boat. As number one torpedo exploded, Buzz yelled, "Fire Two!" Once again, the fish blasted from the tube splashing into the water. The crew of the tug began hammering with axes, trying to cut the tow ropes that connected the boat to a line of barges, but they could not cut them all before the torpedo struck and exploded. The bow of the tug jumped up nearly ten feet before falling back into the ocean, fully a blaze.

Buzz smiled as he flew past the burning hulk, searching for more targets. Every weapon on the 113 was firing on the helpless barges as they ran into each other with their tug boat gone. Geysers of water rocketed skyward as a destroyer fired five-inch shells at the menacing devil boats. Lt. Commers, feeling safe, was well aware the skipper of a destroyer was focused on chasing down the 113. Quickly he fired a spread of two torpedoes at the starboard side. As he turned hard to parallel the ship, both torpedoes found their mark. Instantly, the ship slowed and began to list. Men ran around the decks screaming as escaping steam from the boilers burned them horribly. Minutes later an internal explosion tore their ship apart, sending it to the bottom.

With that destroyer out of the way, Buzz spun the 113 around nearly on its side in front of another tug boat. Buzz didn't want the tug right now, he smelled blood and was not going to be stopped. He aimed the bow of the 113 at a damaged troop transport filled with Japanese marines. Kowalski and Stockey hammered away with their machine guns, as Johnson tore up the unarmored engine compartment with his 20mm cannon. Fires began to rage, sending plumes of black smoke skyward, as the stern of the vessel began to quickly settle. As Buzz passed by the side of the transport, Johnson kept punching holes in the thin hull with his cannon. In no time the transport was beginning to turn over as water gushed into every compartment. Men swam as fast as they could from the sinking vessel, only to be in the way of the next oncoming tug boat and its barges.

A huge geyser of water tossed the 113 as one of the light cruisers began firing its ten-inch guns. The ship had its massive searchlights scanning the water, attempting to catch the PT boat in its powerful beam so their gunners could see it. Several more geysers of water sent columns of water over the 113 as Buzz turned in every direction, trying to break loose from the attacking ship. Shrapnel from the exploding shells whizzed by his head as he turned one more time, attempting to set up for a torpedo attack, but the skipper of the cruiser was not going to allow that to happen. Guns blazed on both sides before Johnson was seriously wounded. Hollerman tried to get the 20mm working, but it had been too badly damaged to fire. Torpedoman Kester was lying dead near the engine room and Olean lay wounded near torpedo tube three. Crowder was yelling through the voice tube that they were taking on water in the engine room from damage to the starboard hull. He had rigged a pump to keep the level down, but things were not looking good. Turning on the smoke generator located on the rear of the boat, Buzz sent the 113 into a series of twists and turns, trying to get lost in the smoke before breaking away.

Exiting from the smoke, all Buzz could see was the front quarter deck of the cruiser dead ahead. Knowing he had just Ordman left on the torpedo crew, he slammed his fist down on the button for tube number four, but nothing happened. Making a quick turn to line up tube three, he punched the button on the console. The fish flew from the tube right on the money, heading straight for the bow of the cruiser.

Turning back hard to starboard, Buzz counted down the time to impact. Seconds later the torpedo ripped into the cruiser sending a ball of flame skyward.

As Buzz turned to make his way back toward Tulagi, another destroyer began firing in his direction. Shrapnel from the explosion tore into the engine room, disabling engine number three, and shattering most of the electrical circuits on the boat. Buzz knew the water would take over the engine room soon, so he turned the boat back toward New Georgia, hoping to find landfall before the 113 gave out.

Before Buzz could think, Crowder was standing beside of him. "The engine room is on fire, were going to blow!"

Trailing a column of smoke, Buzz threw the throttles for the last two engines forward one last time, sending them up onto a coral reef that ripped a hole in the hull about twenty yards from shore. Killing the engines, Buzz yelled out. "Get off, get off, she's going to blow!"

The survivors jumped into the water, pulling injured men behind them as the 113 became a blazing inferno. As Buzz walked ashore, one of the gas tanks erupted like the fourth of July, ripping what was left of the gallant boat to pieces.

There had been no time to get the weapons out of the locker down below. All they had for fire power on this Japanese held island was the sidearms several of the men wore, along with the chief's cannon.

By 0100, the battle was over and the surface of the slot was filled with burning wreckage. Scanning the slot with his binoculars, it appeared another PT boat was engulfed in flames several hundred yards out to sea. Closer in, the flames of the 113 illuminated the waters well enough to count at least fifteen sharks searching for food. They were an equal opportunity hunter and it did not make any difference if the body was American or Japanese. Tonight, the dreaded predators ate well, and were still on the search for more.

With the 113 gone, Buzz counted up his losses. Kester, and Olean were dead, Hollerman and Sims were badly injured, but both would survive. They had given the Japanese one hell of a fight tonight damaging a cruiser, sinking a tug boat and its heavy barge, along with a troop transport and two landing crafts. Not a bad night's work, but he had lost some of his men, and the boat he had loved from day one back at Melville.

As dawn crept over the slot, most of the wreckage had already sunk or had been pulled down stream by the heavy current. The engines of the 113 were still partially visible sitting on the coral reef. Eventually, the heavy seas would push them into the abyss along with the other debris of this war.

A heavy overcast dawn with intermittent rain kept search planes grounded until midday. It was nearly 1300hrs. when a spotter plane observed the crew of the 113 waving at them from shore. The pilot dipped his wings in recognition, as he called in the location of the stranded crew before continuing his lonely search for other survivors. At 1345hrs., PT 142 glided along the shore to pick up the marooned crew. They were all thankful and happy but would not forget the friends they had lost that night.

Arriving back to Tulagi, the crew was checked over by the medical staff and received first aid treatment for any wounds they had suffered during the battle. After a hot shower and a good meal, most of the crew found a safe place to sleep until it was decided what would happen next since their boat had been destroyed.

Buzz was told to report to Commander Reddings hut at 1430hrs. Upon arriving, Commander Reddings stood up and reached out to shake hands. "From what I have heard from some of the other skippers, you kicked the Japs pretty good out there last night. Congratulations on a job well done."

Buzz shook his head. "Yeah, it got a little hot out there. Too many targets and too many ships to fight, and they gave us hell. I'm sorry I lost the 113 and five crew members, sir. She was a great boat from the day I climbed aboard her at Melville. They called her a jinxed boat, but she and the crew proved them all wrong. Those guys that died last night fought like hell, they were true heroes."

Commander Reddings nodded his head in agreement. After a moment of silence, the Commander looked intently at Buzz. "And what about you, Buzz? Are you ready for a trip home, or R and R some place like Hawaii? Remember the navy tradition, when you lose a boat in combat, you're allowed a break away from the action. Just tell me where you want to go, and I'll have the orders cut within the hour."

Buzz looked up at Commander Reddings, "And my crew, what happens to them?"

"They'll fill in on other boats behind casualties. It won't take long and they'll all have new families out here," Commander Reddings replied, not sure what to make of Buzz.

"If I stay, can I have them all back? Can you get us another Elco boat soon?" Buzz inquired anxiously.

Commander Reddings looked sternly at Buzz. "If you stay, I can't guarantee when I can get you a sweet break away from here, but it's your decision. As far as a boat goes, I have three arriving in the morning. An older Elco numbered 110, and two newer Elco's numbered 120 and 121. They're all outfitted like the 113, and they already have a fifty cal. mounted on the fore-deck. Say the word and you can have your pick."

Buzz grinned. "The only problem we had with the 113 was that her engines were a bit tired when we got her, but she never gave us a problem. There was no doubt an overhaul was in the near future for her. So give me the 120 and my old crew, and we'll start working her up until you can fill out the rest of the crew."

Commander Reddings smiled. "Damn, that is the best news I have heard in a while." After shaking hands, the commander continued. "Buzz, you're a good boat handler and skipper. We may have to talk down the road about having you become a squadron commander and getting off the boat."

Buzz shook his head. "Not going to happen, sir. If I can't be out there where the action is, put me in some back water base where I can count napkins and toilet paper."

Commander Reddings laughed as he threw his pencil at Buzz. "Go round up your crew and get some sleep. Your new boat should be here around 1200hrs. tomorrow."

The crew was excited about staying together and the thought of having a newer boat. Crowder the machinist mate looked at Buzz. "Sir, you need to be a bit kinder to the motors on the 120. They can take some abuse, but try to think 'gentle, I must be gentle,' when you are throwing that baby of mine around out there."

Buzz grabbed Crowder by the neck and kissed him on the cheek. "I promise to be a kinder and gentler skipper. Just give me all she's got when I ask for it."

Laughing, Crowder threw up his hands saying, "Why do I try!"

CHAPTER 8
THE PILOT RETURNS

The Maddox family was rightly proud to have their eldest son Josh return from flight school as a B-17 pilot. The guest list for the homecoming party contained many members of Boston's most elite, and several important politicians that had been friends with the Maddox and Drumond families for generations.

As the women talked society out on the lawn, Alfred had Senators Main and Worthington retire with him to the dark mahogany paneled den for sniffers of cognac.

Alfred looked seriously at Senator Main, "Now Senator, you know how many pounds of fish I told you I could deliver over the last quarter, and I've nearly doubled it. Plus, we have never failed to fill a quota since rationing began. So I would think you and FDR would be happy to repay such a strong connection to the New Deal. I mean, a slight favor would not be too much to ask, would it, sir?"

Senator Worthington stepped forward, "After all Senator Main, Alfred did much to deliver voters in this part of Maine to your big win last fall. I have helped Alfred with many things during my years in the senate, so I think you might do well to take on this request."

Alfred Maddox laughed as he knew both Senators owed him much since they had successfully been elected to office. "You see, Senator Main, this is not a big deal. I have one son being an idiot and fighting the war on wooden boats in the Pacific, and he wouldn't take a hand out if he lost his last pair of underwear."

Senator Main laughed. "Well Alfred, I would like to think our navy can supply your son with new underwear, although we all know how terribly he treated Angeline Stevenson."

Angered by the Senator's comment, Alfred slammed his glass down on his desk. "And we all know she's all but living with that questionable anti-American commodity broker out of New York. That Bellington boy, Swenson Bellington I think it is."

"Yes, yes, we all know Alfred, so what do you need," Senator Main inquired angrily.

"Being here today you are well aware my son Josh is now a B-17 pilot. No matter how much I hate it, I can't change it. I will not have another boy of mine fighting this damn war. I'm doing enough for the war effort right here in Maine to make up the difference. I don't want his brains splattered all over Germany in some ill-fated bombing mission. I want him assigned permanently to MacArthur's air force in Australia. I don't care if he flies mail bags back and forth from Sydney to Melbourne twice a day, but you will see to it he's not assigned to a combat squadron. Do I make myself clear?"

Senator Main laughed. "Is that all you want, Alfred? Why I have taken care of issues like this for many important families since the war began. I will get his orders cut first thing Monday morning. Besides, the General actually owes me a few favors since he arrived in Australia.

Alfred clapped his hands as he smiled. "Now that's what I like to see, a Senator that has his nose to the grindstone, and his finger on the pulse of the war. You take care of my boy, and I damn well guarantee you there will be another check for two hundred thousand in your campaign chest by weeks end."

Josh was excited when he received orders to report to Melbourne, Australia about a week later. He couldn't wait to tell his long-time girl-friend, Anna Marie Borgland, the good news, as they were already discussing future wedding plans.

Two weeks later, Josh flew out of LaGuardia Airport in New York

City on a cross country flight to San Diego, where he would join his squadron for the long flight across the Pacific.

Arriving at Minter Field near Bakersfield, California, the men were assigned aircraft. Josh stood on the ground looking up at B-17 2665, as the hot desert sun reflected off the shiny new aluminum fuselage as it sat on the tarmac. On the first leg of the flight to Hawaii, it would just be Josh, a co-pilot, an engineer from Boeing, and a naval navigator. After refueling in Hawaii, he would pick up his actual crew and weapons.

At 0700hrs. the following morning, aircraft 2665 and five other new B-17s sped down the dusty runway climbing west into the bright morning sky. Josh loved the feel of the big plane as it rose and dropped over invisible waves of air. Reaching an altitude of ten thousand feet, the flight of planes leveled off as the navigator set the final course for Hickam Field.

Josh had just climbed back into the pilot's seat after taking a short break from the controls, as the Islands of Hawaii appeared on the horizon. It had been a grueling fourteen-hour flight, and Josh was ready to set his plane down on solid ground. The plane had performed perfectly, and its fuel consumption was well within guidelines. That meant they would not be burning all the spare fuel they were carrying in the bomb bay. That weight would have to be taken into consideration when he set the tires of 2665 down on the runway. Forty-five minutes later Josh parked the huge aircraft alongside the other B-17s from his flight on the grass near the main runway.

Two days later after Boeing engineers checked over all the B-17s, they were back in the air on their way to New Caledonia where they would refuel before flying on to Australia. Everyone was happy that the weather had been extremely favorable throughout the entire trip. There was nothing worse for a pilot than to have his aircraft damaged by a storm and need to ditch in the Pacific Ocean.

Throughout the long flight, Josh enjoyed getting to know his new co-pilot, Sam Bench. He was a good pilot, and always ready to take control when Josh needed a break. The rest of the crew spent much of the flight training on the new equipment and being on the lookout for Japanese fighters once they closed in on Australia.

Like any man in the military during World War Two, following orders was paramount. Although Josh and his crew were not happy with their assigned mission, they hoped they would be able to eventually rotate out of it and see some action. Flying cover over the southern shipping routes, meant the only enemy ship they would ever see would be a Japanese submarine if it happened to surface.

Day after day, B-17 2665 flew routes across the deep southern Pacific plotted by navigators from Allied headquarters in Melbourne. Sure, there were all kinds of cargo ships and convoys making their way to and from Australia that were important, but Japanese attacks that far south were few and far between. After two months of flying the routes, the only submarines or warships they had seen were American or British.

After another boring four hour search without seeing anything at all, Josh walked into operations to speak with group commander Lt. Colonel Baker,

"Colonel, my guys are going crazy flying the southern supply routes. They need a break from it. Is there any way we could trade jobs for a few weeks so we could get some combat experience? After all, flying those trade routes day in and day out is a waste of a great B-17."

The colonel leaned back in his chair. "Maddox, someone has to fly those routes every day, and believe it or not, it's an important part of our war effort. You just happen to have drawn the short straw and there is nothing I can do about it. You know the routes, you know what the ships look like from the air. We would have to train crews all over again if we sent you somewhere else. So, you all have a job to do and you need to do it, as Australia and General MacArthur count on you keeping those ships safe. Think about it Maddox, there are men in the states loading those ships that will never get any closer to the war than San Diego. You are part of South Pacific Operations, and you should be proud of that."

Josh left the operations center more depressed than before he walked in the door. Before heading back to the barracks, he decided to get a stiff drink and drown his sorrows. Many of the B-17 crews hung out at a bar called the Oyster Shucker, not far from the main gate of the base. Josh had barely entered the bar when he ran into Sam Bench and gave him the bad news. However, Sam was not upset.

Placing his arm around Josh, Sam smiled. "You see that guy at the corner table with the crazy cowboy hat on? Well, he's the guy that assigns B-17's to combat missions every day. I already spoke with him about our dilemma. He says some senator placed orders in your file not allowing you to fly combat missions. However, he stated that for fifty bucks those papers could get lost forever. He's done it before and not one word has been said by anyone."

Before Sam could say another word, Josh had walked up to the man in the cowboy hat. "My name is Josh Maddox, I fly the 2665. I hear you can make documents disappear and I need a favor."

Removing the cowboy hat the man wiped his forehead. "Well, the documents in your file happen to come from a Senator Main. He's big stuff in Washington and on the appropriations committee, I don't know if I want to cross him."

Josh shook his head. "The bastard is a friend of my fathers, which is exactly how that damn order ended up in my file, and I want it out!"

Standing up, the man took Josh by the arm. After they walked outside the bar the man turned back toward Josh. "My name is Stamp, Master Sergeant Earl Stamp. Usually, I'll take care of a mess like this for fifty—"

Before he could finish, Josh shoved a hundred dollars inside his shirt. "I don't have it right now, but after payday there's another fifty bucks coming your way if you get the orders changed. Do we have a deal, Master Sergeant?"

Beaming from ear to ear, Sgt. Stamp smiled. "Have your crew ready to fly at 1200hrs tomorrow. I have a bombing mission to New Guinea that's short one plane. You will be bombing Salamaua on the north coast of the island. If you do this well, I have a real tough nut coming up on

Monday that will be right down your alley. Just get me that other fifty bucks when you can."

At 1130hrs the following day, Josh watched as the arming crew finished loading his bomb bay with hundred-pound bombs. For the first time, Josh felt like he was doing something special. At 1200hrs, ten B-17s took to the air heading off to the northwest. Flying over the Own Stanley Mountain range was always treacherous. Winds and rain buffeted the area daily, and you had to be on oxygen to climb over the 13,500 ft. mountains.

After clearing the mountains and the heavy clouds, a panoramic view of the South Pacific opened up in front of them. The crews had an outstanding view of the lush green Pacific islands that dotted the ocean as far as the eye could see. They could see varying shades of blue and turquoise as the warm ocean waters rolled over coral reefs then plunged hundreds of feet under the dark blue water.

Quickly, the group leader turned the squadron to the east, as they dropped to five thousand feet hugging the coast line. Minutes later they were over Salamaua where the Japanese had been caught off guard. Sailors and dock workers scrambled in every direction, attempting to flee the lethal rain of death that was about to fall upon them. Brave soldiers ran for antiaircraft batteries that had been installed near the pier, but were never able to get off a shot before the bombs were upon them.

Explosions from the first five planes rocked the coastal town as Josh approached, turning over control of his lumbering bomber to Ward, his bombardier. Moments later Josh pulled up the nose of his B-17 after Ward called out, "Bombs away!"

The plane shook from the shock waves created by the huge explosions beneath them. Two Japanese ammunition ships were torn to pieces as the bombs detonated directly on their decks. Pieces of the ships were seen hundreds of feet in the air, damaging one B-17 directly behind Josh.

Climbing back to 13,500 feet, Josh looked back toward Salamaua. All he could see were thick, black, greasy clouds of burning oil and ammunition climbing ever higher, blotting out much of the New Guinea coast. Forty thousand pounds of bombs had all but obliterated the military base, tank farm and harbor. How many civilians had been killed would never be known, but there was no way to warn them without alerting the Japanese to the upcoming raid.

Arriving back at the airfield, the entire crew of 2665 was celebrating their first successful bombing raid. After shaking hands with the crew, Josh walked over to a jeep that was parked nearby. Master Sergeant Stamp stepped from the jeep and walked over to greet Josh.

"Well, I hear the mission was a job well done. Congratulations, you got one under your belt, but the next mission won't be so easy. Tomorrow morning, you and three other B-17s will depart here at 0600hrs. You will take off without a bomb load and fly to Port Moresby on the coast of Southern New Guinea. There, you will fuel up and take on four thousand pounds of bombs. You will fly northeast and attack Tonolei Harbor near Buin on Bougainville. After you drop your bombs, swing out to sea, return to Port Moresby, fuel up and come on home. Any questions?

Josh looked over the maps he was handed. "Sounds like a tough job, Sergeant."

"It is. We tried it a week ago with five planes. Only two made it back, and they were shot all to hell. But we need to knock out the harbor and warehouses soon. We need accuracy here, so bombing needs to be from about 4,000 feet. Good luck, Lieutenant, this is how careers and medals are made. The Sergeant Major responded as he fired up the jeep and drove off.

At 1600hrs, Josh gave the crew a run down on the plan. Then they listened to Major Fleming explain how each aircraft would be going in to Buin to drop their payloads. When he had completed the briefing he looked over the crews. "Some of you will not be coming back. Some of you will probably be captured if you bail out. Name, rank and serial number is all you will give them. The fighters will be up when we come out of Buin, so be on your best behavior and shoot the bastards down. Best of luck gentlemen!"

Not much was said across the intercom system of the 2665 on the way to Port Moresby. After fueling and getting back in the air, several of the men asked Josh what he was going to paint on the nose of the plane for their mascot and identification name.

Tom Carney the tail gunner spoke up. "I think when we get back, we should name her Bougainville Betty."

Everyone laughed and agreed that would be a good name for the bomber. Josh smiled as he said to himself, "Bougainville Betty if we get back. If we get back."

Josh became more concerned when they ran into a rain squall about a hundred miles out of Buin. It was pretty thick stuff and if it didn't clear, they would never be able to see their targets or turning points. They could run into one another and blow the planes to pieces without doing any damage to the Japanese. Finally, the navigator came on the intercom.

"Lieutenant, I can see clearing at about 3800 feet. It looks like Major Fleming is heading into the same hole I observed. It might be our best shot."

Knowing the Major had taken the same course relieved some of the butterfly's Josh was feeling. Pushing the wheel forward, Josh called Ward. "When I straighten out the ship it's yours. Take us into the target and drop our load."

Ward never responded, as he was already looking through the Norden bomb site, attempting to line up a hit on the fuel tanks near a small railroad repair shop. Smiling, Ward called out. "Bombs away, now get us the hell out of here, flak is coming at us fast!"

Josh could feel the explosions from the bombs on the fuselage as he pulled back on the wheel, throwing power to the engines. The B-17 began to climb beautifully as he swung out over Tonolei Harbor, heading for the open ocean.

Moments later, cries seemed to come from every gunner. Bogies at nine o'clock, bogies at two o'clock high, bogies at eleven o'clock high. Josh could feel the vibration on the wheel as every machine gun on board the B-17 hammered away at the attacking Zeroes. To his right he could see a B-17 streaming smoke from its port engines as the pilot continued pouring fuel to the two engines that remained. Seconds later the image was replaced by a massive fire ball as the plane disintegrated, wiping out the entire crew.

Josh watched a Zero in front of the 2665 explode as the top turret gunner tore into the fuel tanks. To his right, another Zero rolled over and dove for the sea after getting caught between the machine guns of the 2665 and Major Fleming's Fortress.

Moments later, Josh could see the Plexiglas nose of the 2665 explode as a Zero pilot blasted it with his 20 mm cannon. He knew immediately that his nose gunner was dead and the plane would no longer operate the way it was supposed to, as wind gushed in through the massive hole. Attempting to gain altitude made the engines strain as the aircraft shuddered.

"I'm hit, I'm hit," came the scream over the intercom as the belly gunner was struck by one of two attacking Zeros. Little by little the 2665 was being overwhelmed and torn to pieces with fewer guns to fight the determined enemy.

Several bullets ripped through the window near Sam Bench, hitting him in the throat and tearing into an electrical control panel on the back wall of the cockpit. Most of the gauges on the control panel quit working as Josh fought with all his strength to keep his aircraft in the sky, but he was quickly losing the battle.

Seeing a Sandy beach on the south side of Bougainville, Josh dropped his speed and pushed the wheel forward. The plane groaned as smoke poured from engines two and three. They had hit the target but now had lost the battle. He could not be sure how many men were alive, but he realized he needed to save their lives if he could. Just as the B-17 was about to hit the water, Josh pulled back on the wheel bringing the nose up one last time. The 2665 did a perfect belly flop on the water and skidded up on the beach. With the fire spreading along the port wing, everyone left on the plane ran to an exit to escape. Moments later the 2665 exploded in a fire ball.

What had started that morning as a crew of ten, was now down to just five. Both waist gunners along with the tail gunner and the navigator had survived. There was no doubt in the minds of any of the survivors, that the war was now over for them. As a truck load of Japanese soldiers came charging down the beach, Josh removed his pistol from its holster and threw it as hard as he could into the channel. Nodding his head in agreement, Roy Shapiro the navigator, similarly tossed his side arm into the deep water.

Looking at Josh, Roy commented as he raised his hands. "At least these guys don't have a problem with Jews. I guess that's worth something."

Within minutes, the five men were searched and forced onto the back of another truck as they were driven off to captivity.

The 120 was in need of a good cleaning as it had been used for crew training near the Panama Canal for the past several months. Ensign Speidel and Chief Petrovski put the crew to work, as Buzz focused on ordering all the equipment it took to make a PT boat an efficient combat vessel.

Over the next several days, Commander Reddings began sending crew replacements. First to arrive was Carl Zumwalde, a 20mm man. He was a retread that had been wounded several months ago and was ready for reassignment. Then came Andy Rice and Charlie Ansel, a couple of torpedo men that were survivors from a lost boat over at Rendova. Gabe Ridman a new man to PT boats arrived next. He had been a gunner's mate on an LST that couldn't get along with his skipper. When he volunteered for PT boats, they gladly transferred him. Lastly was Julian Stegura, a combination cook, medic and signal man, that had worked tramp steamers prior to the war. He and Chief Petrovski enjoyed swapping stories from the good old days almost instantly.

Buzz was rather concerned with Ridman after reading his file. After securing the boat for the night, he and Ensign Speidel sat down with Ridman for an explanation of his complaints.

Ridman looked seriously at Buzz, "Sir, that son-of-a-bitch has no business being in charge of any vessel in this man's navy. He ran us aground twice, rammed a PT boat over at Rendova causing a lot of damage, and then blamed the PT boat skipper for the accident. We were clearly entering the harbor way too fast. Then, when we were attacked by a couple of Zeros while in transit from a supply ship anchored off Rendova, he gave me a reprimand for firing before being fired upon. He claimed he could not recognize the planes as Zeros, and that I was trigger happy. Well sir, those planes he could not identify killed one of our deck workers and destroyed supplies in our hold. The next week while moving wounded men off a destroyer, we were once again attacked by three Zeroes. I pointed them out and began firing, as did the ship. We dropped one of the bastards, but once again he claimed he could not make them out as Zeros and I was once again trigger happy. He wrote me up for endangering the destroyer and our vessel for firing before the planes could be recognized as enemy aircraft. Sir, I know a Jap plane when I see one and I studied those charts very well, and I have never been wrong. But none of that mattered and he had me reassigned to land duty in a kitchen. Yes sir, I raised hell and was almost insubordinate, but I want to fight not peel potatoes for the duration of the war. So, finally Commander Reddings told me he could either put me on a wooden boat where I might get killed, or he could send me back to the states to train new men. So I chose the PT boat option, much to the dismay of Captain Knight. So Skipper, here I am, ready to fight if you will let me do so."

Buzz smiled at the rather upset sailor. "You'll be backing up Zumwalde on the 20mm, or any machine gunner that goes down. You guys can work out a plan for operations on the 20mm. That's the only job I have open, take it or leave it."

Ridman nodded his head. "I'll take the job, sir. I don't know much about these boats, but I'll learn fast. You can count on me."

With the crew intact, Buzz and Ensign Speidel ran through several battle scenarios over the next few days to make sure everyone knew their jobs. With all the work completed, Buzz took the 120 out to sea for a serious shake down run. The engines were snappier than those on the 113, and the factory mounted .50 caliber machine gun on the fore-deck was more solid. Returning to Tulagi he reported that the 120 was ready for service.

Commander Reddings was extremely happy to have the 120 ready for action. There was a small convoy with Seabees, construction material, and other supplies coming up the slot from Guadalcanal, needing an escort on the way to the New Georgia Islands.

The following morning after loading depth charges on their decks, the four escort boats left Tulagi at 0600hrs. It would be a short trip to Guadalcanal, where the convoy was being protected by several destroyers and a couple of armed sea tugs. Running in daylight, the skippers of the PT boats were more concerned with enemy aircraft and submarines than surface vessels.

Buzz patrolled the port side of the convoy as they got underway. About an hour into the trip, Stockey observed three aircraft dead ahead at twelve o'clock. Everyone tensed up as they appeared to be Zeros, but they never approached the convoy. After several minutes the pilots turned to the northwest, disappearing over the mountain peaks of Santa Isabel.

Mid-afternoon Andy Rice spotted a periscope paralleling the 120 off its starboard rear quarter. After watching it for several minutes, Buzz became anxious.

After radioing the other boats, Buzz called out. "General quarters, man your battle stations!"

Charlie Ansel and the Chief prepared the first depth charge for attack as Buzz swung the 120 hard to starboard, reversing their course. The skipper of the submarine began a dive as soon as Buzz made his turn. Ensign Speidel held his hand in the air as they passed over where they suspected the sub to be turning. As he dropped his arm he yelled out, "Roll cans!"

With the help of Ordman and Ridman, the men slid five cans overboard in less than a minute. The water behind the 120 blew skyward as the depth charges exploded about a hundred feet below the surface. As Buzz swung the boat hard to port for another attack, a Dauntless SBD dive bomber appeared out of the south. From the quick maneuvering of the pilot, it was apparent he could see the silhouette of the escaping sub against the lighter colored coral rocks below. After one final adjustment, the pilot nosed his aircraft over, dropping to about five hundred feet when he released the two-hundred-pound bombs he was carrying.

Every man in the convoy watched with anticipation as both weapons exploded in unison, sending a huge geyser of water a good fifty feet into the air. Instantly, a trail of oil could be seen on the surface as the skipper of the sub attempted to deal with the damage to his boat. As the pilot of the SBD circled slowly, watching to see what was going to happen next, his back seat gunner was waving toward the 120 and then pointing up. Moments later, the damaged sub broke through the waves listing to port. Several crew members exited the conning tower making a run toward the deck gun, but never made it, as Kowalski mowed them down with his fifty caliber machine gun.

Buzz spun around to look at Zumwaldt, who was already aiming his 20mm toward the stricken vessel. "Engine room, pump that mother full of rounds!"

Before Zumwaldt could fire a round, an explosion directly behind the conning tower lifted the boat into the air several feet, setting it back down on an exposed coral reef. Flames and smoke rose from the tower, and a major split in the hull appeared aft of the tower. Immediately, the sub rolled over hard on the port side and began sliding back into the deeper water, as several crew members attempted to escape the inferno from the torpedo loading doors on the top of the fore-deck. Neither Buzz nor the pilot of the SBD took any further action against the Japanese crew that had ceased to be any form of threat.

As Buzz rejoined the convoy, the SBD vanished off into a cloud bank to the east. Several minutes later, Lt. Commers called Buzz from the 118, notifying him that the sub had slipped off the reef and had gone down. It appeared that six men had survived and were swimming toward a small uninhabited coral island in the Russell Group. He notified air-sea rescue as to the location of the would-be prisoners.

Approaching Rendova, three Zeros and a Kate dive bomber came in low over Vangunu island. Every weapon in the convoy opened fire on the attacking aircraft. The pilot of the Kate dropped down quickly, aiming to place his bomb inside a tank landing craft. The skipper of the lumbering and heavily laden flat-bottomed ship attempted to take whatever evasive action he could, for what it was worth. The five-hundred-pound bomb dropped into the open bay, detonating on the steel cargo floor. Flames and debris from exploding shells sailed skyward as the ship instantly began to sink into the Solomon Sea. As a Zero came racing by to machine gun what few survivors there were, the team of Wickman, Stockey and Kowalski shredded the aluminum fuselage. With flames raging from the engine bonnet, the ill-fated Zero's left wing struck the water, cartwheeling the aircraft about fifty yards before it broke up.

Quickly, Chief Petrovski assisted in tossing cargo nets into the water, so survivors from the landing craft could crawl up to the deck of the 120. The remaining Japanese planes turned northwest toward Rabaul with its sprawling airfields.

By 1700hrs. the balance of the convoy was safe and sound in the harbor of Rendova where anxious dock workers began unloading the precious cargo. Buzz found an empty pier where he could unload the survivors from the tank ship, and get medical care for the wounded. As the sun began to end its journey across the Pacific for another day, four PT boats raced back toward Tulagi, hoping they would not be the last in line to refuel.

As with all islands in the Pacific, the day arrived when the war had passed by Tulagi. Everything pertaining to PT boats was packed up for the move to the rapidly expanding base at Rendova. For the PT sailors, it was sad to see Tulagi become a backwater storage facility. With all essential materials removed, the navy would remove it from its list of active islands, and Tulagi would be forgotten. The jungle would once more reclaim the muddy paths and repair areas, and the natives would secure the well-built huts for themselves. The soldiers and sailors on both sides of the conflict will have moved on, becoming memories and stories for future native generations.

Rendova was a far cry from the muddy trails of Tulagi. Roads were paved with crushed coral, streets had names, and there were rows of well-built and perfectly painted Quonset huts. There was a naval administration in place that attempted to keep things organized and running like any naval base back in the states. It would take a few days for the new crews to get accustomed to the structure and discipline in place at that type of facility, compared to the more casual atmosphere on Tulagi.

The first visitor to the docking pier of the 120 was Captain Knight. Walking up to Buzz, he pointed at Ridman who was helping tear down the 20mm for cleaning.

"I want that man off this boat, and off this island no later than 2200hrs. tomorrow. I will not put up with his attitude or failure to comply with naval regulations. Do I make myself clear, Lieutenant?"

Buss shook his head. "No sir, he is legally assigned to the 120 and will remain so unless I find a reason to get rid of him. He has proven to be a good sailor and a qualified PT man so far. If you have a problem with that, go see Commander Reddings."

Angered by that response the irate captain jumped in his jeep and was gone. Ridman walked over to Buzz as he wiped down a piece of the weapon. "Thank you, sir, but I don't want you getting in trouble because of me. If you want me gone, just say so and I'll pack my sea bag."

Buzz smiled as he slapped Ridman on the shoulder. "You're a member of the 120 and so it shall stay, sailor. Just stay sober, stay away from him, and keep your nose clean when you're ashore. You do that and you'll be just fine. Now, get that gun operating."

Ridman smiled, "You got it, sir. There will be no problems from me. I found a home here and won't ever take it for granted."

Since arriving in the Pacific, Buzz had received very little mail from home, which did not surprise him in the least. He was stunned when Chief Petrovski handed him a letter from his mother.

Looking up at the chief, Buzz shook his head. "Has to be bad news of some sort, she would never write just to say hello."

Sitting down on the fore-deck Buzz ripped open the envelope and recognized his mother's private stationary immediately. The letter was one page and very short.

"Dear Buzz, I hate to inform you of this sad news. Josh has been shot down on a mission to Bougainville. Pilots from the other planes said he landed his plane on the beach, and he and the crew were taken prisoner. You must go find him and bring him home. Do what you must do, but save your brother. Mother."

Chief Petrovski sat down next to Buzz. "Just as you suspected, it was bad news?"

"Go ahead and read it, Chief. There's nothing I can do about this," Buzz said, as he shook his head. "Josh had no business flying a B-17 or any other combat aircraft. He's not a survivor, and surely not the type of guy that will stand up to the Japs. She doesn't say how long ago he was shot down, so he could be long dead already."

Placing the letter back in the envelope, the chief handed it to Buzz. "What are you going to do, Skipper?"

Standing up, Buzz looked up as three Corsair fighters streaked in low from the east. "Hell, we are not even close to taking Bougainville from the Japs yet. All we can do is our jobs, Chief. Beat the Japs back one day at a time, and when we get that far we'll see what happens."

Buzz had a hard time sleeping that night, as he thought about Josh being tortured by the ruthless Japanese security forces. Although trying to comply with his mother's request sounded like a good idea, in all honesty, Buzz knew it was not. There were many other sailors, soldiers and airmen that were now POW's, and attempting to rescue one man in these dangerous islands was sheer lunacy. Possibly one day he would get a chance to look for Josh, but for now, winning the war came first, and he could never run away from his obligations to the navy or his crew.

The following evening, the 120 followed seven other boats out of Rendova harbor at 2030hrs, then headed east on the south side of New Georgia into Blackett Straits. Coast watchers had reported a large convoy heading southeast toward Ghizo Island.

Every channel, and every strait in this section of the Solomon's was filled with uncharted coral reefs just waiting to rip a hole in the bottom of a boat or shred the propellers. Fighting the enemy here was tough, but attempting to make a high-speed exit from a battle was equally dangerous. Tonight Commander Reddings was at the helm of PT 130 that was equipped with an experimental radar system. The problem was, many parts of the radar system could not take the pounding handed out by a PT Boat at high speed, so skippers had a tendency to ignore calls from the lead boat.

Tonight was the type of night no PT skipper enjoyed. The sky was heavy overcast and small rain squalls drifted back and forth over Blackett Straits. But somewhere out there was the Tokyo Express, and it had to be stopped, severely damaged, or turned around.

Near the coastline of Simba Island, Buzz joined the 118 and 98 boats as they took up station about two hundred yards apart. With the big engines muffled, Buzz backed off the throttles until they were at idling speed. Ensign Speidel stood beside Buzz, staring out into the blackness that appeared to be enclosing the 120 from all the other human beings on earth.

"Skipper, I can't see a thing, what the hell do we do?"

Buzz looked over at his XO. "You can breathe, Speidel. It's almost good fresh air out here."

"Almost good air, sir?" the young ensign inquired with a grin.

"Yeah, no matter what I do, we keep getting exhaust fumes from the 118 every once in a while, so wherever the hell Commers is, he's close enough for that," Buzz replied. Though he always tried to display a calm demeanor and good attitude to the crew, at the same time he was nervous tonight. The last thing you ever wanted to do was take off after a target and slam into one of your own boats.

At 2245hrs, Commander Reddings reported a large blip on his radar coming southwest down Blackett Straits at a speed of 25 knots. They had to be destroyers, as they were moving too fast to be supply barges. Buzz was positive they would continue on the same course right through Ferguson Passage. He knew the coral reefs on each side of the passage made it nearly impossible for a destroyer to make a wide turn and then reverse course while PT boats were attacking the Tokyo Express.

Seconds later, Commander Reddings reported a larger blip on his radar to the northwest in Wilson Strait doing 15 knots. As it began a slow southerly turn around the west side of Ghizo, every skipper knew this was their target. Carefully, the remaining boats began crossing Blackett Straits to join the 130 and 128 that were sitting just south of Kolombangara. Buzz knew every boat crossing the strait would have to move slow and cautiously. Otherwise, they would risk the watch crews on the destroyers seeing their phosphorescent wake, giving away their presence and causing all hell to break lose. Watching the straits, Ensign Speidel observed the silhouettes of the 118 and 98 boats heading out across the channel and disappearing once again into the darkness. Knowing the last two boats were somewhere off the starboard beam of the 120, Buzz shoved the throttles for engines one and three forward, keeping number two in reserve. This would help keep the wake of the boat down to a minimum. As of now few Japanese ships had radar, so they relied on visual contact on nights like this.

They were somewhere near the middle of Blackett Strait when Ansel called out, "Destroyer coming dead ahead at our two o'clock!"

From the cockpit, Buzz was just able to see the mast moving against the dark sky. Knowing there was only one way to avoid contact, Buzz threw the wheel over hard to port, harder than he ever had before, as he engaged engine number two. If it all worked out as Buzz had planned in those short seconds, the 120 would end up paralleling the enemy vessel, but how close they would be was anyone's guess. It was intimidating as hell for the crew as they stood motionless with their mouths open, watching the massive steel plates of the destroyer's hull gliding past them just six feet away from their wooden hull. Buzz held tightly to the wheel until the stern of the ship passed them by.

Ensign Speidel slapped Buzz on the back as he laughed. "If you have a clean pair of underwear down below, I for one could sure use them."

Spinning the wheel to starboard so they could complete their run across Blackett Straits, Buzz looked up at his XO.

"Well, I may be needing those myself, but you're welcome to them when I'm done."

Both men laughed for a moment before they once again trailed the boats ahead of them at very close quarters.

As they neared the southwest shore of Ghizo, Commander Reddings called out. "Radar is gone and I can't track the convoy. Firing three flares."

The trails of the red flares flying from the 130 were not hard to miss on a night like this. Instantly, every gunner in the Tokyo Express opened fire whether they could see a target or not.

Slamming his throttles forward, Buzz shot by the 118 that appeared to be having engine problems. Buzz went after a barge that had broken from the convoy when the flares went off. Wickman, Kowalski and Zumwaldt hammered away with their weapons, working the boat over fairly well as they passed by. After spinning the boat around for a second pass, Stockey was able to fire on the damaged barge. Moments later, an explosion on board the barge sent a ball of flame into the sky, illuminating the channel. Bringing the 120 back toward the southwest, Buzz charged after a smaller craft that only had one machine gun firing. Zumwaldt placed a 20mm shell right at the base of the machine gun, blowing a large hole in the deck. Now the slow moving vessel was at the mercy of the 120 and the 118, which appeared to be moving just fine now. In a matter of minutes, the small enemy boat slipped below the waves.

By now, barges were burning all over the channel, and resistance from enemy machine guns had been all but wiped out. Japanese soldiers and sailors climbed off the transports to escape the inferno rapidly engulfing the desperately needed supplies they were carrying.

Several small Japanese patrol boats from Ghizo came out to save what was left of the convoy, only to realize they had to run or be destroyed.

Lt. Debbins, the skipper of the 98, was at the far southern end of the channel when he called out, "Two destroyers heading northwest of our position, making full speed."

Feeling like the seven boats had won the day, Commander Reddings ordered the boats to retreat back into Wilson Strait as their ammunition levels were beginning to run low.

Without a response from the 102 boat, the commander was unwilling to leave. He realized that if there were two destroyers, it was possible that all five ships that went through Ferguson passage could be coming back to the rescue. Just as Commander Reddings ordered the boats to make a quick swing into the channel, their questions about the 102 boat were answered. Gunners on the leading destroyers began pounding a target near Vella Lavella. Moments later, the one hundred octane fuel of a PT boat exploded. It was evident that the boat had run aground on a reef or sandbar and was hopelessly stuck. The only hope at this point was that the crew had been able to abandon their boat and swim for shore.

Arriving back at Rendova, Commander Reddings immediately put in a request for Search and Rescue to go out at first light to look for possible survivors.

Buzz was extremely tired as he stretched out on his cot. It had been a difficult mission made even harder by the prevailing weather conditions. As he began to unwind, thoughts of Josh in the hands of the brutal Japanese marines would not allow him to sleep. He knew his brother would do everything possible to take care of his crew, just as he did on the fishing boats. Consequently, Josh could push that too far and lose his own life in the process. His mother was right, Josh and his crew needed to be rescued, but such a mission was still too far out of reach.

The following morning, the air-sea rescue division reported they had found no sign of the 102 crew, but some of the wreckage from the boat was still afloat within the coral reefs. PT crews were always told to hunker down until dark, then wait for patrolling PT boats to find them.

But if they were alive, why didn't they attempt to signal the slow-moving float planes.

Captain Knight was unsatisfied with the search results. Since there was no word regarding another convoy, he decided to send several boats out to Vella Lavella to harass the enemy and search the area for survivors. After explaining the mission he assigned the 120, 111, 118 and the 130 with repaired radar, to sail at 2030hrs.

Commander Reddings ordered the skippers to run unmuffled at high speed until they reached Parara Island. Creeping cautiously through the narrow channel separating Parara and Arundel Islands, Buzz could tell his crew was tense as he muffled his Packard engines. They all remembered the close call with the destroyer in Blackett Straits, and Buzz was about to negotiate a turn to the southwest, taking them right back into the dangerous waters. Luckily, a few stars dotted the otherwise dark sky tonight, allowing them to recognize features that posed a threat.

Chief Petrovski stood behind Buzz and Ensign Speidel in the cockpit as he watched the 111 enter the straits. "I used to think these waters were dark when I worked on tramp steamers back in the day. But on this damn boat everything seems a whole lot darker."

Buzz smiled, "Yeah Chief, but back then you weren't thinking about being sliced in half or shelled by a destroyer. All you had to worry about if you went into the water were sharks and head hunters."

The chief laughed as he shook his head. "Damn college boys always have an answer. But me and my .45 can deal with head hunters, it's the sharks you can't beat no matter who you are."

The conversation drifted off and everyone manned their battle stations as the 120 followed the convoy deeper into enemy waters. Approaching Vonavona Island southeast of Ghizo, Commander Reddings picked up two small bogies on his radar. They were not only here to search for the crew of the 102, but they were also to harass the enemy every way possible. So he ordered Buzz and Lt. Commers to continue on to Vella Lavella, while he and the 111 went after the barges.

Lt. Commers and Buzz stayed in close contact via TBS radio (Talk between Ships) as they charged up Wilson Straits with their engines un-muffled once again. They began to slow down and muffle their engines when they were about two miles from the beginning of their search point. Every eye on the boats searched the blackness looking for any enemy vessels that could attack them. But suddenly the sound of an approaching aircraft at a very low altitude caught the attention of every man. All the gunners swung their weapons skyward attempting to seek out the plane before it could attack. Moments later, flames from the exhaust port of a Japanese Aichi two seat float plane, commonly called a Jake, gave away its position. It was turning north into Wilson Passage from Baga Island, flying less than a hundred feet above the water at nearly stall speed.

It was evident that the pilot observed the PT boats mere seconds before a hail of gun fire came his way, and he began pouring power to the engine while attempting to pull the nose up and turn east. But that maneuver exposed his underside to every gunner below. Pieces of metal were ripped from the plane as machine gun bullets and cannon rounds found their target.

As flames began to pour from the engine and oil coolers, Buzz could see a hundred-pound bomb hanging from the rack. Quickly, he pulled back on the throttles while turning sharply to port, hoping to avoid any damaging debris from an aerial detonation. Unfortunately, before Buzz could get the 120 away, the plane and bomb detonated in a massive fire ball that lit up the channel with an eerie glow for several hundred yards around.

In the shower of flying shrapnel, two mufflers were ripped off the boat, and a third had a massive hole in it. Torpedoman Ordman reported the firing mechanism for number four torpedo was ripped off, and Crowder reported a small hole in the hull, well above the water line. Ridman also reported damage to the 20mm pedestal, keeping the weapon from traversing to port.

After a head count was completed, Buzz was amazed that no one had been killed or injured. He felt it had to be a miracle considering the sheer quantity of debris that struck the boat and flew overhead. But there was no doubt the crew was shaken and needed to get their heads back in the game. Buzz and Lt. Commers made several slow circles in the channel, searching the sky and horizon for anymore low flying aircraft before proceeding.

Confident the Jake had been a lone patrol plane, they once again pulled in closer to the shore, as close to the reef as they dared. Seeing debris from the 102 in the water near the shore, the large spotlights on both boats were turned on so they could scan the shore line.

Chief Petrovski worked the light back and forth before yelling out. "Back up, Skipper. I see somebody!"

After Buzz backed up about fifteen feet, the chief placed his light on a man leaning against a coconut tree. Looking through the binoculars, Ensign Speidel reported, "He's one of ours!"

Without hesitation or being ordered to do so, Ansel and Rice tossed the life raft into the water and began paddling to shore, being careful not to hit a reef and shred their little boat. They spoke with the man for a moment before they loaded him into the raft. Rice stayed near the raft as Ansel removed the officer's pistol and disappeared into the jungle. After a long excruciating wait, especially with those bright lights giving away their positions, Ansel returned with two more men that appeared to be badly wounded. Setting them down he ran back into the jungle for just a moment before returning with one more survivor that appeared to be in pretty good shape. The 118 boat sent their raft ashore to help extricate the wounded, so the 120 crew could make a dash back to the boat without returning.

Just as the men were pulling the rafts back onto the decks, a swarm of Japanese Marines appeared on the shoreline, firing their weapons and setting up a mortar tube.

Buzz yelled at the chief. "Light those bastards up!"

Once more the large light illuminated the dark shoreline giving the gunners on both boats ample targets to engage. With the enemy fire suppressed, the 120 and 118 began turning back toward Blackett Straits, just as the 111 and 130 arrived on scene.

Commander Reddings was happy with what they had accomplished during the patrol and ordered everyone back to base.

The man they had seen by the tree was Ensign Toros and he relayed what had happened to the 102. He reported that before they were attacked, they were already taking on water from a major rip in the hull, and they knew the boat was lost. When they saw the destroyers coming, the entire crew bailed off and swam to shore, with a few men carrying weapons from the locker. As they sat on shore watching their boat burn, a small Japanese patrol came through the jungle, making a tremendous amount of noise. The crew of the 102 was able to kill or injure most of them, but a couple were able to escape. Early in the morning a larger patrol came down the island and attacked the crew, killing most of the men. He stated that he and the other three men were the only survivors. Looking up at Commander Reddings, he began to cry.

"Sir, we prayed you would not forget us. When we saw the battle with the plane, it was like the hand of God swept that Jake out of the sky allowing the boats to come and get us. Thank you. Thank you all."

Very inclement weather closed down operations for the next two days. Even the coast watchers could not see what was going on with the rain and low clouds. With the 120 now repaired, Buzz crawled into his rack and took the longest nap he had taken since college, warning everyone that he had his pistol under his pillow and would happily shoot the first man that woke him. With the waves rocking the boat and the sound of rain up on the deck, it was the perfect recipe for the sound and restful sleep he so badly needed.

Over the next few weeks, the PT squadrons had pretty much put the loss of the 102 boat behind them, and were once again operating at the top of their game. With the boats working in teams, they had tremendous luck striking at the Tokyo Express with very few injuries, and no boats lost to enemy fire. Buzz could not have been happier with the operation of the 120 and his veteran crew. Everyone pitched in where needed during a mission and no one ever complained. As he saw it, they were operating like a well-oiled machine.

At about 2130 on the night of July 31, 1943, fifteen boats sailed out of Rendova after a tip from the coast watchers. Their mission was to hunt down the Tokyo Express that was said to be making a late night run. The course that had been reported would bring the convoy south of Vella Lavella, where they could hug the shoreline, then squeeze through the narrow channel separating Vella Lavella and Mbava, before breaking out into Blackett Straits north of Ranongga Island. The odds were the convoy was headed toward Kolombangara, where it was estimated nearly twelve thousand Japanese were still holding their position.

Commander Reddings had once again turned off his malfunctioning radar by the time the boats had reached Parara Island from the southeast. Regrettably, by now the coast watchers on Vella Lavella had lost sight of the convoy due to heavy rain squalls that were moving through the area, but a British submarine reported the convoy nearing the southeastern point of Vella Lavella doing fifteen knots.

With the boats operating in two squadrons, Commander Reddings decided the best thing he could do was to set up a picket line in Blackett Strait with his eight boats, stretching from the south coast of Kolombangara to just west of Ghizo. The 130, 98, 111 and 118 boats would handle the north end of the watch. The 120, 162, 169 and 109 boats would handle the south end of the precarious line. The other seven boats patrolled farther to the north in Blackett Straits, making runs from Wilson Straits north to the slot and back down again. If anything came that way it was sure to be seen.

As Buzz idled the 120 slowly toward Ghizo, Lt. Speidel peered into the darkness, shaking his head.

"Skipper, it's just so black out there, by now I should be able to see the outline of the mountains on the island, and I can't see shit."

Chief Petrovski entered the cockpit and leaned over toward Buzz. "Skipper, the men are nervous as hell and it gets worse every time one of those damn rain showers comes through. No one can see a damn thing. Do you even know where the 162 is right now?"

"I can't lie to you, Chief. I lost track of her about twenty minutes ago, and I'm sure the 169 and 109 are even farther south, or at least they should be. Keep your eyes open."

Around midnight, the 111 boat spotted several destroyers and a cruiser exiting Wilson Strait, sailing due east across Blackett Straits toward Kohingo Island.

Commander Reddings ordered all boats in the area to attack the Japanese ships. Spotters on the Japanese ships noticed the PT boats closing on them at nearly the same time and were preparing for a fight. Deck guns on the ships roared as machine guns and twenty-millimeter cannons on the PT boats hammered away at the steel monsters. Torpedoes sprang from well-greased tubes causing the ships to twist and turn to avoid them. Angry skippers claimed their torpedoes struck ships, but as in the past, many failed to detonate. By the time the enemy ships sailed into the channel separating Kohingo and Vonavona Islands, the PT boats had expended thirty torpedoes without being able to document one destructive hit. Dismayed by the situation and not seeing any transports, Commander Reddings radioed Rendova of the situation. The decision was made to have all boats that had expended their torpedoes to return to base, and allow the rest to continue searching for the convoy.

Since Buzz was in the southern group, he had not been involved in the action, but had watched the fireworks from a distance. By now, no one had a clue what had happened to the convoy, and everyone's nerves were on edge. Had the Japanese turned back? Had the convoy broken up and delivered to several smaller islands? Or, were they hiding in coves somewhere along hundreds of miles of shoreline? Buzz in the 120, along with the 162, began checking coves along the north side of Ghizo without any luck. Far to the south, Lt. j.g. John Kennedy was idling the 109 slowly near the entrance to Ferguson Passage, a favorite spot for enemy ships and convoys to pass through. Kennedy stood at the controls in the cockpit along with Ensign Leonard Thom, scanning the darkness for any signs of activity, but it was so dark it was impossible to see what might be coming at them until it was too late. At one point as the young ensign scanned the straits, he looked over at Kennedy.

"Skipper, there's a lot of water out there."

Kennedy responded with a smile, "Yeah Lenny, and that's just the top of it."

Around 0130hrs, skippers from the 169 boat and the 157 from another squadron, decided to begin patrolling farther north up the strait, leaving Kennedy and the 109 as the last boat patrolling on station where they had originally been assigned. At 0200hrs, a lookout on the 109 yelled out, "Destroyer at two o'clock!"

Kennedy turned just in time to see a Japanese destroyer bearing down on the starboard side of his vessel at full speed. Spinning the wheel hard to starboard and slamming the throttles forward, Kennedy hoped to fire his torpedoes and avoid a collision. Although Kennedy made a valiant move to avoid the crash, the destroyer made contact before the 109 could fully respond.

The Destroyer Amagiri sliced through the 109 boat, rupturing the fuel tanks. The stern of the boat containing the heavy engines sank nearly immediately. The bow of the boat stayed upright for several hours, allowing the crew to assemble on the deck. The crew searched the water around the bow until it was clear that two men had perished in the crash.

Buzz was the last boat to return from the mission, running on just one engine to conserve what little fuel was left in the tanks. With the boats secured, the crews began making their way ashore for some well-deserved sleep. As Buzz followed his men, he noticed several of the skippers around Captain Knight who was seated in a jeep near the pier.

"Maddox, glad to see you made it back. We were concerned about you and the 109 boat. Did you happen to see the 109 on your way back? Tell us what happened as far as you know it," the anxious officer inquired as he stared intently at Buzz.

"Well sir, my number three engine started to sputter a bit when we were still patrolling to the north in Blackett Straits. My motor mac told me the fuel line was partially plugged, and he couldn't tear it down while we were underway. But he also informed me that our fuel level was low, and there was no way we could make it back home running on all three engines. I heard the skippers of the 162 and 169 on the TBS radio report that they were low on fuel as well and heading home. We hadn't seen any action all night, as we had been too far south for the torpedo attack. So Ensign Speidel and I felt it was a good idea to drop the number three engine and head home, considering the fuel situation we were in. As we were nearing the passage between Arundel and Parara, we saw a large sheet of flame go up from Blackett Straits far to the south, then it settled down into what appeared to be fire on the water. I'm guessing it was near Ferguson Passage. With one engine gone and being extremely low on fuel, we were in no condition to run down there, and possibly get into a running fight, so we decided to continue home on two engines until we were about fifty miles out. Then we cut it down to just our middle engine. We watched the 162 and 169 disappear into the darkness ahead of us when we were passing Mbanga. But we never saw the 109 all the way back," Buzz reported, realizing they were missing one of their boats.

Captain Knight shook his head. "Yeah, both the 162 and 169 skippers reported what appeared to be an explosion down to the south, but they had the same issue, not enough fuel to check it out. I'll call air sea rescue and see if they can find anything in the morning. As they say gentlemen, it's a hell of a war!"

With all the boats separated by miles of water, in the dark and low on fuel, Captain Knight understood that his skippers had no way of investigating, and could never be sure from their position if it had been the 109 boat they saw, or an accident within the Tokyo Express.

Unfortunately, the bow of the 109 had turned over during the night, so the morning air patrol reported it as a damaged barge floating in Ferguson Passage.

Seven days later after swimming to several islands, the survivors of the 109 were rescued with the help of island natives. Regrettably, two men were lost in the initial collision. Everyone on Rendova gave the missing crew a rousing welcome when they returned. Very seldom did a crew that large ever return after being gone so long. The southwest Pacific was a harsh area of the world to be lost in as it was, but adding in the Japanese, the odds of survival were dramatically less.

Skippers of the boats that had been involved in the torpedo attack that night returned to Rendova angrier than they had been in a long time. They could not believe they had expended thirty torpedoes and not even damaged a single ship. Morale was noticeably low for several weeks, with threats of mutiny when they were given a new mission to go on. The skippers allowed their men to vent what were legitimate frustrations, but always managed to have them ready when it came time to sail.

Within a month the boats had the new Mark 13 torpedoes which were faster and much more dependable. Crews enjoyed finally being able to hunt the enemy and attack the way PT boats were designed to do, and they began taking a serious toll on Japanese shipping.

CHAPTER 10
TRAITOR

Near the small town of Kieta on the northern coast of Bougainville, the Japanese had constructed a small POW camp. The wire enclosures had been designed to hold about twenty prisoners. Today it held thirteen allied prisoners, consisting of three U.S. Navy fighter pilots and five British sailors, along with Josh and his four men. Every day they were taken from the enclosure to work on various building projects for the Japanese Army. Luckily, they were fed by native tribes, since most native island foods were still plentiful, and they caught more fish than they needed for themselves. This allowed the prisoners to keep up a fairly good diet considering the hard labor required of them.

That also made the Japanese happy, as they did not have to share their dwindling supplies which were continually ending up on the bottom of the Pacific by the ton. However, the island commander, Colonel Etsuji Numora, was already demanding weekly quotas of food from the islanders to supplement their rations.

Knowing there was no way to escape the island, all of the prisoners decided that attempting to escape from the compound would accomplish nothing, and only bring down the hostility of their captors. So a type of peace was set in place for a time, and the torture and beatings were no longer daily rituals.

On two occasions, Josh had shown a Japanese sailor how to repair the engine on his small patrol boat. He knew the boat could be used to announce the location of allied war ships, but Josh also realized that knowing the harbor and equipment could pay dividends down the road.

The sergeant in charge of the work detail was Hideo Kokawa from Yokosuka, Japan. His father, grandfather, and great grandfather, had all spent their lives in defense of their homeland. He was a tough military man from top to bottom, but resented having to wear the rank of an enlisted staff. He had applied four times to attend the Eta Jima Military Academy, and been solidly turned downed each time. It was obvious to his men and the prisoners, that he despised Colonel Numora, a man who had no military history in his family, and had been accepted to Eta Jima on his first attempt. The last slap in the face to Sgt. Kokawa was being assigned to a construction battalion on Bougainville. He often complained to the prisoners that his talents were being wasted guarding an enemy work detail. He explained how a true Samurai would take his own life before surrendering to the enemy. For that reason he looked down on his charges, but did not punish them for surrendering. Often, he showed them a knife he carried in his boot so he could commit seppuku, a form of hari kari, where you split your belly open allowing your entrails to fall out. He relished dying that way in battle as a tribute to his ancestors and the emperor.

To the men in the stockade, they would just as soon put a bullet right between his eyes. Not quite as messy and honorable, but just as fatal.

One morning the men were loaded onto a Japanese landing craft that sailed northeast before rounding the tip of the island where it took a southerly course. Fauro Island, along with Shortland Island, guarded the southeasterly approach to Bougainville. Any invading force would need to deal with each of these islands, so the Japanese were wasting no energy re-enforcing every aspect of their defenses.

As soon as the men were unloaded, the engineers put them to work mixing a new, more solid type of concrete, capable of taking massive explosive hits when re-enforced with rod and wire. As the men were mixing their third batch around midday, Josh was overwhelmed. Standing by the head engineer, Capt. Soto, was Swenson Bellington, his one-time friend, and the new boyfriend of Angeline Stevenson. His mother had mentioned the relationship to him in several letters she had written before he was shot down. The two men walked together, amiably discussing different features of the bunker complex they were constructing. Josh did everything possible to hide, so Bellington would not see him during the visit. Josh knew without a doubt that his one time buddy Swenson Bellington, would have him killed in a heartbeat to protect what he was obviously doing, and the huge sums of money he was no doubt collecting from the enemy.

About mid-afternoon, a large float plane arrived to take Bellington and his aide out of the war zone and back to the safety of whatever rat hole he was hiding in. Josh tried to make himself believe that Angeline was clueless as to what her boyfriend was up to. After all, if it meant a new necklace or ring on her finger, who was she to question where the money came from.

However, it was clear that the allies were well aware of the defenses being built on the islands. Nearly every other day reconnaissance aircraft flew overhead, taking photos of the progress. This made all the prisoners nervous as they were sure that B-17's from New Guinea or Australia were going to start dropping bombs, and they were located right at the target.

Nevertheless, construction continued at a frenetic pace with more concrete being poured each day. Soon, landing craft arrived delivering artillery and mortar equipment to be placed in the new bunkers. The men felt like traitors for building the massive structures that would slaughter their countrymen when they came ashore, but it was build or be shot.

On a cloudy afternoon when the men had just finished mixing a new batch of concrete, the Japanese workers on the bunkers began to yell and run. Looking up, Josh saw three carrier based naval F4U Corsair fighter bombers making a wide circle before beginning their run.

The first pilot dropped his first hundred-pound bomb on the newest unfinished bunker, blowing out the back wall. As he prepared to climb, he strafed a fuel truck that exploded instantly.

The second pilot dropped both his hundred-pound bombs on one of the finished bunkers. There was a cloud of dust, but the bunker was not damaged. He finished his run by strafing several vehicles used by the construction workers.

The third pilot dropped one bomb on the landing craft that was tied up in the harbor, and the other on a pile of construction materials, including bags of the new concrete mix. He then strafed several construction workers that had decided to run for cover in a new spot.

The first pilot returned, firing his six machine guns at anything he could destroy. His last bomb dropped right on target, wiping out the cement factory and igniting a fire in a fuel storage tank.

Josh and the men shook hands before crawling out of a slit trench they had used for cover. Slowly they walked around surveying the damage, and it was immense.

Sgt. Kokawa walked up to his workers. "This has been done by your navy, you will need to pay a price. You will spend the night here without food or shelter. You will work until sundown today and every day until this mess is cleaned up. The guards watching you may not be as sympathetic as I am. They will shoot you if you do not cooperate!"

After kicking a piece of debris, he and several other engineers walked over to a patrol boat that had been sent to pick them up.

Immediately, everything arriving on the island was camouflaged to hide it from the roving aircraft patrols. It took the men over a week of hard labor to remove all the debris from that attack, and begin building the new concrete factory with equipment arriving from the Island of New Britain.

Josh was careful to keep close watch every time any type of boat arrived at the pier. The last thing he wanted was to be caught off guard by Swenson.

About a month after the bombing raid, a large Japanese freighter dropped anchor between Fauro and Shortland Islands. Landing barges began the task of unloading steel beams, concrete bags, lumber, re-enforcing rod, and tons of other construction material. There was little doubt the Japanese intended to make these islands impregnable to allied guns and bombs.

The prisoners began discussing how they could refuse to do the work as defined in the Geneva Convention, and not be murdered by the Japanese, though they all realized Sgt. Kokawa would have no problem lining them up against a bunker to be shot for refusing to work.

Aboard the freighter, Swenson sat with the officers of the ship in their ward room, sipping sake after a delicious meal of steak. The food and equipment were being supplied by one of the Bellington family holding companies located in South Korea. The Japanese were paying top dollar to the Bellington's, who chose to fulfill orders for equipment to keep their factories from being destroyed or taken over. Korean slave labor supplied by the Japanese military kept costs to a minimum, allowing the Bellington's to reap a huge financial reward where no taxes would ever need to be paid. All financial arrangements were being handled through a bank in Italy supplied by Benito Mussolini, a signer to the Axis agreement along with Japan and Germany. Life for the Bellington's could not be any sweeter.

CHAPTER 11
SWENSON BELLINGTON

There were not too many people around the Kennebunkport area that hadn't heard of the Bellington family. Oscar Bellington had been a ruthless lumber man back in the late 1800's, playing every dirty trick in the book to destroy his competition. There were very few people that attempted to stand up to him or get the law involved, because retribution was always swift and lethal.

His only son Oliver had grown up in the middle of it all, learning from the best how to intimidate and wreck the good fortune of any competitor that stood in his way. By 1935, Oliver took over the reins of the family business, running it with an iron fist. There were very few politicians in the New England states that Oliver did not have tucked away in his hip pocket. He hated President Franklin Roosevelt with a passion, the one politician he could never manage to sink his claws into. When FDR was Secretary of the Navy, he had signed contracts with several lumber companies to supply logs and other lumber materials for new ship building quays needed by the navy. He had overlooked Bellington Lumber, and never supplied an explanation that was sufficient for the family. The loss of those contracts had cost Bellington Lumber over a million dollars in easy revenue.

Furthermore, as tension with Japan increased in the Pacific, FDR had ordered embargo's on everything from oil, scrap iron, forest goods and many other products, in an attempt to bring Japan to the conference table. Many of those products had sailed across the Pacific on cargo ships owned by the Bellington consortium. Those ships now sat empty in ports up and down the west coast, as Oliver searched far and wide for any country willing to sign shipping contracts with him. Although Korea was annexed by the Japanese Empire in 1910, they allowed large individual companies in Seoul to continue operation, since the companies were forced to pay much of their profits to Tokyo. It did not take long for Oliver to sign contracts with the Jeong Company for deliveries of oil and building products.

After December 7, 1941, oil, rubber and many other products were cut off from Korea, once again causing pain to the Bellington pocket book.

In 1942, Oliver sent his son Swenson to Korea, to see if they could work out deals that would keep the Bellington shipping operation in the black. Japanese officials were excited, yet nervous, regarding an American businessman dealing with a company they controlled. They insisted they be allowed to sit in on any conferences pertaining to business deals.

When Tokyo realized the Bellington family was totally willing to disregard the embargo's placed upon Japan and Korea in order to make a profit, they were more than willing to take advantage of their good fortune. It quickly became clear that the Bellington's would happily supply ingredients for high strength concrete mix documented as cattle supplements; high tensile strength barbed wire documented as livestock fencing; and many more items for a good profit. Immediately, Swenson signed the contracts and sailed back to the United States, carrying with him a half million dollar down payment.

Swenson was born with one leg an inch shorter than the other, and had worn a raised platform shoe on his right foot since he was a child. Consequently, he was not eligible for the draft, and the military would not allow him to enlist. He flaunted his so-called good fortune at every social gathering he attended. Many of the well to do young ladies in his social circle enjoyed the fact that Swenson would not be swept away for military service, and could always be counted on for escort duty. He knew which families owned businesses his father was interested in, and always made special effort to court the proper daughters.

When word had spread throughout Kennebunkport that Buzz Maddox had walked away from Angeline Stevenson, Oliver's ears perked right up. There was nothing he wanted more than to gain control of the Stevenson's lumber and shipping holdings, but Mathew Stevenson wanted nothing to do with the Bellington name. But if Oliver could get the brokenhearted Angeline to fall in love with his handsome son, he would have his foot in the door. For Swenson, the thought of taking Angeline away from Buzz Maddox permanently, was a mountain he would eagerly climb.

Two weeks after Buzz was solidly into PT boat training, Swenson approached Angeline at a social event at the local Eagles Club. It did not take long for Swenson to convince the forlorn young lady that Buzz was all in the past, and her future now rested on his shoulders. She was totally taken in by stories of long exotic ocean trips to Korea, and his dealings with foreign dignitaries. She quickly realized this was the man that would be able to give her the world someday, not just the eastern corner of the United States.

After long dinners at the Stevenson mansion, Swenson and Mathew would discuss deals for raw materials that would pay handsomely. Of course, Mathew Stevenson was totally into following the war effort, so Swenson had to explain exactly how all the raw materials would be helping produce war materials that would build America's war machine.

Within no time an agreement was signed, allowing shipments of material from a mine in Idaho to a concrete plant in Tacoma, Washington. Concrete from the plant was being purchased by the war department, but only the special high strength product designed by Japanese engineers was leaving on ships for Korea as farm goods.

It took an office full of workers to forge and create documents that were acceptable to the War Production Board, which routinely audited companies monitoring production levels on a regular basis. No one in the office had any idea as to the authenticity of the work they were creating. When an audit team wished to tour the cement factory, Swenson arranged the meeting, and changed production in the plant for that particular day. When the audit team chose to look into the manufacturing of barbed wire from the Bellington plant in Colorado, Swenson once again set up the tour and changed to making the lighter weight wire he was contracted to produce for a few days. Not one top official working in the plants ever saw the actual contracts that were awarded to the Bellington family. They just worked off purchase orders produced in the Bellington office in Augusta, Maine.

Laundering the money coming from the Japanese and illegal Korean interests was a bit tougher, but for a good down payment, the Mafia and corrupt union bosses gladly worked out the finer details. Only once in early 1944 did a new young union official question an influx of three quarters of a million dollars in cash that could not be easily explained by his bosses. The following day he was taken out for lunch to discuss a new job opening and promotion, but never returned. Workers in the office were told he accepted an immediate transfer to a west coast union office that was having problems.

In late June of 1944, Swenson was contacted by a high-ranking German official working out of the Mexican Consulate. He wanted Swenson to come to Rio de Janeiro, Brazil, for a very important meeting. All the travel documents were delivered to Swenson by a private courier, and he would be travelling under the name of Franko Marsell.

Arriving in Rio, Swenson immediately checked into his hotel as planned. At 5:00pm, two men came to his door looking for Franko Marsell. After Swenson showed the men his identification papers, he was whisked away in a darkened Mercedes. Forty minutes later, the car pulled up to a mansion on a hill overlooking the city.

The men escorted Swenson into a large wood paneled office, where a tall blonde man stood behind the desk smoking a pipe. After waving off the escorts the man pointed toward an over-stuffed red leather chair.

"Have a seat, Mr. Marsell. It was good that you agreed to see me on such short notice, but time is of the essence in this matter." After pouring two glasses of Cognac, he handed one to Swenson.

"Sip it, Marsell, enjoy the flavor. This bottle came from the private stock of Herman Goering, and is said to be two hundred years old, and taken from a Monastery in Italy."

Swenson nearly choked with his first sip when he heard the name Herman Goering mentioned.

Looking out the large window to the right of the desk the man continued. "Ah, you must enjoy the night life of Rio while you're here. You see the lights of the city are magnificent, not like Paris where everything is darkened because of the war. I will make arrangements for a special dinner tomorrow night with shall I say, a few gorgeous escorts."

Nodding his head, Swenson smiled, "I would be honored to be your guest for such an occasion. Now, what is it I can do for you?"

Sitting down behind the desk and relighting his cigar, the man began. "My name is Gerhardt Keisinger, and I am a member of an organization called Odessa. We are responsible for keeping Adolph Hitler and the Third Reich safe and alive at all costs. We know it is possible we might still lose this war, as the Allies now have a foothold in France. The Fuhrer says we have some new and powerful weapons coming soon that will turn the tide of battle, but in all honesty, I do not think they will make that much of a difference. So, my organization sent me here to contact you."

After finishing the Cognac, Swenson leaned forward. "What does all of this have to do with me, just an American industrialist?"

Laughing, Keisinger shook his head. "And a very good liar to say the least. Mr. Marsell, Berlin knows all about your contacts and dealings with the Japanese government, and we are most impressed. What we want you to do is fill this wish list."

Swenson leaned forward, taking several typed pages of construction materials from Mr. Keisinger. After looking over the list, he shook his head. "This is quite the list, and some of these items are hard to find. Many are actually controlled by the War Production Board. Can you tell me what you are building and where the construction is going to be completed? I may have a few ideas we could employ to mitigate some of the challenges."

Smiling, Keisinger stood up from the desk and walked over to an easel that was sitting in the corner of the room. Pulling back a white sheet, he revealed a map of Argentina. Pointing his finger at the map, he continued. "We will be building here, at Santiago del Estero." Removing the map from the easel, he uncovered a diagram of a large building complex surrounded by a large wall. "This is where we will take the Fuhrer if we need to get him out of Germany. This is where the Third Reich will continue to operate, despite losses sustained in the war. We have already moved millions of dollars in Reich's Gold to finance our operation. We have the workers in place to take care of construction, we just need a man of your talents to get us the supplies." Stepping toward Swenson, Keisinger continued. "Do you know what would happen to you if the FBI found out what you're doing? You and your entire family would be branded as traitors and end up in prison. If you supply us with what we need, you will be paid royally, more than enough to last you and Miss Stevenson two life times."

Swenson swallowed hard when he realized Odessa and the Third Reich knew more about him than he ever imagined was possible. Looking coldly into Keisinger's dark gray eyes, Swenson spoke.

"If I do this, you must agree to leave my family alone, not speak with the FBI, and not bring Miss Stevenson into the picture."

Keisinger nodded. "Mr. Marsell, if you cooperate, we could never go to the FBI without implicating ourselves and our plans. They would be on us like a hungry dog on a bone. Your family and Miss Stevenson will not be in harm's way. We do not care where you get the supplies, just begin to get us items one through fifty over the next two months, and in that order. We will tell you when we want the next group, and so on. Your profits after paying for the equipment can go to a Swiss bank account that you can break open after the war is over, and no one will ever know the difference."

Nodding his head, Swenson responded. "And what am I to be paid?"

Keisinger laughed as he clapped his hands together. "First off, the FBI will never be on your tail. We can fix all of that so you'll not spend the rest of your life in prison for being a traitor. Second, we will pay you in increments, as you need to pay the bills for material. By the time we are finished, there will be two million dollars in the account, that only you can access. Does that sound like a deal, Mr. Marsell?"

After a moment of thought, Swenson nodded his head. "Fine, I agree. Just tell me who my contact man will be in Argentina, and I will get what you need immediately."

Keisinger smiled as he walked back to the desk. Pulling out an envelope, he handed it to Swenson.

All you need to know is in here, and there is fifty thousand American dollars for your time and trouble. By all means, bring the lovely Miss Stevenson down to enjoy the beaches one day, and we can talk more as construction moves forward."

Returning to his room, Swenson sat down on his bed, attempting to clear his head. He was no longer involved with just the Japanese, now he was also involved with the most dangerous men in the entire world. Men that would stop at nothing to get what they wanted, regardless the consequences.

The following morning, Swenson began ordering construction materials from companies he was aware of in Brazil and Chili, that his father had held shipping contracts with before the war began. He realized quickly that this was not going to be an easy project, but now the very lives of those he cared about were on the line, and there was no turning back.

Returning to Kennebunkport, all Swenson wanted was to spend some quality time with Angeline and maybe take a small vacation, but that was not going to be the case. The second day home, as Swenson parked his car near the Bellington Company offices in Augusta, two men dressed in dark suits approached him.

The taller of the two men reached out to shake hands with Swenson. "Mr. Marsell, my name is Heinrich and this is Klaus. Just so you are aware, we will be watching you, monitoring your phone calls and keeping record of who you meet and talk with. We are American citizens, but we were also part of the German-American Bund that operated out in the open until the war began. We still have many followers operating quietly across the United States. All we want is your cooperation, as Mr. Keisinger pointed out to you. We will attempt to be out of sight as much as possible, but know we will always be just a heartbeat away in some fashion. We do not wish for anyone to get hurt, so please just do as you were told."

After tipping his hat, Heinrich spoke out loudly. "Thank you for your directions, sir. We surely would have been lost in Augusta without your help."

After the men drove off, Swenson leaned back against his car as he felt his knees begin to buckle. He knew full well that the German-American Bund was monitored closely by the FBI and other law enforcement officials. He could feel the noose tightening around his throat, and now there was no way out of the deal he had gotten himself into from the very beginning.

CHAPTER 12
CONVOY'S AND TARGETS

The crew of the 120 had stayed busy attacking the Tokyo Express and any other shipping that the Japanese attempted to send up into the slot. Although a few men had been slightly wounded, Buzz was thankful he had not lost a man over a long period of time. Several other skippers were not so lucky, as their boats had been sunk or too badly damaged to be repaired. It was always sad to see the stripped-down hulk of a PT boat towed out to sea and set on fire. But now, new boats were arriving regularly, out pacing losses, and new squadrons were now picking up some of the slack piling up behind the overworked crews.

The boats were now beginning to move farther northwest in the Solomon's, attacking targets in the Treasury and Shortland Islands, as far north as Buka Island, just beyond Bougainville. Here the waters became more treacherous, as they began running into open ocean where larger Japanese ships operated at will.

The skippers of five boats including the 120 were called into a planning meeting for a night time attack in the Treasury Islands, where the Japanese were constructing bases on Mono Island. They would sail from Rendova through the New Georgia Islands, around the north side of Ghizo Island, then south of Baga Island they would enter the slot and pass through the Shortland Islands to their target.

The skippers were fairly familiar with the area they would be passing through, as they had fought battles there before. They were to sail at 2130hrs, the same time another squadron was leaving for a mission near Choiseul.

Ensign Speidel was at the controls as the squadron left Rendova. Buzz spent time talking with the crew in their battle stations as the 120 skimmed the nearly placid waters of the Solomon Sea. With a partly cloudy sky, it was easy to make out the islands and the boats they were travelling with all the way to Vella Lavella, where they ran into a heavy rain squall.

Buzz took command of the 120 as the wind picked up the farther they sailed into the slot. He kept a sharp eye on the wakes of the two boats off his port beam, and the three off his starboard. It was apparent that all the skippers were doing the same, as a nearly perfect interval was being maintained.

Entering the Shortland Islands, Commander Reddings, skippering the 130, ordered everyone into single file with engines muffled. Quickly, the tension on the boat rose a thousand percent as each man scanned the darkness, searching for any signs of Japanese movement.

Chief Petrovski stood next to Buzz, watching the wake of the 117 boat directly in front of them, calling out changes in course as they moved forward. Ensign Speidel dropped down to the chart room to monitor radio traffic and keep an eye on the maps they were provided.

About thirty minutes later, Ensign Speidel jumped back up to speak to Buzz. "Mono Island approaching to starboard in about five minutes, we're passing Stirling right now."

Buzz nodded his head in acknowledgment as he backed off the outboard throttles. As Mono Island came into view, Commander Reddings led the boats closer to shore and began turning northeast along the north coast, where the unloading of equipment was supposed to be taking place.

Suddenly a flare from the island illuminated the night sky directly above the six PT boats. Every weapon on the boats opened fire as the flare also silhouetted several Japanese barges anchored close to shore. Buzz cranked the wheel hard to port making a wide turn in the channel before heading closer. Kowalski on the bow .50 and Stockey on the starboard .50 both opened fire on a heavily laden landing craft that was anchored about a hundred yards off shore, as Ridman blasted away with the .20mm toward a large pier where a group of trucks were parked. In seconds, the trucks were ablaze as men dove into the water. With fuel tanks on the landing craft exploding, the shore was well illuminated, providing ample opportunities for every gunner on the 120.

All along the line of PT boats, explosions from anchored barges lit up the night sky. Flames from stock piles of burning equipment on shore, gave ample light for the gunners on the boats to attack any target that came into range. After a forty-five minute attack that left the harbor in shambles, Commander Reddings led his squadron back toward Rendova.

Taking stock of the damage, Wickman on the port .50 was hit in the arm by a bullet that required eight stitches. Yamry sewed him up, and had him back in action by the time they reached Ghizo Island.

Captain Knight was excited about the raid and what they had accomplished. Aerial photographs taken the next morning confirmed what the skippers had reported.

After photography experts located at Port Moresby in New Guinea looked over all the aerial photographs from the morning fly overs, they were surprised to see a cargo ship anchored of Fauro Island. That would be a great target for the PT boats the next evening.

With so many boats down for repair and a lack of highly experienced men due to injuries and deaths, Captain Knight asked Buzz and Commander Reddings if their crews were up to another long mission that evening. After conferring with the crews, both officers informed the captain that the men were totally ready.

Using a large map of the Solomon's, the captain once again dropped his pointer on the Shortland Islands, southeast of Bougainville.

"Recon photos show a large freight transport anchored in a small bay on the north side of Fauro Island. According to a coast watcher on Magusaini, workers have been slowly unloading construction equipment from the vessel, as natives cut palms to camouflage it. We want that ship destroyed tonight before they can unload anymore equipment.

At high tide the water in the bay runs about fifty feet, so you should be able to send her to the bottom with torpedoes. You will sail at 2200hrs. Follow New Georgia's southern coast line and turn north between New Georgia and Kolombangara. Cross the slot passing between Choiseul and Vagiena. Follow the north coast of Choiseul until you get to Bougainville Straits. Turning south, you can slip between all the small islands covering your approach. If the Japs do see you, they won't know where the hell you are headed in time to stop you. Hit the bay from the north and retreat as you think best. Any questions?" The captain asked as he watched his six skippers carefully studying their maps.

After looking over at his men, Commander Reddings nodded his head, "We're good to go, sir."

At 2130hrs, Buzz and Chief Petrovski walked around the 120 one more time, just to be sure all the men understood the mission. As a sustained wind of nearly twenty knots blew north out of the Solomon Sea, the boats would be encountering side waves of six to ten feet as they started the mission, but things would improve as they turned north, allowing them to travel with the waves. At 2200hrs, with Commander Reddings at the helm of the 130, the flotilla headed out of Rendova harbor.

Stars were plentiful as the six boats plowed through heavy seas, sending large plumes of water off the sharp bows of their boats. This is where Buzz was in his glory. It reminded him of the waves they encountered nearly every day in the northern Atlantic while fishing. He loved watching the water break off the bow of the 120, and the two boats to his left. Keeping a boat on course and in the correct formation with seas like this was not for an amateur boat handler.

As the coast of New Georgia broke off to the north, the seas became better, but the crews understood they were entering far more dangerous waters as they now sailed in single file.

Buzz handed the helm over to his capable XO Ensign Speidel, as he and Chief Petrovski used binoculars to scan the shorelines for Japanese patrol boats. Buzz loved watching Kowalski on the forward .50 machine gun, as he slowly traversed side to side looking for enemy targets. Crossing the slot, Stockey pointed out flames on the water to the north of Kolombangara. Ridman reported a small Japanese barge moving west toward Blackett Strait, but he was sure with the windy conditions, no one on the low riding barge could see them.

As they began passing by Vagiena Island, both Stockey and Wickman reported two Japanese float planes paralleling the coast of Choiseul. Seconds later it was clear the pilots had seen the flotilla of PT boats, as they changed course and dropped down to about five hundred feet.

Quickly, Buzz warned all the other boats over the TBS radio of the impending attack. Within a minute every machine gun and .20 mm cannon on the group of boats let loose with a stream of fire. Tracers filled the dark sky, arcing in every direction as the gunners swung their weapons to keep contact with the attackers. A ball of flame lit up the sky as the fuel tanks on the lead plane erupted. The second pilot turned quickly to the east, hoping to avoid most of the deadly fire and drop his hundred pound bomb on or near the 133 boat that brought up the rear of the flotilla. Buzz and Lt. Grissom of the 127 broke their formation, allowing their gunners to keep pressure on the attacking plane as Lt. Hudson swung the 133 side to side, making his boat a more difficult target.

The pilot roared skyward, attempting to break off the attack just as flames began leaping from his engine cowling. As the engine sputtered and quit, the plane nosed over, diving full speed into the channel below where it exploded.

Although float planes rarely did much damage to PT boats, Buzz always gave their pilots an 'A' for effort, as they seldom ran from a fight.

With the island of Choiseul now on their port side and blocking the wind somewhat, the boats were only encountering three-to-four-foot swells as they continued forward.

Commander Reddings slowed the flotilla to fifteen knots and muffled engines, as the boats weaved through the narrow channels separating countless small islands and coral atolls. Everyone stayed tight in single file formation in the main channel, as there were hundreds of coral reefs boarding the narrow waterway.

With everything set as planned, Commander Reddings appointed Buzz and Lt. Grissom to attack with torpedoes, as the rest of the boats attacked the Japanese base with machine guns and cannon fire.

Entering the open deep waters north of Fauro, Buzz and Lt. Grissom broke from the flotilla, racing directly toward the bay. Wanting to make sure they hit the target, both skippers waited until they were 1300 yards away before firing two torpedoes. The four fish jumped from their tubes running hot on course toward the side of the freighter, as tracers from machine guns on board the ship opened up on the attacking boats. Moments later the night sky turned a brilliant orange and yellow as flames leapt from the burning ship. Buzz smiled as he counted four solid torpedo hits against the thin hull of the freighter.

Inside the crew quarters of the ship, men jumped from their bunks, running out of the cabins toward the railing, hoping to jump clear of the growing inferno that was consuming their vessel.

Swenson Bellington was tossed from his bunk when the second torpedo hit. Dazed and with a tremendous headache, he stumbled toward the door as flames were already climbing as high as the walkway outside his cabin. The ship was listing hard to port after the torpedoes had blown out all the supporting bulkheads below the main deck. Burning oil covered the water directly below his cabin, while machine gun bullets from the PT boats were striking all around the superstructure of the ship. Realizing the only place free of massive fires was the fan tail of the ship, Swenson quickly began pushing hot debris out of the way as he made his way aft. Climbing down one deck, he suddenly realized he was trapped as flames were climbing higher, burning away the thick layers of paint that had been applied over the years. Not wanting to burn, Swenson jumped over the rear railing, landing in the water, where the burning oil had not yet taken over. He swam toward the entrance of the bay, where he crawled up onto several large rocks. He sat there in awe as he watched the freighter break apart and sink into the bay, hissing and moaning, like some prehistoric monster. Looking back at the base, all he could see were fires from buildings, trucks and construction equipment. All of the machine guns had now been silenced as the PT boats sat offshore, firing at anything that appeared to be a logical target.

In the small building deeper into the jungle where the prisoners were kept, Josh jumped up and down as he yelled, "Give 'em hell, Buzz! You whip their sorry—"

Suddenly, he was pulled to the floor by one of his fellow POW's. "Knock that shit off, you want to piss off the Japs? They'll come over here and kill us all if you keep that up! Besides, you have no idea if that's your brother out there anyway."

Josh rolled on the floor and laughed as several machine gun bullets zipped through the walls of their hut. "Oh yeah, Buzz is out there, I can feel him close by." Standing up again, he gazed at the inferno out in the bay, just as one of the boats came in close to pump .20mm rounds into one of the buildings. Laughing once again, he said, "The hull says it's the 120 boat, I just bet that's my brother. No one else would have the balls to make a maneuver like that. You stick it to 'em, Buzz!" he called again as several more machine gun bullets made him dive for the floor.

A minute later the six boats disappeared from sight, heading southeast down the slot.

The following morning Capt. Numura, Sgt. Kokawa, Swenson Bellington and Commander Wanishi, the captain of the ship, surveyed the damage.

"I'm afraid there's not much more we can accomplish here. What the bombers do not destroy, now those evil devil boats destroy. I have lost too many men to continue trying to build here. We must work harder on Bougainville to defend it," Capt. Numura stated, as he looked at the charred remains of one of his men.

"Well, I can tell you for a fact, my company cannot afford losses like this. We will have to find another way," Swenson replied as he watched the POW's picking up the bodies for burial.

Commander Wanishi stared angrily at the remains of his ship protruding from the oil-soaked bay. "We must begin to think of defending the Philippines. When the burials are completed, we will head back to Kieta by barge. From there we will take the POW's north to the Philippines and begin reinforcing many islands."

One week later several barges arrived at night, removing Swenson Bellington, Commander Wanishi and his surviving crew members. Josh and the rest of the POW's were placed on the second barge, heading for the island of New Britain. On the extreme northern tip of the island, near the city of Rabaul, lay the massive Japanese naval base. There, the small band of POW's were placed in a stockade with about twenty more men.

In a conference at Rabaul, it was decided to move the POW's to the island of Mindanao in the Philippines, which was in need of fortifications.

Over the next few weeks, PT boats ran countless missions in the waters around Bougainville, attacking Japanese shipping and performing surveillance work with the Marines.

While the 120 was laid up with an engine problem, Buzz and the crew were looking forward to a few days of rest before getting back into the battle. However, that was not to happen. The night before the engine was to be torn down, Commander Reddings came to the boat where Buzz was sleeping.

After shaking Buzz a few times, Commander Reddings was finally able to wake his trusted skipper. Buzz sat up on the edge of his bunk as he looked strangely at his commander and friend. Sitting down beside Buzz, Commander Reddings spoke up.

"Buzz the 117 boat was sent to the Island of Alu in the Shortland Islands to pick up a marine raider party. Part of the raider party got off the island and swam to the 117. As the Japs rushed down onto the beach, the rest of the marines high tailed it back into the jungle and are still there. The 117 suffered damage to the fuel system and is floating in Bougainville Straits. I know your number three engine is really sick, but you're all I have left to rescue them. The fuel system can be repaired if they have the parts, so you can take them with you and drop them off, and then try getting the rest of the marines out of there. If the 117 is there at day break, they all become POW's and the marines on the island will be destroyed. I can't force you out with a bad engine, but will you help us?"

Buzz shook his head. "Commander, we were told not to refuel this afternoon, so we have enough fuel to get us there, hopefully grab the marines quickly, and start back before we run out of fuel. If the 117 has lost a lot of fuel, there's no way she can tow us back. There is a possibility that you could end up with two boats dead in the slot, out of fuel, with wounded marines on board and no way to get home, but for damn sure we're going."

As Buzz jumped up from his bunk, Commander Reddings said, "Get out there, get it done and let me worry about getting you home."

As Buzz woke up Ensign Speidel, he nodded his head. "Can't ask for a better offer than that, sir."

In less than a half hour the crew of the 120 had brought on extra ammunition from a supply building near the pier. Crowder and the Chief had managed to get the center engine running fairly well, while Buzz had reviewed the charts with Yamry and Ensign Speidel. Just prior to sailing, motor technicians from the engine repair shop delivered parts for the 117.

As Chief Petrovski strapped on his .45 six-shooter, Buzz idled the 120 away from the pier into the Solomon Sea. With light winds and nothing more than two-foot swells, the 120 sailed across the waters of the Solomon Islands at a respectable 33 knots, although Crowder kept reminding Buzz that the harder he ran the engines, the quicker his center engine may come completely apart.

Entering Bougainville Straits, Buzz muffled the engines and placed every man not tied to a weapon forward, to search for the 117. This was a night Buzz was praying for some stars or a little moonlight, but God was having no part of it. After nearly three quarters of an hour of searching and burning precious fuel, Buzz did what he hadn't wanted to do, he broke radio silence.

"Blue Hound Two , this is Blue Hound Three, do you copy? Over," Buzz said softly into the mic.

A moment later he had a return. "Blue Hound Three, we copy. We got caught in an ocean current pulling us out of the channel. Look north of Masamasa closer to Pirumeri. All seems quiet but if we drift any closer to shore, we may be in big trouble. Over."

Buzz nodded as he looked down at the chart Yamry had in his hands. Shoving the throttles forward, Buzz could not believe how far the 117 had drifted in such a short time, but it also meant the 120 was burning precious fuel they did not have to spare.

Rounding the northwest corner of Masamasa Island, Stockey called down to Buzz from his machine gun tube. "There she is, sir, about your ten o'clock and a quarter mile in."

Idling up alongside the 117, Buzz could smell fuel and see a definite sheen on the water. It not only meant the 117 had way less fuel than they expected, but one spark could send the boat and everyone on board to pieces. It was clear by the looks on the faces of the crew and marines they carried that everyone was scared. Signaling for the lieutenant in charge of the marines, Buzz found out what frequency to use when calling the raiders when he arrived offshore. Looking at his watch he called over to Lt. Emery. "Eddie, dawn is just two hours away, I'll get back here as quickly as I can, hang tight!"

When he was finished speaking, Chief Petrovski and Andy Rice pushed the two boats apart as Buzz backed away slowly.

Closing in on Alu Island, Buzz felt the boat shudder as steam came up from the engine bay. The chief quickly ran back to investigate. Returning to the cockpit, he shook his head. Our middle engine is gone, sir. A push rod came right up through a valve cover, so there is nothing more Crowder can do but take it off line."

Taking a deep breath, Buzz idled the 120 within a mile of Alu Island. "Flamingo Road, this is Blue Hound Three. We are ready for you with just two engines, tell us where we need to go, over."

"Blue Hound Three I don't care if you have a sail and a parrot to blow it, we need off this island, taking too many casualties. Need assistance to get men to your boat, over," Sgt. Nevis returned.

Buzz looked over at the chief, "Take Yamry, Ordman, Rice and two rafts. Get those bastards off that beach as quickly as you can."

Nodding his head, the chief stepped forward, extending his hand. "Just in case, sir. It's been nice serving with you. Thanks for giving me the chance to get into this war and be the sailor I was meant to be."

Buzz shook his hand as he nodded his head. "Get your ass back here, Chief, and that's an order."

A second later, Ensign Speidel came up from the radio room holding a chart. Pointing to a section of beach just around the east side of the island he said. "They'll be there in ten, we should have our rafts in the water before that."

Buzz maneuvered the 120 the last two hundred yards before giving the chief a signal to go. Before the rafts made the beach, marines were running into the water attempting to help some of the less seriously wounded men with them. Ordman and Yamry loaded the first raft with seriously wounded men before pushing it back out into the surf. Rice was just loading a man when he was struck in the shoulder by a bullet, as several Japanese soldiers charged onto the evacuation beach.

The chief knelt down pulling his .45 from its holster. In several seconds, four Japanese soldiers laid dead, and one was holding his neck as blood ran from the gaping wound. Directing several marines to help with the raft, the chief quickly reloaded his pistol and commenced engaging more Japanese soldiers running down onto the beach. Running over to the marine private that was carrying the radio, the chief pulled the hand set lose.

"Blue Hound Three, the balance of our men are in the water or are in rafts. Rake the beach or we all die tonight!"

Seconds later, every weapon on the 120 opened up on the beach and nearby jungle. The chief stood in knee high water a short distance from shore, knocking down several Japanese soldiers attempting to assemble a light nambu machine gun at the edge of the surf. Shoving the pistol into its holster with two shots left, the chief ran into deeper water before swimming back to the boat. He helped hand up several of the wounded men, until one of the marines yelled out in pain. Looking to his right, he saw a large shark preparing to make a second attack on the severely wounded man. Pulling out his pistol, the chief fired his last two bullets into the head of the shark. The wounded animal spun around for a moment before sinking into the channel. The only problem was, that amount of blood would attract more sharks in minutes. Several other marines on board the 120 were firing at sharks as they raised the last men aboard. As the chief rolled onto the deck, he quickly reloaded his pistol, walked to the edge of the boat, firing all six shots at sharks that came close to the side of the 120.

A corporal nearby looked up at the chief. "Damn Chief, there ain't no one left in the water."

As Chief Petrovski reloaded his western style .45, he replied. "Son, I hate sharks, like Wyatt Earp hated criminals. You got a problem with that?"

Backing away from the chief, the man never said another word as he stared at the massive pistol the veteran sailor was holding.

While attempting to maintain some type of order on the boat with all the wounded marines, Buzz looked down at the lifeless body of Ensign Speidel near the steps leading to the chart room. Angrily, he began yelling for Chief Petrovski as he turned the boat away from the island and shoved the throttles forward. As the chief pushed his way into the cockpit, he called out, "What the hell, Skipper?"

Buzz shook his head. "A freak shot from one of the Japanese. The bullet hit the ensign in the back of the head and killed him instantly. You're my second in command the rest of the night, Chief. Find out how many other casualties we have before we find out the hard way!"

Instantly, the chief took off, searching out the crew on the congested bloody deck. Returning minutes later he reported, "Ordman is dead, a bullet through his throat. Ansel has a bullet wound to the upper arm, but one of the marine corpsmen is already stitching him up, so he'll be fine, sir"

Buzz nodded as he grabbed the mic from the radio set, "Blue Hound Two, this is Blue Hound Three, what is your position and are you able to move?"

Moments later Lt. Emery angrily responded. "Blue Hound Three, we've purged the system and have power, but as the tide went down the bow became lodged on a rock pile and we can't break free. We need a pull and fast as dawn is near, and the tide continues to pull back. We're about a hundred yards west of last contact."

Throwing the mic down, Buzz poured power to his two remaining engines as he said, "That's great, just fucking great!"

Slowing down into the Bougainville Strait, Chief Petrovski scanned the horizon searching for the 117. After several anxious moments, he punched Buzz in the arm. "To your 1100 o'clock and about two hundred yards away. Too damn close to Pirumeri Island."

Grabbing his binoculars, Buzz could see the forlorn PT boat with the bow raised up on the rock pile. Closing the throttles, Buzz carefully idled up to the 117 where Lt. Emory was standing on the rear deck.

"It's just rock, Buzz, it's not coral. Give me a pull and I'll start backing off slowly. We should be just fine."

Kowalski and Stegura tossed the heavy rope to the 117 crew as they attached it to the Sampson post on the front of the 120. When they were ready, Kowalski waved to Buzz.

Buzz eased the engines carefully into reverse and began pulling as Lt. Emory did the same. The 117 slipped back about a foot before coming to a sudden stop. Angry that the boat had not come all the way off, Buzz pushed his throttles forward nearly half way. The engines from the 120 screamed as the props kicked up mud and water from the shallow bay. The 117 shuddered and moaned as five giant Packard engines strained to pull her free from the rock pile.

With fuel beginning to become a major issue now, snipers on Pirumeri began firing at the American vessels. Kowalski, Stockey and gunners from the 117 began answering the call with machine gun fire. Although they had no idea where the snipers were, but at least it kept their heads down.

A sniper bullet snapped against Stockey's machine gun tub, ricocheting the bullet just inches away from Buzz's head. There was no doubt in Stockey's mind that the close call was the end of the line for his skipper. Screaming a list of obscenities, Buzz threw the throttles all the way forward, sending full power to his two massive engines. He had read reports that doing so could literally rip the back end off of a PT boat when it was stuck, but dawn was beginning to break over the Solomon Islands, and it was do or die, literally.

With a sudden boom, the 117 flew backwards off the rock pile, following the 120 toward the center of the channel. Quickly Stegura slammed an axe onto the rope, cutting the 120 loose from the 117 that was coming back at them at full speed. With the tow rope removed, Buzz spun the wheel hard to starboard, allowing the 117 to slide by them, missing the port side by about a foot.

When the 120 came to a stop, Chief Petrovski looked over at Buzz, "You know, Skipper, I wanted to get into this war. But I think I've had about enough for one day. Let's go home!"

Smiling, Buzz shifted the 120 into forward gear, following the 117 away from the Shortland Islands, heading southeast down the slot with Choiseul to their port side. Buzz picked up the mic. and called out, "Hornet's Nest, this is Blue Hound Three, do you copy?"

A moment later Commander Reddings replied. "Blue Hound Three do you have Blue Hound Two with you?"

"Yes sir, only slightly worse for wear, we are southeast in the slot near Charlie Shoals. Tanks about gone, what can you give us, over?" Buzz replied, as the sun rose higher from the eastern horizon.

"Help's on the way, keep your heading, watch the skies, overhead," Commander Reddings replied before cutting off.

About ten minutes later the engines coughed several times before the 120 ran the three massive fuel tanks dry. Lt. Emery spun his boat around, pulling up beside the 120.

"Should we rig for a tow, Buzz? I don't think we'll get very far on the fumes I have left." Lt. Emory called over from his cockpit, as his number one engine coughed.

Buzz smiled. "Shut them down, Eddie, you're going nowhere fast. That way you won't have to purge them again."

With the engines of the 117 turned off, all they could hear was the wind, sounds of water lapping against the wooden hulls, and the soft moans of the wounded marines.

About fifteen minutes later a frustrated marine sergeant walked up to Buzz.

"Some help you guys were. Now we're sitting ducks for any Jap ship that comes out to see what's going on. They should have sent us skippers that knew what the hell they were doing. What the hell is your plan, Lieutenant? I have men here that need hospital care and you're lounging around like it's Fourth of July at the beach!"

Suddenly Wickman called out, "Two aircraft at three o'clock, dropping down from about 5,000 feet. Not sure whose they are yet."

Both Buzz and Lt. Emory yelled out for battle stations, but told the men to wait for orders to fire. Buzz had his jaw clamped shut so hard it was giving him a headache as he watched the aircraft with his binoculars. He couldn't figure out why they were separating as they dropped down to about 500 feet. Finally, Buzz smiled as he yelled out. "Corsairs, they're corsairs. Hold your fire."

Shortly, the two marine fighters were making wide circular patterns around the stranded boats as they kept an eye out for marauding enemy planes or patrol boats.

A cheer went up from the marines, knowing it was their guys overhead looking out for them. About a half hour later, one of the pilots radioed Lt. Emory.

"Thunder One to Blue Hound Two, American destroyer escort and two Peter Tares coming to your position about twenty miles east. Peter Tares will take badly wounded and head for home, destroyer will give you a tow. We'll stay on board."

About a half hour later, the men could see the mast of the destroyer escort coming over the horizon. It was a welcome relief as the hot burning sun only made matters worse for the wounded.

Finally, the 130 and 129 came alongside the stranded boats, taking all the wounded men and corpsmen back to Rendova. With the transfer completed, the destroyer crew threw down heavy tow ropes to the stranded boats, taking them in tow. The two fighters stayed with the small convoy, patrolling the skies all the way back to Rendova.

With the 120 safely tied up to the pier, Commander Reddings walked up to the boat.

"Permission to come aboard, skipper?"

Saluting his senior officer, Buzz nodded his head. "Permission granted, sir."

Commander Reddings stepped on board the 120, shaking his head. Corpsmen from the hospital were still removing bodies of marines that died during the night, along with bloody bandages, empty plasma containers and morphine syringes that littered the deck. The cockpit, along with Buzz's shirt were splattered with Ensign Speidel's blood. Bullet holes from Japanese machine guns had torn holes all over the starboard side and torpedo tubes of the 120.

Walking up to Buzz, Commander Reddings held out his hand. "Outstanding job, Buzz, although I heard you lost two men, including your XO. It looks like the 120 took a bit of a beating and the loss of an engine. Maybe—"

Before he could finish, Buzz cut him off. "Sir, if you're going to say the 120 needs to be retired, you're absolutely wrong. She needs a new engine, and we need two new men. But while she's in the engine shop, my men can help the carpenter crew take care of the holes. We want the 120 back, sir!"

Nodding his head, Commander Reddings looked over at Buzz. "Alright, we'll get her repaired, then. Come down to my shack first thing in the morning and we'll fill out your crew from my replacement list."

As the commander jumped back into his jeep and drove off, Buzz patted the top of the number two torpedo tube. "You aren't going out to pasture just yet, old girl, you've got lots of war to fight yet."

The following morning, Buzz and Chief Petrovski arrived at the operations shack at 0830. Sitting in a chair near the door with his sea bag at his side was a young freckle faced, red headed ensign. He jumped to attention and saluted as Buzz walked past. "Ensign Will Gruenke ready to join your crew, sir!"

Buzz returned the salute and stared at the man for a moment. "Take a seat, Ensign. I'll be back shortly."

Walking into Commander Reddings office, Buzz exploded, "Are you for real, sir? I have underwear older than that kid. Do you expect the battled hardened crew of the 120 to respect this snot nosed kid? I doubt he has any experience except sailing boats in the bath tub? Come on, sir, I can take a joke like anybody else, but this time you got to be kidding!"

Command Reddings looked sternly at Buzz. "Maddox, he came in yesterday on a C-47 with fifteen other new men. He was the only officer in the bunch and you need an executive officer and he needs a home. You take him and train him and make him into a qualified boat handler."

Buzz shook his head. In case you've forgotten, sir, there's a war on out there and we end up right in the thick of it every damn day. I don't have time to start working with a green XO that has never been in so much as a bar room brawl. Come on sir, there must be someone else on this base you can give me."

Angrily, Commander Reddings jumped up from his chair, walked over to Buzz and yelled, "Attention!"

As Buzz snapped to attention, the commander stood face to face with Buzz. "Listen up, Maddox. You may be one of the best boat handlers I've ever seen, you get better results than half the skippers on Rendova, and I always considered you a friend as well as a subordinate. So, this is the way it is. Get the ensign up to speed and do your job, or I'll send you back to Tulagi where you can run a supply barge for the duration. Do you understand me?"

Looking at the fire in his commanders eyes, Buzz knew his only response had to be in the affirmative. Bringing his right arm up to his forehead and saluting, Buzz replied, "Aye, aye sir!"

Commander Reddings backed up about two feet before replying. "My clerk will give you the name of your new torpedo man before you leave. I cannot believe we had to have this conversation, and if this ever happens again, say hello to Tulagi like I said. You are dismissed!"

Walking out of the office, the petty officer at the replacement desk handed Buzz a slip of paper with the name Lopez, Juan written on it. "I already gave the name to your chief. He should be at your boat by the time you arrive, sir."

Without saying a word, Buzz took the piece of paper and walked up to a very nervous Ensign Gruenke. "Follow me, Ensign, and I'll show you to your new home that's temporarily under construction. Then I'll see if we can't round up a boat so we can get out on the water and see what you've got."

Without saying a word, the ensign followed Buzz back to the 120. Chief Petrovski was sitting on the number four torpedo tube watching the crew as they worked on repairing the battle damage. "Want me to show him where he bunks, Skipper?"

"Yeah Chief, that would be fine. I'm going to go see if I can't grab a boat so we can do some training. I'll be back shortly." Buzz motioned for Crowder to follow him as they walked down the wharf.

At the repair docks, Buzz was able to get the 299 boat that was waiting to have a new radar unit installed. With Crowder in the engine room, Buzz fired up the Packard engines. With warm up completed, Buzz idled the boat over to the 120.

The crew stopped working on the 120 as they looked over at Buzz and Crowder. They watched intently as the chief, Lopez and their new executive officer climbed on board. After a moment of silence, Buzz yelled out. "Do you idiots need a written invitation?"

The men hooped and hollered as they dropped their tools and ran to the 299, taking up their battle positions. Moments later, Buzz had the 299 turned around and was idling out to sea.

After Buzz cleared several coral reefs, he called out, "Alright Ensign, take the helm and put her through some exercises.'

Half-smiling and overjoyed to be at the controls of a PT boat again, Ensign Gruenke slammed the throttles forward while doing a hard turn to starboard, followed by a sharp turn to port, where the boat bounced heavily over its own wake. About ten minutes later, Zumwaldt yelled out, "Bandits at ten o'clock and diving!"

Instantly, the gunners began hammering away at the Zeros as they dropped down from about ten thousand feet. The ensign began evasive maneuvers, charging the boat from left to right, followed by a sudden one hundred and eighty degree turn. The pilot of the first Zero dropped his hundred-pound bomb short of the port side by a good fifteen yards, but Wickman stayed with the Zero the entire way, ripping up the under belly of the aircraft. Moments later the plane turned on its side cart-wheeling into the Pacific. Zumwaldt found it difficult to get a good aim with the way Gruenke was maneuvering the boat, but he kept firing, hoping he was going to hit something.

Finally, after completing the last quick turn, Zumwaldt found his mark, shattering the prop of the third fighter. The pilot opened his canopy to bail out, just as the engine exploded. The pilot of the second plane missed the PT boat with his bomb by at least twenty yards, before attempting to escape by flying just above the surface of the waves.

Buzz watched the parachute of the Japanese pilot as it dropped down into the water. "Go get him, Ensign. Don't let him swim all the way back to Tokyo."

Ensign Gruenke smiled, knowing he had just earned the respect of Buzz and the rest of the crew in a battle that lasted less than ten minutes.

Lopez and Andy Rice raced to the front of the boat with a pike, ready to fish the pilot out of the water. As the 299 idled up to the angry pilot, the man pulled out his pistol, firing at the rescue team.

Wickman aimed his .50 caliber about fifteen feet away from the pilot and fired a quick blast. The stunned pilot threw away his pistol as he shook his fist at Wickman and yelled.

Chief Petrovski laughed as he leaned against Wickman's machine gun tub. "Now, I didn't get all of what he said, but the last part was very derogatory about your mother."

Wickman laughed as he watched Lopez and Rice fish the angry pilot out of the water. "You know, Chief, if Florence Wickman had heard him swear like that, she would have washed his mouth out with soap and sent him off to bed without supper. Honestly, he's probably better off with us!"

The chief laughed heartily as he walked forward to search their new prisoner.

Heading back to port, Buzz pointed out the two reefs to his new XO that disappeared at high tide, but could rip the bottom out of a boat at low tide. With the boat tied up, the crew shook hands with their new executive officer before returning back to work on the 120.

After a moment of thought, Buzz walked up to his new XO. Looks like you get to fill out the after action report today. You did a bang up job of handling the 299 to say the least. I know you must have heard some of what I said to Commander Reddings. I'd like to apologize for bad mouthing you without giving you the benefit of the doubt and the chance to prove yourself. Welcome to the South Pacific, Ensign."

With the 299 back in the shop, Buzz and his crew were able to have some free time to relax before the 120 was again ready to go after the Japanese. However, Buzz, Will and Yamry spent hours going over charts and making notations. Although it's a tough rigorous job, Lopez and the rest of the torpedo crew practiced loading and unloading torpedoes at least once a day from the repaired tubes. After several arguments with the veterans, Lopez learned quickly he needed to reduce the amount of grease he was putting in the tubes before loading a torpedo. Using a lot of grease like he was doing would create a large sheet of flame when the torpedo left the tube, notifying every enemy ship within twenty miles of their position.

The rest of the torpedo team had to laugh as Lopez autographed the war head on each torpedo. He wrote, "Compliments of Juan Lopez, Sacramento, California."

CHAPTER 13
FLEEING FROM MANILA

As American and British POW's continued building reinforced fortifications on the island of Mindanao, Swenson Bellington was able to procure an elegant hotel room in Manila.

He was wined and dined by Japanese officers and government officials on a regular basis. He ate luxurious meals served by white jacketed waiters, as soothing Japanese melodies filled the air. Many evenings after such a delectable meal, there never was a problem having local officials provide him with one or more exquisite Philippine beauties for an evening of adult entertainment back at his hotel room.

Tonight however, Swenson decided to return to his hotel alone. Standing in his darkened room, he looked down from his fifth floor window onto the nearly quiet waterfront streets of Manila. It was all too apparent that the lives of the Filipino residents of Manila no longer measured up to the refined and calculated lives of their Japanese conquerors.

No longer did Manila fit its prewar designation as, 'Pearl of the Orient.' Now the streets were filthy and it was not unusual to find bodies lying in alleys, or floating along the shoreline of the bay. The streets no longer hummed with colorful taxis, shiny American cars, or packed tourist buses. Today, shabbily dressed people pushed carts filled with refuse thrown out by Japanese military wives, or the carcass of a dog they had been able to find to butcher as food for their family. The lot of the Filipino people had taken a sharp turn into total poverty since the Japanese invaders had thrown out the Americans. Anyone identified as working for the American Government quickly disappeared, along with their families. There was little tolerance for Filipinos that spoke against the Japanese occupation, or those that attempted to run black market operations. At this point, the Japanese military was running what was known as, 'A War of Annihilation.'

Since arriving in the Philippines nearly six months ago, Swenson had seen a huge change in the attitude of Japanese officers and soldiers working on front line defenses. They were tense and beginning to display the actions of an army that was starting to taste defeat.

They no longer controlled much of the Pacific, and shipments of supplies were becoming fewer and farther between, as American submarines were beginning to place a strangle hold on the archipelago. Swenson was well aware that the time would come when they would take out their frustrations on any foreigners, no matter what they had done to help their war effort, even if they had good relations with operatives in the third Reich.

On the evening of November 23, 1944, Thanksgiving back in the United States, Swenson enjoyed a superb seven course meal put on by the headquarters staff of General Tomoyuki Yamashita. As the wait staff prepared to clean the tables, Swenson retired to the elegant flower gardens with the general staff officers. While sipping very fine rice wine, the general regaled his guests with stories of triumph and reduction of civilian dissent. His junior officers would yell with delight, slapping each other on the back when they heard of tribal leaders and local mayors being beheaded for failure to comply with dictates of the Imperial Japanese Government.

Although Swenson knew what he was doing would be seen as treason back in the United States, it did not compare to the barbaric actions of the Japanese military. After General Yamashita told how the mayor of one town and his entire family were burned at the stake in the center of town after being disemboweled, Swenson felt sick. However the sickening feeling quickly turned to fear, when he was poked in the side by a young lieutenant for failing to applaud the story. The lieutenant and his friends gave Swenson a very displeased look for failure to take part in the frivolity.

After politely turning down an escort for the night, Swenson walked silently back to his hotel on Roxas Boulevard. There was a nagging feeling in the back of his mind that if he did not leave Manila soon, some vengeful young officer would ceremoniously murder him one day. He even wondered if officials from Odessa were still watching him, or if had they turned observation over to the brutal Japanese Kempeitai. Walking into his room, Swenson once again peered out the window overlooking the bay. He began to realize that his life was not going to be worth a plug nickel if he stayed in Manila. The problem was, any ships sailing to and from Korea regardless of the flag, were now coming under constant submarine attack. Attempting to get a flight on a Japanese military transport was a total death wish, as American based carrier fighters were sweeping the skies across the Pacific clear of any Japanese aircraft.

After a few moments of thought, Swenson's attention was drawn to an old tramp steamer flying the Spanish flag, that was currently tied up to one of the piers. Although Spain had announced early on that it was taking a neutral position in this war, everyone knew Francisco Franko's victory in the Spanish Civil War was owed entirely to Adolph Hitler. So, with Spain's neutrality and former ties to the Philippine Islands, they had been allowed to continue delivering food supplies.

After changing into some work clothing, Swenson walked down to the front lobby of the hotel to find it empty. After making sure there were no soldiers patrolling near the hotel, he slid out the door, making his way down onto the wharf. A small crew of men were just finishing unloading the last of the cargo onto a small truck. Standing nearby checking each item off the manifest, was a tall older man wearing a naval captain's hat.

As Swenson approached, the man pulled a pistol from his belt and glared, looking menacing. "What are you doing here and what do you want? I'll turn you over to the Japanese officials!"

Realizing he might have made a serious mistake, Swenson attempted to smile as he waved his hand. "I'm not here to cause you any problems. I'm here to see if we can work out some sort of a business deal."

Lowering his pistol, the captain looked strangely at Swenson. "You are an American in Manila, so how does that work out? Are you one of those that has not been caught yet and is trying to escape? Were you an American soldier, because if you were, I want nothing to do with you!"

Swenson took a deep breath. "I have been getting building materials to the Japanese for the last two years through our plant in Korea. But now, no ships are getting through. I know the allies are going to eventually tighten the noose around Manila, and not even you will be allowed in. I now realize the allies are going to win this war and I need to find a way out of here if I'm going to survive."

The captain shook his head. "What? And you expect me to help you? There is nothing I can do for you. If the Japanese find you on board my vessel before sailing, they will seize my ship and feed me and my crew to the sharks. Please leave the wharf now before we are caught speaking."

Swenson was not ready to play this hand yet, but quickly realized he had no choice. "Captain, I will pay you five thousand American dollars to get me to Spain, or as close to the United States as you can. I will not cause you any problems, and I will eat whatever you choose to feed me in my cabin, or wherever else you can hide me."

The captain looked at the ground for a moment before replying. "Here is my only deal. My next cargo stop is in Cuba to pick up sugar cane. But you will have to figure out how to deal with the Panamanian officials, as you are not on my ships roster. You will give me the five thousand dollars up front, and another two thousand when we arrive in Havana. If you travel with me all the way to Bilbao, Spain, I cannot guarantee you will not be arrested on the wharf, as you have no papers. There is a small cabin next to mine you can use. As you said, I will deliver your meals. It will be a long trip, but you must stay out of site as best you can. Once we arrive in Cuba, you are on your own."

Breathing a sigh of relief, Swenson nodded his head. "I know how to deal with the Panamanian Officers, that is not a problem. And yes, from Cuba I can find my own way, as my family has contacts in Havana. The price of seven thousand American dollars is not a problem. I will go back to my room and pack what I can in one bag and be back in about an hour. I will have your payment with me when I arrive."

Placing the pistol back in its holster the captain smiled. "Then we have a deal, senor. I shall be on the aft deck when you arrive, and the quicker you return the better."

Swenson was stuffing everything he wanted to take with him into a large canvas duffel bag when there was a knock on his door. A feeling of dread raced down his spine as he stared at the door. A moment later there was another knock followed by the voice of Lieutenant Chiba, a supervisor from the local Kempeitai detachment.

Opening the door Swenson smiled at the young officer. "Can I help you, Lieutenant, it's getting late and I was just getting ready for bed."

The Lieutenant stared at him for a moment before stepping forward, brushing Swenson to the side. Looking down at the mess on the bed and the packed duffel bag, the officer spun around quickly pulling his pistol out from its holster. "Where are you going Mr. Bellington? I know you are not scheduled to return to Mindanao for another week. You were seen coming back into the hotel about twenty minutes ago, where were you? You can tell me now, or we can go down to my headquarters to discuss it. I'm sure General Yamashita would like to know what his American engineer is up to, or maybe even my contacts from Odessa that arrived by submarine yesterday. They are not a trusting people, and I'm sure they might be interested in what you are doing also."

Swenson shook his head as he reached for a smaller bag on his bed. "Let me show you something Lieutenant, I think you will understand completely."

Pushing Swenson's hand to the side, Lt. Chiba stepped back. "I will check it out!"

The Lieutenants eyes stared in disbelief when he saw more bundles of American and Japanese money than he had ever seen before.

As he dumped out the bag, Swenson slammed his fist into the side of Lt. Chiba's head. As the officer's feet buckled, Swenson grabbed the pistol from his hand. Scared and unsure of what to do next, Swenson pounded the butt of the pistol into the lieutenant's head over and over until blood ran from a massive wound on the back of the skull. Realizing he had just killed an officer of the Imperial Japanese Kempeitai, Swenson began to panic. He knew the Japanese would torture him unmercifully before finally putting a bullet in the back of his head, and they may very well go after his family back home.

Then there was Odessa to contemplate. Although he had managed to supply them with nearly eighty percent of the materials they requested for their project in Argentina, to many questions were being asked by suppliers, and he no longer had adequate answers. Now that the Allies were overrunning France, there was no doubt they would be getting more anxious about completing their new compound. Swenson knew full well they would crush anyone that stood in their way. If he was going to run from the Japanese, he would have to run from Odessa at the same time.

After a moment of thought, Swenson placed the money back in the bag and set it by the door with his duffel bag. Walking to the table by the window, he picked up a coal oil lamp the hotels now had for guests to use when the power went out, which was most evenings. After splashing the fuel around the room, he started a fire near the door of the bathroom. That would give him enough time to get to the main floor by using the back stairway across the hall, before the room exploded in flames.

Moving rapidly down the stairs, Swenson arrived near the lobby just as the explosion rocked the building. Lieutenant Chiba's two aids and the counter clerk rushed up the front stair case as they began yelling for everyone to evacuate. Storming out the front door Swenson ran out into the middle of the street waving his arms yelling, "Fire, Fire!"

As the nearby soldiers ran excitedly toward the hotel, Swenson turned and cautiously made his way down the walkway to the wharf.

Arriving by the ship, he watched dock workers beginning to pull the mooring lines loose from the large steel anchoring posts. The captain of the ship was standing at the top of the gang plank, hurriedly signaling for him to climb aboard.

Shaking his head, the captain clearly angry said. "Where have you been. I told you to be back in an hour, and we were told to sail fifteen minutes ago. I've been worried we would be stuck here in Manila if the navy withdrew our orders to sail. We would all have been taken to a detention camp for the duration of the war. Now get inside and stay quiet, I'll be back in a while to pick up my down payment."

Swenson sat on his lumpy mattress as he tried to make his hands stop shaking. When the tug boats began pulling the ship away from the pier, he stood up and looked out the dirty window back toward the hotel. Flames were shooting out of several rooms now as the fire was spreading quickly. A small detachment of fire fighters were just arriving as the ship got underway. Swenson's heart rate began to settle down as the ship passed the island of Corregidor and sailed out into the deep dark waters of the Pacific Ocean.

Swenson was looking at a six-month-old copy of the New York Times that was laying on a shelf in the room when the captain knocked on his door. Opening the door, Swenson observed a much more relaxed officer than he had experienced about two hours earlier.

Walking into the room, the captain handed Swenson a bottle of rum. "Well sir, it looks as though we have left Manila behind and are on our way across the wide Pacific. So, I've been wondering, you looked very nervous when you climbed on board my vessel. Did you have any-thing to do with all the excitement taking place along the pier?"

After Swenson poured several glasses of rum, he handed one to the captain. "I'm not sure I know what you're talking about. I was running so fast to get to the ship, I wasn't paying much attention to what was going on."

The captain laughed as he sampled the rum. "Only a deaf and blind man would not have heard the explosion and seen all the soldiers running toward one of the hotels. Are you deaf and blind, senor?"

Taking a large swallow of the strong rum, Swenson replied. "I sometimes find it best to keep my eyes shut and my nose to the ground. That way I know very little of what is actually going on around me. It has kept me alive in this war so far."

When he was finished speaking, Swenson walked over to a small steel night stand where he pulled out a paper bag from the top drawer, handing it to the captain. "You may count it if you wish, but I assure you each bundle contains ten one-hundred-dollar bills as promised. Cooperate with me when we pass through the Panama Canal, and it will make you an additional thousand dollars when we arrive in Cuba."

Smiling, the captain raised his glass. "To Cuba," he said, before drinking down the rest of his rum.

Swenson smiled broadly as he raised his glass in return. "Yes, to Cuba!"

The trip across the Pacific was slow and rough, as storms coming up from the south produced copious amounts of wind and rain. The storms actually calmed Swenson's mind, since he knew that neither Japanese, British nor American patrol ships would stop and search a ship under these conditions.

The captain made sure Swenson was fed decently each day, and allowed him to take walks along the narrow walkway above the fantail each afternoon when weather permitted.

On the twelfth day of the voyage, the captain walked up to Swenson as he stood on the walkway watching several cargo ships heading west. "We have permission to traverse the canal at 2200hrs. this evening. I trust you have a good story ready for the officials, as I do not want to be detained and investigated. My company would not look favorably on creating problems for the Panamanian officials."

Swenson smiled. "Just go along with what I say and all will be fine. You have nothing to fear, Captain. I would do nothing to put you in danger."

At 2200hrs. Swenson arrived on the bridge wearing a dark business suit. He shook hands with the Panamanian officials when they came on board. "My name is Swenson Bellington, my father owns Bellington Shipping out of New Jersey. You will see that my name is not on the manifest, as I asked for a chance to ride with the ship before it left Bilbao at the last moment. My father is always looking for new shipping companies to purchase, and I thought this one could be a good buy."

After looking over Swenson's credentials, the senior inspector smiled. "I have never met your father personally, and we have examined many of his ships as they pass through the canal. It's nice to finally put a face to the company. Welcome to Panama, Mr. Bellington, we should have the ship cleared and on its way in just a few minutes."

The captain looked at the inspectors. "It shall be interesting to see if Mr. Bellington decides to purchase our company. That will definitely give us more cargo to transport, and that means more money in my pocket."

The inspector laughed as he handed the captain the ships documents. "Yes, I'm sure things have been very tough with this damn war on." After shaking hands, the inspection crew departed the ship onto a waiting tug boat.

As they cleared the canal, the captain followed Swenson back to his cabin. "I trust I earned that extra thousand dollars we spoke about?"

Nodding his head, Swenson almost had to laugh. "Yes, you will receive it when we arrive in Cuba as promised. Captain, you have kept all your promises and helped me escape a bad situation. I thank you for your hospitality and will not forget it."

The captain looked seriously at Swenson. "There was a moment in Manila when I thought of sailing without you. I had no idea what you were about, or what kind of trouble you were in. But I knew whatever it was, it involved the Japanese Government, and that scared the hell out of me. Needless to say, the thought of seven thousand American dollars in my pocket made me take the chance. I'm glad I took the chance, and best of luck to you when we reach Cuba." After sharing a drink, the captain went on to finish his rounds of the ship.

Three days later the tough looking steamer sailed into the Port of Havana. After shaking hands with the captain and handing him a bag containing his final payment, Swenson stated.

"Captain, the three thousand I promised you is all there, plus an additional five hundred dollars so you will forget I ever sailed on your vessel."

The captain smiled as he tucked the bag into the pocket of his rain jacket. "Good luck, sir. And you can be sure no one will ever know you sailed with me from Manila, nor have I ever laid eyes on you. Be safe my friend."

Swenson smiled as he walked down the gangway at a brisk pace, searching for a cab that would take him to his father's sugar cane warehouse.

Arriving at the warehouse, Swenson walked up to the manager he knew very well. "Carlos, how have you been. It's been close to a year since we have spoken."

Surprised to see Swenson in Cuba, Carlos quickly shook hands with his old friend. "I did not know you were going to be here in Havana. Did your father send you down here to check on my operation? I assure you, everything is in order as Mr. Bellington demands."

Patting his old friend on the back, Swenson looked out at the ship that was being loaded with sugar cane. "No, I came down here on the yacht of a friend, but he's not ready to go back to the states just yet, and I need to get back to work. When is that ship sailing and where is it going?"

"You are in luck, my friend. It sails at 0800hrs. tomorrow and will unload in Miami. So you can be back in the states by noon," Carlos explained with a smile.

Swenson breathed a sigh of relief as he climbed aboard his father's freighter the following morning. It would be nice to be back in the United States where he didn't need to be afraid anymore. After all, no one he could think of had any idea of his dealings with the Japanese or Odessa. He would return to Kennebunkport, get back into one of his father's operations. He would marry Angeline Stevenson, have a family, and live the rest of his life in luxury.

After a lengthy train ride up the east coast from Miami, the train finally arrived in Kennebunkport three days later. Stepping off the train, Swenson was excited to see his parents and Angeline waiting on the platform. After a long wonderful dinner, Swenson and his father retired to the den for brandy as was always the custom in the Bellington home.

After taking a sip of brandy, Swenson's father looked over at him, his expression deadly serious. "Son, is there anyone that knows what you were doing with the Japanese? This is a delicate situation and we need to get out ahead of it if there are issues."

Swenson smiled as he shook his head. "No sir, there isn't a soul that knows I was out there designing and supplying hardware for construction projects. I got out of Manila well before any western people arrived, and every reporter had long since been banned from the Philippine Islands. I found safe passage out of Manila, and I can guarantee you the captain of the ship will never tell anyone I was on his vessel."

After a moment of silence, Swenson looked at his father. "Sir, is there a problem?"

Getting up slowly from his black leather chair, the old man looked out the window toward the flower garden. "If you are right, there is nothing to be afraid of from the Japanese. However, your dealings with Odessa are a more serious issue. Once they get a scent, they are on the trail like a dog on a bone. They will never stop looking for anyone that has crossed them. I hope you have covered your trail well, because if you are wrong, all hell will be dumped upon this family and we will be labeled traitors for all time, and that is only if Odessa does not murder us all first."

After lighting a cigar, Oliver Bellington turned to face his son. "But Swenson, you have always been trustworthy, and I believe you know what you are talking about. So, let's put it all behind us and go forward. I have several new ideas for our corporation, and we need to start making wedding plans so you and Angeline can get married. Taking control of the Stevenson operation is a priority, and you are the key to that door."

After shaking hands and having another glass of brandy, the two men joined the rest of the family in the living room for lively conversation, including plans for a wedding that would be the highlight of the years social calendar.

After the senior Bellington's went off to bed, Swenson and Angeline walked quietly through the flower garden. When they reached the gazebo, Angeline sat down while looking intently at her handsome boyfriend. "Tell me, Swenson, what were you doing the whole time you were out west? I wish I could have joined you. I have never seen Washington and Oregon, it would have been a grand time. I would not have minded spending time by myself during the day while you were working. Plus, on the weekends, we could have traveled around and seen all the sights I read about. Where did you stay when you were out there so long?"

Swenson took a deep breath as he sat down beside Angeline. "Honey, there were times I stayed in mining camps way up in the mountains that had no phone service, or regular mail delivery. Things were pretty primitive. But it was something I needed to do if we were going to find new ore deposits. There were also times I went from the mining camps to the logging camps to see how those operations were working out. Sweetheart, there were times I was out in the wilderness for a month or more. It would not have been very nice for you."

Taking hold of Swenson's hand, Angeline smiled. "Yes, I can understand that now, but I missed you very much. But now you are home and we can plan our wedding, so I can see an entirely new life on the horizon and I'm so looking forward to it. Father has said many times that he's happy we're getting together, as he'll have a smart business man to handle the affairs of all his companies when he's no longer able to do so."

Swenson could not help smiling at Angeline's last comment. He knew he could have nearly any young high society woman in New England that he wanted, but adding the Stevenson fortune to the Bellington conglomeration was a total dream come true.

CHAPTER 14
GOODBYE RENDOVA

As fighting continued on the Island of Bougainville well into January of 1944, it was essential to find a base farther north for the boats to operate from and continue attacking Japanese shipping. Since the Allies were preparing to invade the islands of New Britain and New Ireland in the Bismark Archipelago, it was decided to move a large part of PT operations out of the Solomon's.

On June 30,1943, American marines had cleared out Woodlark Island in the Trobriand Island group after a week of battle. Seabees immediately began building three airstrips on the island, as well as a crude PT base at Guasopa Bay, reminiscent of the Tulagi Base.

On July 5, three squadrons of PT Boats, including the 120, sailed from Rendova for the last time heading northwest into the open Solomon Sea. They would rendezvous with a large fuel tanker about midway during the trip to refuel. The ship was rigged so six boats could refuel at one time from its massive tanks. Seas were extremely calm as Buzz idled the 120 up to the tanker to refuel his thirsty boat. The torpedo men were in charge of handling the fuel line, so the gunners could stay at their positions in case of an air raid. The boat took on fuel at such a quick rate it almost stunned the crew. Back at Rendova, they would have had to spin cranks on fifty-five-gallon drums for hours to fill their fuel tanks. This was a much better situation.

With all the boats topped off, they continued their voyage northwest, heading deeper into enemy waters. It was exactly what the veterans had experienced when they sailed into Rendova. They had been surrounded by hostile Japanese land, sea and air units that attacked them at will until they were driven north up the slot. Now they would be dealing with desperate Japanese forces being squeezed from every direction as the Allied drive to the Bismark Archipelago quickened.

It was early evening when the PT convoy arrived in Guasopa Bay. Thankfully, the tanker was on station to fuel the boats one more time before it sailed off to take its place in the invasion of New Britain. Since most of the construction at the base was concerned with repair shops, a fueling pier, and supply buildings, there were no crew quarters ashore.

Buzz was completely fine with that, so if the Japanese decided to send down bombers to strike the new neighbors, the gunners could man their stations quickly.

For the first few days the crews studied maps, depth charts and the location of enemy bases in the group of islands.

Since the main Japanese base for the south Pacific was located at Rabaul on the northern tip of New Britain, it would not be unexpected to deal with high-flying long-range bombers and quick raiding heavy Japanese ships. The nights of attacking the slow-moving Tokyo Express were over. Now they would be patrolling the open Solomon Sea to the north, and raiding Japanese held islands to the south and west. There would also be the chance of running into Japanese subs attempting to resupply or evacuate men off the islands. Incredibly, that was the very first action the 120 and 117 boats experienced late one night during their first patrol. While sailing southeast out of Woodlark Island into the main body of islands, Dick Wickman reported seeing a periscope about fifty yards off the port bow before it submerged. A half hour later the bow gunner on the 117 reported a periscope sailing in the reverse direction before again submerging. It was clear to Buzz and Lt. Emory that the skipper of the sub was hoping to surface somewhere nearby, but the PT boats were keeping him submerged. They decided to patrol farther to the south near Normandy Island before making a quick run back to the north, and hopefully catching him on the surface. The night was quiet with winds gusting to about ten miles an hour, with moderate cloud cover over head. Kowalski and Stockey enjoyed watching a group of dolphins on the starboard side keeping pace with the boat as they dove and breached the surface over and over. Zumwaldt on the rear .20mm reported a small barge circling a nearby island before disappearing into a dark channel. Buzz decided not to give chase as the prospect of a supply submarine sounded a whole lot better.

About thirty minutes later, Buzz and Lt. Emory muffled their engines while dropping their speed down to 15 knots. Everyone on the starboard side of the boat scanned the dark island coast lines looking for the silhouette of a half-submerged submarine.

Forty minutes later, Lt. Emory reported the sub sitting stationary with workers on the deck off Murua Island.

Instantly, Lt. Emory spun his wheel hard to port and poured fuel to his engines. After making a wide turn, he raced back toward the island, firing two torpedoes at the well exposed side of the submarine. Seeing the PT boat charging toward them, the Japanese crew began running toward the deck gun, only to be cut down by the 117's machine gunners, before they could get there. Moments later, the two torpedoes slammed against the side of the sub, sending geysers of water and flame a good thirty feet in the air. Flames roared from the open hatches on the conning tower, as men with flames covering their uniforms dove into the water and swam toward shore. Several minutes later the submarine exploded and broke in two. The aft section sank almost immediately as the bow appeared to roll with the waves for a few moments before gliding to the bottom.

Several machine guns and small artillery piece on shore began firing at the boats. Buzz and Lt. Emory made several passes along the shoreline, allowing their gunners to engage the enemy batteries. As the fire died down, the skippers made a turn to the northwest, heading back to base as dawn was beginning to break over the Pacific.

Over the next few days, heavy bombers from Rabaul attacked Woodlark Island, making the airstrips their primary targets. On the second attack, three escorting fighters dove on the PT Base.

Thankfully, since a patrolling U.S. destroyer had warned the island of the impending attack, there were only two boats caught in the bay. The other sixteen boats had made it out to sea and were able to fire at the attackers. One burning Zero spun upside down before crashing into the jungle, the second pilot realizing his plane was going down, aimed for PT-98 that was still tied to the pier. A massive fire ball rolled skyward as hundreds of gallons of high-grade aviation fuel and unexploded ordinance all detonated at once. Large pieces of hot shrapnel tore into the engine room of PT-121 that was tied up about fifty feet away, rupturing a fuel line. In minutes the half-filled fuel tanks on the 121 blew apart in a blinding flash. Burning fuel and oil covered the water near the pier as thick black smoke rose above the island. Several sailors that had attempted to save the 121 were killed by shrapnel from the massive wall of debris that scattered over a hundred yards.

The third pilot made a strafing run on the island as men ran for cover, before climbing to the south and escaping the heavy anti-aircraft fire.

As the bombers finished attacking two airfields, they turned to the north to begin their trip back to Rabaul. However, six marine Corsairs from the third field streaked into the afternoon sky, attempting to seek revenge. With the Japanese fighter planes now gone, the fighters were able to bring down four bombers before the balance of the flight disappeared into a large cloud bank.

Buzz stood in the cockpit scanning the skies for Japanese planes as he circled the 120 about a mile off the coast of Woodlark Island. As he turned back toward the east, he could see the large plumes of smoke rising from the burning PT boats and airfields. The loss of four planes and their crews was a small price to pay for the massive damage the Japanese had inflicted on the new bases being constructed on Woodlark Island. However, Buzz was well aware of how far American forces had moved across the Pacific already, and he knew it was just a matter of time until they moved on to the Philippines and this part of the South Pacific would be nothing but back water.

Buzz had no idea just how correct he was. On September 12, 1943, one squadron of boats was ordered to move to Aitape on the northern coast of New Guinea. Once again, the boats sailed with a naval tanker and two destroyer escorts for the 1200-mile journey through waters still being contested by the Japanese.

The base at Aitape was still under construction when the squadron arrived. A second squadron of PT boats had also traveled from Milne Bay to help make up the advance fleet. Much like in the Solomon's, they would be working behind enemy lines, attacking shipping in the Bismark Sea and attempting to reinforce New Britain and New Ireland. As the Japanese continued building new airfields scattered through out New Britain, PT crews understood they would be under air attack more than they ever had before.

Three days after arriving at Aitape, the 120, 301 and the old 99 boat from Milne Bay were assigned their first patrol. They were to run northeast to Wavulu Island, then south east to Manus Island, then west back to the coast of New Guinea where they would turn northwest back toward Aitape. There were many small islands and atolls the Japanese convoys loved to settle into during the day, before moving on to New Britain under the cover of darkness.

Ensign Gruenke manned the helm as the 120 cleared the harbor heading out into the Bismark Sea. The night air was uncomfortably hot and moisture laden as a million stars dotted the crystal clear sky overhead. Although Buzz was not truly happy with the idea, most of the crew had removed their shirts and were wearing just their kapok vests above their waists. Chief Petrovski had found several men at their duty stations without their steel helmets, and given them a royal butt chewing. He knew that if they were attacked, the time it took to grab their helmets before they began firing, could be the difference of getting back to Aitape at dawn or treading water all night in a shark infested cove.

Nearing Wavulu Island, Buzz ordered all boats to slow to fifteen knots and muffle their engines. Slowly the three boats closed to within a hundred yards of the island as everyone with binoculars scanned the shoreline, looking for any sign of enemy activity.

Buzz and Ensign Gruenke kept a close watch on the sea in front of them, lest they run into a marauding destroyer by surprise. Rounding the north side of the island, Chief Petrovski pointed out some small lights in a cove. At first Buzz dismissed them, until he saw the muzzle flash of a rifle on the beach. Spinning the 120 around, and with the 99 directly behind him, Buzz threw open the mufflers, switched on the search light and charged forward. Instantly, rifle fire erupted over a wide section of coast line.

Wickman, Stockey and Kowalski began firing their machine guns as the 120 closed to within thirty yards of the cove before turning east. The spot lights from both boats brilliantly illuminated a Japanese Tug boat and a small barge tied up for the night. Making wild quick turns, both Buzz and Lt. Newman of the 301 set up their next pass, allowing the 20mm gunners to have a clear field of fire. Both gunners hammered away as machine gunners continued spraying the shore line wherever they saw movement. Just as the 99 began its run, the fuel tank on the tug exploded, sending debris and men into the air. With all the machine guns firing, the light skinned barge had taken countless hits, piercing the hull. It was already settling into the muddy bottom of the cove.

Buzz smiled as he set a course back out to deeper water, knowing the Japanese had now been properly introduced to the crews from Aitape. It was good to hear none of the boats had suffered any casualties or major damage. But now it was evident that there was a convoy hiding among the islands. Quickly, Lt. Emery sent a flash message back to Aitape requesting more boats and lining up air patrols for the following morning.

After a short run toward Manus Island, Buzz once again ordered all engines muffled as he dropped speed to ten knots. Instead of searching the coast of the big island, Buzz led his little flotilla into the group of islands directly east of Manus. He knew if the Japanese were going to hide barges, this would be the place to do it. The channels were narrow and filled with coral reefs and rock piles. The remains of two PT boats were easily visible sitting half submerged on underwater obstacles. There was no way to make a wide turn without getting out of the narrow and shallow channels, and making a high speed run was a pure recipe for disaster. Buzz was sure there were many props and rudders lying at the bottom of these channels.

Although Ensign Gruenke had seen some action, being in so close to these islands without true safe escape routes made him nervous. As he scanned an island to their port side, Chief Petrovski walked up to him.

"Sir, there is no way you can see a damn thing the way your hands are shaking. If you don't stop it, the Japs are going to hear your bones rattling and be on to our position."

Smiling at the chief, Ensign Gruenke replied. "This has never happened before, Chief. I just can't get past it tonight. It's like walking into a haunted house."

The chief smiled as he placed his hand on Gruenke's trembling shoulder. "Take a deep breath, sir. For all intents and purposes you are in a haunted house. Thousands of natives and mariners have died in these waters over the centuries. Their bones litter these waters from Manus all the way to New Ireland. That's why all the sharks down here are so damn healthy."

Will laughed as he watched the chief pull his pistol out of its holster as he looked over the side of the boat.

"Chief, somehow I don't think there's a shark out here with your name on it."

Laughing, he holstered his weapon. "Yeah, I'm probably too tough and rubbery for their liking anyway."

With the ensign calmed down, the chief made his way back toward the .20mm mount to check on the gun crew.

While continuing to scan the islands, Ensign Gruenke leaned back against Stockey's gun tub. Seconds later, Stockey leaned over, tapping him on the shoulder. "Check out your eleven o'clock, sir. Is that a damn destroyer cruising slow to the south?"

After studying it for a moment, Ensign Gruenke replied. "Sure is!"

Quickly the XO rounded the gun tub jumping down into the

cockpit. "Buzz, the channel coming up ahead to starboard, at your ten o'clock we have ourselves a destroyer heading south at about ten knots."

Picking up his binoculars, Buzz studied the channel for a moment. "We most certainly do, Mr. Gruenke. Take the helm, back off to five knots and hold our course!"

Quickly Buzz and Yamry studied the charts while making notations on a scrap of paper. When they were finished, Buzz grabbed the radio mic. "Blue Shepherd this is Dog One. We have mother hen southeast Manus, bridal channel vectoring due south. Channel is too narrow to make a greeting, request you send sky walker a.s.a.p. Please advise."

Seconds later, Buzz had a reply. "Dog One, heavy squall over area, sky walker possible when squall moves north, no way of knowing how long that could be. Be careful, but give mother hen hot eggs, will send sky walker when possible."

Shaking his head, Buzz picked up the hand set for the TBS radio. After explaining the situation he told the three boats to line up for a rear attack on the destroyer.

With everyone in agreement, Buzz unmuffled the engine and threw the throttles wide open. Swinging hard to starboard, Buzz entered the channel with the 301 and 99 screaming right up his stern.

Chief Petrovski called out, "Skipper, it will be a short run, we're at 6500 yards right now."

Nodding his head, Buzz knew he could only fire his port torpedo tubes since they were firing at such a narrow target. At 5,000 yards he yelled, "Fire one and three!"

With the torpedoes away, Buzz swung the 120 hard to starboard to make a pass of the slow-moving destroyer just as the 301 let lose its torpedoes. Buzz heard three sharp explosions as the rear of the destroyer raised up out of the water.

Lt. Warranton, skipper of the 99, made a wide turn to starboard to pass the crippled, burning destroyer, but made a fatal mistake. Instead of following Buzz and the 301 boat down the channel, he turned into another narrow waterway, attempting to make a quick turn for a broadside torpedo attack on the Japanese ship. Suddenly, the 99 shuddered to an immediate stop as the props were torn from the shaft and a large coral rock ripped open the bottom of the boat.

Sailors on the fore-deck of the Japanese ship wasted no time turning their five-inch front mount in the direction of the stranded boat. The first round slammed into the corral rock of a nearby atoll as the crew of the 99 began jumping into the warm waters to get away from their stranded boat.

The second round struck directly on top of the doomed boat igniting the fuel tanks. A brilliant wall of yellow and red flames rolled skyward as debris flew in every direction. Having the gun sighted in on the target, the Japanese gunners continued sending shells in concentric patterns all around the burning hulk in order to kill the crew.

Buzz knew full well attempting to save any crew members was sheer suicide, as he would sacrifice two more boats and the lives of over twenty-five men.

Although the commander of the destroyer had destroyed the stranded PT boat, that was not the answer to his problems. Flames from the fire in the engine room continued spreading until they reached a fuel bunker. A massive explosion rocked the destroyer as it became lodged on a coral reef. Wounded and desperate sailors quickly jumped overboard before the vessel rolled off the reef and sank.

Although the flotilla was to be back before dawn, Buzz continued patrolling the area until he felt he could safely return to check on the 99 and see if there were any survivors to pick up.

Instead, what they saw sickened the entire crew. The water in the cove was red with blood as fifteen to twenty sharks thrashed and ripped at the remains of the crew from the 99 boat and the destroyer. As they watched, two sharks swam past the 120 to join the frenzy. But Chief Petrovski quickly fired his large pistol, hitting the lead shark in the head. As it spun around and bled, the second shark attacked it with a vengeance. The chief quickly dispatched the second shark with two more shots. Of course it didn't take long to attract more sharks from the depths, as blood from the sharks coupled with that of American and Japanese sailors was spreading with the current.

As Buzz placed his engines in reverse, Ridman stood by the number three torpedo tube, yelling at Ensign Gruenke as he pointed toward the small island.

About two hundred yards south of the bloody feeding frenzy, one of the crew members was running along the shoreline waving his arms. Quickly, Chief Petrovski and Stegura tossed a life raft over board and paddled toward the island. Understanding he was the lone survivor, the men quickly paddled back to the 120 as Stockey and Kowalski stood on deck with rifles doing anti-shark patrol.

With everyone safely on deck, Buzz turned to the northwest, taking the crew home. The survivor was checked over by Yamry but he couldn't find any physical injuries. The man never said a word all the way back as he sat beside number four torpedo tube. Charlie Ansel recognized him as one of the torpedo crew, and attempted to strike up a conversation to no avail. The shocked sailor refused to get off the 120 when they arrived back at Aitape. It took three corpsmen nearly half an hour to get him off the boat and on to a stretcher. There was no doubt his war in the Pacific was over, but it would never be over in his mind.

As the crew of the 120 cleaned the boat, Ensign Gruenke walked up to Chief Petrovski. "Chief, there are even more bones in the water after last night. I don't ever want to see anything like that again."

The chief nodded his head. "Sir, the best thing you can do for yourself is to go get drunk before you sack out this morning. If you don't, you'll revisit it over and over and it will haunt you, and take away your sharp edge when we go back into combat."

About 1130hrs. Ensign Gruenke and the chief polished off a bottle of cheap whiskey before laying on the deck and falling asleep. The problem was, the ensign now found it easier to fall asleep each day after polishing off at least a pint of whatever he could get his hands on.

Seeing the sudden change in his XO, Buzz began to realize how different his entire crew was since they started this war.

The chief always slept with his .45 under whatever he was using for a pillow. Kowalski slept with his forty-five semi-automatic on his chest, and didn't roll over all night long. Crowder slept with a bayonet at his right side no matter where he slept. Stockey was sleeping with a hand grenade after he downed at least four bottles of beer. Yamry was sleeping with a homemade weapon that appeared to be a large straight razor firmly embedded in a baseball bat. Stegura slept with a razor-sharp Japanese machete he had found in the jungle on Rendova.

Buzz knew his crew drank as much as most other boat crews he had come across. He never chastised any of them as long as they were ready to perform their jobs when called upon. The rule he had made back at Melville regarding drinking and drunks on board his boat had been abandoned by the time they arrived at Rendova. The Pacific was a tough place to fight a war. But fighting it from the wooden deck of a PT boat where you saw the horrors of war face to face was something most men could not handle. He knew they would all have to come to grips with their issues once the war was over, and Buzz knew he was no different than the rest of his crew.

On December 15, 1943, operation 'Director' was launched against New Britain. American and other allied forces landed on the southern beaches near Arawe. It would be a long and hard-fought battle until remnants of the Japanese forces finally surrendered on August, 21, 1945. Now the PT crews stationed at Aitape were busier than normal. Huge convoys of Japanese ships laden with equipment and men crossed the Bismarck Sea hoping to dislodge the American forces. Planes flew cover missions out of Rabaul attempting to keep American subs, PT boats and destroyers from sinking their precious cargo.

With the focus on saving New Britain, the Japanese had begun setting up large naval bases at the deep-water ports of Seeadler Harbor on Manus and Hyane Harbor on Los Negros, and air bases on every small island in the cluster. The only way to effectively deal with these bases was by air strikes or PT boat attacks.

Carrier based planes struck the small airbases daily, cratering runways and destroying grounded aircraft. Nevertheless, the Japanese rebuilt the bases nearly as fast as they were damaged, and the pipeline bringing in new aircraft from Japanese factories was now much shorter than it had been six months earlier.

Every day Australian coast watchers and scout planes radioed in countless messages confirming ship movements and air craft dispersal. With so many targets and so few boats, headquarters at Aitape had a tough job meeting all the requests for attacks. Plus many of the boats were getting old and were in need of heavy overhaul or scraping. Buzz realized it was only a matter of time before the 120 was going to be put out to pasture as it was starting to show its age, and the engines would no longer kick out a solid thirty knots at times.

On December 23, word came that a large convoy of Japanese ships were closing in on Seeadler Harbor, and MacArthur wanted them put out of action. At 1900hrs, eight boats left Aitape under the command of Commander Esselman, who had just been reassigned from the base at Ferguson Island. He was a no-nonsense commander that expected each crew member to give everything they had and then reach into their pockets and dig out some more.

The wind was blowing out of the north at ten knots, and the boats were easily handling the seven-foot swells of the dark Bismarck Sea. Overhead, the sky was partially cloudy with just a crescent moon bathing the surface of the sea in a light bluish hue. It would be a glamorous evening if you were on a cruise ship with your sweetheart, something you would write home about on your next postcard.

But this was no romantic cruise, and Buzz could feel the tension in the air as the crew checked and rechecked their weaponry. Looking to his right, Buzz could see Stockey sitting behind his .50 caliber leaning against the back wall of his tub, slowly scanning the heavens for telltale signs of enemy float planes. To his left, Wickman nervously maneuvered his .50 caliber from left to right as he glared into the darkening night, swearing from time to time.

On the fore-deck, Kowalski was sitting against the front of the chart house with Stegura, using binoculars to search the empty ocean in front of them. Zumwaldt was standing near the controls of his .20mm cannon on the aft deck, searching the skies, while his loader, Gabe Ridman smoked cigarette after cigarette as he paced back and forth along number three torpedo tube. The torpedo crew appeared to be the most relaxed, or so it seemed, as they sat huddled on the deck next to tube number four. Below, Buzz could see Yamry bathed in red light as he looked over charts and spoke on the TBS radio to the navigator on Commander Esselman's boat.

Chief Petrovski had gone to the rear to check on things in the engine room with Crowder, and Ensign Gruenke was leaning on the back wall of the cockpit, just to the left of Buzz, scanning the skies as he hummed a song Buzz didn't recognize. No matter what the crew was doing, each man was alone with his own thoughts and fears as the 120 rushed forward toward enemy contact at a steady twenty knots. Although number one engine was given a clean bill of health by the mechanics, tonight Buzz was watching the gauges closely as he feared a gremlin was hiding in the engine. Out in the middle of the Bismarck Sea while under attack by Japanese war ships, was not a good place for an engine to fail.

Following Commander Esselman's slight course change, Buzz could feel the hair on the back of his neck stand up and scratch against his shirt collar. The farther north they sailed, the darker it became, as clouds began to move in from the west. If it wasn't for the phosphorescent wakes of the boats in front of the 120, Buzz would have had a hard time making out their silhouettes.

Turning to his left, Buzz called out, "Ensign, make a quick check on the crew. Make sure they're on top of their game. We don't need anyone nodding off.

Without saying a word, Ensign Gruenke jumped out of the cockpit disappearing into the darkness, as he made his way aft.

Returning about ten minutes later with the chief, Will stood aside of Buzz. "Sir, they are wound about as tight as a watch can be but they're ready."

Buzz nodded his head as he pointed toward a red flare that had just been fired at their one o'clock.

"Theirs or ours, sir?" Chief Petrovski inquired, as he felt his skin begin to crawl.

"No way of knowing, Chief, but I can assure you that we'll be in the thick of it too damn soon," Buzz replied as he looked over the gauges for engine one again.

Seconds later, a star shell streaked across the horizon, followed by the brilliant illumination of muzzle flashes as the big guns began to roar.

Moments later, Commander Esselman reported a destroyer dead ahead, and that he was beginning a torpedo run. Quickly, the rest of the boats broke formation and began searching for targets.

As one of the commander's torpedoes struck the bow of the destroyer, the blast silhouetted a large landing ship sailing on the far side of the damaged destroyer. Buzz turned hard to starboard, racing past the front of the burning destroyer, lining up for a broad side torpedo attack.

Ensign Gruenke looked at the gyro for a moment before calling out, "We're too close Skipper, we're under six thousand yards!"

Angrily, Buzz turned hard to port, giving his gunners an opportunity to fire on the slow-moving ship. Circling around behind the transport, Buzz observed another landing ship ahead. As he set a course for it, Ensign Gruenke called out, "Ten thousand yards and closing sir, we're all good!"

Instantly, Buzz punched the buttons for torpedoes one and two as he held the wheel tight. Both torpedoes launched from their tubes with an explosive whoosh, with hardly any telltale flame as they left the tubes. It was evident that no one on the transport had seen them launch their torpedoes. Moments later, a wall of flame and debris raced skyward as both torpedoes found their mark. One fuel tank ruptured, sending a cascade of burning fuel all around the starboard side as the wounded ship began to list.

Happy with their first attack, Buzz raced into the center of the convoy, allowing his gunners to strafe tugs and barges that couldn't run away and didn't have many guns on board to defend themselves. Making a sharp turn to starboard, Buzz watched another PT boat attack a Japanese patrol boat setting it on fire.

All around the convoy, ships, barges, and landing vessels were aflame. Gunners on destroyers fired non-stop at the racing PT boats with their three and five-inch guns. Plumes of water washed over the 120 from near misses, as Buzz charged forward toward his next target, a tug boat that was attempting to escape to the north with a large barge tied to it.

Wickman and Kowalski strafed the small control bridge with their machine guns while Zumwaldt poured 20mm rounds into the engine room. Smoke began pouring from the tug as it went dead in the water. Men on board the barge worked feverishly to cut the ropes securing it to the tug. But before they could finish their task, they were cut down by deadly machine gun fire from Stockey and Kowalski.

As Buzz began accelerating, he heard a sharp bang and the boat slowed noticeably. Looking down at his gauges, Buzz realized that the gremlin in engine one had made itself known. The tachometer showed the engine was no longer running.

Angrily, Buzz made a starboard turn in an attempt to break clear of the heavy fighting. However, seconds later Ansel yelled out, "Bandits at ten o'clock." Looking up to the east, Buzz watched three Aichi dive bomber float planes dropping down toward the battle. One of them without a doubt was heading straight toward the 120.

Buzz began evasive action as the gunners fired all they had at the slow diving seaplane. The pilot attempted to predict their next move and dropped his hundred-pound bomb, missing the 120 by about fifteen yards. However, as the pilot began to climb, a .20mm shell from Zumwaldt's weapon slammed into the engine compartment, blowing the prop off the engine. With little fanfare, the plane fell nearly straight down, slamming into the ocean breaking the aircraft apart.

Seconds later, Wickman called out, "Six fighters at two o'clock!" Spinning around, Buzz could see the planes diving into the battle and was somewhat dumbfounded. It had been a long time since he had seen Zero fighters engaging in night action, but these were desperate times for the Japanese. The pilot of the fourth plane in the formation swung hard toward the south to begin firing at the 120 with his .20 mm cannons.

Unable to gain full power, Buzz began swinging the 120 from side to side, attempting to avoid the explosive rounds that were slamming into the water all around them. Regrettably, the pilot was able to strike the hull of the 120 just below torpedo tube number three. Instantly, a cloud of steam arose from the side of the boat, telling Buzz that the cooling jackets for his last two engines had been hit.

Just as quickly, Crowder exited the engine room followed by a stream of black smoke. As he told everyone to move forward, he yelled out to Buzz, "The fuel line is ruptured and there's no way to put that fire out. We need to get the hell off this boat!"

As the engines of the 120 sputtered for the last time, and clouds of smoke began billowing from the engine compartment, Ensign Gruenke yelled at the chief and Andy Rice, "Get those rafts in the water."

Knowing his beloved 120 had given all she could and was destined for the bottom of the Bismarck Sea, Buzz yelled at his crew, "Abandon ship, she's going to blow any minute, get the hell off!"

Yamry came top side, handing out weapons from the emergency locker as he made his way to the port side of the boat. After saluting Buzz, he jumped off the deck and swam for the raft that Ansel was holding onto about five yards from the boat.

After completing a head count, Buzz and Ensign Gruenke slipped off the side of their sinking boat into the warm tropical water. However, as the ensign looked to the east, he could see the pilot of the Zero was making a wide turn toward the south to come back and strafe the survivors. In an instant, he climbed back on board the 120, jumping into Wickman's gun tub.

Buzz yelled frantically "Will, get the hell of the boat, that damn thing is going to explode. Get the hell off, that's an order!"

Ignoring Buzz's demands, Ensign Gruenke charged the twin .50 caliber machine guns, and began firing at the diving aircraft. Following the tracers, it was evident he was striking the diving plane near the wing roots where the unarmored fuel tanks were located. Nevertheless, it was also evident that the pilot had the ensign directly in his sites. Cannon fire from the Zero ripped into the gun tub shredding the steel, spraying the ensign with lethal shrapnel, but he never quit firing.

Suddenly there was a blinding flash in the sky as the fuel tanks of the Zero detonated. As if in slow motion, remnants of the aircraft slowly drifted over the ocean as they were carried by the westerly wind.

With a loud groan, the 120 began rolling over on its port side with Ensign Gruenke still in the gun tub. The chief jumped out of the life raft, joining Buzz as they swam back to the boat to extricate the ensign from the twisted steel.

Without any heavy tools to pry with, they could not get his right leg free of the twisted gun mount, and the 120 was beginning to roll over at a steady pace.

Taking a full breath of air, Buzz went under water to try one more time to save the brave young officer from drowning. Coming back to the surface out of air, Buzz and the chief watched in horror as they saw the ensigns right arm swinging at the water before disappearing forever.

Flames roared across the bottom of the 120's engine room, heading straight for the fuel bunkers. Buzz yelled at the crew to paddle as fast as they could, as he and the chief swam faster than either of them thought possible. Several minutes later the bunkers exploded, sending a massive ball of flame skyward, and a wave of shrapnel nearly twenty yards out into the ocean.

With the 120 gone, and everyone else safely in the rafts, Buzz and Chief Petrovski climbed aboard the rubber boats to avoid any contact with roaming sharks. The crew sat quietly in anger as they watched flames consume the wooden flotsam that remained on the surface.

After several minutes Yamry spoke up. "Which way do you want us to paddle, Skipper?"

Shaking his head, Buzz replied, "West toward Los Angeles would be best. Let's go home."

Everyone sat still not knowing quite how to deal with what their skipper had just told them. After a moment, Buzz pulled a compass from his life jacket. "South is to our right, but there is no way we can paddle all the way back to New Guinea, no matter how hard we try. The battle is still going on, so let's hope we get picked up by one of our boats when they decide to leave. Otherwise, our best hope is to be spotted by one of our subs in the morning, or a roving patrol plane checking out the floating wreckage. Save your strength men, we may be out here for a while."

About a half hour later, Lopez called out. "Skipper, either my eyes are playing tricks on me, or there is some sort of large raft coming toward us from our port side."

Buzz stared into the blackness for a minute or more before replying, "Yeah, I see it, and there are men on top of it. Get your weapons ready in case we have to fight."

Quickly, everyone pointed their guns toward the raft as they ducked down as low as they could. As the large raft approached, more men stood up and began yelling in Japanese as they shook their weapons in the air."

"Hold your fire men, hold your fire, let them get a bit closer."

As the men waited, Buzz could hear the unmuffled engines of a PT boat off to his left. Grabbing the flare gun from the raft, he fired a red sky flare toward the sound of the engines.

Just as the first Japanese sailor fired at the rafts, he was met by a hail of machine gun fire from PT-323. In seconds, the big raft began to sink as the bodies floated across the top of the Bismarck Sea.

When the 323 was about fifty yards away, the skipper flipped on his search light, allowing his crew to prepare to take on survivors. It took less than five minutes for the crew of the 120 to scamper up the cargo net hanging over the side of the rescue boat.

The skipper never searched the area looking for Japanese survivors, as sharks attracted by the blood were already arriving to indulge themselves.

Buzz sat on the fore-deck leaning against the front of the chart room. No matter how hard he tried, he could not erase the thought of Ensign Gruenke's arm pulling on the gun tubs twisted framework as he was taken down by the boat. Closing his eyes, Buzz remembered the day he was assigned the young ensign, and how he had worked every possible angle to keep him from being assigned to the 120. The worst part was that Will had heard every word he had said to Commander Reddings. He was sure his XO had gotten over it, but he was just as sure he had never forgotten it either. The crew, including Buzz and the chief, quickly came to trust him, as they realized he was a skilled boat handler and statistician. However, by now everyone had become somewhat hardened to the loss of a crew member, and Buzz was no different. But this was painful, as he had never truly found a way to apologize for his actions, and now he never could. He would make sure Ensign Gruenke's family received a hand written letter explaining what kind of a true PT man he had become, and how he died saving the lives of his crew. Buzz was determined to make sure Gruenke was awarded the Navy Cross for his bravery. It would never replace the son the family had lost, but at least they would know he died a hero.

Several days after returning to Aitape, Captain Cushmann, the commander of New Guinea PT Operations called Buzz into his office. "Maddox, Captain Reddings gave me your after action report, and the recommendation for the Navy Cross for Ensign Gruenke. I'm not sure I can approve this, and I'm actually feeling that the Bronze Star would be more appropriate."

Buzz shook his head. "Sir, I received a Bronze Star when we were at Rendova, and I appreciated it very much. But I'm still alive, and I'll be getting another boat in a few days. Sir, I've seen men die in combat all too often. He never even flinched when he realized we were going to be strafed. He climbed aboard the 120 and gave every inch of his life to shoot down that aircraft before it could attack us in the rafts. In my opinion, sir, that boy deserves the Navy Cross and then some."

Captain Cushmann sat behind his desk looking up at Buzz. "Lieutenant, I heard you did everything possible to keep that kid off your boat. Are you feeling some remorse for your actions, is that why you're putting him in for the Navy Cross?"

Buzz shook his head. "Do I feel bad for how I acted? Affirmative, sir. Did I judge his abilities without giving him a chance, yes. But he put that behind him, and did his damnedest to prove to me and the crew that he belonged on a PT boat with the rest of us, and he did it in style. So, no sir, I'm not asking for this award because I let my emotions get the best of me. I'm asking for the award because in my book sir, he was a true hero and willingly gave his life trying to save the rest of the crew from a certain death. And because of his gallantry and despite our vulnerable position in those rafts, we didn't lose one man. In my book that makes him a hero. We all owe him our lives."

Nodding his head, the captain stood up and shook Buzz's hand. "It shall be so, Maddox."

Feeling somewhat relieved that the award was going to go through, Buzz walked over to the tent he was sharing with several other boat skippers. Sitting down at the small wooden desk, Buzz looked at the blank sheet of paper in front of him. How did he write a letter of this nature on Christmas Eve? Obviously, the family would not receive the letter until well into January, but just the thought of writing it during this special holiday season seemed nearly sacrilegious. After taking a deep breath, he began writing,

> *Dear Mr. and Mrs. Gruenke,*
>
> *I regret to inform you that your son, Ensign Willard Gruenke, died in combat in the early morning hours of 24 December 1943. We were involved in attacking a large Japanese convoy that was attempting to re-enforce their soldiers on the Island of New Britan. Will and I were at the controls of PT-120 searching for enemy targets when*

we lost our number one engine. Due to our lack of speed, the 120 sustained further damage, causing a massive fire in the engine room. Within minutes, the fuel system was destroyed. As the fire was spreading quickly, I gave orders to abandon ship because there was little doubt that the fuel tanks were going to explode at any time.

As we left the boat and climbed into rafts, a Japanese fighter plane dove on our position. Immediately, and against my orders, Will scrambled out of the raft and climbed back onto the boat where he began firing at the attacking plane with the port fifty caliber machine guns. He and the Zero exchanged fire for several minutes, with Will taking heavy shrapnel as the plane exploded. Regrettably, damage caused by the cannons on the plane mangled the railings and steel plates around the gun tub, causing Will's left leg to become entangled in the debris. We tried to get him free, but with no tools we couldn't bend the steel plates back out of the way before the boat capsized, then exploded.

Will died a true hero, saving the lives of the rest of the crew. He will be receiving the Navy Cross for his heroic actions. Every member of PT-120 sends their deepest sympathy at the loss of your son. He was an extremely capable officer and good friend to every member of the crew.
Lieutenant Brian Maddox U.S.N.

After finishing the letter, Buzz walked it over to the mail box near the command office. As the sun began to set, Buzz grabbed a can of beer from the small officer's hut before walking down toward the pier. Although it was Christmas Eve, the war did not stop. Off in the distance, Buzz could see flashes across the horizon where heavy ships were exchanging blows with their massive guns. It took several moments before the rumble of the explosions would finally reach the north shore of New Guinea where Buzz was seated on a stack of empty pallets. To his left, four boats from squadron six were preparing to sail on the nightly coast patrol, searching for Japanese submarines. Buzz watched intently as the PT boats idled off into the darkness, unaware of what they might run into out on the open ocean this sacred night.

It did not take long before Chief Petrovski walked up alongside of him, carrying a six pack of soda pop. "Mind if I join you, Skipper. I have plenty of nontoxic libation that is nearly ice cold."

Buzz laughed as he motioned for his chief to sit down. "Funny, I only took one beer as I thought getting drunk on Christmas Eve was a sure ticket to hell. My mother would never allow any heavy drinking until the afternoon of Christmas Day. She was quite the stickler for protocol around the Maddox home. If she saw me now, sitting out here on pallets drinking beer on Christmas Eve, wearing cut off pants, bare feet, unshaven, with my shirt untucked, she would punch that ticket to hell herself."

The chief laughed as he opened the first can. "Well, Skipper, she could punch mine also. If you go, I'm sure as hell going too, and there's no two ways about it."

Buzz shook his head after taking another swallow of beer. "Chief, we have fought our way half way across the Pacific already, and we still have a long way to go. What do you think our odds are?"

After thinking for a minute, the chief replied. "Whoever thought some baby lying in a manger filled with straw, after being hunted down by some evil king, and forced to flee on the back of a donkey, would ever change the entire world in just thirty years of living, but he did."

Buzz turned to look at his friend. "Chief, I never took you for a religious man."

Laughing a little, the Chief crushed the empty can and opened a second. "When I was growing up, my mother probably was a lot like your mom. Church every Sunday, plus Sunday School, dressed prim and proper so everything looked good for the neighbors. But my dad was a drunken son of a bitch. He beat me and my sister any chance he got. I left home after my freshman year in high school and never looked back. My sister joined a convent to escape, though she says she's very happy."

"Then what?" Buzz inquired.

"Well, I roamed around a while, eventually got married, had a daughter, and joined the Navy. I destroyed my marriage by getting drunk way too often. We tried to reconcile, but too much damage was already done. But somehow some of those lessons from Sunday School stuck with me. Then you kind of know the rest of my story already. So, I still try to avoid the booze and stay sober, although it has been a bit tough with this damn war, and everything we see out there. But tonight, I thought about my daughter, wherever she is, maybe opening gifts with her kids, making a special dinner, and heading off to Midnight Mass with her family. So tonight I decided to have soft drinks in her honor."

Buzz patted his chief on the shoulder as he smiled. "You're a good man, Petrovski, a damn good man. Now hand me one of those cans if you don't mind."

After opening the bright red can, Buzz looked over at the chief. "You never really answered my question. What do you think our chances are of surviving this damn war?"

Shaking his head, the chief replied. "Damn, I wish I knew the answer to that, Skipper. Every time we sail it feels like a little piece of my luck stays back here on the pier, and eventually my luck is going to run out no matter how hard I try, and there won't be anything I'll be able to do. Just make me one promise, Skipper. Don't let the sharks get me. Shoot me first if you have to. I just don't want to die being torn to pieces by those powerful jaws. Will you promise me that? I don't want to die that way!"

Buzz could feel the honesty and the fear in Petrovski's voice as he starred out to sea. Nodding his head Buzz replied.

"You have my word, old friend, you have my word."

Just as a brilliant flash arched across the northern horizon, Buzz looked down at his watch. "Merry Christmas, Chief. Glad to have you with me tonight."

The chief smiled as he and Buzz shook hands. "Merry Christmas, Skipper. The best gift I ever got was from you, allowing me to join your crew and be the man I hadn't been for a long time. Someday, maybe I can hold my grandkids on my knee and tell them what their grandpa did in World War Two. And I won't have to fib or make things up, because I manned up and did the job. Though a whole lot of people would never believe the stories we can tell."

Buzz nodded his head. "That's a fact, Chief, that's a fact!"

The men watched for nearly fifteen minutes as heavy fire rolled back and forth across the horizon. Every so often when the wind blew from the north, they could hear the rumble of the battle.

"Somewhere out in that horrible blackness men are dying tonight, Chief," Buzz said, in a hushed tone. After watching the next round of fire, Buzz looked up into the clear sky above them where the southern cross constellation shone so brightly. Continuing, he added, "Sad to say there's no good will toward men out on that restless sea tonight. No angels, no shepherds, no wise men, just the blackness of hell in those dark hostile waters for the losers. God help them."

Nodding his head, Chief Petrovski made the sign of the cross as he replied, "Amen to that Skipper, the poor bastards."

Slowly, the Chief slid down from the pallets. "Skipper, I'm going to turn in. I wish you the best Christmas ever, and hope we can all celebrate at home in 1945."

Shaking hands with his chief once more, Buzz replied. "Go get some sleep, Chief, and Merry Christmas. I think I'll watch the fireworks for a while longer."

About fifteen minutes later, a massive explosion sent a fire ball high up into the dark night sky. Buzz knew full well a ship had exploded, probably killing everyone on board.

"I wonder if those men even realized it was Christmas Day before they died." Buzz said out loud before walking back toward his tent.

The following morning after breakfast, Buzz ran into Commander Reddings. "Maddox, come over to my office. I have something for you."

When they entered the office, the commander smiled. "First off, do you want another Elco configured like the 120, or do you want a new model configured more or less as a gun boat."

Without any thought, Buzz replied. "I want the old-style boat, sir."

"Fine, then the 303 is yours. She'll arrive from Milne Bay tomorrow morning, and has only been in the Pacific about a month. Secondly, I have papers here promoting you to Lt. Commander, Buzz. Now, you'll lead a squadron every time you go out. You'll have six boats. The 298, 304, 312, 316, 317 and your 303 boat. Congratulations, Maddox, you've earned it and then some. Also, your new XO will arrive with the boat. He is Ensign Stuart Kirkman. He has seen some action and appears to be a good boat handler. Put him to work and get the 303 ready to lead your new squadron.

CHAPTER 15
A GOLDEN FIND

Josh Maddox and the filthy crew of POW's that now numbered twenty-five, continued working day after day with Japanese construction teams on the island of Mindanao. Their latest assignment was to lengthen and pave the new runway with a combination of concrete and crushed coral. It was back breaking work, but the men never complained to their captors. They knew if they were placed on a transport for Japan, the odds of ever being seen again were very low.

On the afternoon of November 21,1944, a Japanese Nakajima Ki-34 Army transport plane rolled to a stop on the old dirt runway. Several high-ranking Army officials exited the plane, along with Swenson Bellington's top aide Evan Burns. Josh took cover behind a road grader just twenty yards away, watching the arrival ceremony. He was curious that he had not seen Swenson himself for quite a while, but Evan Burns was just as guilty and underhanded.

Captain Numura walked up to the dignitaries and shook hands. After several moments of discussion, the guests were taken to a large tent that had been erected earlier in the day for cold drinks and rice cakes. About an hour later, the men loaded into two half-tracks that would take them on a tour of the new defensive positions on the island.

About 1700hrs, the half-tracks returned to the air strip. The officers rolled out several blue prints on the hood of the lead half-track, as they discussed future construction projects. Happy with what they had seen, they all took time to get their photos taken in front of the half-track with Capt. Numura. After several rounds of hand shaking, the delegation returned to the transport plane for the flight back to Manila. That evening Josh lay on his thatched mat, seething with anger, knowing American boys were going to die because of those bunkers.

He knew Swenson and his firm were not only designing them, they were also unlawfully supplying the necessary materials. When the plane arrived that morning, Josh had felt like rushing one of the guards, taking away his weapon, and shooting Burns before anyone could stop him. But he was sure in his weakened condition, he would have never been able to hold the weapon steady long enough to shoot accurately. Even after seeing Swenson and Burns so many times on the islands, it was still hard to believe someone he had grown up with could have sold out his country this way. Josh had explained to all the other POW's about Swenson and Burns, just in case he didn't survive the war. One way or the other, he wanted to make sure the Bellington's paid for their acts of treason.

Through out the months of December and January of 1945, American carrier-based fighter bombers attacked Mindanao incessantly, destroying equipment and blowing craters in the new runways. Planes that had been dispersed to Mindanao by the Japanese General Staff, had been caught on the ground in the early raids and destroyed. Due to a shortage of planes and trained pilots, Captain Numura was told it could take weeks or months before any more aircraft could be sent to the island.

Since all the concrete had been used, craters on the runways were filled with either plain dirt excavated near the airfield, or crushed coral if the rock crushers were operating. Day by day things were beginning to deteriorate for the construction crews and POW's. Japanese Marines assigned to the island were beginning to confiscate most of the rations being delivered at night by landing craft, leaving very little for the POW's and civilian slave laborers.

Adding to the desperation on the island, large American war ships were now shelling the island at night with their large caliber weapons. For hours on end, fourteen and sixteen-inch shells weighing more than most cars, pummeled the island. Palm trees were shredded or broken off, massive craters finished off the airfields, and many defensive installations were decimated. Artillery sitting in the jungle waiting to be placed into bunkers or dugouts was smashed, ammunition stock piles were wiped out, and the marines were taking heavy casualties. Josh was sure he and his fellow POW's were going to be wiped out by their own navy before they had the chance to be rescued.

Toward the end of January, the prisoners were awakened one morning to the sound of small arms fire and a lot of yelling. The men huddled on the floor of their huts, shaking with fear, not knowing what was going on, or if the Japanese would toss grenades into the huts to kill all the POW's before they evacuated.

When the firing ended, Josh could hear the sounds of men speaking Spanish near their hut. Carefully, he stood up and walked to the window that was crisscrossed with barbed wire. Looking out into the yard, he observed ten well-armed men wearing American military uniforms mixed with civilian clothing. Throwing caution to the wind, he yelled out. "Hey, we are POW's, get us the hell out of here!"

Before he could say another word, several men ran to the hut, ripped off the make shift lock and opened the door. Josh and the other prisoners stood frozen in place, not sure what to make of the hostile looking men standing outside the hut.

Finally, a tall man with a broad smile walked up to the door and spoke in perfect English. "I am Lieutenant Edward Romero, United States Army. I am the leader of the guerrilla operation here on Mindanao. We were unaware that any more POW's existed on the island. I'll need to contact my superiors to arrange transportation for all of you. We'll give you some of our rations, and leave five men to keep you safe, while the rest of us meet up with the balance of our force. You are free to roam about the camp, but don't journey into the jungle as you may get shot."

The guerrillas shook hands with all the prisoners, bandaged injuries, and handed out quinine pills before handing over the bulk of their K-Rations to the hungry prisoners.

After eating some of the rations, Josh and several of the men walked over to the huts where the Japanese guards and officers had lived. They ransacked the buildings looking for anything of value the soldiers might have left behind. Josh went straight for Captain Numura's hut that was nestled under several low hanging palm trees.

Going through the desk, Josh found a small photo album filled with photos from many different islands. Incredibly, there were a bunch of photos taken with Swenson Bellington and other high-ranking officers. After showing the photos to the men that had been shot down with him, they ripped apart the file cabinet, and the rest of the captain's quarters, searching for any other paper work that would tie Swenson to the Japanese military. It didn't take long for them to find shipping manifests and letters signed by Swenson on his father's company stationary. Finding a small leather bag under the desk, Josh carefully placed most of the evidence they had collected inside. The balance of it he gave to Sgt. Sanmore, his long-trusted crew chief, just in case something happened to him and his bag. They felt it best not to put all their eggs in one basket.

About 1400hrs, Lt. Romero returned with several American sailors. After a quick round of boisterous hugs, the men were escorted to the west side of the island, where two PT boats sat idling off shore. In quick order, the men were taken by rafts out to the waiting boats. Once everyone was aboard, the skippers turned to the south, heading toward an aircraft carrier where the prisoners would be deposited.

As PT-237 roared across the sea, Josh walked up to the cockpit. "Skipper, can I ask you a question?"

Looking over at the bedraggled pilot, he replied, "Ask whatever you want, sir, we're at your service."

Josh smiled as a tear ran down his face. "My brother, he's a PT boat skipper, or at least he was the last time I heard from him. Have you ever heard of Lieutenant j.g. Brian, Buzz Maddox?"

The skipper laughed, "I guess you have been out of contact for a while. He's now Lt. Commander Buzz Maddox and has his own squadron. He's still in New Guinea tearing up the Japanese in the Bismarck Sea. I would think he should be joining us up this way before too long. We have a lot of work to do here in the archipelago. I actually served with him back at the beginning of our operations on the island of Tulagi. I found out quick that your brother is one of the best boat handlers in the Pacific, and a very good friend of mine. I can't wait until he gets here."

Josh smiled, happy to know his kid brother was still alive and doing well. "Just curious about something. You say he's a great boat handler, has he lost any boats yet?"

The skipper laughed as he made a course correction with the wheel. "Oh yeah, he's lost two in action, but he's always been able to save most of his crew. If you don't fight, you'll never lose a boat. I've lost one so far, and this baby has been repaired a few times already. It's a tough war out here in the islands, and the Japs hate the hell out of the PT fleet. They go after us with everything they've got, but somehow we manage to survive to fight another day."

The skipper quit talking as the boats roared past the back of a destroyer and began maneuvering to line up on the side of the U.S.S. Lexington. Quickly, the POW's began transferring to the carrier, allowing the PT boats to get clear of the big ship so it could maneuver if it came under attack.

As Josh prepared to leave, he looked over at the skipper. "When you see Buzz, let him know I survived and I'll see him when he gets home."

With a big smile, the skipper replied, "Good as done!" Then he and the XO saluted as Josh stepped aboard the carrier.

Josh stood on the huge steel platform for a moment, watching the two PT boats race away across the Philippine Sea. He turned toward a young ensign standing nearby. "My brother is a PT skipper in New Guinea. I never realized how small those damn boats are until today. Fighting steel with wood, these guys are some damn brave men."

Nodding in agreement, the ensign replied, "I was on one destroyer that went down, but there is no way you could get me on a wooden boat loaded with all the fuel and ammunition they carry. You are correct, sir, they are braver men than I am."

After showers and haircuts, each POW was seen by the ships doctor. The medical staff were surprised to find the men in better shape than they expected. Since all the prisoners were suffering from some degree of malnutrition, the doctor put them on diets that would help them regain their strength without causing them any harm.

Three days later the Coast Guard operated resupply ship FS-141 pulled aside the Lexington. After all the supplies were transferred to the carrier, the POW's were transferred to the supply ship that was bound for Pearl Harbor. FS-141 was placed in a convoy of ten ships protected by four destroyers for the six-day trip back across the Pacific.

At Pearl Harbor, Josh saw a familiar looking smoke stack on a ship anchored in the east lock. He was sure it was the logo of the Bellington Shipping Company. After questioning several officers, he was told the ship had been bound for Korea when it broke down in the northern Pacific. When it was rescued by a U.S. Naval tug, the ship was searched and found to be carrying a cargo that was considered contraband by the War Department. The crew had been released, but the ship and its officers were being detained under orders of the U.S. Attorney General's Office.

Before returning to his quarters, Josh went to the Western Union Office on base to send a telegram to his father.

"Need to talk to your attorney stop *set up meeting with F.B.I. upon my return* stop *do you know whereabouts of Swenson B.* stop *imperative we know but keep still* stop *sailing from P.H. In morning. Josh."*

Josh knew his father would be totally confused by the telegram, but he also knew he would follow through with the meeting without question. From this point forward, Josh knew he would have to guard everything he had in that small bag with his life. It was all that was needed to take down one of the wealthiest families in the country, and create a scandal that would rock the New York elite.

Arriving in San Francisco ten days later, Josh and his crew were taken to Fairfield-Suisan Army Base about fifty-four miles away. The men went through an intensive debriefing by intelligence officers. Unfortunately, everything they had with them was searched and cataloged.

It was about 2100hrs, when Josh was escorted to an interrogation room, where two FBI agents and several high-ranking Army intelligence officers were seated at a long table. Over in the corner with armed guards on each side of him, was a dejected looking Sgt. Sanmore.

Before anyone could say a word. Josh spoke up. "Sgt. Sanmore did nothing wrong. I just asked him to carry some of the evidence, so if something happened to me, he could get the balance to the proper authorities, and that would be you people."

One of the FBI agents stood up, pacing back and forth. "All your questions at Pearl Harbor, and the text of the telegram you sent had us spinning in circles. What was your plan, Captain Maddox?"

Sitting down Josh began. "I first saw Bellington when we were working on the islands around New Georgia. I always hid when he was around so he wouldn't see me. I knew if he recognized me, the Japanese would have executed me immediately.

I never saw him on Mindanao. There were several times Evan Burns arrived for inspections, but he had changed a bit. He was no longer the carefree bastard I grew up with. He was now more nervous and impatient. I had heard him mention Manila a few times to Capt. Numura, so I figured that's where he and Swenson were living, but I couldn't be sure.

When we were set free on Mindanao, we ransacked every building the Japanese had occupied looking for souvenirs or anything that looked valuable. Going through the office, I found the photo album. Other guys digging through the file cabinets handed me files they thought were worth looking at. I placed what I wanted in the black bag you went through, and as I said, gave the rest to the Sergeant for safe keeping."

The FBI agent leaned against the wall. "And what was your plan?"

"As the telegram stated, I wanted to sit down with the FBI and my father's attorney for my own protection when I got home. I was going to give them everything we brought back from Mindanao, and tell them about the ship at Pearl. I thought that was the best way to handle it," Josh replied, wishing he had not sent the damn telegram.

The other FBI agent leaned forward in his chair. "Tell us what your dealings are with a Miss Angeline Stevenson?"

Not able to control himself, Josh busted out laughing. "I never had much to do with her, as she was quite a bit younger than me. But my brother Buzz had a hate, love relationship with her over several years. Before he went off to school at Melville, he told her they had nothing, never would have anything, and she should go out and get a real life. Her family was damn upset as they had intended for the Maddox and Stevenson families to join together in a major financial conglomeration. But Buzz was never interested in big money, or a spoiled, sniveling tramp like her. It didn't take long for Swenson to go sniffing around Angeline, after she let it be known Buzz had left her high and dry. I went off to the Air Corp about that time and lost touch with that entire mess."

Colonel Brinkman looked over at Josh. "After you turned Swenson in, what were you hoping to gain?"

"Nothing, sir. I just wanted to see a traitor tried and sent to prison for the rest of his life. If more of his family were involved, I want them arrested, tried and sent to prison as well. Sir, I lost five crew members when we were shot down. My brother has had two boats shot out from underneath him, and I'm sure lost several crew members himself. Men are dying out there every damn day, and this son of a bitch is helping to make that possible. If I could, I would love to put a bullet right into his evil brain," Josh replied angrily, as he stared coldly at the Colonel.

"Maddox, I believe you would, but you'll never get the chance of course. The Army insists you testify against Bellington, as the sergeant has already agreed to do. But you cannot discuss this with your family when you get back home. They know nothing of it since the FBI jumped on the telegram and destroyed it," Col. Brinkman replied.

Before Josh could say a word, the FBI agent leaning against the wall spoke up. "Bellington is in the wind, and we don't have a clue where he might be. Can you help us with that?"

Josh thought for a moment. "The family owns a large place up in Canada somewhere, and a home down near Boston. Those are the only places I know of, but with his money and his dad's connections, he could be anywhere. And believe me, old man Bellington will do whatever it takes to keep Swenson free, including lying to the authorities. He's a ruthless son-of-a-bitch."

By midnight, the question-and-answer session had come to an end. The following morning Josh boarded a train heading east for Maine, while Sgt. Sanmore headed north toward Montana.

Arriving in Kennebunkport, Josh was happy to see his family again. They had a wonderful dinner that evening, and hung on every word Josh told them about being a POW, lest the news about Swenson Bellington.

After a three week leave, Josh was assigned to the Presque Isle Army Air Corp base, at Presque Ilse, Maine. With his experience flying over the open ocean, he spent the next several months patrolling the Atlantic, covering the coast lines from Maine to Nova Scotia, and providing air cover for convoys coming and going to Europe. He was credited with the sinking of one German U-Boat in February of 1945.

With Germany surrendering on May, 7 1945, Josh was transferred to Panama where he patrolled the western approaches to the canal until July first 1945, when he was discharged from the military due to malaria.

Back in Kennebunkport, Josh decided that working in the family fishing business was not such a bad idea. Carl took over the business end of the company while Josh worked with the boat crews. He soon came to love the sea again, and the adrenaline rush when they ran into a big catch.

By this time the FBI had arrested Swenson's father and the family attorney for their part in supplying the Japanese with contraband. The Bellington Corporation, and all family bank accounts were seized by the government. But as yet, the FBI hadn't been able to locate Swenson.

On a cold October day as a stiff wind blew out of the northwest, Josh and the veteran crew of the Lady Bee, prepared to sail out to sea to catch some North Atlantic Cod. As usual, Clyde Foxmeier, the skipper of the Lady Bee, was at the helm, gently guiding the vessel out of the cramped harbor. Once they reached the breakwater, he carefully shoved the throttles forward as he kept a watchful eye on his engine gauges. Seeing his powerful diesel engines were operating properly, he gave the throttles another nudge forward, bringing his sturdy craft up to twenty knots.

Today, they would be fishing about one hundred fifty miles south of Yarmouth, Nova Scotia, where they had enjoyed good luck on many occasions.

The sky was partly cloudy and the temperature was hanging in the high forties as the bow of the Lady Bee plowed through the six-to-eight-foot swells like a dashing greyhound. Josh sat in the right-hand seat drinking coffee and trading barbs with his favorite skipper. Clyde had been terribly wounded during the invasion of North Africa in 1943, when the landing ship he was operating was struck by a German eighty-eight shell as they approached the beach. After being released from the hospital the navy discharged him, so he went looking for a job operating fishing a boat. He was the best hire his brother had made in a long time.

As they neared the fishing grounds, the winds began to die down, bringing the ocean to four foot swells, perfect for cod fishing. With all the booms lowered and the nets released, Clyde began his first run. Reaching the north end of the feeding banks the nets were completely empty. Moving a bit more to the east, Clyde began another run. He could feel the engines bogging down as they were pulling more weight. Josh smiled and patted Clyde on the back, knowing they were making a nice catch. Clearing the feeding banks, Clyde brought the boat to a stop allowing the booms to be brought up so the nets could be emptied. The crew cheered when they saw the nets brimming with hundreds of cod waiting to be dumped into the Lady Bee's holds.

With the nets emptied, Clyde turned north once again to cover the same area. However, as the nets began to place a drag on the engines, there was a loud bang, followed by a column of smoke coming from the engine room. Several men ran toward the open hatch to give their mechanic a hand.

After several frightful minutes, one of the crew members came running to the bridge. "The fuel transfer pump exploded. The fire is out, but Stan is burned really bad. We need to get him to a hospital or he's not going to make it."

Josh ran to the engine room to see what could be done to get the engines working again. After looking over the damage, he knew there was nothing anyone on board could do to get the engines running without new parts.

Returning back to the bridge, he heard Clyde on the radio calling out an S.O.S. over and over without getting any response. After the fourth try Clyde looked at Josh. "Can we fix her up, Boss?"

Josh shook his head. "There's so much damage, trying to jury rig one engine could blow this boat clear out of the water. All we can do is keep calling for help until someone hears us. But I'm afraid Stan won't survive, he's burned over fifty percent of his body. The guys are doing what they can for him."

As the sun set behind gathering storm clouds in the western sky, Clyde inquired. "Boss, do we turn on the running lights or do we keep them off to preserve the batteries?"

Josh shook his head. "If we keep everything off, we could be hit by a ship and ripped in half. Turn on just the bow and aft lights, every half hour spin the search light in a slow three sixty turn. Keep calling for help every ten minutes. Shut down everything else that consumes power, even the ice machines. If we can't get out of here soon, we'll need to deep six our catch."

Near midnight, lightening flashed across the western sky as heavy wind driven rain began to blow unceasingly across the frigid waters of the Atlantic. According to the gauge on the ships console they were getting gusts of over forty-five miles per hour. The cod in the hold were helping to keep the Lady Bee low in the water, so the odds of capsizing were slim, but the men needed to bucket water from deck areas where it could not flow back into the ocean.

Crew members cleaned cod from the hold, and cooked them on the propane stove in the galley, so food was not a problem for the nervous crew.

By dawn, the boat had drifted about forty miles northeast which was bringing them a bit closer to Nova Scotia, but farther away from home. Once they passed Sable Point, they would drift out into the middle of the Atlantic Ocean where they would face larger waves and the serious prospect of being lost at sea.

As night fall began to settle over the storm-tossed sea, Clyde once more checked the power levels of the batteries. "Josh, I'm afraid we'll run out of power before dawn, what do you want us to do? As you know, without batteries, we have no radio."

Josh nodded his head as he braced himself for a large wave that was about to slam into the Lady Bee. After the boat dropped into the trough, he looked at Clyde. "We'll call for help every twenty minutes, but we need to keep the bow and aft lights burning, it would be too dangerous to shut them off. I'll take the first watch until midnight, go get some rest."

About 1130hrs, Josh picked up the radio mic and took a deep breath. After repeating the emergency call twice, he placed the mic back on the shelf and sat down in the captain's chair. It was nice to see the winds had dropped back down below thirty miles an hour, so the boat would not drift out to sea quite so quick. Just as he was going to look over the ocean charts once more, the radio crackled to life.

"Lady Bee this is the Canadian Coast Guard cutter, City of Ottawa. We heard your call and are sailing toward your position. Request you turn on all lights regardless of battery condition. We have you on radar and should be at your position in about forty minutes. Do you have medical problems?"

Smiling with relief, Josh keyed the mic. "Negative, but we have one fatality wrapped in a tarp."

Moments later the City of Ottawa replied, "Roger that, stand by!"

Clyde had just climbed back onto the bridge as Josh set down the mic. "Wake the men, Clyde. Get them in their wet suits, we have a coast guard cutter coming in about forty minutes."

Clyde spun around without saying a word as he charged back down into the crew quarters.

Returning several minutes later, he picked up a set of binoculars and began scanning the seas to the northeast. About ten minutes later, he called out. "Search light approaching at our nine o'clock, Boss."

Picking up the mic, Josh called the cutter. "City of Ottawa, this is the Lady Bee. We see your search light off our port beam."

"Roger that Lady Bee, we have you in sight. Will circle your craft once to make sure none of the rigging is torn lose. Then we'll approach on your starboard side to drop off a pilot."

The crew watched eagerly as the large cutter circled the Lady Bee, with its huge spot lights moving up and down the rigging. When the skipper of the cutter was satisfied, he idled his vessel carefully up to the starboard side, where an officer jumped safely into the arms of the Lady Bee's crew.

With the tow line connected, the City of Ottawa turned northwest, sailing toward the port of Lunenburg. The coast guard pilot took the helm of the Lady Bee as he watched the lights of the cutter in front of him. For the first time in two days, Josh felt relieved as he was finally going to be able to call his father to let him know the crew and boat were just fine. He knew everyone in Kennebunkport was well aware by now that they were missing at sea.

Arriving at Lunenburg, the cutter brought the Lady Bee up to the dock of a sea food broker. After examining the fish in the hull, he made Josh a good offer for the catch. The cold ocean water surrounding the fish had kept the load from spoiling. The body of Stan Wigman was removed from the cooler where Josh had placed him, and taken to a local mortuary, where the body would be prepared for transport back to Kennebunkport when the boat was repaired.

Once the fish were unloaded, a small tug pulled the Lady Bee over to a ship repair shop. After a careful examination of the damage, Josh was told it would take three days to make all the repairs to his vessel.

Josh put the crew up in a small hotel just down the street from the wharf. On the second day, Josh and Clyde decided to walk about a mile to a pub they had heard about. When they were halfway there, Josh froze in his tracks. Crossing the street in front of them, just twenty yards away was Swenson Bellington.

Josh pushed Clyde into the doorway of a small clothing shop, as he watched Swenson walk up the small hill past the business district. Backing into the shop, Josh looked at the startled woman.

"Miss, do you have a local police department?" Josh hurriedly inquired.

With a deep Irish accent the woman replied, "Why yes, we have a very good constable here. He's a real no nonsense man to say the very least, if you know what I mean."

Josh nodded his head. "Good. Do you know how to get ahold of him this time of day?"

Laughing, the woman smiled, "Aye yes, he and his deputy would be over at McHale's, just two doors down, finishing their lunch right about now. They are very prompt about that, they never want to miss the lunch time pool tournament."

Before the woman could say another word, Josh grabbed Clyde by the arm, pulling him back out onto the street. "Go get the constable and bring him over here. I'm going to follow Swenson."

Clyde ran into McHale's just as the constable was preparing to leave. Looking up at the large man with a thick red mustache and eye brows, Clyde quickly told him what was going on.

Squinting with one eye, the constable replied. "A traitor to the United States you say. Well, let's go have us a look young man, we can figure it out when we catch up with your boss."

Turning up the street Swenson had followed, they saw Josh about fifty yards ahead standing behind a street light post. Looking at the skeptical constable, Josh pointed toward a blue Ford pickup truck with its hood open.

"He's in front of the truck working under the hood. There's no doubt in my mind he's armed, so we'll have to be very careful when we approach him," Josh explained nervously.

"Son, you won't be approaching anyone, that's the job of my deputy and myself. You two stay right here and let us do our jobs," the constable warned, as he stuck his huge index finger into Josh's chest.

As the constable unzipped his jacket, Josh observed a military .45 pistol on his belt, along with several cases for spare magazines. Josh was glad to see the constable was being serious about the situation, because he knew Swenson would never be taken without a fight.

Making a wide berth around the truck, the constable rested his right hand on the butt of his pistol as he called out. "Mr. Bellington, step away from the truck and let me see your hands!"

Josh knew Swenson was saying something back, but the open hood muffled the words.

He watched the constable shake his head and yell back. "Step back away from the truck like I said and let me see your hands. Let's get this over with, so we can all go about our business."

In a split second, Swenson spun around and ran toward a nearby garage as he pulled a pistol from under his jacket. He quickly fired two shots at the deputy before lunging toward an open door.

The constable and his deputy took cover behind the truck as they pointed their weapons at the open door.

"Mr. Bellington, there's no place for you to hide. Put down your weapon and come out with your hands up. It's all over, son!"

Hearing the breaking of glass, the deputy charged toward the open door only to find the garage empty. Swenson had smashed the south facing window and climbed out, disappearing into a small thicket of over grown weeds and small trees.

The constable and his deputy ran around the garage with Josh and Clyde in close pursuit.

Holstering his weapon the constable said calmly. "Well, now we have a man hunt on our hands. We'll need to call for help from our local posse. If he's here, my men will find him."

Over the next few days, the posse searched every part of Lunenburg and Bridgewater, without any sign of Swenson. With all the repairs completed on the Lady Bee, Josh had the mortuary deliver the casket with Stan Wigman's remains. After Clyde had assembled the crew, Josh announced he was not sailing back with them. He handed Clyde a note to give to his father when they arrived back in Kennebunkport. Josh removed a shot gun and a box of shells from the Lady Bee's emergency cabinet and walked ashore. He had to find Swenson one way or the other.

Everyone knew Swenson was a very self-sufficient individual that could think on his feet. After all, he would not have been able to work his way around war department officials as well as he did, without having a knack for underhanded operations. But Josh was determined to find him one way or the other.

The following day, a man's body was discovered half buried in the sand by a parking area near the ocean a mile north of Lunenburg. According to the paperwork in the man's jacket, he had been working for a small freight company. With the truck missing, officials suspected Swenson would be driving northwest toward the city of Amherst where he could cross into New Brunswick. They found the abandoned truck several days later in St. Johns, near a wharf on the Bay of Fundy.

It was evident that Swenson had made a perfect escape and was now at large. As St. John's is only about ten miles from the United States border, Canadian officials sent out wanted notices to officials in the United States as well as all Canadian Provinces.

Renting an old pickup truck, Josh spent the next two weeks driving the highways between St. John's and Kennebunkport. He stopped at cafes, gas stations and small grocery stores talking to people about Swenson. Josh drove on countless muddy backroads, searching deserted cabins or lumber camps for any sign of Swenson, but came up empty in every case.

Arriving back in Kennebunkport, he observed a fishing boat named Donna M. out of Nova Scotia, tied up to a fueling pier. Parking the truck, Josh walked down to the pier to speak with the crew. An old skipper named Josiah was standing on the pier watching the dock workers as they pumped fuel into his boat.

"Running a bit low on fuel?" Josh inquired, as he smiled at the skipper.

"Aye, to be sure young man. When I get my tanks topped off, I'm heading back to St. John's with a nice load of halibut," the man replied with a toothless grin.

"St. Johns you say. When was the last time you were there?" Josh inquired, as the man counted out money to pay the dock worker for the fuel.

"Well, let me think a minute. We finished rebuilding two of our pumps and then took the Donna M out for a few trial runs before heading out for the halibut. So we were in and out of the docks several times over the past few weeks. Sorry, I can't be more specific, the memory isn't what it used to be. Why is it so important?" The skipper inquired, as he stepped from the pier back onto his boat.

Taking a photo of Swenson out of his jacket pocket, he handed it to the skipper. "Did you ever see this man in St. John's hanging around the pier when you were working on your boat or anything?"

"Aye, I did. He was a rather rude fend impatient young man, with no sense of understanding to say the least. He wanted me to bring him here to Kennebunkport, and for a handsome sum, I might add. But I told him a catch of halibut paid more. I also told him I wasn't sure I would come this far west, but the halibut kept me coming." The skipper shook his head as he handed the photo back to Josh. "The truth is, money or not, I recognize trouble when I see it and I wanted no part of it."

"Is it possible another boat might have brought him here?" Josh inquired.

"Aye, that is always a possibility for sure. There were three other boats getting ready to head out when we left. Any one of them could have given him a ride, and may have for the kind of money he was offering. I'm not much into being a water taxi and I've always found it to be way more trouble than it was worth. And with his attitude, I probably would have tossed him overboard anyway. Nice talking with you, I need to get moving now. Good luck with your search." With a nod of his head and a tip of his dirty cap, the skipper turned his attention back to his boat.

Josh stood on the dock watching the Donna M. head back out to sea. There was no doubt in his mind that Swenson had beaten him back to Kennebunkport and was long gone. Walking back to the truck, he was determined to drive over to the Stevenson's house and talk to Angelina. She may be a lot of things, but one thing she never was good at was lying or keeping a secret. Josh knew it wouldn't take long to find out if Swenson had been there to see her.

Arriving in Kennebunkport, Clyde and the crew were surprised by the homecoming they received. Every local dignitary shook hands with the crew that had been considered lost, and now returned safe and sound. The dock area was full of well-wishers, family and photographers that wanted photos of the men for their stories. Even a reporter from CBS News came by to get an interview for their weekend report.

Clyde walked over to Alfred, handing him the note from Josh. After reading the note, Alfred took Clyde and Carl for a walk away from all the hoopla. The three men talked for nearly an hour regarding Swenson and Josh's plan to look for him. Carl was sure the search would come up empty, but he understood his brothers desire to find the traitor.

Josh was ready to kick in the front door of the Stevenson home after knocking three times. Finally, one of the maids opened the door, looking at Josh with disgust.

"Can I help you, Mr. Maddox? You certainly appear to be impatient this afternoon."

Before she could say another word, Josh brushed by her and walked into the large foyer. "Where is Angeline? You find her and you bring her down here right away!" Josh demanded angrily.

Before another word was spoken, Angeline appeared at the top of the large stair case. "What do you mean by coming in here and raising so much trouble. I have a mind to call the police and have you removed from our house. You have no right to barge in here like this. I dare say you are more of an animal than your younger brother," Angeline stated angrily as she made her way down to the foyer.

When they were standing face to face, Josh grabbed her by the arms. "Where the hell is Swenson Bellington?"

"Quite dead I presume, and I don't much care. I have not heard from him for some time, and any decent man worth loving me would never walk away without giving me some reason. Now, I don't want you here, and I don't care where Mr. Bellington is, and if you do not let go of me at once, I will have Miss Spade call the police!"

Letting go of Angeline's arms, Josh nodded his head. "Alright, let's play it your way. But that son-of-a-bitch will be found one way or the other and if you know something it's best you speak up or you'll be going down with him, I promise you that!" Josh threatened.

"Get out," Angeline demanded, as she shook with anger. "Get out of this house right now!"

Climbing into the old truck, Josh realized he had misjudged Angeline Stevenson. Despite being a selfish, self-centered arrogant bitch, she had also become a well-crafted liar. She knew full well where Swenson was, and obviously felt threatened by Josh's sudden appearance. He knew it was just a matter of time before he had the information he needed to bring Swenson Bellington to justice.

As Josh drove from the long circle driveway, he was unaware of two men sitting in a blue Chevrolet about a half block to the south. As the truck disappeared down the wide tree-lined street, the Chevrolet slowly drove up the driveway to the front door of the Stevenson mansion.

Miss Spade gasped as she answered the door. She had seen the two men before when they had come to visit Mathew Stevenson, and it had not been a pleasant visit.

"Mr. Stevenson is not home, and I do not expect him to be back for several days, so you will have to come back another time."

As Miss Spade attempted to close the door, the taller of the two men put his foot in the way, before pushing the heavy door open. Angeline was just walking through the foyer with a cup of coffee as the men barged in.

"Well, well, if it isn't Miss Stevenson. Is your boyfriend here in the house, or should we just search ourselves? Oh, excuse me, my name is Heinrich and this is my associate, Klaus. We have been here before talking with your father, and he was not much help. But now we know your boyfriend is indeed back here in Kennebunkport. So, do you wish to tell us where he is?"

Knowing enough to be scared of these two men, Angeline set her cup on a small table before approaching them. "I know who you are, and I know you threatened my father. Mr. Bellington is not here and has not been here. I do not know where he is, and I would not tell you if I did. So, get out of our house or I will have Miss Spade call the police."

Klaus walked over to Miss Spade, who was terribly frightened. Placing his pistol against her cheek, he replied. "Oh, I don't think Miss Spade will call the police if we ask her not to."

Heinrich turned to his partner. "Klaus, we do not have to act like we mean to cause them harm. After all, I'm quite sure Miss Stevenson realizes what the consequences would be if she lied to us." Turning back toward Angeline, Heinrich bowed. "Have a good day young lady. We will be talking with you again soon, very soon."

Without saying another word, the two men turned and left. Angeline walked over to the stairway and sat down as she shook uncontrollably. She fully realized the Odessa was not going to play games and they would get the answers they wanted no matter who got hurt.

CHAPTER 16
THE ENEMY ISN'T DEAD

When General Douglas MacArthur began his war to send the Japanese back to Tokyo, the only logical place to begin was the island of New Guinea. On the Southern Coast of the large island laid the city of Port Moresby, already firmly controlled by experienced Japanese marines and army infantry, just eighty miles across the Torres Strait from Australia.

The enemy was already extremely busy building airfields, tent cities, wharfs and warehouses, all for the eventual invasion of Australia. General MacArthur realized he either had to stop the Japanese right where they were, or prepare to move the Southwest Pacific Headquarters out of Australia. During several meetings with the American, Australian and New Zealand general command, MacArthur made it quite clear there would not be another evacuation as there had been from Manila. It was time to fight, and he was taking the war to the enemy.

The battle for Port Moresby was long and bloody, but allied air power flying just a short distance from Australia made the real difference. The only way for the Japanese to retreat from the southern plains of New Guinea, was an overland route across the Owen Stanley Mountain range called the Kokoda trail. It was a rugged trail covered by wet triple canopy jungle, with elevations reaching to eight thousand feet. The floor of the trail was filled with twisted tree roots and deep washouts that could break a man's ankle or leg if they were not extremely careful. The route across the mountains to Popondetta on the north coast was one hundred and thirty-nine miles. Throughout the long and arduous trip, allied aircraft strafed and bombed the long columns of escaping soldiers. Many seriously wounded soldiers were left behind on the side of the trail to fend for themselves, or commit hari kari, as it was impossible to carry litters over the rough terrain. Many merciful soldiers killed their comrades rather than see them suffer or die to the ravages of the animals that prowled the jungle at night.

As the survivors descended the mountains, nothing was sacred to them. They butchered farm animals, while murdering and raping villagers on their desperate search for food.

Upon reaching Popondetta, it took commanders weeks to get the former well-trained soldiers and marines back into any form of military discipline. However, this was not the last of hell many of these men would see. Slowly, they were introduced into new units of tough battle-hardened marines that were now occupying the towns of Lae, Hansa Bay, Wewak, Madang and Salamaua on the north coast of New Guinea.

As the allies prepared to attack areas on the north coast to establish bases, General MacArthur realized his army could not go up against areas fortified with these tough Japanese forces. He pointed to locations on the map that were not heavily controlled by the Japanese, but could be used for invasions that would cost fewer American lives.

He stated they would bypass Japanese strongholds, cut them off from ground resupply, set up naval blockades, and pound them from the air with no hope of withdrawal. He stated that starvation was his Allie, and the best weapon he had among the allied forces now.

Little by little these strong points became bases of pure misery for the Japanese, as bodies piled up, and diseases like cholera, typhus and dysentery spread like wildfire. Soon, starvation and disease were killing men quicker than bullets.

Some of the tougher Japanese marines broke free of the blockade, choosing to find food and relief farther up in the mountains. Soon there was no place along the north coast or lower mountain plains free from the desperate, marauding Japanese marines.

For the PT crews arriving at their new hastily constructed bases on the New Guinea coast, life was also pure misery. Severe storms tossed the Bismarck Sea for nearly a week after Christmas. Heavy winds with gusts over fifty miles an hour pounded the north coast. Waves as high as fifteen feet damaged piers and destroyed buildings close to the sea. Crews were required to check on their boats every half hour to assure the mooring lines were still intact. Many of the poorly constructed huts on the base at Aitape were torn apart by the wind, forcing men to cram everything they owned into the newer sturdy Quonset Huts built by the Seabees.

Up in the mountains where Japanese survivors attempted to find refuge in caves or reinforced huts built by natives, things were much worse. They had run out of food, and hunting in weather like this was totally impossible. The men had been soaked by the driving rains for days on end, causing trench foot to become a major problem. It had reached a point where they no longer had any dry fuel to start fires in the caves to stay warm or to dry their clothing. Desperation grew as they realized their last chance of survival was to attack the PT boat base at Aitape that was hunkered down with the storm.

Around two in the morning, four Japanese sappers blew the barbed wire fence on the southeast side of the base. After killing three Marine sentries, twenty Japanese soldiers attacked the base, searching for rations, medical supplies or anything else that would make their pathetic existence more tolerable.

Much to the surprise of the Japanese attackers, off duty Marines and PT crews responded quickly to repel the attack, despite the horrible conditions. Realizing they were not going to accomplish their original objectives, ten Japanese marines smashed into the small hospital, grabbing any type of medical equipment they could carry, while pulling four nurses out the back door.

By three o'clock, Aitape was quiet once more, with the bodies of twelve enemy marines lined up near the back fence. The American forces had suffered seven casualties, but regrettably, four nurses were now missing and were somewhere out in the dark jungle with the murderous enemy.

Everyone realized that attempting to go after the Japanese in the middle of the night in a dark jungle during a driving storm was suicide. However, by dawn, Marine Raider Captain Ramey had assembled a team of thirty men to begin the search.

Buzz and Lt. Mews from the 316 boat armed their men from the Marine ammunition building and prepared to join the search. When the newly promoted Captain Reddings found out about their plans, he came looking for them in the ammunition building.

As he walked in the door, Stockey yelled out, "Attention!"

Every man snapped to attention as they watched their new Captain walk straight up to Buzz.

"Maddox, you best explain to me exactly what the hell you're planning to do!"

"Sir, there are four nurses out there with those Japs, and we need to get them back. There's only thirty marines in the strike force, and we have no idea how many Japanese they're going to run into. Outfitting our crew will add nearly another thirty men to the force, which just might make the difference between success and failure," Buzz explained, as he jammed several more grenades into a pouch on his belt.

Shaking his head, the angry captain yelled all the more, "Tell me, Maddox, how do I explain to headquarters that I lost two complete boat crews chasing down some ragged Japanese marines that probably number into the hundreds. Can you answer me that question?"

Before Buzz could say another word, Lt. Mews spoke up. "Sir, those nurses go through hell trying to keep us patched up and somehow find ways to get medical supplies when no one else can. Do you really want us to stand down?"

After taking a look at the well-armed boat crews around him, he looked back over to Buzz. "I have a feeling that no matter what I say you're all going to go anyway, risking courts martial, which will just make matters worse. " Taking in a deep breath he looked at his two officers. "Alright, get out there and find them. But if you don't accomplish the mission in forty-eight hours, I want you back here. The weather is supposed to improve out there in the Bismarck Sea, and I may need your boats. Secondly, I don't want you going with the marines contingent. You can cover more ground if you follow another trail up into the mountains. Let's not put all our eggs in one basket."

Nodding his head, Buzz replied. "That was our plan from the very beginning, sir. Looking at the dead out by the fence, I don't think they'll be travelling too fast. They all appear to be in tough medical condition. We'll get them, sir, I promise you that."

Several minutes later, Buzz led his men out through the blown wire, but took a more southeasterly course up into the mountains. About an hour into their trek, Chief Petrovski found a Japanese canteen laying on the ground alongside the narrow jungle trail. Emptying it out, he tasted the liquid. "It's fresh water, Commander. I would say we're on the right trail."

Encouraged by their find, the men moved quicker up the slimy, muddy trail, knowing as each minute passed, the situation of the nurses was becoming more dire.

As the afternoon slowly turned to dusk, heavy damp clouds drifted into the thick jungle from across the Bismarck Sea, making visibility next to nothing. Coming across a small village that had been evacuated by its inhabitants, the men carefully searched each hut before reporting to Buzz that everything was quiet. Although several huts had dry fuel for a fire, the chief explained that any type of smoke could bring way too many Japanese down on them before they could react.

Buzz and Lt. Mews set up a schedule for guard duty that allowed all the men to get some sleep before moving on up the mountain in the morning. About 0500hrs. Ansel heard noise coming down the trail into the village. Slowly, he backed away from his position so he could notify the sentry closest to the hut where Buzz and Lt. Mews were sleeping. About five minutes later, two Japanese marines walked cautiously into the village, knowing something was not right. As one of the soldiers pulled his bayonet, Lopez grabbed him from behind slicing his throat. Before the second man could respond, a crew member from the 316 struck him in the head with a large rock.

After pulling them off to the side and out of sight, their bodies were searched from top to bottom. One of the men was carrying several fresh United State Navy medical bandages in his back pack. The men knew they had taken the right trail, and were now closing in on their nurses.

In the predawn light, Buzz set his men forward once again, searching for the enemy soldiers that attacked their base. About midday, Stockey made a grisly discovery as he was walking point. On the left side of the trail was one of the nurses, tied to a tree and disemboweled. After cutting her down and covering here with a poncho, Lt. Mews said a few prayers over her body as the balance of the men stood quietly with their helmets off. When the lieutenant was finished, Kowalski placed his helmet on his head saying. "They all die, that's the way it has to be, they all die!"

All the men slapped Kowalski on the back as they began moving back up the trail. By late afternoon, Torpedoman Fulton from the 316 was walking point. Hearing voices in front of him, he motioned for Buzz to come forward.

Slowly Buzz, Fulton and Chief Petrovski worked their way forward inches at a time until they could see into a small clearing where there was a large cave opening. Just inside the cave they could see the other three nurses sitting on the ground tied to a large log. In the clearing were about fifteen soldiers talking back and forth as they watched three other men skinning a wild boar.

Buzz sent Fulton back down the trail to bring the others forward. Once they were gathered around, Buzz pointed out where he wanted each man to go. He told them to wait until they saw the chief walk into the clearing, then take out the soldier closest to the cave. They all thought the plan was a bit crazy, but knew it was best not to argue with the chief.

Quickly, the chief removed his combat equipment, shoes and shirt.

After rolling his dungarees up to his knees, he spread mud over his chest, arms, face and legs. With his .45 pistol jammed into his waistband he grabbed his canteen. As he entered the clearing, he began singing ninety-nine bottles of beer on the shelf, as he waved his canteen in the air as if he were drunk. Several of the Japanese soldiers stood up, laughing at the chief as if he were a lunatic. A young lieutenant walked toward the chief, yelling at him in Japanese.

The chief smiled as he handed the canteen toward the officer. "Hell yeah, have a drink, ya never knew when you're going to die."

However, the officer was more interested in the huge pistol the chief was carrying. After pointing at it several times, the chief smiled. "Oh, you like my gun? After pulling it slowly from his pants, he began to hand it toward the smiling lieutenant. Before the man could react, the chief cracked the heavy revolver across the bridge of his nose. With blood flowing from the massive cut, the chief spun sideways, firing a round into the head of the soldier by the cave.

Immediately, all the men around the clearing opened fire. In mere seconds, every Japanese outside the cave was dead. The chief dove into the cave firing his last five rounds into the dark opening. Buzz and Stockey ran head long into the cave, firing their Thompson machine guns. With a smile, Buzz pitched the chief another Thompson he had strapped to his back. Moments later, several men cut the nurses lose from the log and pulled them away.

When Lt. Mews dropped down beside Buzz, he inquired. "Are there more inside?"

Nodding his head, Buzz replied, "Yeah, we heard them yelling back and forth several times. How much plastic did you bring with you."

"Enough to collapse this cave twice over," Mews responded as he began to remove his pack.

Quickly, the men rigged the blocks of explosives in several areas near the mouth of the cave. With all the detonators and wires attached, Mews rolled out all the wire he had around the left side of the large opening.

As he began to wire the small switch, Buzz asked. "Is that all the wire you brought? With all the plastic we have in there it's going to be suicide to set that off!"

Mews smiled, "Turn the switch and dive into the brush. I should be fine."

"Unless you fall down on a damn snake!" Buzz replied with a slight laugh.

"Yeah, well then you can be a good commander and suck out the venom, now get your ass out of here so we can finish this," Mews stated as he placed his hand on the switch.

Counting to three, the lieutenant threw the switch and jumped behind some logs that were laying nearby. A massive roar shook the mountainside as dirt, rock and shredded trees flew through the air. The ground all around the cave rumbled and shook as tons of rock and dirt crashed down, filling the cave entrance for eternity.

As the cloud of dirt settled, Lieutenant Mews stood up brushing himself off. Slowly he walked over to Kowalski slapping him on the shoulder. "Like you said, Ski, they all die!"

Buzz kept everyone where they were for a short time to make sure no other Japanese came to check on what had happened. When he felt everything was safe, they back tracked down the trail toward the empty village where they had stayed at the night before.

When they came to the poncho covering the young nurse, Buzz had the men cut some solid pieces of bamboo from a nearby tree. After constructing a make shift stretcher, the men placed the body on top of it for the trip back down the mountain.

As dusk settled over the Owen Stanley Range, the tired men shared their rations with the nurses before taking up guard positions as they had the night before. Buzz placed the women in a small hut next to the one he was in, but they refused. They insisted they sleep near the men as they were armed, and the last thing they wanted was to be alone with all the jungle noises around them. When the head nurse laid down beside Wickman, she reached into his holster, pulled out his pistol, and placed it next to her under the poncho one of the men had given her. She looked up at Wickman and said, "No offense sailor, I just need to feel safe tonight."

Wickman smiled as he handed her a second magazine for the weapon. "The safer the better, Ma'am!"

As the sun rose in the east, it burned off the remnants of the storm that had battered the north coast of the island for over a week. Slowly, the caravan made their way down the muddy, slippery trail heading back to Aitape. About halfway down they ran into the marine raiders that had started out before them. Seeing the nurses, Captain Ramey walked up to Buzz.

"Commander, it appears you accomplished what we could not. Every damn trail we found took us nowhere. We killed a half dozen nearly starved Japs last night when they attempted to shoot their way into our camp, but that was the only contact we had. We heard the huge explosion yesterday afternoon, but weren't sure who created it. We knew it was far above our position and just figured we would head east this morning to find another trail. One of my runners told me you guys were out here, and it was probably a good thing in the long run."

Buzz smiled as the two men shook hands. "Hell Captain, we didn't have a clue where we were going. We just knew you went toward the west, so we would try to the east. We probably killed twenty or more. We have no idea how many of them backed up into the cave before we blew it, but believe me, they're sealed in there forever." After shaking hands with Lt. Mews, the men continued their trek back to their base.

Captain Reddings was relieved to see his filthy mud covered boat crews walk back into the base intact. He hugged each of the nurses before shaking hands with all his men. "I couldn't be prouder of each and every one of you. I'll admit I was angry as hell when you left, but I owe you guys a real apology. Bringing three out of four back was more than I had ever thought was possible. So, were you involved in that massive explosion yesterday afternoon?"

All the men laughed as Lt. Mews stepped forward. "Sir, we had to seal that big cave. I wasn't sure how much plastic to use, so I used everything that was in the bag."

Captain Reddings laughed as he slapped his lieutenant on the shoulder. "I have to guess the Japanese Emperor felt that rumble in Tokyo. The ground here just shook before we saw that massive cloud of dust and debris rolling up from the mountainside. Job well done men. Go clean up, get some hot chow, dry clothing and a good night's sleep. It looks like you will be back in action tomorrow."

Buzz accompanied the body of Lt. Cheryl Sandberg to the morgue area. He told the attendants what to expect before they opened the poncho. Before leaving he placed his hand on the poncho and said, "Rest well Lieutenant, may God be with you."

The following morning the boat crews were busy cleaning up all the debris that had collected on the boats, plus reinstalling the machine guns and .20mm cannon, and removing all the torpedoes to get any debris out of the tubes that may have been driven in by the winds. By noon, Buzz had heard from every boat in his squadron they were ready to sail.

About 1400hrs, squadron seven sailed from Aitape to patrol through the small islands that helped make up the Bismark Archipelago. As they approached the islands to the north of Manus Island they were stunned. It was apparent that the Japanese command had decided to either reinforce New Britain, or pull troops out during the storm. Bodies of Japanese Marines and sailors were floating over miles of open ocean. Most of them had already been ravaged by sharks as body parts floated everywhere. Near the island of Balvan, they discovered an overturned landing craft stuck on a sand bar. Farther to the north, near Rambutyo, they found another landing craft grounded on a coral reef with the starboard side ripped loose from the deck plates. It had either been involved in a major collision, or it might have been tossed by the high waves into the coral reef and ripped apart. Either way, it appeared there were no survivors to be found.

As they turned toward the west, a B-17 flying reconnaissance over the Bismarck Sea reported an overturned medium size barge floating about two hundred miles due east of Rambutyo with no survivors in sight. Buzz felt sick when he thought about the slaughter that took place in the Bismarck Sea without a shot being fired. True, they were the enemy, but none of those men had any chance of survival in such a tremendous storm, especially in the midst of shark infested waters.

After completing a patrol through the northern islands, Buzz sailed south toward Sisi Island located just off the southeast corner of Manus. Kowalski reported some type of craft listing hard to starboard floating south of the island. Slowly, the boats spread out and prepared for a fight as Lt. Mews idled the 316 up to the side of the Japanese patrol boat. Every gunner on the 316 stood ready to fight as one of the torpedo men scanned the wreckage with the spot light. Buzz brought the 303 up along the port side, adding his spotlight to the search. Seeing no sign of life, Buzz had Zumwaldt and the .20mm gunner on the 316 boat pump rounds into the engine room to sink it.

As flames began to roll from the engine room, the vessel began to creak and moan as it settled further into the water. As the flotilla of boats sailed back toward Aitape, the patrol boat turned over on its port side and slid down into the depths.

Buzz's first mission as a squadron commander was safer than most patrols were. However, it gave a good indication to the brass at MacArthur's headquarters, that the Japanese were starting to become increasingly desperate, as they attempted to withdraw to a more manageable position.

Several days later, squadron seven sailed from Aitape for the last time, heading north to the Island of Palawan in the Philippine Islands. With MacArthur now in Japan's backyard, everyone knew the war in the Pacific was beginnings its final phase. But were the Japanese ready to accept that fate?

CHAPTER 17
THE PHILIPPINES

The sounds of the Seabee's construction equipment could be heard all around the new PT base on the island of Palawan when squadron seven arrived. It was one of seventeen new bases being constructed throughout the Philippine Archipelago. There was definitely a need for that many bases, as the Archipelago consisted of seventy-six hundred islands, of which slightly over two thousand are inhabited. It would be a tough job for the Marines and Army soldiers that had not yet joined the fight in the Pacific to clean out every Japanese stronghold.

Although General MacArthur had said, "I will return," the Japanese were insisting he would not, and they were determined to keep him out. That led the Japanese to set up bases or surveillance outposts on thousands of islands.

Every day more of the jungle disappeared, as heavy equipment continued grading runways, and using crushed coral rock to pave them along with aircraft parking areas. Two experienced marine fighter squadrons and a company of marine raiders were going to share Palawan with the PT crews.

The marine raiders knew they were going to have to get along with the sailors, as it would be the PT boats that would land them on islands, provide fire support, and retrieve them when it was time to leave.

Since it would be about a week before the raiders stepped foot on Palawan, Buzz kept his squadron busy, raiding islands, destroying piers, blowing up stocks of supplies piled in huts close to the water, and sinking all the barges and landing craft they could find. Every skipper in the squadron was able to turn in good reports as the Japanese were not expecting them to hit so quickly since the airfields were not ready.

On a bright Sunday morning, a large troop transport anchored up off the south coast of Palawan. As landing craft were lowered into the ocean, they immediately began ferrying marine raiders and all their equipment ashore. Several specialized landing ships came closer to shore allowing fuel trucks and equipment for the airfield to be unloaded. Buzz took the 303 along with the 304 and 298 out to sea to provide cover for the landing ships. The last thing anyone wanted was for a Japanese submarine to sneak in and sink these ships with their valuable cargo. By 1500hrs, the ships had been unloaded and were sailing to the south with destroyer escort.

The following morning marine Corsair and Hellcat fighters landed on the new airstrips. By late afternoon they were followed by Helldiver dive bombers and several PBY-5 Catalina flying boats.

Palawan had quickly become the largest and most powerful base Buzz and many PT crews had ever been stationed at. The island also contained a guerrilla force made up of about one hundred natives, and former Philippine and American army members that had taken to the jungle after the fall of Corregidor. They were well armed, well led, and more than willing to fight the Japanese wherever they could find them. Whenever they moved out, they were followed by a dedicated group of women providing medical care and well-cooked food.

The guerrilla force was led by a man named Marcel Castillo, who had been a major in the Filipino Army, and knew General MacArthur well. Japanese General Tomoyuki Yamashita had led the attack against the Philippines and was now Military Governor. Yamashita hated Castillo so much, the general offered a bounty of one hundred thousand Filipino Pesos for his capture. In response to the bounty, Castillo offered a bounty of twenty pigs, twelve goats and a hundred pounds of rice to anyone that could lead his force to the capture of Yamashita. He had vowed he would oversee the hanging of Yamashita in Manila.

Buzz became acquainted with Castillo quickly, as the first mission for squadron seven was to land fifty members of the guerrilla force on Boracay Island at 2200hrs. The landing party would be split up between the 303, 316 and 317 boats. The remaining three boats would provide cover during the landings. After the force was ashore, the boats were to withdraw to patrol the perimeter of the island, avoiding all enemy contact, and return for pickup at 2330hrs.

Major Castillo stood in the cockpit next to Buzz and Lt. Kirkman for the first half of the trip without saying a word. As they passed Busuanga Island, he turned toward Buzz.

"I hear you have been a skipper since the Tulagi days, and have lost two boats in combat. Yet still you remain in the Pacific, why is that, Commander Maddox?"

After scanning the southern shore of Busuanga with binoculars, Buzz replied. "There's a war to fight out here, and as long as PT boats are a part of it, I'm going to stay right where I am."

After a moment of thought, the major said, "What will you do when the Japanese are defeated? What are your plans?"

Buzz smiled as he looked over at his XO. "Well, like most men out here, I have a pretty little nurse waiting for me back home. I'm going to marry her, have a family, and live a quiet life doing something, though that part of my plan is still up in the air. What about you, Major?"

After looking up toward the star-filled sky, he smiled. "Like you, I hope to get remarried. My first wife was killed by the Japanese. Then I hope to be part of rebuilding the Philippine Army, to make sure nothing like this ever happens to my homeland again. Too many people have been butchered by the Japanese for no reason. This can never happen again! Now I will check on my men to make sure they are ready to go."

After the major left the cockpit, Buzz looked over at Lt. Kirkman. "Has to be tough fighting to take back your own soil, and seeing your people slaughtered by the invaders. I can't imagine ever fighting across the western plains, trying to throw the invader back into the Pacific, while seeing the destruction they could have done to places like Los

Angeles or Seattle. Worst of all would be to see your family and friends massacred. What an awful thought!"

Lt. Kirkman scanned the horizon with binoculars for a moment before looking over at Buzz. "Yeah, we can never allow America to be invaded or attacked like that, this war came close enough. No one should ever forget the sacrifice that was made out here to win this damn war!"

Buzz had the squadron muffle their engines as they passed between Mindoro and Panay, as there were several smaller islands they would need to pass by. It was impossible to know if there were any Japanese coast watchers keeping close watch on the channel tonight.

Looking down at his small radar screen, Buzz could see the coastlines of the islands, but there didn't appear to be any vessels moving about. After clearing the channel, Chief Petrovski had the guerrilla team assemble on the foredeck.

All eyes were on the coastline of Boracay, searching for any signs of enemy activity. Buzz hoped the intelligence report was correct and that the sandy beach extended nearly a hundred yards out to sea or they could severely damage their hulls.

With the throttles nearly shut down, the bow of the 303 came to a soft stop about fifteen yards from shore. Quickly, the raiding party from all three boats raced ashore, disappearing into the dark jungle. Opening up the throttles in reverse, the 303 easily backed out into deeper water. After waiting a few minutes to see if there was any combat, Buzz turned northwest, sailing between Mindoro and Boracay where sharp coral outcroppings were a real problem at low tide, like tonight. Buzz could feel the tension among the crew as they sailed slowly between the reefs. After clearing Boracay on their port side, Stockey reported two low flying aircraft at their two o'clock. There was no doubt they were Japanese float planes flying a nightly patrol through the islands.

Buzz backed off the throttles, bringing the 303 to a near standstill as he watched the float planes stay on course, flying away to the northwest. Once they were out of sight, Buzz slowly continued his patrol, hoping to avoid all enemy contact.

Completing a circle through the islands north of Boracay, Buzz turned his squadron south, heading back toward the pickup site. It was 2320hrs. when Kowalski and the chief reported a signal from the shore requesting pick up. Slowly, the same three boats approached the shore, knowing the tide had gone farther out. It was easy for the men to see smaller coral reefs that had been under water earlier. Holding his breath, Buzz brought the 303 to a stop about ten yards farther out to sea than when he had unloaded. Without hesitation, the raiding party charged out from the jungle and into the water.

With everyone on board, Buzz ordered the boats to back out carefully. Lt. Ebersal, skipper of the 317 boat reported he had scraped up against a coral piling on the way out to sea, but was not having any flooding problems. Turning to the southwest, Buzz brought his squadron back out through the islands and into the open sea. With their engines unmuffled, the squadron returned to their base on the southern coast of Palawan.

Major Castillo reported to Captain Reddings that the mission had gone off as planned, and they had picked up all the intelligence they were hoping for. Buzz reported that the 317 had scraped paint from the hull but otherwise all boats returned intact. Two days later, squadron seven, along with two landing craft left Palawan at 2030hrs, for a return trip to Boracay.

However, tonight as they began their run through the channel, a Japanese float plane slipped down out of the clouds dropping a hundred-pound bomb near one of the landing crafts. Luckily, the bomb dropped far to the right without causing any damage. Every gun in the squadron opened fire on the float plane as the pilot attempted to pull back up into the clouds. But the pilot was unlucky, and moments later the plane exploded in a ball of fire, dropping debris over one of the small islands.

Major Castillo was noticeably upset that every island nearby was now fully aware that a flotilla with landing craft was in the area. He stood stoically on the back of the landing craft next to the boatswain scanning the south shore of Boracay. When the convoy reached the landing beach, Buzz notified the boatswains to go ashore as all six PT boats sat off shore ready to supply fire if needed.

The one hundred men from Major Castillo's guerrilla unit ran ashore, pulling two 37mm anti-tank guns with them. The landing craft, along with boats 298, 304 and 312, stood off shore waiting for recovery, while Buzz took the 316 and 317 with him up the west coast of the island to supply fire power for the raiders.

At 2345hrs, the raiders struck a Japanese supply base near the northwest corner of the island. Buzz could hear the crumpf, crumpf, crumpf, of the 37mm. guns as they engaged targets. Fires popped up around the base, allowing the boats to make out targets they could attack. The machine guns and 20mm cannons quickly added their strength to the fight. By now it appeared the entire corner of the island was on fire, as small explosions from stock piles of fuel and ammunition bunkers exploded.

Two trucks parked on the small wharf loaded with fuel were attacked by the PT boats. Seconds later they burst into flames, ripping out a large section of the wharf. In the light of the flames, Lt. Mews pointed out a medium sized barge that had been set afloat when the trucks exploded. Immediately, the .20mm gunners took the barge under fire. In short order the fuel tanks ruptured sending a large ball of fire skyward. As the raiders withdrew into the jungle and the PT boats turned to leave, the burning stern of the barge settled down onto a large reef with its propellers facing skyward. Slowly the bow settled on the sandy bottom of the beach, signaling a clear sign of victory for the PT crews.

Arriving back at the landing beach, the raiders were already moving quickly toward the landing craft with their cannons in tow, while gunners on the PT boats fired at Japanese marines attempting to stop the getaway. Three minutes after going ashore to pick up the marines, the landing crafts were backing away from the beaches toward the protection of the PT boats.

Realizing every Japanese unit from the Philippines to Tokyo was now aware of what was going on, Buzz wasted no time bringing his flotilla through the channel out into the Philippine Sea where they could fight if need be.

Arriving back at Palawan, Buzz learned that five of the guerrillas were killed and three badly wounded. Although the Japanese clearly lost many more men, Major Castillo took the loss of his comrades very hard. However, he knew it would not take long to rebuild his force from volunteers on nearby islands.

Without delay, Squadron seven continued making their presence known to the Japanese on a daily basis. They once again were attacking convoys as they did in the Solomon's. They continued landing Major Castillo's men on island after island where they caused severe damage and captured high value targets.

On a dark rainy Wednesday afternoon, Buzz was called into the operations hut by Captain Reddings. As Buzz walked in, he observed the Captain and Commander Esselman from Squadron Two studying a large map that lay across a wooden table. Looking up from the map, Captain Reddings motioned Buzz over toward the table. "Commander, we have a serious problem, and it has to be handled quickly, and by that, I mean tonight, regardless of the weather." Pointing toward Negros Island, he continued. "Two days ago, a specialized group of army rangers parachuted onto the island. Their mission was to destroy a radar installation that was being constructed on the high ground west of Dumaguete, then evacuate the island by submarine the following night. The men were already on the way out for pick up when the sub came under attack by four Vals. They did not sink the sub, but caused some serious damage. The skipper had to submerge halfway before sailing into a heavy rain squall. Some of the rangers were killed, the rest made it back to shore where they were instantly captured by the Japs."

Moving his hand across the map he pointed to a town named Bais, farther up the east coast from Dumaguete. "This is where the captured rangers are being held. Tokyo Rose has been reporting for the last twenty-four hours that they will all be executed Friday at noon. We cannot permit that to happen! There is another group of rangers on their way here, and you will take them to rescue the others tomorrow night."

Buzz nodded his head, "How many rangers are we talking about, sir?"

"You will have three boats carrying twenty men a piece landing on the beach north of Bais. There is a rather good beach there but it's narrow to say the least. We'll have rebels lighting your way in, they know where the reefs are, follow their markers and you'll be just fine. They'll lead the rangers to the stockade where the prisoners are being held. You'll then wait offshore for the order to pick them up. Get in as quick as you can, load them up, and get out."

"Sir, we have Cebu and Bohol islands just a few miles away, and they're crawling with Japs. There's no way we can just sit off shore and wait, we'll be sitting ducks for an air or destroyer attack. We're going to have to leave the area and group up in the open water of the Sulu Sea west of Mindanao. It's the only safe place to be if we're attacked and need to make a run for it."

"Run! Did you hear what I just said!" Captain Reddings replied in a loud voice. "Maddox, you can't run, you can't play cat and mouse. When they're ready to go you need to be there right that damn minute. Do I make myself clear!"

"Yes sir, I understand your orders. But we're going to have seven eighty-foot boats out in a three-mile-wide channel filled with coral reefs. If we have to scatter, we'll lose boats and crews, so I need to ask, sir. What amount of loss will be permitted if we're going to consider this mission a success?"

Captain Reddings walked over and went nose to nose with Buzz. "Maddox, squadron seven has the most experienced skippers of nearly every squadron in the Philippines. If you can't make this work, who the hell am I supposed to send in there? Oh sure, we could bomb the fuck out of the base and just kill them all, and that would solve the blasted problem, but we're sure as hell not going to do that."

Buzz was somewhat taken back by the captain's forceful direction.

They had locked horns before, but never had the man taken that tone with him. After looking over the map, Buzz looked his captain eye to eye. "We'll do it, sir!"

Gathering the skippers together Buzz laid out the organizational details. When he was finished speaking, every skipper agreed it was pure and simple a suicide mission for the PT crews, and none of them liked their odds.

Buzz was called back to operations late in the afternoon to meet Captain Nemke, the lead officer of the ranger team they would be putting ashore. Throughout the discussion, Buzz pulled no punches, he repeatedly told Captain Nemke and Captain Reddings the odds of getting off the island without major losses were slim to none.

Finally, Capt. Nemke held up his hand. "This mission comes from the very top. It was laid out and planned by MacArthur's top brass. There is no arguing, there is no changing plans, there is no walking away from it. We go at 2100hrs. tomorrow night. Have your men ready, Maddox!"

Throughout the day on Thursday, the skippers of Squadron Seven worked on evacuation plans, air attack plans and surface threats. When everyone had their say, Buzz stood up and looked over the concerned faces of his men.

"Alright, here it is men. The 303, 304 and 312 will carry the rangers." Turning toward Lt. Mews, he continued. "Lane, you will keep the 317 boat with you in the Sulu Sea." Turning to Lt. Jake Royce from the 298 boat, he smiled. "Jake, you're going to be my bird dog. I want you to stand fast in the channel between Negros and Mindanao and provide cover for whatever comes our way. You'll need to watch east and west for any trouble coming through the channels. This isn't pretty, but it's the best plan we've come up with so far. After we land the rangers, we're going to move south of Bohol where we have deeper wider water. We can race back for a pickup when the call comes in, and still have at least some room to maneuver if needed." Looking back over at Lt. Mews,

Buzz said, "Lane, you and Ebersal are our back up. Keep your hands on the throttles!"

Thursday evening at 2130hrs, four trucks drove up to the pier where Buzz and his skippers stood at the ready by their boats. Once the rangers were loaded, Buzz turned toward Capt. Nemke. "With all due respect, sir, you are now on my turf and I give the orders here. The skippers of these boats know the plan we have laid out, and they will do as they have been told. We will get you in and we will do everything possible to get you out, regardless of the circumstances. You just do your part and leave the command of these boats to me. Understood?"

Captain Nemke was clearly angered by his attitude, but was also slightly overwhelmed at the sight of the seven boats heading out into the dark South China Sea, with every man at their assigned battle station. Turning to Buzz he nodded his head. "It's all yours, Maddox."

When the boats were about three miles west of the south shore of Negros, Buzz grabbed the TBS mic. "Green Star to Constellation, muffle up. Black Moon, drop off."

Captain Nemke watched nervously as the 316 and 317 turned toward the south and slowly disappeared into the total blackness. A few miles more he watched the 298 boat that had been running aside of Buzz turn east and begin slowing down.

Turning to Lt. Kirkman, the captain asked. "Does Maddox know what the hell he's doing? We're all alone out here now, and we've got zero coverage!"

Lieutenant Kirkman put down his binoculars for a moment and replied. "Sir, the Japs have us totally surrounded, we've got them right where we want them."

Shaking his head, the captain walked up to the foredeck where many of his men were waiting.

Staring down at his watch, Buzz knew they were right on schedule for the landing, and there was no sign of any Japanese planes or vessels. Turning north, the three boats moved slowly through the narrow channel in single file. Off to the northwest, streaks of lightning raced across the massive thunderheads that were continuing to build. At times it was hard to tell if the rumbling they heard was thunder or the sound of artillery. However, as there were no ground explosions, the crew wrote it off as strictly thunder, but kept up their constant vigilance. Passing Bais on the port side, Buzz once more picked up the mic.

"Green Star to Orion, let's begin our run."

Immediately, the three boats turned east toward the shoreline. Chief Petrovski had all the rangers move forward, as Lt. Kirkman pointed out the small lights the rebels had planted on the shore and on three small coral reefs. Buzz closed the throttles on the two outboard engines, using just the center engine to power the boat forward. When the bow slid into the soft sand, the rangers jumped from the boat and dashed through the knee-deep water while following the native rebels into the jungle.

With the rangers ashore, Buzz led the boats to a position off the southeastern point of the island, near where the 298 boat was patrolling.

It did not take long for the sound of mortar and artillery explosions to displace the calmness of the South Pacific night. All along the eastern shore the sound of machine guns and small arms fire could be heard among the constant barrage of mortars. Flares lit up the night sky above the jungle as the marines and Japanese soldiers fought in close quarters, all too often in hand-to-hand combat. By now Buzz was sure the plan to rescue the captured marines had all but fallen apart.

About a half hour later, a call from the rangers to be pulled off the beach came over the radio. Immediately, Buzz led the 316 and 317 boats back into the narrow channel where he knew the desperate rangers would soon be rushing onto the beach. Just as the boats began their slow turn toward the shore, a mortar round landed right above the fuel tanks on the 217 boat. The wooden vessel exploded in a large ball of flame that lit up the channel as if it were the middle of the day. A constant barrage of mortar rounds rained down on the rendezvous point, sending geysers of water into the air.

Buzz had been on the bow of the 303 guiding Lt. Kirkman forward since the guiding flares were no longer burning. When the 317 exploded, the force of the blast had been large enough to throw him off the boat, and he landed about ten yards from the burning wreckage. Coming back to the surface, Buzz could see a man struggling to pull another crew member away from the burning fuel. As Buzz swam toward the struggling sailors, he yelled up to Kirkman, "Get the hell out of here!"

By now, a constant barrage of mortar rounds was beginning to crash all around the waiting boats.

Lieutenant Kirkman spun the wheel hard to starboard and threw the throttles open, heading north up the narrow channel with the 316 boat right on his tail.

Gasping for air, Buzz realized Lt. Ebersal had already pulled one man clear of the fire and was attempting to grab a second man that was unconscious. Mortar rounds continued slamming into the shallow bay, as Buzz and Lieutenant Ebersal pulled other survivors up onto the beach and into the jungle. The first man the lieutenant had pulled away from the fire was his forward deck gunner Wexseth. He had been stunned when he slammed into the water, but was now doing fairly well. The second was Chief Fitzgiven, who definitely had a broken arm and several severe burns.

Within seconds, several rangers came running up to them. A sergeant that had been on the 303 looked down at Buzz.

"It was an ambush, sir, they were waiting for us. The captain is dead, and I'm not sure where the lieutenant is. Last time I saw him, he was attempting to break off the fight and get back into the jungle with about twenty men. I've got fifteen here with me and I don't know where any more of the guys are at! How the hell do we get off this fucking island, sir?"

Lt. Ebersal looked up at the sergeant as Buzz and Wexseth attended to the chief. "Where the hell is the leader of the rebels? How many men does he have?"

"He's over by the beach, I'll go get him," the sergeant replied as he took off running.

Minutes later the sergeant returned with a young man of about twenty years old that looked more nervous than the American rangers. Lt. Ebersal walked up to the man. "What's your name, and how many men do you have in your band?"

"My name is Ramos, I have just ten men with me," the shaking man replied as he ducked each time a mortar round slammed into the jungle.

Buzz angrily walked over to Ramos. "We were told you would have a sizable team of men here to help us. What the hell is going on?"

Ramos looked down for a moment. "Up near Bacolod, Aquino has a force of over two hundred men with mortars and a shortwave radio. But they refuse to work with me as Aquino will not let me be in command. He is a stubborn angry man and I shall piss on his grave when he dies."

Getting angrier by the second, Buzz grabbed Ramos by the shirt collar. "Where do we find Aquino, how far away from here is he?"

Before Ramos could reply, one of his men came forward. "I know where his camp is, my sister is his wife. I can take you there, it's about a half day walk, his radio reaches Palawan easily."

Shaking his head, he looked over at the sergeant. "Do any of your men here have a radio, we need to call our boats."

"Yes sir, give me just a minute, my radio man is on the beach," the sergeant replied as he sent a runner to get the soldier.

Shortly a corporal with a radio came running up to Buzz. "Tell me the frequency sir, and I can dial you up pronto."

Buzz had to smile at the young soldier that still appeared to have a sense of humor. When the radio man had reset the frequencies. he handed the handset to Buzz.

"Orion this is Green Star, Orion this is Green Star. Do you copy? Over," Buzz said calmly.

"Green Star this is Orion, go ahead, over." Lt. Mews came back immediately.

"Orion, pick up Stars and return to Moon. Fill Moon Walker in.

Will be in touch via short wave, plan on two stars for return. Do you copy, over?" Buzz questioned.

"Roger on the copy, will proceed, over," Lt. Mews replied as he signaled Lt. Kirkman to follow him back down the channel to pick up the rest of the boats.

With the boats on the way home, Buzz looked at the sergeant. "We have a man here too injured to do much walking. I will take Lt. Ebersal and Wexseth with me to find the other rebels. Can you take care of my wounded man, and do you have any weapons we can use?"

The sergeant nodded his head. "I have a medic and three wounded men, sir. We can put them all together. I have two Thompson's and an M1 carbine my wounded will not be using, with lots of ammo if that will do, sir."

Slapping the sergeant on the shoulder, Buzz smiled, "That will work just fine."

Twenty minutes later a Filipino named Ernesto, led Buzz, Lt. Ebersal and Wexseth on a trail that rose to about a thousand feet above sea level before dropping down into a lush jungle valley leading northeast. As dawn broke over the island, several Japanese Zeros patrolled the skies, forcing the men to seek cover several times, slowing down their progress.

Around noon, Buzz noticed all the chirping and noise normally associated with a lush jungle valley had disappeared. Even the wind ceased blowing, as if it knew it was time to get out of the valley.

Before any of them could realize what was happening, a large group of veteran Japanese marines descended on the four men from several directions. The leader of the Japanese patrol walked up to Buzz. "Commander, you and your men are my prisoners. You are operating behind enemy lines, so you may be executed per the Geneva Convention Rules you Americans like to scream about. And so it shall be done."

CHAPTER 18
ISLAND FEVER

Captain Reddings was nervously walking on the pier at Palawan as the remaining six PT boats from squadron seven idled into the harbor. As Lt. Kirkman jumped off the 303, Capt. Reddings was in his face. "Son, you best have one hell of an explanation for everything that went wrong, or I'll guarantee you your next assignment will be maintenance of bathrooms on an aircraft carrier up in the Aleutians. Now, what the hell went wrong!"

Before the young lieutenant could reply, Lt. Mews came forward, pushing Lt. Kirkman to the side. "Back off, Captain! You know as well as I do this mission smelled like shit before we even left the harbor. We had a ranger captain hell bent to take on the world with just sixty men on an island that had probably two hundred times that many men just sitting around drinking Saki. You have a high command back in Australia that hasn't got a clue what's going on up here, making plans that aren't feasible one way or the other. They get them rubber stamped by MacArthur's office, send some poor schmuck up here to tell you which way the wind is blowing, you kiss their asses and then send good men out to die, and then you threaten the first returning officer with punishment and everyone is happy. Well sir, you have a mess out there no one back in Australia is ever going to be able to fix, so they'll just write it off and forget the mission ever existed. But you sir, you lost one boat and most of its crew, along with the skipper of the 303, not to mention sixty army rangers. How do you plan to sleep tonight?"

Captain Reddings glared back at Lt. Mews. "Consider yourself on report and no longer in command of the 316. Go ahead and get cleaned up, get some food and I'll have the shore patrol escort you to the brig at 1300hrs. And how I sleep is no concern of yours, Lieutenant!"

As the captain returned to his jeep, the men from the boats stood dumbfounded on the pier. Suddenly, they found themselves with a squadron commander missing in action, their assistant commander headed to the brig, while they were all mourning friends killed when the 317 exploded, and there was nothing any one of them could do about it.

After taking a deep breath and collecting his thoughts, Lt. Mews turned to face the men. After looking at their expectant and worried faces, he called out, "Attention!" When the men had assumed the position, Lt. Mews looked down at the pier for a moment before speaking. "Gentlemen, I don't know how this is all going to work out, but I believe the captain will come to his senses before this day is over. For now I want you all to get some hot chow, get some sleep, and get these boats serviced and ready to roll. Your squadron commander is out there, so when you get the call, go out there and get him and bring Commander Maddox home.

Turning to Lt. Kirkland, he continued. "Kirk, you're the skipper of the 303 until further notice. Take charge and do what Buzz would expect of you." Stepping up to the 316, he shook hands with his XO. Ensign Sturmm, you have not been around here very long, but you are a PT officer and a graduate of Melville. I'm placing you in charge of the 316. If you have any questions get a hold of Lt. Kirkland, he can square you away. Son, take care of my crew."

Before dismissing the men, Lt. Mews shook his finger at them. "Gentlemen, you are all veteran PT crews and I expect you to act accordingly. I don't want to hear of any disobedience or problems regarding the captain." After forcing a smile he saluted them and said, "If I don't go with you to rescue Commander Maddox, I wish you God speed. Dismissed!"

As Lt. Mews walked swiftly off the pier, the men stood silently for several minutes taking in everything they had just been told. Finally,

Chief Petrovski climbed up on the bow of the 303. "Men, you heard our squadron XO, and you know what's expected of us. Now let's get to it."

Slowly, the dejected sailors began walking up the pier not knowing what the fate of the squadron might be.

Showered, shaved and wearing a clean uniform, Lt. Mews presented himself to the shore patrol officer outside the brig at 1250hrs. Saluting, he stated boldly, "Lt. Mews reporting for house arrest and brig time as ordered by Captain Reddings."

The Lt. Commander in charge of the shore patrol looked at the warrior in front of him.

"Understood Lieutenant, and I hate to be a jerk about this, but prisoners do not have the right to salute, or wear rank insignia's, sir."

Dropping his arm down, Lt. Mews nodded his head. "You're absolutely correct, Commander, and I'm sorry for putting you in that position. Get me my brig clothes, assign me to my bunk, and you won't hear another word from me, sir."

Laying on his bunk, Lt. Mews worried about the men on Negros Island and how they were going to be eventually rescued, or if the captain was even going to make an attempt. He was sure the captain was not interested in Buzz's request for pickup in forty-eight hours. It made him physically sick, but there was nothing anyone on Palawan could say or do that would make a difference.

The following morning while Lt. Mews sat on his bunk eating his breakfast of cold powdered eggs and nearly raw bacon, the morning brig officer walked up to the makeshift cell. "Lt. Mews you are to come with us immediately. The captain wants to see you straight up."

Lt. Mews laughed as he chewed on the rubbery bacon. "What's the matter, does Captain Reddings want to officially hand me the iced coffee I ordered with my breakfast?"

The Lt. Commander was not amused by the smart comments he had just heard, or the fact that Lt. Mews was not getting up from his bunk. "This is a direct order, Lieutenant. You will get up, you will grab your cover, and you will come with us, now!"

After placing the regulation service cap that all enlisted men wear on his head, Lt. Mews stood up, placing his hands through the bars. When he was cuffed, he stood back so the door could be opened. A petty officer from the shore patrol helped Lt. Mews into the back of the jeep for the short ride over to the operations office.

Walking into the outer office, it was clear something strange was going on, as there were men there from the naval air detachment. After a several minute wait, a Chief Petty Officer Lt. Mews had never seen before, walked out of the captains office. After throwing his hands up in the air, he turned toward the shore patrol sailor sitting next to Lt. Mews. "Good God man where the hell did you leave your brains this morning. What is this officer doing in brig blues? You best get him back to the brig, get him dressed in his proper uniform, and get him back here before Captain Agnew wants to see him. For Christ's sake, what is wrong you?"

Before the men could turn to walk back out, the door to the captain's office swung open. Lt. Mews recognized the captain as one of the top officers of the naval air wing on the island. The Chief Petty Officer yelled, "Attention!"

Captain Agnew stood by the office door for a moment, visibly angry before returning the salute. Stepping forward he shook his head in disgust as he stared at the handcuffed, unshaven officer wearing the wrinkled blue dungarees that he had slept in all night. Walking up to the shore patrol petty officer that had just entered the building, the captain yelled. "Is this some sort of a joke, Petty Officer? Because if it is, I'm not laughing one bit. Get those damn cuffs off, take him back to the brig, get him cleaned up, shaved and properly dressed, and then bring him back here in an hour. Can you do that, Petty Officer, or do I need to send some of my men to handle this situation!"

Snapping to attention and saluting, the petty officer replied. "No sir, we can get this accomplished!"

Returning the salute, the captain nodded his head. "Good, now get your ass moving!"

In just over an hour the brig crew returned Lt. Mews to the command center in his khaki uniform wearing his insignia's. Captain Agnew was looking over a map in the outer office as they walked in. "Wonderful, this time you brought me an officer I can identify. Lt. Mews, come into my office!"

When the door was closed, the captain walked behind his desk. "Lieutenant, I am Captain Agnew of Naval Fighter Wing 318 across the way. Last night around midnight, I received a message from Admiral Moorhead over in New Guinea. He told me Captain Reddings had requested he be replaced due to health reasons. There will be a flight coming over from New Guinea later today or tomorrow morning with a Captain Robesky on board that will take over the PT base. But for now, I'm in charge and I don't know a damn thing about PT operations. Nevertheless, I'm also aware of a mess that took place yesterday that needs some immediate attention, and you're smack dab in the middle of it. Come over here to this map and give me a quick rundown."

When Lt. Mews had finished his briefing, Captain Agnew walked back and forth the across the office several times, deep in thought. "Tell me, how will Commander Maddox contact us?"

"The rebels told Maddox that this Aquino guy has a shortwave radio. Lt. Maddox told me he would call us in two days with information on a new rendezvous point. We are down to about thirty-six hours right now," Lt. Mews responded, hoping the captain would agree with the plan.

After a moment of thought, Capt. Agnew looked seriously at Lt. Mews. "First off, do you trust the rebels, and can you accomplish the mission with just five boats?"

Feeling a sense of relief, Lt. Mews nodded his head. "Sir, we have to trust the rebels all the time, and hell yes we can accomplish the mission with five boats. Just let us do our jobs."

"Alright then, Mews, you will assume your role as Squadron XO. Who will be in charge of Commander Maddox's boat?" Captain Agnew inquired, feeling relieved that there was a way to clean up the failed mission.

"Lt. Kirkland can handle the boat and crew just fine. And if I may be so bold sir, I would like you to allow Chief Petrovski to be the XO for now. That man knows the crew, and knows more about handling PT boats than half the skippers in this man's navy!"

Laughing slightly, Captain Agnew nodded his head. "Make it so, Lieutenant. Also, I wish to inform you that all charges have been dropped against you, and there will be no mention of what happened with Captain Reddings in your jacket."

Stepping onto the pier from the brig jeep, Lt. Mews felt like he had just won the war all by himself. The men came running from every boat to shake hands with their squadron XO. The skippers explained about all the extra ammunition and medical supplies they had brought aboard, along with a doctor from the hospital that had agreed to join the operation to treat as many injured as he could.

Early that evening, a C-47 Dakota dropped down onto Palawan carrying Capt. Robesky and his staff, along with a reporter and photographer from the New York Post.

The news crew was not privy to the plans for the rescue for security reasons, and were kept busy photographing aircraft and interviewing pilots about their exploits against Japanese fighters.

Back on Negros, Buzz quickly realized there was no way to fight their way out of the situation they were in, and directed his men to lower their weapons to the ground and not attempt anything stupid. As Buzz stood back up, his internal sense of caution unmistakably told him there was someone else out in the valley, keeping a close eye on what was going on, and that things were going to happen very fast.

While raising his hands, Buzz looked at the Japanese officer. "We are all wearing the uniforms and insignia's of a combatant. The Geneva Convention says we have the right to be treated as POW's and that we cannot be executed."

The officer scoffed as he slammed his finger into Buzz's chest. "You and your men were clearly involved with the battle near Bais. You have also been in touch with the Filipino rebels as is evident since you are travelling with one of them. Our headquarters has marked them all for annihilation for the many Japanese they have killed, so being with them makes you guilty of insurgency also. Either way you look at it, Commander, you have given us permission to treat you as armed guerrillas."

The officer directed one of his men to line up the Americans beside the trail as he organized ten of his men into a firing squad. Before another word could be said, the tall kunai grass around the trail exploded in a fury of steel from every direction. Birds shrieked throughout the valley as hundreds of them flew in every direction seeking safety. Buzz threw himself to the ground, covering Lt. Ebersal's wounded chief.

In a matter of a minute, the sounds of fighting disappeared from the valley, as they echoed off the surrounding hills. Buzz slowly looked up as the sound of approaching men caught his attention. One by one, guerrillas with wildly painted faces emerged from the protection of the kunai grass. They kept their weapons pointed at the Americans, until a man wearing an American army shirt with the sleeves removed walked into the circle of fighters. He looked down at his brother-in-law and shook his head. "Tell me, did Ramos let you leave, or did you grow balls and leave on your own?"

Buzz and Lt. Ebersal stood up, holding onto their weapons. Slowly Aquino stepped forward and smiled. "If you are looking for your boat that blew apart in the bay, I can assure you, it cannot be found up here in this valley. What else might you be looking for now that we have saved your lives? And what are we to do with this piece of crap from Ramos's sorry rebels that you have dropped on us."

Angered by the in-fighting, Buzz walked up to Aquino. "Enough of the family feud. We need your help badly and we are willing to help you, in any way we can."

Aquino laughed as he looked down at his nervous brother-in-law. "Well, I suppose my dear wife would be angry if we left him out here to die, so I suppose we should go to my camp." Looking at his men he yelled, "Grab anything we can use!"

About an hour later, Aquino led everyone back into his camp that was about five hundred feet above the valley. The rock formations around the camp made it impossible to be seen from the valley floor below, which made it very easy to defend the base. About a hundred feet above the camp site was a large natural ledge, allowing a man to view the entire valley, and Panay Island across the narrow channel.

As Buzz sat down on a log across from Aquino, he could tell the Filipino guerrilla leader was not in a good mood. After a moment of thought, Buzz spoke up.

"Aquino, we know you have a short-wave radio. We need your help to line up a rendezvous with my squadron. How can we go about doing that?"

Shaking his head, Aquino stood up and paced. After kicking a small rock across the ground, he looked down at Buzz.

"You come to my island to save the soldiers that are most likely dead now. You deal with a snake like Ramos who has no way of helping you. Now you want Aquino to make things right for the mighty Americans. I don't see a way of doing that. You slapped me in the face and said I am not worth dealing with. Now that Ramos has failed, here you are with your hand out. So, Commander, tell me what you can do for me if I decide to help you. Can you get me a place at the table with MacArthur when the Japanese surrender?"

Buzz shook his head. "There is no way I can guarantee you that. Look—"

Before Buzz could finish, Aquino turned and walked away. "Then you and I have nothing to talk about. My men will take you back to Ramos. Good luck, Commander."

Lieutenant Ebersal stood up. "We can get you weapons and food, all you will need, what would you like?"

Aquino laughed. "Weapons? We can get all we want by killing the Japanese, and food is plentiful here in the jungle, so that offer is worthless. Get me at the table with MacArthur and we can make a deal, that is all I want!"

Buzz was getting angrier by the second. Jumping up to his feet, he looked up at the stubborn chief. "Look Aquino, what do you think MacArthur is going to think of you when he learns that you failed to help stranded rangers and PT sailors. He won't want you near him at the surrender table, you will be an embarrassment to him."

Angered by the remark, Aquino turned back toward one of the small huts that had been built along the rock face. Stopping at the door, he looked back toward the naval officers. "You are no friend of MacArthur's and you are no friend of mine. I will rest now, you should be gone when I awake!"

Buzz could not believe what he was hearing from Aquino. Turning toward Lt. Ebersal, he asked. "Well, what's our next move, it's apparent we'll get no help from this one."

After a moment of thought, the lieutenant responded. "Let's find the short-wave radio and make the call ourselves. I'm sure Ernesto can figure out a place where we can make a rendezvous along the north coast."

After listening to the conversation, Ernesto stood up. "The radio is in the watch area above us. I have seen it used many times. But the guards up there will never let you touch it without Aquino's permission. They will shoot you first!"

Picking up his Thompson, Buzz walked near the hut Aquino had entered. Raising the weapon, Buzz fired off a long burst toward the roof. Seconds later, Aquino burst from the hut with a Japanese machine gun in his hand. Glaring at Buzz, the guerrilla leader snarled as he shook with anger.

"You come into my camp and make demands, you shoot into my hut, you insult me and expect my help. Now you have pushed me over the edge. My men will throw you out of my camp and let the Japanese kill you, I no longer care."

Buzz walked forward, placing the barrel of his weapon up against

Aquino's chest. "We are also done, Aquino. You either tell your people to let us use that radio and call for help, or by God, I will kill you where you stand, and let MacArthur be damned!"

Staring at Buzz with fear in his eye, he replied, "I believe you would. However, I feel you have no belief in the Filipino people."

Pushing the barrel of the weapon tighter up against Aquino, Buzz yelled angrily, "I respect the Filipino people and pity them for what they've gone through, and I will do everything possible to help them when I can. But I have no time for a self-serving son-of-a-bitch that refuses to cooperate when the chips are down. Now, you either let us use the radio or kiss your sorry ass goodbye!"

After dropping the machine gun, Aquino nodded his head. "Come with me, I'll let you use our radio, but you must tell MacArthur I co-operated."

"Yeah fine, I'll tell him the next time we have tea. I'm sure he'll be most excited to hear the news." Buzz stated sarcastically.

Walking up the rocky path to the watch area, Aquino pointed toward a small cave where the radio sat. Aside of the radio was one of Aquino's men. He looked at Buzz and Lt. Ebersal, "Who do you want me to call?"

After Lt. Ebersal tossed the man a pack of Lucky Strike cigarettes, he inquired. "Where would there be a good spot on the north coast for PT boats to do a rescue?"

One of the men scanning the valley below spoke up, "Lieutenant, I would recommend a small cove south of Bacolod. The palms hang low over the water and there are very few Japanese in the area. We keep driving them away. Plus, it will not take as long to get the rest of your people there if they are still alive. We can mark the landing site for your boats."

Buzz turned toward Aquino. "Now that is the kind of cooperation MacArthur would expect."

Lt. Ebersal studied his watch for a moment. "If we move at first light to gather up whatever is left of the landing party, we could be back to the cove by 1900hrs. We should have the boats here at 2000hrs. What do you think, Buzz?"

"That's fine unless we run into heavy Japanese resistance, and if that happens it's anybody's guess. Yeah, go ahead make the call."

After the radio man had changed the frequencies, Lt. Ebersal picked up the mic. "Moon Walker this is Green Star, do you copy? Over."

Several seconds later, Lt. Mews replied. "Green Star this is Orion, copy you."

"Orion, will give you coordinates minus DiMaggio's ERA for 1943 on the last coordinate. Need you there by closing time of Macy's tomorrow. Bring entire constellation." After reading off the coordinates the radio man handed him, they waited for a reply.

"Green Star this is Orion, needed help with the ERA but we got it. We'll be there, over."

Buzz laughed as he slapped the lieutenant on the back. "Not sure where you came up with that. I sure wouldn't have known the answer."

Smiling, Lt. Ebersal handed the mic back to the radio man, as he looked at Buzz. "So, you're a Dodgers fan then?"

As they walked back down the rocky trail, Buzz called out, "Bean town, if it's all the same to you, Lieutenant!"

As dawn broke over the valley, Aquino led seventy of his men out of the fortress, followed by Buzz and Lt. Ebersal. Wexseth went with twenty guerrillas to make sure the cove was secure.

As Aquino's men reached the south end of the valley where it drops the thousand feet back toward the beach, they found Japanese beginning to dig in all the way down the hillside.

Buzz sat down with Aquino, "Is there another way down there?"

Pulling out a map, he pointed to an area along the water where the boats had originally landed. "We can access the beach from a small trail about two hundred yards north of us. Once we get down by the channel, we will have to walk along a rock cliff in about eighteen inches of water, less if the tide is running out. It will take you right up to where your men should be. Bringing up wounded will be tough, but we cannot battle the Japs the way they are dug in on the main trail."

Buzz turned to Ernesto. "Do you think this will work, do you know the trail?

After running his finger over the map he looked at Aquino. "You are right, it is dangerous and slow going. But we can probably pull them out right under the noses of the Japanese."

Quickly, Aquino set up a defensive perimeter with his men, as Ernesto led Buzz and Lt. Ebersal down the slippery rough trail. Within minutes, they were standing on a small sandy beach directly below the towering rock cliff. With the tide going out, the men had to walk in water about a foot deep for a hundred fifty yards, before the beach began to rise up from the channel.

Kneeling down behind several large boulders, Buzz scanned the beach before moving forward. It was clear to see the rangers were still in control of the beach and several more had now made their way back out of the jungle.

Quickly, Buzz and Lt. Ebersal walked onto the beach, staying close to the rock wall where most of the rangers had dug in to stay out of view of the Japanese mortar crews. After talking with the sergeant, Buzz signaled the able-bodied men to begin following Ernesto back toward the steep trail. The medic had made up five litters from tree branches and palm fronds for his wounded patients. When Ernesto returned, Buzz sent the ten marine litter carriers, along with the medic and radio operator next. When they were halfway toward the rugged trail, Buzz lead Lt. Ebersal and the sergeant into the water.

It was tough hauling the litters up the trail as it took several tight turns and every inch of it was wet and slimy. Arriving at the top, Buzz was happy to see all the wounded had survived the treacherous climb. After taking a head count, it was clear they had lost eighteen rangers, and failed to repatriate the ten men they originally came for. Taking into consideration the loss of the 317 boat, by his count, thirty-one men had perished for nothing, and they were still not off the island.

Under Aquino's direction, his men broke from the defensive perimeter to begin leading the survivors across the island toward the landing site. About forty-five minutes later, the men dropped to their knees as the sound of artillery and mortars filled the air. It was apparent the Japanese had started their push to clear out the rangers they figured were still on the beach. When the Japanese realized they were gone, they would no doubt begin a major search of the island.

Arriving in Aquino's camp, the tired marines were finally able to get some hot food and a few hours of well-deserved sleep. The normally quiet Japanese encampment near Bacolod, had spread out around the northern section of the valley, searching for the rangers and rebel forces. Several low flying Zeros from nearby Cebu Island were adding to the search, as they flew patterns east to west less than a hundred feet above the kunai grass.

Aquino watched the action with a set of binoculars for a while before turning to Buzz. "You have placed us in danger, Commander. We have not seen this much activity from the Japs on this end of the island for quite some time. All we wanted to do was help you, and now look at what you have caused."

Without saying a word, Buzz carefully made his way up to the lookout station. Sitting down by the radio operator, Buzz asked. "Can you tune in the PT base for a real short message?"

The man shook his head. "Not without Aquino's permission, he'll have me shot if he found out."

Buzz smiled. "Look, what Aquino does not know will not hurt him. In fact, letting me use the radio will help you and Aquino. You have nothing to lose, my friend."

After a moment of thought, the man changed the radio frequency handing the mic to Buzz. Pushing down the talk button Buzz began. "Moon Walker this is Green Star, over."

Seconds later, a voice Buzz did not recognize came back. "Go ahead Green Star, this is Moon Walker, over."

"Tell Orion go ahead as planned. He may want to add fire flies, we have some bugs. Do you copy, over," Buzz replied slowly.

"Orion already planned on that, anything else? Over," the sailor on Palawan explained.

Smiling, Buzz simply said, "Roger that. Over and out."

As darkness settled over the Philippine Islands, Lt. Mews stood on the pier having a conference with the skippers that were going on the rescue mission. When he had finished, he walked back toward the 316 boat where his crew waited for him.

He stopped as he watched a jeep approach the pier. Captain Robesky exited the jeep, followed by Sheila Conroy, an award-winning writer from the New York Post, and one of her camera operators. After exchanging a salute, the captain took Lt. Mews off to the side.

"Are all the skippers aware of what their jobs are tonight? Can we pull this thing off?"

Lt. Mews nodded his head. "The men know what they're supposed to do, and I believe we can get out there, get them off the beach and get back here by dawn. It's not a slam dunk by any means, sir, but we'll get the job done one way or the other. We'll give it all we've got, sir."

Captain Robesky nodded his head. "I can't argue with that. Carry on, Lieutenant."

Before Lieutenant Mews could get to the 316, Sheila Conroy spoke up. "Excuse me, but if you two men are not too busy, what do we have to do so we can go along on this mission. Either me, or one of my camera people to catch the rescue on film? The story is just what my readers are hungry for. And after all, MacArthur asked me to come out here to capture what you men are doing."

Without looking at the captain, Lt. Mews responded. "Ma'am, there are ten to fifteen thousand Japanese out there that would like to see this mission fail and see these boats at the bottom of the Pacific. Once we sail past the northern tip of Palawan, we'll be in Japanese held waters. God knows what can go wrong out there. The only people I want on these decks tonight, are men that can fire a weapon or kill Japs with a knife or bayonet. Anyone else on board will just be in the way and cause us problems. These men are always at the bloody end of the spear and never complain. To a man, they are all volunteers, no one ever ordered them to become part of a PT crew. When these guys die, they usually die alone and under terrible conditions, or are blown to smithereens in an explosion. Most often, their bodies are not recovered so their families never have a grave to visit. So ma'am, when we pull away from this pier, I want to know I gave each and every one of these men the best chance of coming back home. If you don't like it, discuss it with MacArthur next time you see him!"

As Lt. Mews jumped up on the 316 boat, Sheila Conroy looked at Captain Robesky. "He's certainly a rude officer. I could have made his name a household topic back in the states. And what do I get for my efforts, a slap in the face."

Before the Captain could respond, Lt. Mews signaled the skippers to fire up their engines. Miss Conroy put her hand over her chest and stared wide-eyed at the boats. "My God, I can feel my chest throb from the roar of those boats. It's incredible, it's so awesome."

Slowly, each boat backed away from the pier and turned toward the open sea while muffling their engines. Miss Conroy walked out to the end of the pier watching the boats slowly disappear into the blackness. When she could no longer see any of the boats, she turned toward Captain Robesky. "No lights, not even the lit end of a cigarette. My God, it's like they sailed off the end of the earth. What kind of men do that?"

"PT crews, Miss Conroy. Some of the bravest and least talked about heroes in this damn war. And like Lt. Mews said, every one of them is a damned volunteer. To be honest, I wish I were going with them. My guts will churn all night wondering what's happening to those men. And you can bet I'll be standing here on the pier in the morning hoping like hell they all come back," Captain Robesky stated boldly.

"Yes, I can imagine that sending five boats out there not knowing what they might run into is a tough thing to do," Miss Conroy stated.

Captain Robesky looked down at Sheila Conroy. "You don't get it,

Ma'am. I can replace those boats from a large surplus of PT boats coming off the assembly line. What turns my stomach is the loss of those men. That's what keeps me awake, night after night. I have already written enough letters to parents and wives to last me a life time. It's not the boats, Miss Conroy. It's the men that will haunt my dreams for the rest of my life."

Rounding the northern tip of Palawan, the boats began to battle fifteen-foot waves as they raced across the open waters of the Sulu Sea. Each time the bow of a boat smashed through the large waves, a sheet of salt water sprayed back over the boats. Every man was wearing a poncho, attempting to stay somewhat dry as they mentally prepared themselves for the upcoming rescue.

At 2100hrs, Aquino's men began leading the rangers down toward the beach, while Ramos and a few of his men prepared the small torches they would use to light the landing area. Suddenly, Ernesto came running down the hill toward the beach. "Small Jap tanks, two of them, with about a hundred infantry coming south down the dirt road above the beach!"

Buzz ran up the steep embankment with about thirty of Aquino's men. They laid down in the tall grass, watching the column cautiously move down the narrow jungle road, as several men set up a captured Japanese Nambu light machine gun and a type 92 heavy machine gun.

Buzz was next to a man named Salizar, that was second in command to Aquino. After a moment of thought, Salizar said. "That road is very narrow and the sand very lose. If we blow the first tank, the second cannot go to the right to bypass it, because it will roll down the hill onto the beach. If it goes left around the burning tank, it will surely get caught up in the muck and get stuck. What do you want us to do?"

"Those are type 95 Ha-Go tanks. Their armor is very light. If your anti-tank gunner can hit the lead tank in the turret near the cannon, that thing will go up like the fourth of July," Buzz explained.

Salizar looked at Buzz, rather confused. "Like the fourth of July? What are you talking about, Commander?"

Buzz had to laugh when he realized he was talking to a man that had no idea about American history. "I mean it will blow the hell out of the tank and we'll get a real fireworks display."

Salizar nodded his head and smiled as he motioned for a man with a Japanese anti-tank weapon to come forward. After Salizar explained what he wanted done, he turned toward Buzz. "If he backs up and tries to leave, we can try another anti-tank round. By that time the machine guns and my men should be able to do considerable damage to the infantry."

Buzz nodded his head as he slapped Salizar on the back. "Sounds like a plan to me."

When the tanks were about fifteen yards away, Salizar tapped his gunner on his shoulder. The rocket screamed from the weapon, slamming into the tank directly beside the cannon. The explosion tore a hole in the turret, igniting the ammunition. Slowly, the rolling inferno came to a stop with half the turret missing. The commander of the second tank had his driver back up several feet, before attempting to circle to the left around the burning wreck. Water and muck flew from the rear of the tank as the driver continued pouring power to the mud filled tracks. With a loud bang, the track on the right side disintegrated, sending a shower of steel flying rearward into the infantry behind. Bodies fell as men screamed in pain, but the angry officers continued motioning their men forward around the disabled tanks.

Since the cannon and machine gun on the stuck tank were still operable, Salizar had his anti-tank gunner fire another rocket into the side of the tank where the tread had been. The powerful rocket once again penetrated the light armor, striking a shelf filled with shells. A massive fire ball roared skyward as Salizar's machine gun operators opened up on the confused infantry.

As promised by Orion, several F8 Hellcat fighter bombers adapted for night fighting, screamed in from the channel, strafing the infantry, and firing rockets into the sand bank where some of the men were attempting to seek cover. Looking over his shoulder, Buzz could see silhouettes of PT boats out in the channel that were beginning to add their fire power to the battle. Crawling back through the tall grass, Buzz began making his way back toward the beach. He had gone about ten yards, when three Japanese soldiers began firing at him from the sandy bank.

Rolling over to his left side, he could see an infantryman hunched over, searching the tall grass. Taking careful aim, Buzz pulled the trigger of his Thompson. He watched the man roll down the hill as the other men began firing in his direction. Buzz returned fire as he attempted to crawl back toward a couple of small trees half way down the steep bank. Reaching into his shirt he pulled out a hand grenade he had taken from a box up in Aquino's camp before they left.

After crawling away from the trees toward a natural depression, Buzz pulled the pin on the grenade and stared over the rim of the depression. Sweat rolled down his grimy face as he glared out into the darkness, not exactly sure where his assailants were at. After seeing the muzzle blast of a Japanese 7.7 rifle about five yards away, Buzz hurled the grenade as hard as he could.

After the grenade exploded, Buzz jumped to his feet running as fast as he could toward the two soldiers. One man was definitely dead, but the second man was attempting to get up and grab his rifle. With a quick blast from the Thompson, the man fell backwards out of the hole they had used for cover.

Turning back toward the beach, Buzz ran head long for the sound of a muffled PT boat that was still taking on the last of the rangers. Grabbing hold of the cargo net, Buzz threw the Thompson up toward the deck as he scrambled up the netting. Reaching the deck, one of the torpedo men grabbed him by the belt pulling him in as he called out. "That's it, Skipper, let's get the hell out of here!"

Buzz leaned against the side of the steel plating protecting the cockpit for a minute, trying to catch his breath. A corpsman knelt down beside Buzz and began looking him over.

"You hit, Commander? Anything I can do for you?" he inquired.

Buzz shook his head. "No, I'm fine Corpsman, just out of breath. Do you know the number of the boat we're on?"

"Yes sir, it's the 316 under command of a Lt. Mews. Do you wish to see him?" the corpsman inquired, as he helped Buzz up off the deck.

After smiling at the young corpsman, Buzz said. "I can make it from here, Doc."

Walking the last few feet into the cockpit, Buzz walked up to the side of Lt. Mews and complained. "If this were the 303, we'd be passing out cold beer to a fellow rescued skipper."

Laughing, Lt. Mews shook hands with his friend. "Well sir, if you want to join the 303 boat and leave this slice of heaven, she is somewhere behind us. You can jump off the stern and hope she doesn't run you over and make shark food out of you in this darkness.

Buzz laughed as the radioman handed him a canteen cup of water. After taking a swallow he looked toward the back of the boat. "Do you know if Ebersal and the other two are on your boat?"

"They're on the 304 and safe. Ebersal yelled at me wondering if I had seen you shortly before we pulled out. If you want, go ahead and call the 304 on the TBS radio to let him know you're here. I'm sure he would appreciate it," Lt. Mews replied with a smile.

After talking to Lt. Ebersal for a minute, Buzz walked up toward the front of the boat, picking up a small blanket that was laying on the deck. Finding a spot still open near the chart room windows, Buzz rolled up the blanket for a pillow and laid down. Although the boats were running unmuffled and breaking through fifteen-foot swells, Buzz had no problem closing his eyes and falling asleep.

At 0500hrs, a rain squall was just passing over Palawan as five PT boats slowly sailed into a small cove where their busy base was located. Tired crew members stood by the edge of their boats, waiting to jump ashore to secure the mooring lines. With the mooring lines secured, the weary and dejected rangers picked up their gear and left the boats, walking slowly up to their command center. Buzz jumped from the 316 and ran along the pier until he came to the 303 where the crew was still tying off the boat. Within seconds, the entire crew was on the pier, shaking hands and hugging Buzz.

As Chief Petrovski gave Buzz a bear hug he said. "Believe it or not, Skipper, I was the XO on this mission and I never tossed one man overboard. Apparently, all your counseling has paid off."

Buzz laughed as he pulled the chiefs hat down over his eyes and patted him on the back.

Suddenly, despite all the fanfare, Lt. Kirkland yelled out, "Attention!"

Buzz turned around to see Captain Robesky and Commander Esselman walking down the pier. With a broad smile on his face, Capt. Robesky extended his hand to Buzz.

"Glad you made it back, Maddox. To be honest, there were quite a few people on this island that gave all of you up for dead. It's nice to see they were wrong. However, I spoke with Lt. Ebersal before coming over here. He's asked for R and R since he lost a boat and that's to be expected. However, he has asked to be reassigned in a rear area and does not want to come back to action for the time being. So, you'll have to find a skipper to replace him."

Grabbing hold of Ensign Kirkland, Buzz stated. "Sir, I want Kirkland promoted to Skipper, but that will mean a promotion to Lieutenant Junior Grade. Is that possible?"

Turning toward Commander Esselman, Capt. Robesky stated. "Have the orders cut promoting Kirkman. He can take over one of the two new boats arriving day after tomorrow." After shaking hands with Ensign Kirkman, the Captain continued. "Both boats are Elco's, you can take your pick. Tomorrow, you can start scrounging up a crew from the replacements we have on the island. I expect your boat to be ready for combat in a week. Will that work for you?"

Nodding his head, Ensign Kirkman replied. "The boat and crew will be ready, sir."

"Good, I'll hold you to your word. Maddox, that will mean you need to find a new XO, anyone in mind?"

After a moment of thought, Buzz replied. "I'll grab one of the ensigns off the replacement boats when they arrive. We should be able to bring him up to speed in a matter of days."

"Well then, you men can go back to celebrating and get some hot chow. "Oh, by the way, Maddox, Ebersal leaves for Hawaii at 1600hrs, if you want to say good bye to him. You and your squadron are off duty until 0700hrs day after tomorrow when the new boats come in. Dismissed!" And with that, Captain Robesky turned to walk back to his jeep.

At 1530hrs, Buzz and Lt. Mews walked over to the air strip where they found Lt. Ebersal sitting on a bench by the air operations hut.

As the lieutenant stood up, a silver and white Navy C-47 Dakota was dropping down from the heavy clouds that remained over the island. Lieutenant Ebersal shook hands with his friends as he forced a smile. "Thanks for seeing me off. If you haven't heard, after my R and R, I'll be taking a job back at Pearl. I just can't come back to this. I can't sleep, I can't eat, and my hands never stop shaking. All I can see is the 317 exploding into that ugly ball of flame. Those guys never had a chance. I just can't come back here and do it all over again. I don't mean to chicken out on you like this, but my nerves are shot."

Walking out toward the aircraft assembly area, Buzz replied. "You're not chickening out on us. I doubt if any of us would stay if they lost a boat and complete crew in an instant like that. Eb, go back to Pearl and relax a bit. Take some time to work through all of this and you'll be alright."

Standing at the bottom of the steps leading into the plane, Lt. Ebersal saluted his squadron commander. "Thanks for everything, Buzz, you're a hell of a PT man." Looking over at Lt. Mews, he stated. "Thanks for getting us out of there. If there's anything I can ever do for you, just let me know."

Lt. Mews smiled as they shook hands. "Just get better, Eb."

Grabbing his sea bag, Lt. Ebersal walked up into the plane and disappeared.

Later that evening, Buzz walked out to the 303 and sat down on the roof of the crew quarters. He wondered how he would handle the loss of a boat and an entire crew. The hair stood up on the back of his neck just thinking about it. Moments later, he heard Chief Petrovski's voice call out.

"Permission to come aboard, Skipper?"

"Permission granted, Chief. Your company is always welcome," Buzz replied with a smile.

Sitting down beside Buzz, the chief handed him a stick of spearmint gum. "Only flavor they had in the canteen when we got back, but I guess it will do."

Buzz smiled as he unwrapped the gum. "It's been a long time since I've chewed any gum at all, so this smells pretty darn good." After placing the gum in his mouth, Buzz looked at his chief. "So, what's on your mind, Chief. Anything I can do for you?"

After looking up at the stars that were beginning to break through the overcast sky, Chief Petrovski shook his head. "Skipper, we're all getting into the same situation as Lt. Ebersal. We have all seen a lot of combat, and we have seen the ugly remains of it. I thought by now this war would be over. I never imagined we would be sitting here in October of 1944, still fighting the day I met you at the pier back in Melville. Now I hear through the grapevine that a big battle is coming up here in the Philippines, the last big punch against the Japs, and I know we'll be in the middle of it. I'm kind of scared, Skipper. I think my number is coming up, I can feel it in my bones. Did you ever get that feeling?"

Buzz nodded his head. "Do you want to know how many times I've felt that way, Chief? That's exactly why I'm here tonight. Eb got me thinking how lucky we've been for so long, so yeah, there is no doubt our number is coming up one way or the other, but I just can't run from it. I need to do my job and help win this war. But I really am tired of being scared."

Chief Petrovski looked strangely at Buzz. "You scared? Get the hell out of here. You're always a rock out there, you keep us all focused. No sir, I can't buy that you're scared!"

"Chief, do you want to go home? Do you want some R and R? I can get you out of here in a couple of days," Buzz inquired, as he studied the chiefs tired face.

Taking a deep breath, the chief replied, "No, no, I don't want to leave. Besides, I made you a promise at Melville to fight with you to the end. If you're staying, I'm sure as hell staying. Besides, about the time I leave, you'll go off and do something stupid I could have talked you out of, and I'll kick my ass the rest of my miserable life."

Buzz laughed as he punched the chief on the shoulder. "Alright, then let's make an agreement. We ride out the 303 all the way to Tokyo. Then I buy you the best Teriyaki steak in Japan, we split a bottle of Saki and get drunk, then chase a few Geisha girls down the street."

Chief Petrovski laughed heartily as he stuck out his hand to shake on the agreement. "Just so you know, Skipper, I'll have mine medium rare."

Buzz smiled as he slapped the chief on the arm. "Is that the steak or the Geisha?"

Both men laughed at the ridiculous joke as they slid off the roof and began walking back toward their huts. The chief knew Buzz had the utmost respect for women and would never pursue the prostitutes posing as geisha girls targeting the American soldiers. And for the first time in months, Buzz felt like maybe he would get out of this war alive.

The following day, the two PT boats that Captain Robesky had spoken of arrived. Buzz was happy to see PT 323 under the command of his old friend from Melville, Lt. Jake Sterling. The second boat, PT 338 was a newer Elco that had depth charges instead of torpedo tubes three and four. And a 20mm cannon on the bow as well as on the fan tail. Since two ensigns delivered the 338 boat, Buzz took Ensign Holbrook to be his new XO, and Kirkman took Ensign Waters to be the XO on his first boat.

That evening, Buzz and Lt. Sterling had several beers as they discussed their training days at Melville. Buzz was saddened to hear Lt. Doug May had been killed near New Georgia, and Lt. Dick Albrecht had been killed when his boat was sunk near New Guinea. They had been good skippers and top of the line boat handlers, but as he had come to understand, when your number comes up, there is not a damn thing you can do about it.

After a long talk with Captain Robesky, Buzz was able to have the 323 boat assigned to his squadron along with Lt. Kirkman's 338 that was replacing Lt. Ebersal's 317 boat. The captain was aware of several large operations coming their way, and he fully realized having one more boat in Squadron Seven could end up being a blessing. Plus, having a skipper that understood the way Commander Maddox operated would give continuity to the squadron.

Throughout the next seven days, Lt. Kirkman ran training drills day and night until he was sure the 338 was ready to take its place in the fleet. Buzz was along on a training mission when the crew shot down a marauding Japanese Zero north of Palawan without missing a beat. He knew the crew was ready for action, and could be an integral part of Squadron Seven.

CHAPTER 19
MOVING CLOSER TO TOKYO

Over the next few weeks, Captain Robesky only used Squadron Seven for light patrols where they were sure not to run into any heavy action. Although the crews was restless with the reserve roll, Buzz and Lt. Mews knew something big was coming, and they understood the need to keep the squadron intact.

On the night of December 11, 1944, Squadron Seven sailed from Palawan to Mindoro Island. The marines were scheduled to assault the beaches on the west side of the island at 0800hrs on the morning of the twelfth. Since it was a 300-mile trip, and the range of a PT boat at cruising speed was 520 miles, each boat was carrying four fifty-five-gallon drums of fuel on the deck to give them more time in action without having to worry about refueling so soon. Once the island was secured by the marines, the majority of the PT base on Palawan would set up shop near Mangarin on the western coast of Mindoro.

The skippers of Squadron Seven were happy to find all they had to contend with were three and four foot swells all night long. It not only made for a more comfortable ride, but they burned less fuel than expected. They kept topping off their fuel tanks from the barrels, and as each was emptied, the crew punched holes in them and tossed them over board so they would sink quickly and be out of the way, no longer presenting such an easy target for disaster. Arriving near the invasion beaches around 0500hrs, the squadron went to work sinking three Japanese patrol boats, four barges and one small freighter. Two Yokosuka E14Y float planes known as Glens to the American navy, were shot down as they attempted to get involved. Three boats attacked a pier near the town Brgy Ibud, setting five float planes a fire and destroying several Quonset type buildings built near the shore line. The PT boats left the area an inferno as they quickly shot back out to sea at full speed.

Lieutenant Kirkman's 338 boat trailed a midget submarine for a short time before attacking and sinking it with depth charges, about three miles off the coast near Mangarin.

By 0630hrs, the waters off the coast of Mindoro was full of warships of every type. At 0645hrs, battleships and cruisers began sending in a barrage of steel to destroy enemy emplacements all along the coast and farther inland. When the barrage lifted at 0745hrs, tracked amphibious vehicles, known as amtracks, rolled ashore, delivering American marines to their assigned beaches. As the marines pushed inland, tank landing ships approached the beaches, unloading M-4 Sherman tanks, and other rolling stock, all filled with the tools of war.

As the invasion continued, Buzz had his boats patrolling the waters around the fleet, watching for submarines or Japanese torpedo boats that might attempt to hamper the operation.

The crew of the 303 shot down an Aichi MGA float plane that arrived from the north, and the 312 boat shot down another Glen that dropped down out of the clouds, making a torpedo run toward a heavy cruiser. One by one, the boats refueled from a seaplane tender that had accompanied the fleet. The crew found it much easier to accomplish the task then idling up against a tanker as in the past.

Unloading continued all night long putting thousands of men ashore along with countless tons of supplies. Throughout the long night, Buzz had two boats at a time tie up to the sea plane tender and get a couple hours of rest.

The following morning, Seabee's began building a permanent pier near Mangarin where the PT base would be. After nearly two days of nonstop patrolling, Buzz had all the boats tied up to the new pier for a well-deserved night of sleep. A large part of the fleet had now sailed away, and what was left was easily protected by the squadron of destroyers patrolling the waters around Mindoro.

However, around midnight a flight of ten Zeros and five Aichi D3A dive bombers came after what remained of the fleet. One cruiser took a direct hit by a hundred pound bomb on the foredeck, knocking the forward five-inch gun out of commission. A destroyer close by received minor hull damage near the bow from another bomb, but that pilot was unable to escape as rounds from a forty-millimeter anti-aircraft battery ripped off one of his wings. The plane spiraled several times before crashing into the ocean. A third pilot dropped his bomb short of a cruiser patrolling closer to shore. The plane took several hits before the pilot attempted to escape over the top of the PT boat base. However, every gun on the boats was manned and ready. Once the alarm went out, it was a matter of mere seconds before every gunner had the escaping bomber in their sights as they opened fire. The plane exploded in a fire ball as the pilot began a climbing turn to the north. One of the Zero pilots was hit by a five-inch anti-aircraft shell fired by a destroyer that had moved up along the damaged cruiser. The explosion was so bright, it seemed as if the entire bay was illuminated.

As quickly as the attack had begun, it was over. The remaining aircraft turned toward the north heading for their bases on Luzon. It was becoming evident that the Japanese navy had lost most of their experienced pilots over the course of the war. Many of the new pilots made terrible mistakes that quickly cost them their lives. Although two ships received minor damage, the Japanese had lost three Zeros, four dive bombers and eleven aircrew members. Japanese factories were still producing aircraft, but finding men to fly those planes was beginning to become a problem.

Before the Seabee's could finish constructing the new PT base, everything that was scheduled to be transferred from Palawan was sitting on transports waiting to be unloaded.

From their base at Mangarin, crews were easily able to sail the 130 miles to attack Japanese ships entering or exiting Manila Bay, or set up ambushes at night in the narrow channel separating Luzon and Mindoro. There were now six PT bases scattered around the southern Philippine Islands, and they were devastating to Japanese ship movements.

On Squadron Seven's third night attack out of Mangarin, the only enemy they had run into was a float plane that ducked in and out of clouds, but never came within range. Buzz was sure their movements were being broadcast to some Japanese base, but the question was, where?

After passing to the north of the entrance to Manila Bay, Buzz ordered the squadron to turn around. Dropping down to a near idle, Buzz grabbed the TBS radio. "All ducklings, follow mother goose, damage whatever you can and run."

Setting down the microphone he looked at Ensign Holbrook and the chief, "Well, gentlemen, a hunting we shall go." Pushing the throttles forward and opening up the mufflers, the 303 raced forward at nearly full speed into Manila Bay. As Buzz turned to his left to circle Corregidor Island, he spotted an old freighter riding high at anchor. Although the ship was empty, Buzz slammed his hand down onto the buttons for torpedoes one and two. Instantly the two missiles flew from their tubes and smacked down into the water running straight and true. As Buzz spun the wheel hard to starboard, both torpedoes detonated against the freighter. Looking over his shoulder, Buzz could see other fires in the harbor as the skippers were firing on any target they could get in their sites.

Coming around to the northeast side of Corregidor, Buzz spotted a large patrol boat backing out of a pier on the island. Pointing to the boat he yelled, "Get that damn thing!"

Instantly, Stockey, Kowalski and Zumwaldt began hammering away on the rear of the patrol boat. Within seconds, flames erupted from the engine room, and the crew began diving overboard. The crew of the 298 boat that was following Buzz, finished off the patrol boat in short order, blasting holes in the hull. Following Buzz forward to seek more targets, they left the boat a burning wreck along with the refueling station.

Grabbing the microphone for the TBS radio, Buzz called out, "All ducks leave the nest." Without question, every boat in the squadron turned toward the entrance of the bay with their guns still blazing at anything they felt was a target. As the 303 left the bay, Buzz looked back over his shoulder. No matter where he looked, fires were burning and he could see the silhouettes of several ships that were sinking. It was a good way to announce to the neighbors that Squadron Seven was here to stay.

Captain Robesky was excited to hear what the skippers had to say during their debriefing. He had never seen this much excitement from a squadron in a long time. Over the next week, Squadron Seven patrolled the channel between Mindoro and Luzon, while sinking several barges attempting to evacuate soldiers from Boac Island. In the process, they had sunk three barges, one patrol boat, and also damaged a destroyer with a torpedo. Buzz was happy with the way his squadron was working, but what he wanted most was permission to attack Manila Bay again. On December third, Buzz was fully aware that something big was up, but had no idea what it was. All Capt. Robesky kept telling him was that nothing was to get out through the channel leading to Manila, but leave the harbor alone.

So, as had been the custom, on the fifteenth, Buzz led squadron seven back through the channel toward Boac Island, but everything was quiet. he turned south toward a group of small islands where there had been quite a bit of action over the last few weeks, but found nothing.

Lieutenant Sterling on the 323 reported seeing two float planes flying low over the water on a straight east course that would take them to San Pascual. Instantly, Buzz jumped on the idea like a clown takes to big shoes. He knew they could check out San Pascual and the small harbor at Pili as well. The Japs loved the island because of the deep coves, so it sounded like a good place to hunt.

As the sky was slightly overcast, allowing for plenty of starlight, Buzz had the boats cruise in a diagonal line at 25 knots, with roughly a hundred yards between each boat. This gave them the ability to cover a large section of ocean before arriving at San Pascual. Everything was quiet, until the 298 boat on the far-left side of the line, reported a submarine sailing half-submerged running northwest toward Boac Island. Lieutenant Lymon reported he was attacking with torpedoes, with the 312 boat backing him up.

Buzz was confident the two boats could handle the submarine, so he took the rest of the boats forward toward San Pascual, which was now silhouetted against the night sky. Everything appeared quiet along the coastline, so they turned north. Buzz had barely set his course when he saw a large explosion to the northwest, followed by a smaller second explosion, and lots of tracers arcing across the dark sky. Knowing that two of his boats were in trouble, he radioed the rest of the squadron to follow him.

As the 303 closed in, Chief Petrovski stared into the night with his binoculars. He was able to make out a burning PT boat and another boat exchanging fire with a destroyer that was running on a course toward the southwest. Buzz grabbed the TBS mic and said, "316 take the 304 and 323 and get that destroyer, and 338, you follow me."

Immediately, there were PT boats roaring in every direction, with the 316 already firing on the destroyer as they closed on one another. Buzz and Lt. Kirkman ran toward the burning PT boat in the hopes of being able to rescue most of the crew.

Lt. Keppner, skipper of the 312, was just arriving near the fire when Buzz and Lt. Kirkman showed up. Although it was not a great idea with destroyers in the area, Buzz had the chief turn on their big spotlight so they could see what was on the water in front of them, without hitting a survivor. Lt. Kirkman and Lt. Keppner followed suit, scanning the waters with their search lights. The 338 boat instantly observed a raft off their starboard beam. Kowalski sat down on the bow of the 303 pointing straight ahead signaling Buzz to cut back on the engines. Quickly, the torpedo crew tossed cargo nets over the side to help the survivors climb aboard. After a thorough search of the area, it was evident that three men had been lost.

During the rescue operation, everyone heard two large explosions to the southwest, and observed fire on the water. They were hopeful it was the destroyer and not another PT boat. Their worries were put to rest when both Lt. Sterling and Lt. Mews reported firing torpedoes, and both were confident at least one of their fish made contact. Buzz didn't care if they argued all night about whose torpedo did the damage, as long as the ship was gone, that was all that mattered. Lt. Lymon's after action report stated that he and the 312 had become separated during the chase with the submarine. It was during that time that a Japanese patrol boat and destroyer came out of the channel between Boac and Luzon, attacking the 298. Lt. Lyman attempted a torpedo run on the destroyer while continuing to fight off the patrol boat, but that was when they ran into a mine. The explosion ripped a massive hole in the hull of the boat, detonating the fuel tanks. Neither Lt. Lymon or Lt. Keppner, skipper of the 312, could be sure whether their weapons fire destroyed the Japanese patrol boat, or whether the destroyer had rammed it in a hurry to escape the rampaging PT boats. It wouldn't have been the first time a Japanese destroyer rammed one of their own smaller craft to avoid being attacked by PT boats. After finding out there were mines in the area, Buzz decided a raid on the harbor at Pili might not be a good idea after all. The loss of one boat and three crew members was enough for one night. He figured the mines were a result of their attack on Manila Bay.

Squadron Seven arrived back at Mangarin just as the base came under Japanese air attack. Buzz ordered his boats to reverse course and make for the open sea, rather than get attacked at low speed near the pier. Two boats and several Quonset Huts were already burning at the naval base, as well as several planes that had been caught on the ground on the airstrip. Several of the Zeros made strafing runs on the hard charging PT boats, only to find themselves caught in a cross fire they could not escape. Two of the speedy fighters tumbled into the ocean as the balance of the air armada broke off the attack flying to the northeast.

With a large part of the pier destroyed, Buzz had the entire squadron drop anchor about twenty-five yards from shore. They used an infantry landing boat to take off duty crews back and forth to the base. Captain Robesky took in the full after-action report and was satisfied with what he was told. Lieutenant Lymon asked for and received two weeks R and R back in Hawaii. He had been in action just about as long as Buzz, and had just lost his second boat.

Captain Robesky was notified it would take about ten days to replace the three boats that were lost that night, however the piers were rebuilt by the Seabees in just three days.

All the PT crews now knew for sure something was in the making with the amount of fighter and bomber aircraft that were piling up on the airfields. About two hundred front line marines had also been delivered to the island for reasons unknown to anyone, and they camped well away from any other service personnel for security reasons.

All though the boats were kept busy hitting at anything that moved from Panay, Boac, San Pascual and Pili Harbor, Buzz still wanted nothing more than to make another surprise attack on Manila Bay. Every day, intercepted Japanese messages told a story of how many ships were coming and going from the crowded bay, but General MacArthur strictly forbade any more attacks for now.

Once again, Christmas for the PT crews gave them little to celebrate. At 0600hrs, a patrol plane had warned Mangarin of a large flight of attack aircraft coming in their direction from the northeast. Every PT boat scrambled, clearing the harbor before the attackers dropped in from the low hanging clouds. Adding to the excitement, nearly every fighter from the airbase had taken to the skies, hoping to shoot down the attackers before they could destroy everything that was being built up on the island. Buzz watched in fascination as fighters swirled over head in deadly dog fights, trying to out maneuver one another for a kill.

The incoming bombers were the venerable Japanese work horses, land-based Mitsubishi twin engine G3M and G4M aircraft that had been in combat since the beginning of Japan's war in 1937. They were currently making a wide slow turn out to sea to avoid the air battle before making their run west to east over Mindoro.

With little fighter cover around the bombers to keep the PT boats at bay, every gunner on the boats was throwing up everything they had to try and take down the slow aircraft. Several of the bombers were trailing smoke from damaged engines, as a group of ten F6F Hellcats from the Carrier Lexington dropped down out of a rain squall south of Mindoro to assist.

The pilots raced down at incredible speed, firing their six .50 caliber machine guns at the bombers that had no way to defend themselves. Within seconds, five bombers trailing plumes of smoke spiraled into the ocean with a massive blast as their bombs exploded upon impact. Two more exploded in mid-air, sending a shower of debris over the ocean. No matter how the pilots attempted to out run or out maneuver the deadly high-speed Hellcats it was no use. By the time the battle ended, the sky had been swept clean of the Japanese bombers and the base at Mangarin was safe once again. Day by day it was becoming more evident Japan's top air force pilots had been wiped out, as the men now flying the aircraft were very unskilled. The newer pilots were no match for the fast new well armored fighters being produced by America's aircraft factories. The tide of the air war in the Pacific had indeed turned.

To the PT crews that had watched the performance from below, it reminded them of the story they had heard about the air battle that had taken place in the Mariana Islands between June 19 and 20 of 1944. During that battle, American pilots had shot down 300 enemy planes while losing only 29 of their own. It became known to history as the Great Marianas Turkey Shoot.

With the last of the enemy fighters disappearing into a cloud bank north of Mindoro, the American fighters quickly dropped back down to their airfields to refuel and rearm in case a second attack was in the planning. The PT boats patrolled the waters west of Mindoro looking for any Japanese airman that might have survived the onslaught. Only the 312 boat was able to find a wounded navigator afloat several miles from shore. He died from his horrendous burns in the medical station on Mangarin later that evening.

The rest of Christmas Day was rather quiet with just a steady stream of planes flying search grids over the seas to the west and north. Buzz took the time to write letters home to his folks, however he knew that since his brother Josh was home safe and sound, his parents would not have much to write about, if they wrote at all. Of course, sending letters to Connie was the best part of any day. She had sent him a nice box of goodies from Hawaii that was the envy of nearly every man in the squadron. It did not take long for Buzz to pass out the delectable candies and cookies to the appreciative men. There hadn't been much for Buzz to send Connie, so he sent her a bunch of photos one of the men had taken of the 303 and its crew, along with a crucifix Wickman had carved for him from a piece of mahogany. The piece of wood came from a PT boat that had been destroyed by a Japanese bomber while tied up to the pier. It wasn't much, but it was about the best a PT sailor in the Southwest Pacific was capable of doing.

Although squadron seven was operating one boat down due to the loss of the 298, Buzz was extremely happy to receive orders to once again attack Manila Bay on the night of January 3. His orders were to destroy whatever was possible, and also to bring back an accounting of how many major Japanese surface ships were anchored in the harbor or tied up to piers. He was promised the entrance to the bay would be cleared of mines before the squadron attacked.

At 2230hrs. the six boats of Squadron Seven left Mangarin heading due north toward Manila Bay. The seas were moderate with six-foot swells along with a southerly wind of about ten knots. The sky was partly cloudy with just a crescent moon, that should give the boats fairly good cover on their approach, while offering skippers good silhouetting of vessels anchored in the bay.

Buzz was having a hard time keeping his composure as the 303 sliced easily through the dark waves. With the boats running a parallel line across the open ocean, Buzz could see each one of them as he looked from left to right. His heart was pounding like the well lubricated Packard engines that drove the sleek well-armed boats across the surface of the ocean. Forty minutes more and they would be attacking what was left of the pride of the Japanese commerce fleet. Buzz felt the tenseness of his crew as they waited to unleash their weapons in a fury of fire and steel. Every battle they had fought since Tulagi had been a lead up to tonight, and Buzz was not going to allow anything to stop his squadron from giving the Japanese one more solid taste of the devil boats they hated so much.

Ensign Holbrook and Chief Petrovski cautiously scanned the entrance to the bay with their binoculars, looking for the all clear from the partisans that had cleared the mines. Where was the signal? Had the Japanese killed the partisans and set a trap for the PT boats? Were the partisans unable to remove the heavy mines? Buzz's head swam with thoughts of failure, boats burning on the water, his crew swimming for their life in the shark infested waters. Where was the signal? Where the hell was the damn signal?

Just as Buzz was about to turn west and abort the mission, Chief Petrovski yelled out, "I see it, c-l-e-a-r!" Turning to Buzz he said, "Let's send the sons-a-bitches straight to hell, Skipper!"

Buzz immediate swung the wheel hard to starboard as he picked up the TBS radio handset. "Attack! Repeat, attack!"

Buzz hugged the west side of the harbor, looking ahead at a small freighter that was riding low in the water. Not wanting to be out of torpedoes too quickly, he decided to fire just one torpedo at the old ship. Number one torpedo flew from its tube in proper fashion, sailing hot and true toward the middle of the ship. As the 303 turned hard to starboard, a blast send a wall of flame and broken steel sheets skyward. Racing toward the northeast, Ensign Holbrook pointed toward a submarine that was making for the mouth of the bay. Nearly laying the 303 over on its port side, Buzz spun the wheel as hard as he could, but realized he was going to come up too short to fire torpedoes.

Zumwaldt hammered the conning tower of the sub with his 20mm cannon, ripping lose several pieces of the steel plating. Buzz flew past the submarine as if he were riding a thoroughbred race horse. He circled back toward Corregidor, hoping to gain enough space for a torpedo attack. Once more spinning the boat back toward the northwest, Buzz began his run. But by now the skipper of the submarine realized he could not submerge, so he sent his deck gun crew out toward the bow of the submarine to engage the speeding PT boat with their five-inch cannon.

The crew was efficient and fast, as they loaded and fired several rounds in less than a minute. Geysers of water splashed up on the screaming PT boat from near misses as Buzz closed the distance. Kowalski and Wickman began firing a steady stream of machine gun ammunition toward the deck gun until the crew had been killed. As several more men ran to take their place, Buzz hit the buttons for tubes three and four.

Once again, the new torpedoes screamed from their tubes running a course toward the submarine the Japanese skipper could not out maneuver. The torpedoes slammed into the hull of the submarine behind the conning tower, breaking off the rear of the boat with a loud explosion. As the tower settled back in the water, the bow raised skyward, as if it were the head of a whale, then slowly slid below the waves of the bay.

The gunners on the 303 were busy firing at any target that caught their eye as they now raced toward the south where several other ships were already burning. In order to catch his breath, Buzz sailed the 303 out of the bay, circled around Corregidor and rejoined the battle. Ensign Holbrook immediately pointed out a heavy landing ship that was moving toward the north to avoid the attacking PT boats near Manila. Buzz threw the throttles open while gaining quickly on the slow-moving ship. Coming up on the rear of the vessel, Ensign Holbrook watched the gyro. When they were at six thousand yards the young Ensign yelled, "Let her go, Skipper, right up their tail pipe!"

Buzz slammed his hand down on the button, and the motor on number two torpedo sprang to life but failed to exit the tube. All the angry fish could do was shake and rattle in the tube until the motor burned up, and blow the 303 to pieces. As Buzz angrily broke off his attack, Torpedo-men Lopez and Rice scrambled to shut down the screaming motor before the missile could explode.

With a Japanese patrol boat closing on the 303, Buzz had to keep moving to avoid rounds from the three-inch cannon on the foredeck of the hard charging attack vessel. With the torpedo now dead in the tube, and Zumwaldt throwing 20 mm shells at the patrol boat, Buzz spun hard to port to get around a burning freighter. As the 303 screamed alongside the burning ship, Buzz looked back over his shoulder to see if the patrol boat was following him. Happily, the skipper of the patrol boat had failed to follow him, which meant when he was able to swing around the burning ship, he would be able to engage the patrol boat on his own terms.

Completing his high-speed circle around the burning vessel, Buzz came back over to the starboard side of the ship, where the patrol boat was just beginning to make a turn toward the west

Throwing the throttles forward, the 303 charged toward the side of the patrol boat with all three of his machine gunners strafing the side of the boat from stem to stern. As Buzz made a slight turn to the west to parallel the now damaged vessel, Zumwaldt as usual pumped 20mm shells into the hull around the engine room.

Smoke began billowing from the rear of the vessel as flames quickly shot out of the engine room vents. As the crew dove off the burning patrol boat, Buzz turned back toward Corregidor and grabbed the TBS hand set. "Break off, break off, time to leave!"

As the 303 idled outside the bay, Buzz watched nervously to see if all his boats were going to get out alright. First came the 338 followed by the 323 and the 316. Lt. Keppner on the 312 boat was sailing slowly alongside the 304 boat that had sustained severe damage to the rear port quarter, disabling one engine. As the boats surrounded the damaged 304 for the slow trip back home, Buzz learned that six of the crew had been killed, one of them being the executive officer.

Captain Robesky sat nervously in his jeep, alongside Sheila Conroy from the New York Post. Per Mac Arthur's orders, she had once again been allowed to move forward to a new PT base. Several ambulances from the base hospital were also beginning to arrive at the pier after hearing of the damage to PT 304. After much anxiety, everyone on the pier could hear the sound of unmuffled engines coming toward them through the thick fog. All at once the silhouettes of six cautiously moving PT boats broke through the heavy fog bank that had shut down air operations on Mindoro most of the night. Within seconds, six spotlights lit up the pier as if it were mid-day. One by one the tired skippers idled their boats up to the pier, as crew members jumped off to secure their vessels.

Corpsmen and nurses from the hospital ran up to the 304 boat to help unload the wounded and dead, as several other walking wounded from the 323 made their way toward the ambulances.

Finally, Captain Robesky jumped out of the jeep and walked among the crew members, shaking hands, and patting many of them on the back. Arriving near the 303 he shook hands with Buzz. "Well done, Commander. Reconnaissance tells us you left fifteen ships burning and at least three sinking. We could not have asked for a better outcome."

Standing next to Ensign Holbrook, Buzz responded, "We counted six destroyers and two cruisers in the bay. Two of the destroyers were burning when we left and we strafed the deck of one cruiser several times, so it must have some damage. Other than that, there were no other major combat ships in the bay. Nearly every other ship we saw were landing vessels or cargo ships. The 303 did sink a submarine near the north end of the bay. Both Lt. Sterling and I had one misfire torpedo. The 304 took a five-inch shell hit on the port rear quarter. Six men were killed and three more were wounded. The torpedo tube is wrecked and the 20mm was pretty well damaged. Number one engine is gone, a large piece of shrapnel damaged the engine block. But she can be fixed, she still floats. The 323 has some damage to the starboard .50 gun tub, but not bad enough to keep her out of service. Everyone did their job out there tonight, Captain. I'm really proud of Squadron Seven."

Taking Buzz by the arm, the two men walked some distance away from all the listening ears. "Commander, we need to get as many of these boats back into action mechanically and with crews by the fifth. At 0800hrs. on the ninth, marines are going to storm the beaches of Lingayan Gulf. We'll need to have as many boats as possible ready to fight off Japanese resistance. This is top secret so nobody is to know what's happening. All they need to know is that every boat needs to be ready in less than thirty-six hours. You'll be fueling from a tanker and stay on scene until relieved. Make it happen."

As Capt. Robesky walked off, Buzz shook his head. The crews were tired, torpedoes needed to be loaded while bad ones needed to be unloaded and the tubes checked for damage. Ammunition and fuel had to be loaded, and that didn't take into account making repairs on all the small battle damage done by bullets and shrapnel. Healthy crew members from the 304 would need to be transferred to the 323 to fill vacancies left by wounded men, and now the squadron was down to just five operable boats, and there were no more boats on the way over to Mangarin for the next week.

After a shower and hot breakfast, Buzz set about getting the men busy on all the work that was required before they could return to battle. By noon, the mechanics had pulled the damaged engine from the 304 boat and were preparing to drop in an engine from another boat that had been scrapped.

Number two tube on the 303 had sustained too much damage from the misfired torpedo and had to be replaced. By 1400hrs, a refurbished tube had been installed by the crew, and Crowley had it wired into the electrical system. No matter where Buzz looked, the pier was a bee hive of activity and no one was complaining.

By the evening of January 4, Buzz was able to report that he had five boats in good condition ready to go, and the 304 was about forty-eight hours away from being ready, but he needed ten men to bring the crew back up to strength. Buzz also reported that he had sent the crews to bed so they could get some sleep before they had to sail. He assured Capt. Robesky they would be ready to go.

As Buzz turned to leave, the captain stood up from his desk, "Just one more thing Commander. I have orders from Southwest Command that Miss Conroy and two of her camera operators will be on your boat during the invasion action. I'm sorry, Buzz, there's no getting out of it. You'll have to take her along and make things work with a crowded deck."

Although the idea angered Buzz, he simply nodded his head and replied, "Yes, sir!"

The skippers woke their men at 0230hrs on the morning of January 5 for a quick breakfast, before having them ready to sail at 0400. After idling the 303 out from the pier, Buzz turned toward Sheila Conroy. "We didn't have much time to talk about this mission yet, so here's the plan. We'll rendezvous with the fleet as 0500hrs, off the coast of Luzon near Iba. We'll be in the vanguard of the fleet when they arrive at Lingayan Gulf. As the battleships and cruisers begin shore bombardment, we'll lead destroyers into the gulf to make sure we sweep it clean of all enemy resistance, especially submarines. We'll be moving at a high rate of speed and attacking anything and everything we feel needs to be hit. Your crew can film all they want, but we are not making any special runs for them, and they will not interfere with my men while we are in combat. We'll be taking fire, so you and your photographers will wear the helmets you were provided. They are not bullet proof, but they may deflect bullets and shrapnel. You can hide out down below if you feel safer there, I really don't care. Just stay out of our way and let us fight!"

Before she could respond, Buzz turned toward Ensign Holbrook to look over a chart he had brought along from the briefing room. Angered that she was not able to get in a single word, she stomped her foot and walked back toward her camera crew that was sitting on the deck near the number one torpedo tube.

Buzz attempted to do everything he could do to annoy Sheila Conroy, no matter how much she protested. He was happiest when she insisted to get off the 303 when they pulled up alongside a tender to replenish their supplies. She made it perfectly clear General MacArthur was going to hear about his uncooperative attitude when she returned to his headquarters. However, the skipper of the tender made it quite clear she and her crew were not going to stay on his ship. Due to the fact that he outranked Buzz, the skipper of the tender had the last word. The angry Miss Conroy and her crew would remain on the 303.

CHAPTER 20
LINGAYAN GULF

The size of the fleet was impressive, and Buzz loved sailing up between the massive ships as they made their way to the front of the fleet. After passing the lead destroyers, the five boats backed off to twenty knots so they would not get too far ahead. As the early light of dawn was beginning to break over the horizon, Buzz took a few moments to look back over his shoulder. He knew he would never see anything like this sight ever again in his lifetime. Directly behind him was the battleship U.S.S. Pennsylvania, rebuilt after being heavily damaged during the attack on Pearl Harbor, along with the battleship U.S.S. Colorado, and the heavy cruiser U.S.S. Louisville. In the next row were three more battleships and several heavy and light cruisers. Aircraft carriers, transports, liberty ships and landing ships of all type filled the ocean as far as he could see. He wondered what the Japanese felt upon seeing such a massive fleet today, after being so certain they had dealt America a death blow at Pearl Harbor. What Yamamoto had said on that day became true, he feared they had awakened a sleeping giant, filling him with a terrible resolve. Now this armada had driven the Japanese west across the Pacific, in battle after battle, and again today they were going to put another nail in the emperor's coffin.

Reaching the entrance to Lingayan Gulf, Buzz sent his squadron into the bay at high speed as destroyers and destroyer escorts began firing five-inch guns on targets all along the east side of the gulf.

Four Japanese patrol boats charged out of their base at Santiago, attempting to attack the hard charging PT boats. Quickly, Wickman and

Kowalski blew out the windows on the bridge of the lead boat, killing the skipper and his staff. Lt. Mews on the 316 had his 20mm gunner set the engine room of another boat on fire. In less than fifteen minutes, all four boats were burning or beginning to sink. Buzz threw his throttles forward and attacked two more boats tied up to a pier at Caba. As their crews scattered, both boats became ragging infernos. By now, heavy shells from the cruisers and battleships were beginning to pound the coast, destroying everything in sight. Heavy columns of smoke filled the air as fires raged out of control.

Several Japanese Zeros dove down into the bay to drive off the invaders, instead they crashed into the dark blue waters as thousands of anti-aircraft shells raced up into the clear blue sky.

While the crew of the 303 attacked a sea plane that was tied up to a pier near the town of Lingayan, a Zero came screaming down at them from the north. Quickly, the guns turned their attention from the sea plane to the diving aircraft. Buzz threw the throttles wide open as he spun the wheel hard to starboard and then back hard to port. As he repeated the maneuver again, the pilot opened fire. Several bullets struck the roof of the crew quarters and one of Sheila's camera men. When Buzz spun hard to port the next time, Stockey's machine gun ripped the canopy from the aircraft, killing the pilot instantly. The plane swerved low over the 303 before crashing into the beach about two hundred yards away. Moments later, eight dive bombers escorted by ten Zeros dropped down from an altitude of about ten thousand feet to be met by American carrier-based fighters. The sky was alive with screaming aircraft, tracer rounds and smoke trails from planes that were burning as they screamed toward a watery grave.

One Hellcat that was chasing a Zero flew so low over the 303, that the chief was sure he could see how many fillings the pilot had in his mouth when he smiled. Kowalski wasn't so sure it was quite that low, but he felt the heat from engine exhaust as the plane flew on by.

Several pieces of metal from one of the Japanese dive bombers clattered to a stop on the deck of the 303 after it disintegrated in the air about three hundred feet above the boat. Buzz had never seen a free-for-all like this and it was totally mesmerizing. Moments later, a Japanese type 11 PT boat roared out of a small cove heading toward one of the destroyers that was pounding the coast line with its five-inch guns. Unaware of what had happened to the camera operator, Buzz and Lt. Sterling on the 323 gave chase. Bullets from the machine guns and 20mm cannons ripped hunks of metal and wood from the torpedo boat as the experienced skipper attempted to avoid the American attackers. As Buzz made a run passed the stern, he could see all of the gunners slumped over their weapons. It was clear that the skipper was either still insistent on making a torpedo run, or he was going to crash his boat into an American ship. Buzz was certain the skipper was making a kamikaze run with his vessel. Before Buzz could turn the 303 back for another run, he watched the Japanese skipper being torn apart by a burst of .50 machine gun fire from the bow gunner on the 323. As the dead skipper dropped to the deck, he pulled the wheel hard over to port. With the boat running at full speed, it ran headlong toward the rocky shoreline where it exploded in a brilliant ball of flame.

Buzz and Lt. Sterling raced back toward the cove to make sure there were no other Japanese PT boats hiding under palm branches ready to strike. While Lt. Holbrook scanned the cove, Chief Petrovski grabbed Buzz by the arm. "Skipper, one of Miss Conroy's camera men has been killed and the other has shrapnel in his shoulder, but he'll be fine. She's sitting on the deck screaming she wants to go back to base. What do I tell her?"

As Buzz followed the 323 boat back toward the center of the bay, he replied. "She's in it for the long run. When we refuel, she can get off on the tanker, her damn choice. She wanted to see combat, she had her wish fulfilled. Wrap her camera man up in a poncho and take his body below. We can't have his body in the way back there!"

Returning to the fleet, the crew of the 303 was constantly busy as kamikaze planes screamed into the fleet at a furious rate. The noise was deafening as everything from machine guns to five-inch cannons fired their projectiles skyward at an amazing rate. As far as the eye could see, large puffs of black smoke from exploding anti-aircraft shells covered the sky. Deadly shards of steel from the exploding shells screamed across the heavens, ripping the enemy planes to pieces. Burning and damaged planes fell from the sky, leaving greasy columns of black smoke to cover their death spirals.

But still they came. Fighters, dive bombers, torpedo bombers, float planes, even a few small transports, all weighed down with bombs and torpedoes, operated by pilots hoping to become eternal Gods by dying while taking out an American ship for the emperor.

Buzz and all the men on board the large war ships watched in horror, as trained Japanese kamikaze pilots were able to wind their way through the massive flak field and crash into a ship. Many pilots came in low across the water, hoping to rise up at the last minute and slam into the superstructure of a ship, or become a human torpedo and strike a ship right at the water line. Those were the planes the PT crews were now trying to knock out of the air before they could do any serious damage.

Late on the afternoon of the eighth, Chief Petrovski screamed at Buzz as he observed a Japanese dive bomber coming in about ten feet above the water off their starboard bow. Immediately, all the gunners on the 303 began firing at the screaming aircraft. Buzz slammed the throttles forward while spinning the wheel hard to starboard so the pilot would not have a broadside target for his machine guns, but the pilot clearly understood what Buzz was going to do and turned with him, nearly dragging his port wing in the water. Ensign Holbrook stood frozen behind Buzz, watching pieces of the plane being ripped apart by the machine guns and 20mm cannon, but still the flying bomb continued to close on the twisting PT boat.

Buzz knew he had one move left, and if it did not work, the 303 was going to become a blazing inferno. Spinning the wheel hard to port, the 303 was now racing at 42 knots, directly at the deadly missile. The three machine gunners concentrated their fire on the canopy as Buzz counted down in his head. As glass and the aluminum frame work began to be ripped away from the canopy, Buzz spun the wheel hard to starboard and pulled back on the throttles.

As the bow of the 303 dropped back down in the water, the pilot was unable to adjust to the sudden stop and flew directly over the boat, missing the mast by no more than six feet. Immediately, Buzz threw the throttle forward and gave chase. Kowalski on the bow machine gun hammered at the wing root of the port wing, where one of the fuel tanks was located, while Stockey continued firing at the cockpit. Suddenly the plane's left wing dropped down and struck a wave, causing it to cartwheel across the water and explode. Buzz quickly spun the wheel of the 303 hard to port to avoid the wall of shrapnel put up by the disintegrating aircraft. Bringing the 303 back to a straight course, Buzz screamed past a naval transport. Most of the crew was lining the rail, cheering for the 303 that had just saved their ship from possible disaster.

The marines going ashore had met much lighter resistance than anticipated, allowing tons of supplies to reach the beach long before the planners had expected. By January thirteenth, the majority of the massive fleet had sailed off for other duties, but they had taken a beating.

From January third when the fleet began to assemble, until the thirteenth, forty-nine ships sustained minor to extensive damage while four had been sunk by Japanese kamikazes. It is unknown how many aircraft attacked the fleet, but it is estimated to be well into the hundreds.

Just about every boat in squadron seven had taken some type of damage during the battle, but only the 338 had sustained serious casualties. Three men were killed and two wounded by a diving kamikaze on the eleventh.

Capt. Robesky was extremely happy with the performance of his boats. Squadron seven was being given credit for knocking down at least twenty enemy aircraft. It was entirely possible they had shot down more planes, but in the furious battles that took place, it was impossible to know for sure at times who had shot down which plane.

By nightfall, maintenance crews went to work to repair the damage sustained during the battle. In many cases it just amounted to patching holes from machine gun bullets. Some parts that were beyond fixing were replaced with parts from the 304 boat, as it was decided the damage to its rear quarter was too extensive to repair. During the battle, PT 342 had arrived from New Guinea to fill out squadron seven. The crew that delivered the boat would stay with it, since it was decided the survivors of the 304 would be flown back to Hawaii for R and R.

Although Buzz did not know Lieutenant Makely personally, he was comfortable with the skipper. He had quite a bit of combat experience, and had lost a boat during night battles near Cape Gloucester, where the enemy fought with tenacity while attempting to evacuate troops from New Britain.

Since half the crew on the 342 was new to the South Pacific, Buzz was impressed with the training Lt. Makely was putting them through, so they would be prepared when squadron seven was ready to see action again.

Both Captain Robesky and Buzz were well aware that some of the men of squadron seven were showing signs of battle fatigue. Many of them were drinking way too much and were getting arrested almost on a nightly basis. Fights were breaking out over the smallest things, and way too many men were ending up with injuries that could keep them out of action. As the base at Mangarin was beginning to be torn down for a move to Lingayan Gulf, four members of the crew from PT 316 got drunk and went on a rampage, attempting to steal a small marine transport plane they insisted they were going to use to fly back to Hawaii. When the marine guards attempted to stop the men from taking off, a gun fight broke out, and the aircraft crashed into several trees next to the runway and exploded. One marine was killed and two of PT 316's crew were burned beyond recognition. The other two crew members had been able to jump from the plane before it exploded and ran into the jungle.

The following morning Capt. Robesky put together search crews to find the other two men and bring them in for court martial. Buzz took the crew of the 303 to search the east side of the airfield where an emergency hospital had been constructed. They had no sooner begun their search, when head nurse Commander Beth Bell came running up to Buzz from the back of the hospital.

Buzz grabbed her as she stumbled forward with blood on her uniform and the right side of her face. She struggled to break free, and continued screaming something no one could understand.

"Commander, are you alright? What happened to you?" Buzz inquired, as he finally was able to sit the terrified woman on the ground.

As she continued to shake, Commander Bell looked up at Buzz. "Those two men came into the hospital just before dawn looking for something to eat. They were still drunk as all hell and wouldn't listen to anything we told them. They hit me with the butt of a pistol, knifed a marine that tried to help us, and then took two of our newest nurses out the door with them. Buzz, I'm afraid they're going to hurt those women very badly if they're not captured quickly. Those girls don't deserve this!"

Helping the commander get up, Buzz handed her over to Ed Yamry. "Commander, we'll find your nurses, make no mistake about that. Ed, walk her back and get her bandaged, then join up with us. We'll be heading in a northeasterly direction."

Knowing that the two men were now more dangerous and desperate than originally thought, the crew of the 303 began searching through the jungle as if they were on the trail of the enemy.

Chief Petrovski took point, watching for any signs of the two men as they moved forward. He pointed out broken branches, pieces of cloth, small droplets of blood on green foliage and foot prints in the wet mud. Cresting a small rise about three hundred yards from the hospital, a shot rang out, striking a tree about six inches from torpedo man Ansel. The men dropped to their knees as Buzz made his way to the front of his crew. Looking over the terrain below them, he saw one of the men standing behind a stack of fallen trees, looking back toward him, holding a marine issue M1 Carbine.

After moving behind a tree, Buzz called out to the sailor. "Look, this doesn't need to end up in a gun fight, and no one needs to die today.

Put down your weapon, let the nurses go, and we can put an end to this madness!"

After a moment of silence the man yelled back. "We mean no harm to the nurses. We just want to get the hell off this island and go back home. That kamikaze out there just barely missed our boat, and I could see him smiling as he passed over head. We ain't putting up with that crap again. We've done our share for the war and you know it, we just want to go home!"

Taking a deep breath, Buzz continued. "The nurses, where are they? I need to see them before this goes any farther."

Buzz could see the man conferring with his partner who was a short distance away behind some fallen logs. After several exchanges, one of the nurses came forward with her hands bound behind her back and dry blood on her right cheek. There was no doubt she was terrified out of her mind.

Looking over at Ensign Kirkman, Buzz whispered, "We need a plan and I'm all out. If we attempt to surround them, they'll kill those women in a heartbeat, they're not screwing around and they're not really in their right minds!"

Before Kirkman could respond, the man with the rifle called out. "Commander Maddox, are you still there? You wanted to see one of the nurses, so here she is. Now it's your turn. Have your men drop their weapons, fall back to the hospital and get us a plane to Pearl. We'll let the nurses go when we get there. Their lives are in your hands, Commander, just like ours were out on that damn boat."

"What's your name, sailor? I'd like to know who I'm talking to," Buzz asked, in order to keep the conversation going.

"Don't screw with me, Commander. You know who was killed in the plane, so you know who we are!" the sailor angrily called back.

"No, we don't know who was killed in the plane. When it exploded, they were torn apart and badly burned. We didn't find their dog tags in the wreckage," Buzz replied, hoping the sailor would fall for his story.

After a long pause, the sailor called out, "Stellmach, Gunners Mate

Arnold Stellmach, Commander. My partner is Torpedo Man Michael Ridell. If that satisfies you we're ready for a deal and it better be pretty damn quick!" Without another word, the nurse was pulled down behind the pile of logs.

Buzz turned toward the chief. "Petrovski, take Stockey and Kowalski and see if you can find a way to get around them from our right. Be damn careful, though. One wrong move and those nurses are dead. Those guys are operating on a short string." Turning to Kowalski, Buzz continued. "Give Lopez your Thompson, take his M1. If all else fails, kill them before they can kill the nurses."

After trading weapons, Kowalski crawled back to Buzz. "Sir, I can get in position to take them out as you requested, but when will I know it's time to shoot?"

Buzz smiled slightly. "Fair question, Kowalski." After a moment of thought, Ensign Kirkland pulled a flare gun from his pack.

Nodding his head, Buzz stated. "You may not see the flare, but when you hear the pop, take them down!"

Without saying another word, Kowalski jumped up dashing off to catch up with the chief.

Turning back toward the hill and seaman Stellmach, Buzz called out. "Listen Stellmach, I don't think you're going to get a plane ride back to Hawaii or anywhere else. What you need to do is let the nurses go and we'll work to get you the best deal possible. You're trapped now and you know it. There's about two hundred men out searching for you, and some of them may not be as willing to deal as I am. You need to make up your minds quick before things get worse than they are already!"

Laughing, seaman Stellmach replied. "Get any worse? Look, we know we're going to Portsmith Naval Prison for a long time, maybe even life if we don't get the firing squad. I'm not going home and I'm never seeing my daughter again. What the hell is going to be worse.?"

As Stellmach quit talking, Kowalski grabbed the chief by the arm. He pointed through a break in the underbrush where he had a clear sight of the men and the nurses behind the logs. Quietly, he cut off several small branches with his survival knife before settling into a spot that he knew gave him the best field of fire.

Satisfied that Kowalski was ready to fire when signaled, the chief led Stockey a bit farther to the north, hoping to find a great spot from which to jump in and grab the nurses when the shooting began. However, they suddenly came face to face with seaman Ridell, who had quickly decided to escape farther into the jungle with one of the nurses. Without hesitation, Ridell placed his knife up to the nurse's throat.

"Chief, you may kill me and I don't much care anymore, but if you want to see this lovely young woman stay alive, put down your weapons and get the hell out of my way!"

Stockey backed up several steps, holding up one of his hands as he calmly said. "No one has to die here, Ridell. I know you, we played poker together, got drunk together, you're a good sailor."

Laughing, Ridell looked coldly at Stockey. "That was a hundred years ago. We've been on raid after raid, and killed more of the enemy than some marines do in their whole career. No one cares, no one asks when we've had enough, no one up in those ivory offices back at Pearl give a damn about Stockey and Ridell. No one! Well, I ain't going back out there to fight kamikazes, or be ripped up by sharks or watch men burn to death as we sink their barges. No, no more. Ridell is done and Ridell doesn't care how the hell it ends anymore. I dreamed of going back to Pittsburgh to work in my dad's repair shop and someday take it over. But Jesus, my hands shake so damn bad now, I can barely brush my teeth without making a mess. How am I ever going to put a carburetor back together again? Tell me, what am I supposed to do now, Stockey?"

Chief Petrovski knew in his heart there was no good way to end this confrontation. Slowly, as Stockey and Ridell argued back and forth, he pulled his .45 pistol from its holster and held it close to his side.

As Ridell began to cry, the chief spoke calmly, "Come on, Ridell, drop the knife. Let's get you some help, it's never too late for that."

Shaking his head, Ridell laughed before screaming, "Do you think Nimitz gives a damn? Do you?"

In an instant, Ridell raised his knife, preparing to plunge it into the nurse's chest, but instead, the sound of a single blast from the chief's pistol echoed through the jungle. Ridell fell backwards, dropping the knife as a large hole appeared on his forehead.

The nurse dropped to her knees screaming, as the sound of Kowalski's M1 cracked. Stellmach flew backwards before slamming into a tree. Slowly, his limp body slid to the ground as blood flowed from a massive wound in his throat. The blood covered nurse he was holding scrambled across the ground, attempting to put as much distance as she could from the man that had been about to kill her.

Buzz and the crew of the 303 walked down the hill and came upon the terrified crying nurses and the bloody bodies of men they had served with for months.

Kowalski looked at Buzz, "He pulled his knife and was going to slash her throat after the chief killed Ridell. I couldn't wait for the flare gun, sir."

Buzz nodded his head. "No problem, Kowalski. I couldn't see what Stellmach was up to anymore, that's why I picked you for the job. I knew you would make the right decision."

Using water from their canteens, the men washed as much blood as they could from the nurses. Zumwaldt and Yamry escorted them back to the hospital, while the rest of the crew placed the bodies of the two men on ponchos and carried them up to the small mortuary near the airfield.

Walking back toward the PT base, Buzz walked up to the chief. "You did well, my friend, that had to be a tough decision."

Shaking his head, Chief Petrovski replied, "Skipper, I could see the terror in his eyes. The look of a combat veteran that has seen way too much. I could sense the fear he was feeling, knowing they had gone too far and there was no turning back. Never did I think I would use my pistol against another American sailor, no matter the situation. When I get home, it will be retired permanently. Maybe I'll see if some western museum would like to have it. I don't want no part of it anymore, not after today."

That evening as Buzz sat on the 303 by himself, he wondered what his own breaking point was. Would he have enough sense to walk away before he made any serious mistakes that could get someone needlessly killed. He remembered looking down into Stellmach's open eyes as they placed him on the poncho. Even in death, the brilliant blue eyes told a story of pain, fear and sorrow that would haunt his soul through all eternity. Buzz was happy he didn't have to write letters home for the men involved in this incident. What would you say, how could you ever explain it? Or, did you just send the normal telegram to the family that the President of the United States regrets to inform you, blah, blah, blah?"

Their families would never know their sons, brothers, or husbands had broken under the strain of combat. All they would ever know is that they died on some far-off island with a strange name, somewhere in the Pacific. For sure they would be treated as heroes in their community. They might have a park named after them, or a street in the new housing addition. Maybe if they were really lucky, someone would choose to name the local veterans club after them. It really didn't matter to Buzz, because as far as he was concerned, every young man he had served with on a PT boat since arriving at Tulagi were heroes in one way or another. They had seen more horror and pain than any one person should ever be allowed to see in a lifetime.

CHAPTER 21
THE CHASE

It was no surprise to anyone in the Maddox family when two black Fords parked in front of their home several days after Josh returned from Nova Scotia. The FBI agents were more than interested in everything Josh had to tell them regarding his search for Swenson Bellington. There was a sense of embarrassment when the agents realized their belief that Swenson was still in either Nova Scotia, New Brunswick or possibly even Newfoundland was way off base. The thought of having him back in Maine right under their noses did not sit well with them.

After nearly an hour of give and take, agent Sacks looked intently at Josh. "So, tell me, do you have any idea where Bellington has gone and what his next move might be?"

Josh laughed as he shook his head. "If I had the answer to that question, I would be hot on his trail, but for now he's in the wind and I have no clue as to where he might be hiding. However, I do know this, when he's ready to move, he'll take Angeline with him, regardless of what Mathew Stevenson demands of his daughter. Watch her, follow her and eventually you'll find Bellington."

Immediately, Agent Turner asked, "What's happening with Odessa? Any ideas?"

Josh shook his head. "I know nothing about this Odessa you keep referring to. I don't know what Swenson had going with the Germans, although everyone in Kennebunkport knew old man Bellington was a member of the German-American Bund before the war broke out. It appeared he broke all his ties with the organization after Hitler declared war on the United States, but what one says and what one does behind closed doors can be another thing."

Realizing Josh and his father were not giving them what they wanted, the two agents departed the house, but became a nearly integral part in the lives of everyone in Kennebunkport for the next month.

It quickly became apparent that anytime anyone in the Stevenson family left the mansion for any reason, every move they made or anyone they spoke with was being logged by the FBI and Odessa. It almost became a joke in town since these so-called undercover agents were anything but undercover.

It was about three in the morning on a cold rainy night that Mathew Swenson heard a noise in the carriage house that bothered him. Entering the building, he was quickly subdued and pushed against the wall. A man wearing dark clothes whispered in his left ear. "Please be quiet, I'm not here to hurt anyone, I just want to see Angeline."

Turning his head slightly, Mathew replied, "Swenson, is that you?"

Slowly, the man let go off his tight grip and backed away. While removing a black scarf from his face, the man replied. "Yes, Mr. Stevenson. It's me."

Mathew turned around slowly to face Swenson. He hardly recognized him with a full beard and mustache, plus his hair was dyed nearly black. After taking a deep breath, Mathew shook his head.

"I'm sorry, but I'll not allow my daughter to run off with a traitor to our country. You can promise her nothing but fear and constant running. That is no life for a woman of her social stature. So I'm asking you to leave, and I promise that no one will know you were here."

Swenson shook his head. "I'm going up to her room to see her whether you like it or not. It will be her decision, not yours. If you intervene and cause a commotion, there's always a chance that someone may barge in here and people may get hurt. Use some common sense, old man."

After a moment of thought, Mathew Stevenson backed away from the door. "Go, but don't stay long. We are under surveillance every hour of the day. I'm surprised you made it this far."

Without responding, Swenson ran through the foyer and up the long staircase to the second floor. Carefully opening the door to Angeline's bedroom, he could see her sleeping soundly in the large over sized canopy bed that appeared to fill half the room. Removing his glove, he placed his hand over her mouth as he whispered in her ear. "Don't be afraid, Angeline, it's me Swenson!"

Jumping up from a deep sleep, Angeline attempted to pull Swenson's hand away from her mouth, but he kept whispering in her ear to stay calm. Slowly, Angeline calmed down and nodded her head in agreement, as her pulse raced out of control.

Turning her head to face Swenson, she gasped. "My God, is this really you?"

Smiling, Swenson took Angeline into his arms and kissed her. They held each other for several minutes without saying a word. Finally, Angeline pulled back and smiled as she ran her hand over Swenson's dark beard. "It becomes you, sweetheart. Where have you been and how did you get in here? My father will—"

Swenson placed his hand over her lips before she could finish. "Your father knows I'm here, he'll not cause us a problem. Angeline, I must know. Are you willing to run off with me, although it may not be an easy life for a while. My parents are on the run as well, but they'll finance whatever we need to have a comfortable life. Please tell me you still love me and want us to be together."

Angeline grabbed Swenson, pulling him close to her warm body as she kissed him. "Darling, just tell me what to do, where to go and I'll be there. Yes, I want to spend the rest of my life with you, and no can stop me, not even my parents."

Relieved and excited, Swenson sat down on the edge of the bed and laid out his plan for her to escape. She had no problem leaving most of her expensive belongings behind, as Swenson promised to replace them with whatever she wanted. After going over the plan one more time,

Swenson departed the Stevenson carriage house as quickly and quietly as he had arrived.

Over the next week, Angeline packed three medium sized suitcases with items she would carry with her. She packed them in the trunk of her father's Cadillac behind four large boxes of clothing she was donating to a war charity in Boston that was accepting clothing donations for people in Europe.

Arriving at the warehouse, people were pushing carts full of clothing to the building from every direction of the parking lot. A man in his forties walked up to Angeline. "Madam, those boxes are way too heavy for you to carry, why don't you stack them on my cart." As he helped to pull them from the trunk, he whispered, "Let me put those suitcases in the center so no one can see them."

Angeline smiled as she closed the trunk. "This is most gracious of you, thank you for your assistance, I'll be out of here much quicker than I expected."

Disappearing into the massive crowd inside the building, the man quickly removed the suit cases from the cart, handing them to a woman that was preparing to leave through a door on the far side of the building. After dropping off her boxes, Angeline walked back to the Cadillac by herself, carrying a receipt for her donations. There was no doubt in her mind that the bag switch happened so quickly, no one following her would ever have guessed what was taking place.

Over the next couple of days, Angeline went about her business as usual, taking time to have coffee in The Port Coffee Shop, with two of her longtime friends.

On Sunday afternoon, Angeline and her parents attended a social gathering at the church where about two hundred people were in attendance. Rolled up in her large purse was a blue blouse, a pair of worn gray slacks and pair of sandals. After she was in the building for about an hour, she excused herself to go the women's bathroom. Instead, she ducked into a janitorial closet where she changed clothes. She then stuck her over sized purse in a box filled with garbage. Pulling her hair up toward the top of her head, she quickly rolled up a bandanna and tied it in place, as if she were one of the maintenance workers. Leaving the little room, she tossed the box onto a cart filled with other trash, and walked out the back door toward a large incinerator that was already burning.

Unloading the cart, Angeline intentionally tossed one box past the opening of the incinerator. When she went to pick it up, Swenson pulled her into a rusty old green panel truck that was sitting behind the incinerator. After waiting a few minutes to make sure no one was checking on Angeline, the man that had helped her with her clothing donation in Boston drove out of the parking lot.

Over the next three hours, they changed vehicles four different times, while giving Angeline new clothing to wear. After crossing into Canada, they drove to a small town called La Tuque at the edge of the Montagne Tremblante Park, about forty-three hundred feet up in the mountain.

Angeline was taken back by the beauty of the enchanting place, including the charming home set back about a half mile from a small dirt road. It was the perfect spot to start a new life with Swenson.

Willing to go along with Angeline's plans, her parents told acquaintances she had become ill after the church function and was at home in bed.

However, when she missed her next coffee date with her friends, Josh and everyone else in Kennebunkport realized that Angeline had run off to meet Swenson, wherever he may be.

The FBI searched the Stevenson property along with the homes and businesses of all their friends or anyone that had business alliances with the Stevenson family. A very angry Gerhardt Keisinger and his associates from Odessa, were sent away from the Stevenson home by several rather large and well-armed loggers that Mathew had hired for security.

Josh was dumbfounded by the shear speed with which Angeline had disappeared, but he knew in a heartbeat that Swenson had organized the entire operation through his father's contacts. Now it was Josh's turn and he was not about to lose to Swenson or Angeline.

Although the FBI had downplayed the theory that Swenson had disappeared into the wilds of Canada, Josh was not so sure. Immediately, he handed over fifty thousand dollars to a private investigator from Boston named Ira Cartman, with orders to place their focus on all things Canadian.

Three months later, Ira contacted Josh with a bit of information they had discovered. In a small bank in Shawinigan Grand Falls, Quebec Canada, there had been two large deposits received from the Bellington family, into an account for a Franko Marcel. The named matched several purchase orders for construction materials from a firm in Texas that had planned to ship the materials to Argentina before the war ended. All payments came from Bellington accounts in Oregon.

With that information in hand, Josh packed his bags and drove to Montreal to meet Ira and his team. By the time Josh arrived, it was evident to Ira that the FBI was now poking their noses in the same general direction. Josh was determined to beat the FBI to the take down of Swenson Bellington. Studying a map, Ira was convinced that Swenson was living north of Shawinigan Grand Falls in one of the small towns, using the alias Franko Marcel when it was necessary to leave the place they were staying.

For the next three weeks, Ira and Josh spent time in Trois Rivieres, Shawinigan Grand Falls and Jolliette, without any sign of Swenson, Angeline or any of the Bellington family. Turning their attention farther north, one crew went to Parent, and Josh's team went to La Tuque. By the afternoon of the second day, Josh was about to call it quits when he observed an older Mercedes he was sure he had seen before driving north out of town. Careful not to be seen, Josh stayed back about a quarter of a mile until the car drove onto a narrow dirt road leading back into the forest.

After driving into the forest about a hundred yards, Josh found a spot where he could park and camouflage his car. Grabbing weapons from the trunk, Josh and two of Ira's men made their way toward the long dirt road. They then paralleled the road until they came to a large log home sitting on a hill above a large lake. While the two men kept an eye on the cars, Josh made his way around the east side of the house where he could observe the upper deck and large glass windows facing out toward the lake. From time to time he could see people moving back and forth in the house, but was unable to recognize who they might be.

About a half hour later, the sliding glass door to the deck was opened and Josh was stunned to see Angeline and Swenson walk out onto the deck. It was apparent that Angeline was upset about something, and Swenson was attempting to calm her down. Moments later, a man Josh did not know, walked up to the couple, grabbing Angeline by the upper arm and shaking her. The more he spoke, the more she cried until she slapped him and pulled free. She ran across the deck and charged down the wooden stairs until she was a mere thirty yards from where Josh was sitting behind a pile of tree branches.

Angeline picked up a large pine cone as she walked quietly toward the lake. Every few feet she would look back toward the woods as if expecting to see someone. At one point she doubled back and stared into the forest for several minutes before asking timidly, "Is anyone there?"

Josh held his breath until it felt like he was going to explode. Then, hanging her head, Angeline pitched the pine cone into the forest and made her way back up the wooden steps. Reaching the top of the stairs she leaned against the heavy log railing and scanned the forest. Moments later Swenson approached, putting his arms around her. He spoke loud enough for Josh to make out most of what he was saying. He told her it was best they leave the house and catch a freighter to Portugal the following week, as things were once again closing in on them. It was evident that she was unhappy about leaving her castle on the hill, but nonetheless, agreed to the plan.

When they walked back inside the house, Josh made his way back to his men, and then back to the car. That evening, he explained everything to Ira and the rest of the crew. After listening intently, Ira replied. "We can't wait, we must move tomorrow. I saw Keisinger at a gas station outside Parent this morning, so they're on the hunt. It will only be a matter of time before they catch the scent."

After putting a plan together, Josh laid down on the comfortable old sofa in the room they rented for the night. He wondered what it might feel like to have Swenson in his sites, and how he might react if he came across Angeline first. The problem was, Swenson was not going to go down easy, and he would sacrifice Angeline to the point of killing her to buy his freedom.

The following morning at 0500hrs, Josh once again parked the car in the same spot at the edge of the forest and covered it with branches. Josh, Ira and three men would approach the house from the same direction Josh had gone the day before. The other three men from Ira's crew would approach from the west, after hiding their car on an old logging road.

Approaching the log castle, Josh could see the old Mercedes and a black panel truck parked near the front door, but no one appeared to be moving about. At 0520hrs, with all four doors of the house covered by Ira's men, Josh kicked in the front door. Screams came from all around the house, as the well-trained assault team moved quickly to apprehend or disarm the frightened inhabitants.

After Ira shoved Angeline onto the sofa, Josh knelt down to look at her. "It's over Angeline, whatever plans you and Swenson had, are gone forever. He and his family are going to prison for a very long time. Their wealth will be confiscated by the government and you'll be left out in the cold."

Before she could reply, one of Ira's men threw Swenson into an overstuffed chair near a large stone fireplace. His eyes widened and he began to shake as he looked up at Josh.

"What are you going to do to me? I can pay you millions, you fool. I have more money at my disposal than you could ever imagine. Cut my hands lose and we can strike up a deal. Come on, Josh. What the hell have you got to lose, we've been friends forever."

Just as Josh was about to answer, Ira walked into the room. "Well, besides these two we have the senior Bellington's, Swenson's cousin Fred and his wife, and four armed lumber jack looking dudes that were not quite on the ball this morning. What the hell do we do now?"

Suddenly, the sound of three cars entering the driveway caught everyone by surprise. Josh scrambled to the window, pulling back the curtain. "It's Keisinger and it looks like he brought ten goons of his own. Several have automatic weapons, we are so screwed."

Pointing to one of his men, Ira called out. "Take the women to the store room down below. Tie up Swenson and his father in the hallway. The rest of you look for cover away from the windows and be ready to repulse this mob." Looking at the four lumberjacks," Ira continued. "You men haven't done anything wrong yet. So do you want to die like rats, or end up in prison as accessories to treason against the United States? Of course that can be over looked if you want to fight and help us."

One of the men that spoke English, explained the situation to his partners in French. Moments later, the man smiled and replied. "We shall fight, give us our weapons!"

Josh and Ira felt better now that the odds had turned in their favor. Peering out the window, Josh shook his head. "They're just standing by the front car, what the hell are they waiting for?"

"For us, probably. They know we're here, and they know we've seen them. They're just waiting for us to walk out and talk with them. They don't want to begin the shooting if they can help it," Ira explained, as he turned the safety lever from safe to fire on his M-1 Carbine.

"Alright, let's see what's going to happen," Josh said with a smile. Walking out the front door, Josh smiled at Gerhardt Keisinger. "Top of the morning to you, Keisinger. What the hell can we do for you this glorious day."

"Cut the crap, Maddox. Just hand over the Bellington men and Miss Angeline and we'll be on our way and no one gets hurt," Keisinger replied angrily, as he paced back and forth.

"You mean no one gets hurt here. But there will be bloodshed some-where, right?" Josh stated it so boldly, it almost surprised himself.

Keisinger shook his head. "I was told your brother Brian had the smart mouth and you were not much to deal with. Guess I was told wrong."

Josh had to laugh. "You can't grow up around a smart ass like Buzz and not have it rub off a bit. Besides that, I saw Swenson selling equip-ment to the Japanese and living high off the hog while I was a POW, and he's going to pay for it through the justice system, not at the hands of Odessa. And by the way, you're probably lucky you're talking to me and not Buzz. He probably would have shoved a torpedo up your ass and blown you to kingdom come by now."

Josh ducked back inside the house, slamming the heavy oak door shut, as Keisinger and one of his men fired several rounds that shat-tered a narrow window aside of the door frame. Looking up at Ira, Josh smiled, "Was it something I said?"

For the next few minutes, windows shattered and glass flew in every direction as Keisinger's men fired their automatic weapons at the house from every direction. Ira and one of his men carrying a Thompson sub-machine gun were keeping a close eye on the glass deck doors, waiting for them to make a quick attack. As expected, two of Keisinger's men finally ran up on the deck firing at the glass doors. As the heavy glass shattered and fell to the floor, two of the lumberjacks jumped up, firing their shotguns at the intruders until their weapons were empty. As the lumber jacks dropped to the floor to reload, Josh looked out onto the deck. All he could see were two bloody, shredded corpses laying just inches outside the house.

The shooting stopped abruptly, as the sound of more cars and yell-ing men could be heard coming from every direction around the house. Crawling up to one of the windows, Ira could see FBI agents and heavily armed Canadian Mounties descending on the property as if they were a trained army.

Once they had rounded up all of Keisinger's men that were left alive, a tall man wearing a dark jacket with FBI emblazoned on the chest walked up to the house. "Maddox, this is special agent Warren of the FBI. I know you have a small band of well-armed men inside the house, but I also know you don't want to shoot it out with law enforcement, that's not your style. You want justice and so do we, so let me come in so we can bring this mess to an end!"

Josh walked over to the front of the house, pulled back the sofa that had been used as a barricade, and opened the bullet riddled oak door. "Come on in, we'll surrender the Bellington's to you without any problems." Josh said, as he motioned four members of the FBI into the house.

Ira's men along with the lumberjacks stood empty handed in the middle of the living room with their weapons piled on a large table. Pointing to the hallway, Ira announced. "There are the two people you want the most. The rest are in a storage room in the basement, all un-harmed."

Agent Warren looked at Josh. "Does that include Angeline Steven-son?"

Nodding his head Josh replied, "Yes sir, it does."

Making quick work, the FBI agents arrested, cuffed and removed all six fugitives from the house and placed them in the cars lined up in the driveway. Looking at the loggers, agent Warren inquired. "And these guys, did they work for the Bellington's?"

Ira shook his head. "Hell, three of them can't even speak English, and the guy on the end just knows enough to get by. They were told they would make big money to protect these people so it looked like an easy way to make a buck. Cut them lose and tomorrow they'll be back out in the forest cutting trees and eating beans and beef."

"Alright, they can go, but the shotguns stay here," Agent Warren replied as he pointed to the door.

As the FBI departed with the Bellingtons, Josh walked out into the middle of the driveway. "Well Ira, what do you think will happen to them?"

Picking up an empty bullet casing as they began walking back to their cars, Ira shook his head. "You know better than I do how many of our boys died because of them. Hell, I never made it through North Africa before my shoulder was torn up. But I'm guessing they spend a long time behind bars.

Swenson's dealing with the Nazis as well will really pile on the time. I don't think his cousin Fred will be found guilty of much except being stupid. I'm not sure how Angeline will come out of this, her Daddy has pretty deep pockets and good lawyers. She may just get herself ready to walk into your brother's arms."

Josh laughed as he smiled at his good friend. "No way, I think Buzz would rather have another boat shot out from underneath him than come home to that. Besides, it sounds like he's pretty hooked on a hot nurse he met after the Pearl Harbor attack. Somehow, I doubt we'll see much of Buzz back in Kennebunkport, except for an occasional visit."

Arriving back home, Josh sat down with court officials and court reporters, creating pages of depositions that would surely hang Swenson when he went to court. But in the back of his mind he hoped Angeline would get a swift kick in the butt and be set free. After all, she was nothing more than a spoiled, self-centered young woman looking for the next big score from a young wealthy man seeking a trophy wife. She wasn't smart, but that was a role she was certainly cut out for.

CHAPTER 22
LUZON

Nobody was happier than Buzz, when the new base in Lingayan Gulf on the main island of Luzon was ready for occupancy. It had been a long time coming since they began operations on Tulagi in the Solomon Islands. As he guided the 303 over the waves of the South China Sea, he wondered how many boats had been lost, and how many crew members had died to bring them this much closer to the final target of Tokyo, now just 1863 miles to the northeast.

Luzon had been at the forefront of the war in the Pacific from the very beginning, after being attacked by Japanese bombers on December 8, 1941. It had seen the dramatic hold out of General MacArthur on the island fortress of Corregidor, and his daring escape to Australia with the help of Lt. John B. Bulkeley's tired PT Boats.

Most regrettably, it had seen the heart-breaking Bataan Death March where 66,000 Filipino fighters and 10,000 Americans were forced to march sixty-six miles under harsh conditions to Camp O'Donnell. During the march, it's estimated 2,550 Filipinos and 500 Americans died from abuse at the hands of their brutal Japanese captors. When the camp was liberated again, it was estimated that 26,000 Filipinos and 1,500 Americans died of starvation, disease and torture.

It's unknown how many Americans were able to escape Corregidor or other bases as the Japanese closed in. But many did, and they helped train Filipino resistance forces that by wars-end totaled over 260,000 armed combatants. They were so successful that the Japanese were only able to fully control twelve of the forty-eight Philippine provinces.

The dock facilities in Lingayan Bay were some of the best PT crews had experienced during the entire war. Filipino workers joined the Seabees to construct all the facilities that were required. They were willing to do whatever it took to drive the last of the Japanese from their lands.

Buzz looked on with pride as the boats of squadron seven gently slipped into the new docking facility, and tied up to the new heavy piers.

All around the base, the feeling of final victory appeared to be everywhere with the Filipino people, although every American understood that the Japanese would fight to the very end to protect their homeland from invasion. The crews were surprised when their commanders told them part of their job included keeping captured Japanese soldiers safe from retribution of the Filipino population. The islanders were out for blood, and went to any length to get their hands on any members of the Japanese military. The higher the rank the better.

A week after arriving at Lingayan, Buzz woke up so cold during the middle of the night he couldn't stop shivering. He attempted to cover himself with everything he could find in his foot locker but it made no difference. Just as the light of dawn began to fill the small Quonset Hut he shared with nine other officers, Ensign Holbrook knelt down beside Buzz and shook him until he finally woke up.

"Come on, Skipper, get up, you got a bad case of malaria. Man look at you, you're shivering like an Eskimo and your bed is soaked. We need to get you over to sick bay right now!" Ensign Holbrook stated, as he struggled to pull Buzz to his feet.

With the help of several other officers, Holbrook and the chief were finally able to get Buzz onto a cot in the triage department.

One of the doctors took one look at Buzz and shook his head. "How long has he been in this condition?"

Chief Petrovski shook his head. "Doc, he was fine last night when I dropped him off at his hut. We had been down at the boat most of the evening with the crew cleaning and stocking up all the supplies we had been short of. I couldn't believe my eyes when I stopped by to pick him up this morning."

The doctor shook his head. "This man is too bad off for us to deal with, he needs to go to the hospital on New Caledonia right away. I'll get him on the float plane that's leaving in an hour."

The chief and Ensign Holbrook helped carry Buzz's stretcher to the pier where the plane crew took over the loading process. Before Buzz would allow the medical staff to load him, he grabbed for his XO's hand.

"Stu, take care of the crew and the boat. You tell Robesky I'll be back, and I want my boat back. You make him understand that Ensign, I'm coming back!"

"You got it, Skipper, we'll be waiting for you, sir. Go get well and don't worry about the 303. She'll be here when you're ready to take her back," Ensign Holbrook replied, trying to hide the fear that was growing inside him.

As the PBY-5 skimmed across the water before taking to the air, the chief looked over at the ensign. "He ain't coming back, is he sir?"

"He's lost two boats, been wounded several times, and he's lost at least twenty-five pounds. I have a feeling he'll be seeing Connie in Hawaii long before he ever sees the 303 again. I'll go talk to Robesky and try convincing him to give me the 303. I hope to God he's in a good mood this morning!" Ensign Holbrook replied as he slapped the chief on the shoulder.

Standing outside the operations hut, Ensign Holbrook took a deep breath, he figured he was about to get into one of the toughest fights he had been in since arriving in the southwest Pacific, and his stomach was spinning over like a roller coaster.

Stepping into operations, he observed Captain Robesky sitting behind his desk reading a stack of reports. After straightening his shirt and buttoning all but the top button, Holbrook walked over to the desk trying to show a full head of confidence.

"Sir, Ensign Kirkman reporting in, I need to talk to you about the 303 boat."

Captain Robesky continued reading the reports, shaking his head as he replied, "What the hell do you want, Holbrook? Doesn't your skipper have enough for you to do? Go ahead, make it fast?"

Holbrook was surprised that the captain didn't already know that one of his squadron commanders was on his way to New Caledonia with malaria. He knew being the bearer of this bad news was not the way to start this conversation.

"Sir, just about ten minutes ago, Buzz, I mean Lt. Commander Maddox, was loaded on a PBY-5 for the hospital on New Caledonia. He has a real bad case of malaria, sir."

Suddenly, the papers in the captain's hand flew across the desk as he jumped up and glared at Ensign Holbrook. "How the hell do you know this?"

"Sir, I found him this morning in pretty bad shape. The chief and I drove him to the hospital and Dr. Salisman stuck him on the PBY that was preparing to leave. We were not in the hospital for over thirty minutes before the paper work was signed," the ensign responded as he watched the division commander getting angrier by the minute.

"Salisman, you say, I never liked that horse's ass from the day he arrived. We'll have words when you and I are through. So, I suppose you want to take command of the 303, is that what's on your mind?"

"Yes sir, just until Buzz, I mean, the commander returns. I know the crew, they know me, and I think we could keep everything working as it should be, sir." Holbrook replied, as he noticed his hands were beginning to shake.

"And I suppose you expect to get a promotion to Lieutenant j.g. out of thin air, isn't that right Ensign?" Captain Robesky retorted, with his hands firmly fixed on his waist.

Before the ensign could respond, Captain Robesky kicked the trash can below his desk. "Alright Holbrook. I'll have my Yeoman cut the orders for your promotion. I'll promote Lt. Mews to squadron Commander and the rank of Lt. Commander, and I'll find an XO for you by the end of the day. Now get the hell out of here before I change my damn mind!"

After a quick salute, Lieutenant j.g. Holbrook walked at full speed out of the operations hut, where he found the chief sitting on an empty fifty-five-gallon drum, eating a candy bar.

"What did he say, XO?" Chief Petrovski inquired as he studied Holbrooks face.

After kicking the drum Holbrook, glared at the chief. "Is that the way you address a Lieutenant that has just been assigned as your skipper? Snap to attention, sailor and give me my first salute as a senior officer!"

After exchanging salutes, the two men laughed and shook hands. "We'll have a new XO this afternoon, and Lt. Mews will now be squadron commander with Buzzes old rank."

The chief nodded his head. "I like Mews, he's a lot like Buzz, and it won't take us much time to break in a new XO. Let's let the crew know what's happening, and go talk to Commander Mews."

Around 1430hrs, Ensign Bill Hardy reported to the 303 as the new XO. He had very limited experience around New Guinea, but was excited to be on a front-line boat. After a quick meeting with the crew, Holbrook idled the 303 away from the pier turning toward the open ocean along with Kirkland and the 338.

Buzz did not remember much about the first ten days he was in New Caledonia. He lost nearly ten more pounds and looked like a skin covered skeleton. After hearing one of the nurses tell a corpsman that Commander Maddox was being returned to Hawaii before a trip home, Buzz began searching for a way to get back to his crew. He paid another corpsman to buy him candy bars in the PX, and he figured out when was a good time to slip away from his bed and attack the closed kitchen. Although his stomach protested immensely, Buzz was determined to put on weight and stay in the war. The doctors were stunned and somewhat happy when Buzz had gained seven pounds over the next ten days. However, the senior doctor of the ward did not like Buzz, and knew what he was attempting to do. That evening the doctor approached Buzz as he munched on some ice cream pilfered from the kitchen freezer.

"I know what you're up to, Maddox, I've seen if before. You gain weight by any means possible, I send you back to combat, and then a week later you're sick as a dog and right back here in the hospital. Well, I'm wise to it. So your orders are cut for San Francisco, not Hawaii. You've lost two boats, several crew members, and were involved in several island fighting incidents with the marines. You not only have malaria, but you're suffering from combat fatigue. Your war is over!"

Throwing the spoon he had been holding across the floor, Buzz stood up from the edge of his bed. "Let's get one thing clear, doctor. Not you, not MacArthur, not the president himself will keep me from going back to my boat. My temperatures have been stable over the last week and I feel great. I'm going back to Lingayan Gulf with your help, or I'll do it my way. Which way is it going to be, sir?"

The doctor smiled. "I always like the way you people think you can intimidate me. Well, it won't work, Commander Maddox. Many have tried and all have failed. My word here is as good as God's. I hope you enjoy Lombardi Street commander!"

Unable to sleep because of the conversation with the doctor, Buzz walked around the hospital trying to figure out a way to beat the odds. The next evening Buzz put on his uniform and went for the same walk, but this time he left the hospital grounds, walking down to the water front. As he sat on a piling looking up at the stars, a PBY-5 came idling slowly down the channel docking about fifty feet from where Buzz sat. The medical crew on board unloaded several stretchers, before loading them on an ambulance parked close by. After the ambulance left, Buzz jumped off the piling and walked over to one of the crew members that was washing off the windshield of the aircraft.

Offering the man a candy bar Buzz smiled. "Do you go out every night?"

As the man unwrapped the candy, he shook his head. "Naw, we only head out at night if there is a real emergency, and then we don't go out much past the Solomon's because of Japanese air activity. If we need to go out to the Philippines, we usually leave here about 0400hrs, so we can have fighter coverage."

Buzz nodded his head, "Makes sense to me." After flipping the pilot another candy bar, Buzz walked over to a building that had a sign hanging above the door that read 'Commo.'

Walking inside, Buzz had to smile. Sitting at a radio console was Petty Officer Chuck Pride, a good friend of Ed Yamry. He had been wounded on Rendova when an enemy bomb struck the Commo shack. As Buzz walked in, the Petty Officer jumped up and saluted, then smiled and shook hands with Buzz.

"Nice to see you, Commander, congratulations on the promotion. How the hell is Ed? I haven't heard from him for a while."

Buzz sat down in a chair across from the radio console. "Ed is fine, he's always on the ball and roaring to go. You can't beat a radioman like Yamry."

Shaking his head, Chuck Pride looked over at Buzz. "Man, I wanted a boat so bad. I couldn't wait to get out of the Commo shack. Then that damn bomb hit and messed up my leg. I had to fight like hell to stay here and operate the radios, but a least I'm still doing my part for the war. Would you like a cup of coffee, Commander?"

After receiving his hot coffee, Buzz leaned forward. "Anyway you can call the 303 boat from here?"

Shaking his head, the petty officer responded. "Nope, that just isn't possible. I can contact the Commo headquarters on Lingayan, and they can get a message to the 303. This system is so powerful I can contact nearly any operating base station in the Pacific, including the emperor in Tokyo. I can contact a PT boat on TBS radio if they are within a hundred miles, but that's about it."

Buzz shook his head as he stared at the ceiling for a moment. "There has got to be a way to contact the 303 without going through base Commo, but I don't know how to go about it. If I can't figure this out, I'm plain screwed!"

Petty Officer Pride leaned forward, looking at Buzz. "What's the problem, Skipper?"

"It's a long story, but the doctor in charge at the hospital wants to send me back state side because of my malaria. He won't listen to me that it's under control. If I can't figure a way to get past his order, my goose is cooked," Buzz replied, feeling rather down.

Sitting back in his chair, the petty officer smiled. "So, what you're saying is you need orders sending you back to Luzon because you no longer have a medical problem, along with orders to fly you back to Lingayan."

Buzz laughed, "And a partridge in a pear tree, and throw in ten lords a leaping. Yeah, that about does it. I might as well be asking for the moon."

After asking Buzz all the pertinent information about the hospital, including names of doctors and nurses, Petty Officer Pride smiled. "Skipper, there are a hundred guys like you on this island every month that want to get back to their units, but the medical staff refuses to budge. There's an underground black market medical form operation here on New Caledonia that would make the FBI proud. You can't tell a fake from an original, and believe me, officers have tried and failed."

"What kind of bribe do I have to pay for these documents, and how soon can I get them?" Buzz inquired, as a feeling of hope came over him.

Laughing, Petty Officer Pride replied, "To be honest they're not cheap, but an officer should be able to come up with one of the pay plans. Either fifty bucks cash, five cases of whiskey, or ten boxes of Cuban cigars. The deal is non-negotiable and the papers are guaranteed to work."

Before the Petty Officer could say another word, Buzz planted sixty dollars on the desk. "I don't care who gets the tip, just get me off this damn island and back to my boat!"

Placing the money in his pocket, Petty Officer Pride smiled. "Say hi to Yamry when you see him. Now get the hell out of here and remember this conversation never took place."

Jumping up from his chair, Buzz leaned over the desk to shake hands as he winked. "Thanks for the coffee, Petty Officer Grant, it was nice talking to someone from Kennebunkport again, it really passed the time tonight. Tell your Mama hi next time you write to her."

Petty Officer Pride laughed as he shook his head, "Yes sir, she'll enjoy hearing from you."

Without another word, Buzz left the Commo shack and cautiously made his way back to the hospital. Entering the ward, the charge nurse glared at him, "Commander, where have you been. I can't have you roaming the streets of Noumea. I have half a mind of taking that uniform from you and restricting you to the ward. Now get back to bed!"

As Buzz laid down, he was wondering how this underground form operation was going to get medical orders releasing him from the hospital, and orders allowing him to fly out of New Caledonia on the PBY. He hoped everything would go smoothly without anyone getting wise to the operation. It was going to be a complicated maneuver and he was quickly running out of time.

About 1000hrs, the following morning, a nurse walked up to Buzz. "Sir, there's a Captain Luckman here to see you. He's over in the library."

Buzz had no idea who Captain Luckman was, so he was unsure of what was going on. He hoped like hell the captain wasn't here to tell him his plan had fallen through and that he was in big trouble. Entering the library, the captain looked at the nurse.

"I'm sorry miss, but this is a classified interview regarding a combat mission so you'll need to leave the room."

After the door was closed, Capt. Luckman opened a small brief case removing several sheets of paper. "Commander, this first order is releasing you from the hospital. The signature is real, and it's signed by your attending physician. There'll also be a copy placed in your hospital file before 0700hrs. tomorrow morning. The second order is returning you to active duty with squadron seven at Lingayan Bay. It's signed by Admiral Raymond Spruance."

Buzz grabbed the second paper, glaring at the signature. "Admiral Spruance, really? Who the hell is going to believe that?"

The captain smiled, "Better yet, Commander, who is going to question anything signed by Admiral Spruance. Look, don't question anything, Commander. I owe Petty Officer Pride my life. When he asked me for a favor, I didn't think twice, I got you right to the front of the paper pile. Just make sure you're at the pier no later than 2330hrs."

Buzz nodded his head as he folded the documents. "I have a feeling the real Captain Luckman does not exist."

"No sir, he does exist. There just happens to be two of them. One works in the naval hospital in San Diego, and the other is the flight surgeon on the U.S.S. Enterprise. By the time anyone would attempt to unravel this mystery, the war will have long been over, and no one will care anymore. It will become one of many snafus that mysteriously happened on the island of New Caledonia. So now, all I need to do is get out of the hospital, and dump this damn uniform before I get arrested for impersonating an officer," the phony Capt. Luckman responded.

Shaking his head, Buzz inquired. "So, what is your job in this man's navy?"

Before exiting the room, the man smiled, "Boilerman second class, sir, but I'll not tell you more. Good luck, sir."

Buzz had to laugh as the phony Captain Luckman strolled confidently out the front door of the hospital, saluting junior officers like a real pro. Moments later, he disappeared onto the sidewalk, merging into all the other busy naval personnel.

During the afternoon exercise period when all the nurses were busy, Buzz walked over to the medication cart, removing a bottle containing two hundred quinine pills, from one of the back-up supply drawers. He wanted to make sure he had a good supply, just in case his malaria flared up. Trying to get pills from the dispensary on the base at Lingayan might get him sent back to the hospital for good.

After the nurses made their round at 2300hrs, Buzz changed into his uniform, grabbed the pillow case containing the quinine pills and a few other personal items he wanted, then exited the hospital through the ambulance entrance.

It was just after midnight when a flight crew arrived at one of the PBY aircraft and prepared for flight. Buzz ran up to the pilot handing him his orders. "I just received these orders an hour ago, and have been hoping to catch a flight as soon as possible. Are you going anywhere near Lingayan Bay"

After reading the orders, the pilot nodded. "It will be our second stop on this run, so yeah, we've got room for you. Hop on board and buckle up, we'll be out of here very shortly."

Buzz watched the pilot fold up the orders and place them in a manila folder next to the co-pilots seat without asking any questions Within minutes the PBY was climbing into the clear starlit sky. A half-moon cast a bluish hue upon the deep waters of the Pacific Ocean, as ships of all sizes sailed in and out of the huge harbor of Noumea. Settling back into his seat, Buzz pulled his hat down over his eyes, folded his arms across his chest, and leaned his head against the bulkhead. He knew if the crew thought he was sleeping, they wouldn't bother him unless it was an emergency. Feeling relieved by his timely escape Buzz easily dozed off for real from time to time during the long flight.

The sun was shining brightly as one of the crew members shook Buzz by the arm.

"We're getting ready to set down at Davao on Mindanao, sir. Get yourself situated. Our next stop after that is your base at Lingayan."

It did not take long for the crew to unload several cases of military cargo, and then help three marines onboard that were headed back to Noumea for medical attention. In short order, the PBY-5 was once again airborne, flying over familiar islands where the crew of the 303 had battled the Japanese on many occasions. About a half hour later the radio operator walked back to Buzz, "Last stop Lingayan Gulf in about ten minutes, sir."

Smiling, Buzz sat up straight and tightened his seat belt. Looking out the window he could see crews working on their PT Boats under the dazzling sun. It was good to be home, he just hoped he could get the 303 back.

Approaching the operations hut, Buzz observed Lt. Holbrook walking toward the pier carrying some paper work. "Hey, Holbrook how the hell are you?" Buzz called out.

After shaking hands, Lt. Holbrook explained everything that was going on with crew assignments since he left. Buzz wasn't sure how this was going to work since so many people had to be shuffled around, but he had to get the 303 back no matter what it took.

Captain Robesky looked up from his desk as Buzz walked through the door. "Maddox, I didn't think I would be seeing you back soon, if ever. I never received orders on your return from Noumea, so this is a surprise to say the least."

Reaching into the pillow case, Buzz removed the fake orders he had been given. He knew this was the time everything could fall apart if it was going to happen.

Captain Robesky looked over the orders and nodded his head. "Looks like everything is in order. But this is interesting, I see the orders are signed by Admiral Spruance. I thought the Admiral was out at sea with the fifth fleet these days. I didn't know he was working on low level job assignments in Noumea. Well, maybe he was on shore for a meeting at Southwest Headquarters and decided to keep his hand involved in replacement orders. What do you think, Maddox?"

Buzz shrugged his shoulders. "Don't know, sir, this is what the nurse handed me late yesterday afternoon, I never questioned them, I was just glad to be heading home."

With a sly smile on his face, Capt. Robesky nodded his head. "Well, then again, maybe the Admiral stopped by New Caledonia and decided to help out where he could at the hospital since they have been so overwhelmed with malaria cases. You know, that's just the kind of guy he is."

Buzz felt like he was going to vomit as his stomach was tied in knots, because by now he was damn sure the captain knew the orders were about as phony as they came.

Walking over to his assignment board, the captain thought for a moment. "Alright Maddox, you take over the 303, you can have Ensign Hardy as your XO. I'll make Holbrook skipper of the 316 and send Mews over to squadron two as commander. It all works out in the end, thanks to the Admiral."

After exchanging salutes, Buzz was about to leave the operations building when Capt. Robesky stepped in front of him. "Maddox, you best not crap out on me during a mission, because if you do, you just might get the opportunity to explain all of this to your friend Admiral Spruance. Do I make myself clear, Commander?"

Standing eye to eye with the captain, Buzz replied, "I'll never let you or the crew of the 303 down, sir. That's one thing you can take to the bank any day of the year."

Leaving the operations hut, Buzz walked over to the pier to find the crew waiting for him. The chief rushed forward to shake hands. "Tell me, Skipper, you did get the 303 back, didn't you?"

Nodding his head, Buzz smiled. "Yeah, she's all mine. Holbrook will take the 316, and Mews will command second squadron. Now, let's get this thing ready to run."

Buzz went down to the crew quarters to stow his gear and break open the bottle of quinine pills. Suddenly, he was feeling a bit weak and his breathing was labored. But he was sure part of the problem was the exchange he just had with the captain, along with the excitement of being back with his crew. Now all he wanted to do was get behind the wheel of the 303 and get back out to sea.

Back in the hospital at Noumea, as the medical crew made rounds, the doctor stopped at the empty bed of Commander Maddox. Turning toward the charge nurse, he inquired, "And where is our arrogant commander now?"

Both nurses looked at him strangely, before the charge nurse spoke up, "Sir, you discharged him at 0700hrs. this morning. It appears he is on his way back to Lingayan Gulf to resume command of his PT boat."

"Discharge hell! That man is going back home, he's in no shape to continue commanding a PT boat or a rubber boat in my bath tub. He's suffering from classic battle fatigue. Who was stupid enough to sign orders for him to return to combat status. I want to talk to that stupid son-of-a-bitch."

Handing the document to the doctor, the charge nurse replied. "That stupid son-of-a-bitch would be Admiral Raymond Spruance, sir."

"What, oh hell no, that is simply not possible. No, no that can't be. How did the Admiral get involved in this?"

The charge nurse shrugged her shoulders, "Sir, would you like me to have the Commo shack contact the fifth fleet so you can confer with the admiral?"

Angrily throwing up his hands, the doctor yelled, "Are you out of your damn mind? Good God Almighty woman, do you know what kind of mess that would create, questioning the orders of an Admiral. He'd have me inspecting bed pans at Bethesda Naval Hospital until I retired. Damn that Maddox, I knew he was up to no good!"

CHAPTER 23
AS GOOD AS NEW

Several days later another BPY arrived at Lingayan, carrying a short, well-built and tough looking man with bushy gray hair that looked like he could play defensive tackle for any pro football team.

After getting directions from one of the dock workers, the man went straight for the operations building. As he entered, Captain Robesky smiled while extending his right hand. "Chaplain Hammond, it's good to see you again. I heard you were a bit busted up after a Jap air raid on Rendova. How are you doing these days?"

"I'm fine, Gilbert. There are many great doctors on New Caledonia that were able to patch up this old war horse. So, I hear you have two squadrons under your command with men that should have been relieved a long time ago. How are they holding up under the pressure?" The priest asked as he helped himself to a cup of coffee.

"Well Padre, they keep going and doing the job as well as any new sailors could. I'm damn proud of these men." Looking out the window," he continued. "If you want to see for yourself here comes Commander Maddox. He just returned from the hospital with a case of malaria. He's in charge of squadron seven. He's been with us since the Tulagi days, and is one tough boat commander."

Buzz snapped to attention upon entering the command hut. "Good afternoon, Captain, good afternoon, Chaplain. I heard you arrived on the PBY earlier." Turning back to Captain Robesky, Buzz continued. "Sir, all the boats need refueling, and there are a few engine issues we need to clean up. We should be ready for operations by 0800hrs.

Captain Robesky nodded his head, "Sounds good, Commander, get it done."

After Buzz had walked about twenty-yards he heard someone running up behind him. Turning around, he saw the chaplain running to catch up. "You have a brisk pace, Commander. Mind if I come down to the pier to see your boats?"

"Not at all, Padre, but don't have your expectations set too high. These boats are tired and have seen a lot of combat. They are beginning to show their age, but we keep them running as long as we can get parts," Buzz replied matter-of-factly

"Commander, I'm also beginning to show some age, but I keep on going best I can, too," the priest replied as the men continued toward the pier.

Reaching the 303 boat, Fr. Hammond climbed aboard and shook hands with the crew. Turning to Buzz, he smiled. "She looks as sea worthy as any other boat I have seen in the South Pacific. As long as she can fight, what more could you ask for?"

Before Buzz could respond, Chaplin Hammond asked, "So, what faith do you practice commander?"

Buzz laughed as he shook his head. Wiping sweat from his forehead he replied. "Well Padre, my mother would take me and my brothers screaming and yelling all the way to church on Christmas Day and sometimes on Easter. It was quite a sight to behold. My father only went to funerals, he never joined in on the Maddox embarrassment. But it was a Methodist church a few blocks from our home. To be honest, I don't know if I was ever baptized into the religion, or if the location of the building just fit my mother's needs. Religion was not talked about much in the Maddox home."

"Nodding his head, the chaplain continued. "So have you been to services since you've been in the Pacific?"

Buzz shook his head, "I tried the first Christmas I was out here, but it just wasn't the same without my brothers raising hell and my mother slapping us. Damn, what a sight that must have been."

Father Hammond laughed as he patted Buzz on the back. "So, you do believe in God then."

After watching the gunner's mate and the chief reinstall the port machine gun, Buzz nodded his head. "Fact is, Padre, back home there was nothing better than being out at sea on the fishing boat at the crack of dawn and watching the sun come up as we dropped our nets. Watching the colors change in the sky, hearing the cry of the hungry gulls, and feeling the deck roll under your feet with each passing swell, all made you believe some power much larger than all of us was in control of everything that happened in this world. Then pulling up our nets to see the flopping cod, knowing we were feeding a hungry America made life feel as special as hell. But now, after all of this, the sea no longer has that draw. Now I see it red with blood, floating debris, body parts and the hate of one man against another. There is no peace for me on the sea anymore. I'm not sure what belief or faith I have left in my soul. Tomorrow or the next day we'll have a mission where I'll direct the guns of the 303 boat to kill human beings. I don't know, Padre, I just don't have an answer to that question right now."

Although Buzz's conversation with Chaplain Hammond bothered his soul, physically he felt better every day being back on the 303. It was also clear that Captain Robesky had faith in him again, by the severity of the missions he had been assigning to his boat and to squadron seven.

Late one afternoon, Captain Robesky's jeep came flying up to the bow of the 303. The jeep had barely stopped when the captain jumped out. Walking up to Buzz he motioned for the rest of the squadron commanders to assemble on the pier.

Rolling out a map on the hood of his jeep, the captain began. "Gentlemen, last night squadron three tangled with a Japanese convoy here in the Babuyan Islands north of Luzon. It was a bloody mess and both sides took heavy losses and terrible casualties. Fly overs earlier this evening have reported several rafts and floating men in the water. Get up there and rescue whoever you can, and that includes the enemy! I have discharged a landing ship with medical crews to help out. Get moving!"

As soon as the engines were warmed up, squadron seven departed Lingayan Gulf, heading due north into the South China Sea.

The Babuyan Islands cover a large swath of ocean north of Luzon, so the squadron broke into two search parties. Ensign Hardy observed landing ship 2318 a short distance behind, making good time after leaving its base at San Fernando.

Taking the 312 and 316 boats with him, Buzz began patrolling the channels separating Barit, Mabag and Fuga, the largest of the three islands. The rest of the boats continued north toward Irao and Dalvurri Islands.

It was clear to sea by the flotsam, that a battle had taken place here very recently. Buzz ordered all the boats to turn on the spot lights and search the surface of the water for any survivors. Obviously, that could attract Japanese float planes, but that was an issue they would have to contend with if they were going to save lives. About ten minutes into the search, the chief spotted a life raft near the northwest corner of Fuga Island, bouncing up and down on a coral reef. A closer inspection determined it was a Japanese raft normally used on large patrol boats. Although it was empty, it was covered with a tremendous amount of blood. The chief played the spotlight over the shoreline of the island, looking for survivors or bodies but found nothing. The 303, 312 and 316 continued on a north- westerly route following the dark north shore of Fuga Island, but was unable to see any more flotsam or signs of human life.

Farther to the west, the 323, 342 and 336 boats discovered six bodies in the water drifting in the passage between Irao and Dalupri Islands. They were identified as Americans, and they also found debris in the water that had come from a PT boat. The bodies were loaded onto the landing ship, allowing the PT crews to continue their search.

Seeing lights in the water near Pamuktan Island, Buzz spread his boats farther apart and shut down the search lights. With the 312 patrolling closest to shore, it did not take Lt. Keppner much time to report taking small arms fire from Pamuktan. Lieutenant Holbrook on the 316 reported that the lights they had seen on the water were from a small Japanese barge that had been damaged in combat and was stuck on a rock pile. Several Japanese sailors still taking refuge on the barge, began firing on the 316.

Instantly, the twenty-millimeter gunner from the 316 opened fire on the barge, striking it near the engine room that was stuck high up on the rocks. In minutes, fire from the already ruptured fuel tanks exploded, sending a cloud of debris skyward. What was left of the battered barge quickly slipped under the waves.

As the 323, 342 and 336 boats arrived at the passage between Dalupri and Calayan Islands, spotlights fell upon men treading water or clinging to large pieces of floating debris. As Lt Kirkland idled up to several Americans, an Ensign in the water yelled as he pointed to his left. "Japs, those are Japs over there. They've been firing at us all night long. They already killed two of our men."

At first, Lt. Kirkland attempted to ignore the Japanese survivors, directing his boats to areas where more American survivors required their assistance. However, ten Japanese sailors in pretty tough shape and undaunted by the gunners on the PT boats, swam toward the American survivors without causing any problems, hoping they could also be pulled from the water.

When Lt Makely slowed the 342 to pick up several Japanese sailors that were pleading for their help, one of them tossed a grenade that bounced off the hull of the boat exploding in the water. Seeing what had just happened, gunners on the boats opened fire on every Japanese sailor remaining in the water. Lieutenant Sterling stood in the cockpit of the 323 boat, waving his hands and yelling cease fire. He reached up grabbing hold of his port .50 caliber machine gun operator yelling, "Stop it, stop it. Cease fire, dammit!"

The gunner looked over his shoulder yelling, "But Skipper, they're still trying to kill us!"

Leaning against the back of the gun tub, Lt. Sterling shook his head in disgust as the firing ceased. Looking back up at his veteran gunner, the Lieutenant nodded his head. "I know, I know."

Taking hold of the spotlight, the chief of the 323 slowly swung it around the channel looking for any signs of life. The only life he could see now were the ravenous sharks that had arrived on scene with the smell of plentiful blood in the water.

Disturbed over what had just happened, Lt. Sterling turned the 323 back toward the north, so he and the 342 and 336 could patrol up toward Panvitan Island. After searching several smaller channels without any luck, the 303, 312 and 316 boats were now moving toward Babuyan Island.

As dawn broke over the Southwest Pacific, the boats of squadron seven were returning to their base in Lingayan Bay. They had rescued fifteen American, and eight Japanese survivors. The bodies of twenty dead Americans had been loaded on to the landing ship.

After the boats were tied up, Lt. Sterling walked up the pier toward Buzz. We could have rescued more Japanese, but one of the bastards tossed a grenade and every gun on the boats opened fire. I tried to stop them, but it was useless. What the hell are we supposed to do?"

Buzz placed his hand on the Lieutenant's shoulder. "This has been a long war, my friend, and all these men have seen way too much. Talk to them, explain as best you can. But in the end, realize all these men know the war is coming closer to the end. They don't want to die now, keep that in mind."

Several days later, after a quick meeting in the operations office, Buzz ran down toward the pier, yelling at the chief to get the engines warmed up. Waving his arms at the crew of the 312, he told them to get their engines fired up as well.

With the six Packard engines warming up, Buzz ran over to the 312 to give the mission low down to Lt. Keppner. "Air support says a PT boat from squadron two that was picking up a marine recon group has run aground north of the bay near Laoag. They said it looks like she's pretty tight. A tug is on the way from Manila Bay, but they want us out there in case any Jap patrol boats make an unwelcome visit."

As Buzz was explaining the mission, Chaplain Hammond came running. "Commander, may I ride along? I'll stay out of the way and do what you tell me to do."

Turning to the chief, Buzz called out, "Get the padre a helmet, life vest and combat knife." As he turned toward Chaplain Hammond, Buzz stated. "And there'll be no puking on the deck of my boat, Padre. You got that!"

Trying to keep from laughing, Chaplain Hammond saluted and replied, "Got it, Commander!"

With the engines warmed and ready, the two boats roared out of Lingayan Gulf, heading north at thirty knots and breaking through eight-foot swells. Every few minutes Buzz would look over to the chaplain to see how he was doing.

Finally the chief leaned over to Buzz. "Don't worry about him, Skipper. First sign of him turning green, I'll just toss him overboard. As you always say, sir, no one pukes on the deck of the 303."

Buzz laughed harder than he had in a long time as he wiped salt spray from his face with a small towel, "I believe you would, chief, I believe you would."

As they approached Laoag, it was evident the 274 boat was taking on water as it listed to starboard. The skipper of the Higgins model PT boat contacted Buzz on the TBS radio,

"Maddox, that reef extends out nearly thirty feet past my stern. Plus there's a major rock pile just to my port side. I sheered all the props and I got nothing left to move this boat. Will you take my crew off?"

Keying the mic, Buzz replied. "We have a tug on the way, maybe an hour out or so. Keep your crew to man the guns in case we get company. We're standing by, no worries!"

About seventy-five minutes later, the huge ocean tug arrived. After surveying the situation, the recovery crew from the tug walked on top of the reef, carrying ropes and chains. After nearly fifteen minutes of rigging, the crew was sure they were ready to try a recovery.

They had barely begun to put tension on the lines when four Japanese Zeros came diving out of the north. The skipper of the tug dropped all the lines connecting the tug to the 274, so they could back away and be free to maneuver under the air attack. It was evident that all the pilots wanted was the stuck boat, and really didn't want to tangle with three other boats that could out maneuver them and fire accurately on the run. Finally, the first pilot changed directions and came in from the north, low across the water, intending to drop his hundred-pound bomb square on the deck of the 274. What the pilot failed to realize was that the boat was stuck, but not out of commission. The poorly trained pilot flew directly into a barrage of four .50 caliber machine guns and the 20mm canon. In mere seconds, flame shot from the engine cowling as the canopy was ripped from the cockpit. The plane rolled over, slamming into several trees up from the beach where it exploded.

It was impossible to say who had the credit, but moments later, another Zero that was attempting to climb for a second run exploded in midair. The pilot of the third plane swung wide over the island and disappeared from sight for several minutes before he came roaring back at treetop level. The crew on board the 274 had no doubt what was on the mind of the pilot. They immediately dove off the boat, swimming away as fast as they could, Seconds later, the pilot dropped the nose of his screaming Zero and dove at the wounded boat. As the bomb under the Zero exploded, all the fuel left on the aircraft as well as hundreds of gallons of fuel on the PT boat exploded in a massive ball of flame. Buzz could feel the heat from the explosion, although he was nearly a hundred yards away.

The 312 boat was damaged, as one of the water pumps from the 274 slammed into the starboard torpedo tube with such velocity that it nearly cut the tube in half as it ripped right through the live torpedo. The aft 20mm gunner was hit by several pieces of shrapnel, as the barrel from his weapon was torn away by a large unidentified piece of shrapnel from the explosion.

Realizing the target they had been sent to attack was now destroyed, the last pilot climbed to about five thousand feet before setting a heading due north, while trailing an oily cloud of smoke.

With the threat now eliminated, the 303 and 312 moved in quickly to pick up survivors. After a head count was conducted, the skipper was happy so see his entire crew survived, although many of them were bleeding from their ears due to the tremendous blast while they were in the water. This late in the war, that type of injury would allow them a trip back to New Caledonia for treatment, before orders rotating them home.

The skipper of the 274 had several cuts on his arms and back, but refused to go to New Caledonia. The doctors in the small base hospital just stitched him up as they had done to so many PT men since the war began. He was willing to wait for another boat to arrive, as he wanted to be in the Pacific when the war came to an end.

That evening as Buzz sat in the mess tent eating, Chaplain Hammond came and sat down across from him. "They call them kamikazes, or translated, the divine wind. It refers to two typhoons that saved Japan from invasion by the Mongols in 1281. I've heard about their attacks during the invasion of Okinawa, but I was still surprised to see a pilot give up his life today for a grounded wooden PT boat. It's a blessing no one was killed."

"Padre, I have seen these guys die for less than an old wooden boat. They fight like fanatics when they have to know there's no chance of winning. It can be terrifying and it shakes hardened sailors to the core. I watched those pilots hit the fleet during the invasion of Lingayan Gulf. It was horrifying to watch, knowing we could shoot like hell and they still came right on through. That alone will shake your faith," Buzz replied somberly, as he placed his silverware on his tin tray. "If you'll excuse me, I need to talk to my crew about tonight's mission."

Before Buzz could walk off, Fr. Hammond called out. "Skipper, may I go with you tonight?"

After a moment of thought, Buzz replied, "Sure, Padre. You know where the 303 is tied up. Be there by 2330hrs.

Father Hammond was surprised to see twenty marines in full combat gear climbing aboard the 303 when he arrived. Seeing the chaplain standing on the pier, Buzz jumped off the boat.

"We're going to land these guys on Calayan Island. There's a large group of Filipino fighters waiting for us. We'll drop them off, then return home and wait for a call to retrieve them. The 312, 323 and 342 will supply suppressive fire when we go in if need be. If we start taking heavy fire, you'll haul your ass down into the chart room with Yamry, understand?"

Nodding his head, Chaplain Hammond replied, "No problem, Skipper."

At 2350hrs., the four boats left their base in Lingayan Gulf heading north for the Babuyan Islands. The humidity was nearly ninety percent with a high dew point, creating roving clouds of heavy fog that shut out all light from the moon and stars. Tonight, the skippers would have to navigate by using the primitive radar equipment the navy had installed on the 303 and 342. That meant the 312 and 323 would need to stay close enough to the radar boats so they wouldn't get lost, but that also meant the opportunity for a collision in a fog bank was greater than normal. If there was one aspect of tonight's mission that was on the side of the PT crews, it was that with hardly a breeze, the ocean was about as calm as it could be.

Chaplain Hammond stood aside of Buzz in the cockpit, studying the face of the man that was responsible for the 303 and the lives of every man on it. "Been here before, Skipper?"

"Yeah, quite a few times, but we never had to go this far. I'm hoping the fog breaks before we get to Calayan or we may never find the drop zone," Buzz replied, as he carefully watched the fuzzy radar screen.

After a moment of silence, the Chaplain spoke again. "Where you from, Skipper?"

"Kennebunkport, Maine. We have some of the largest fishing fleets on the east coast operating out of there. Not sure I'll go back there when the war is over, though. Where are you from, Padre?" Buzz inquired, enjoying the conversation as it took his mind off their situation.

"I was born in Vermont, but joined the Boston Diocese when I graduated from the seminary. So, we're neighbors of sorts, just a short train ride up the coast. So, why not return to Kennebunkport? I've been there, it's a very nice area," the chaplain inquired as he watched the chief talk to Stockey on the starboard .50 caliber.

"Family issues, Padre. Pretty much burned all those bridges when I left for the navy. Besides, I met a pretty nurse that is stationed at Pearl right now. I don't think she wants to be a fisherman's wife forever." Buzz replied with a grin.

"Ah, I am guessing it might be the odor of fish on the coveralls each day that might make a woman a bit unhappy," the chaplain said with a laugh as he slapped Buzz on the shoulder.

Buzz never answered as he motioned for Ensign Hardy to come forward. "Bill, I can't make out the shore line on this damn screen, and we can't go in any farther. My estimate is we're less than a half mile from shore and there are some ugly reefs out there. Kowalski has motioned he can't see a damn thing from the bow, either. We'll be past the island in a couple of minutes heading into open ocean, and we can't do that. Call everyone on TBS and tell them to begin making a slow 360 degree turn to port, and not to run into one another."

The Ensign had barely dropped down into the chart room when Buzz called out to him. "Damn it, we have enemy contact on radar dead ahead. I'm guessing we have three destroyers coming right at us, and they sure as hell don't know we're here! Tell everyone to turn 90 degrees to port and watch their port side for Dalupri Island, we don't want anyone running aground."

As Buzz began his turn, the sound of a five-inch shell screamed overhead, exploding about a hundred yards in front of the 303. Shaking his head, Buzz gently pushed the throttles forward, hoping to gain enough speed to clear the path of the destroyers, and not run into the 312 which had been directly off the port beam of the 303. If he could make the turn safely, he could crank up the engines and run for the open ocean after clearing Dalupri. That would give him a fighting chance to reverse course and make a torpedo run if all hell broke loose.

Suddenly torpedoman Ansel yelled out, "PT boat on our port beam, ten yards out, the 342, hard to starboard before we hit!"

Buzz spun the wheel over to starboard while throwing the throttles wide open. As the 303 rolled over on its side, Buzz watched the deck of the 342 cross his path as Lt. Makely was spinning his wheel hard to port. Buzz closed his eyes as he waited for the crunching of wood as the boats made heavy contact. Not hearing a sound, Buzz looked back over his shoulder to see the stern of the 342 moving away at flank speed. Looking up on the bow, Buzz saw Kowalski laying on the deck holding on to the machine gun frame work as he prepared for impact.

Buzz called down to ensign Hardy, "Call the 342, make sure they're alright. Find out what happened to the 312 they should have been between us and the 342!

As Buzz finished speaking, two more five-inch shells exploded in their wake, sending a shower of water over the crew of the 303. Chaplain Hammond looked toward the stern of the 303 as he held onto the radio mast. Looking back toward Buzz, he called out, "Those son-of-a-bitches are trying to kill us!"

Chief Petrovski laughed as he gave the chaplain a slap on the back. "That's the name of the game, Padre. Sometimes we just have to maneuver and run like hell, welcome to the world of the 303."

After running the course for another minute, Buzz spun back hard to port heading for open water, hoping Makely hadn't done the same thing.

Three more five-inch shells dropped into the channel about a hundred yards astern of the 303 as the Packard engines roared with the mufflers wide open. Turning to the chief, Buzz exclaimed. "We lost them, they haven't got a clue where the hell we are now. Let's find our lost lambs and head for home."

Unfortunately, that did not take long as the 312 came flying up toward the starboard side of the 303 at nearly full speed. The only thing Zumwaldt could think of to warn Lt. Keppner was to fire a quick blast from his 20mm skyward.

Buzz was happy to see the bow of the 312 drop back into the water as Lt. Keppner closed the throttles. Although he could see Lt. Keppner spinning the wheel over as quickly as possible, Buzz yelled out. "Prepare for impact!"

Seconds later the starboard side of the 312 struck the port side of the 303 sending sparks through the air as the torpedo tubes rubbed against each other. As the 312 came to a stop about fifty yards away, Buzz and the chief ran over to inspect the side of his boat. Shaking his head, Buzz had to smile. "Well, that side needed a paint job anyway, and the body men with some bondo and beer cans can make the tubes look new again."

Chaplain Hammond sat down on the roof of the crew quarters, looking at his shaking hands. After catching his breath, he walked up to the chief. "How can the skipper make a joke after what just happened, we all could have been killed!"

"But we weren't, Padre. Were all still here and both boats are still combat worthy. What more could you ask for? the chief replied, as he looked over at the 312, not allowing the chaplain to see the fear that still gripped his face.

"Buzz stood near the cockpit, still reeling from what could have been a catastrophic collision. Looking over at Ensign Hardy, he said, "That's it!"

Walking over to the control console, Buzz hit the switches, turning on the running lights. He figured they were too far out into deep water for the destroyers to make out the lights in the fog, at least he hoped so.

With the 312 still idling close by, he searched the radar screen for the other two boats, but as usual, nothing was on display.

Several minutes later, Stockey in the starboard .50 gun tub called out, "Skipper, one set of running lights approaching off our starboard beam, coming in nice and slow. It appears another boat is on its port beam running without lights."

Buzz was happy to see Lt. Makely on the 342 had rounded up the 323 and they were both in good shape. When Yamry had plotted a course that would take them back to Lingayan Gulf, west of the Babuyan Island chain, Buzz gave the order to move out.

It was a long trip back, and the crews were very quiet, as the boats once again traveled through heavy cloud banks of fog so thick, they tested the mental strength of each man on board.

Arriving back in Lingayan Gulf, it was clear to the chaplain that the veteran crews of these small wooden fighting boats had been tested to the limit. There was no jovial joking or smart aleck comments. They either went below to sleep, or walked to their assigned huts without saying a word. The stress on their faces said it all.

The following morning at 1000hrs, Buzz was awakened from a sound sleep by one of Captain Robesky's aides. The petty officer informed Buzz that he was to report to operations immediately.

The moment Buzz arrived in the operations hut, Capt. Robesky jumped up from behind his desk. Shaking with anger, the captain stood toe to toe with his squadron seven commander. "Do you want to tell me what the hell happened last night. Your orders were to meet up with the rebels, drop off the marines and get back here. Now tell me, how hard was that order to follow? Colonel Brandt was here at 0700 all over my ass for not getting his men where they were supposed to be. So you better have a damn good explanation and I want it right now, mister!"

"Captain, it was like driving through a can of pea soup last night. We tried to find the cove, but the fog was just too thick. The radar scopes were worthless, and we knew there were shoals and coral reefs all along the west coast of Calayan that would rip the bottom out of a boat. Making matters worse, three Japanese destroyers arrived pumping five-inch shells all over the place, and we couldn't see them or find them on radar. We had to run, there was no other choice."

"Destroyers, my ass, Maddox. My intel states there were no destroyers within a hundred miles of the Babuyan islands last night. You were seeing things, and you let your mind play tricks on you. I would never expect that from a seasoned commander like you. Now listen good, Maddox, you will take all six of your boats out tonight and land those marines as you were told to do. You can leave two of your boats as pickets in the channel in case your mystery destroyers show up again while you make the landing.

If you fail on this mission, I'll bust your sorry ass back to lieutenant and put you in charge of the garbage scow back in New Caledonia, and that's not a threat. And to tell you the truth, Commander, I've never really liked your greater than thou attitude. So even if you complete the mission as you were directed, tomorrow morning when you return, you'll be sent back to New Caledonia to command an ocean-going tug boat. Your PT days are over. Do you understand me?"

Looking straight ahead Buzz replied, "Aye aye, sir, will there be anything else?"

Glaring at Buzz, Capt. Robesky shook his head. "You're dismissed, get the hell out of my office. If you ever make me look bad again, you'll be the sorriest sailor in all the Pacific!"

Exiting the operations hut, Buzz thought he was going to vomit. He could not believe the tongue lashing he had just received, or the promise that he was going to be taken away from his beloved PT boats. Going back to his quarters, Buzz attempted to sleep, but the words of Capt. Robesky went around and around in his head. Getting up he went for a walk and found himself in front of the small chapel the Seabees had just completed. Walking inside, he observed Chaplain Hammond walking back and forth talking to himself.

Looking over his shoulder, the Chaplain called out, "Welcome skipper, I'm trying out my sermon for Sunday's service. Care to hear what I have to say?"

Sitting down on a folding chair, Buzz replied. "I might as well hear it today since I won't be around on Sunday to hear it."

Looking confused, Chaplain Hammond walked over and sat down next to Buzz. "Tell me, my friend, what's going on?"

Slowly Buzz explained his conversation with Capt. Robesky and the final outcome. Totally astonished, the chaplain sat back in his chair. "What are you going to do about it, Buzz? You can't let the man get away with something like this. It's wrong, I was there!"

Shaking his head, Buzz replied, "The man has serious connections here in the Pacific. That's one hornet nest you don't want to kick, Padre. Look, the Japanese can't hold out much longer now that bombers on Saipan and Tinian are striking the homeland. I'll just go to New Caledonia and run the tug and keep my mouth shut until the war is over. At least I'll still be able to command a boat."

Before the chaplain could respond, Chief Petrovski entered the chapel. "Sorry Skipper, but there are a few problems we need to iron out before we sail tonight."

Nodding his head, Buzz turned back toward Chaplain Hammond. "Duty calls, I can't leave anything to the last minute with this raid."

Chief Petrovski walked him over to the 338 boat where the crew had removed the bow machine gun, replacing it with a 37mm light anti-tank weapon, as many boat commanders had done when they could get their hands on such a weapon.

Shaking his head, Buzz looked up at Lt. Kirkland. "Do you plan to run into many tanks out there, Kirk?"

The lieutenant smiled as he patted the barrel of the weapon. "Well, probably not, sir, but if we need to hit any hardened targets on the beach, we'll be ready. Do you mind if we take her out to sea and practice with her a bit. I'd like to see how it works."

Laughing, Buzz shook his head. "No, just don't blow anything up that belongs to our side."

That evening at 2330hrs, Buzz was walking around the boat, checking on each man to make sure they were prepared for the mission. He wondered how he would explain to them tomorrow morning that he was being transferred out. It made him sick, but he fully understood that orders were orders, and every sailor had to comply. Like it or not.

Arriving in the cockpit, he slapped Ensign Hardy on the shoulder, "Roll them over, Bill, let's get them warmed up." Buzz stood near number two torpedo tube, listening to the sound of the sixteen booming Packard engines as they warmed up, taking in the smell of the high-octane exhaust. There was nothing like it anywhere else in the world, and he wanted it to be a memory he would never forget. After checking his watch, he looked forward to see Kowalski standing on the pier, ready to cast off the bow line. After waving his arm he look aft giving Andy Rice the same signal.

As the boat began to back out into the bay, Buzz heard a familiar voice yelling, "Wait for me, wait for me!"

Looking forward, Buzz could see Kowalski giving the chaplain a hand to get on board. Walking back to the cockpit, Chaplain Hammond looked at Buzz. "I wasn't going to go on any more raids after last night, but something in my head told me to get my butt down here. Hope that is alright with you."

Buzz nodded and smiled, "Padre, you are always welcome on the 303."

Walking into the cockpit behind Ensign Hardy, Buzz began adjusting the radar. "All I got is fuzz, I can't see a damn thing."

Leaving Lingayan Gulf, the boats once again turned due north into a massive cloud of fog. Looking aft, he could see the rest of the boats running in a echelon left with Buzz being the lead boat. The problem was, none of the skippers wanted to get lost, so the boats were less than twenty yards apart operating at thirty knots. One small mistake by any one skipper, and there could be a massive collision that could take the lives of many good men.

Buzz had given all the skippers the coordinates they had used to return last night. It would bring the flotilla north around Dalupri on the open ocean, then they would have to muffle down and bring the boats into the channel separating Dalupri and Calayan. Once in the channel, boats 316 and 338 would become picket boats, searching the channel for any Japanese ships, while the rest of the boats took up the operation of landing the twenty marines, and removing some wounded personnel from the island.

Memories of the 312 scraping up against the 303 last night in the fog were still rolling through his mind as Buzz began the turn into the channel. It seemed hard to believe, but it appeared the fog was even heavier in the channel than the night before. Standing at the wheel, Buzz brought the 303 and the column behind him to within a hundred yards of shore, not exactly sure where it was.

Finally, the marine lieutenant on the bow grabbed Kowalski and pointed to a small dull light directly off the port beam. It was evident that someone was swinging a lantern back and forth, attempting to get their attention. After Buzz talked to his skippers on the TBS radio, the 303 and 312 idled in, as the 342 and 323 stood by in case more deck space was required for wounded.

Without saying a word, the marines began jumping off the bow of the 303 into waist deep water, wading ashore.

Instantly, the shore line erupted into a wall of fire. Rifles, machine guns and mortars began firing at the PT boats. The marines in the water dropped their weapons as they began swimming back to the 303. Every gunner on the boats began returning fire as the 312 began backing away from the shore. Torpedoman Ansel and Lopez ran forward to help pull the marines back on deck as the 303 was being hit in every imaginable place by bullets. Ansel screamed as a bullet struck him in the head, causing him to fly back against the bow .50 machine gun as Kowalski hammered away at the unseen enemy on shore. Ed Yamry ran up on deck, carrying a Thompson machine gun to help out, but was immediately cut down by several bullets in the chest.

Buzz slammed the engines into reverse and threw the throttles into fuel power, attempting to get away from the withering fire. Suddenly, a mortar round exploded near the rear of the 312, ripping off the rudders and damaging the prop from the middle engine. The concussion jammed the Vee Drive gear box, so Lt. Keppner could not put his boat in gear. He screamed over the TBS radio for back up, as the current was pushing his boat back toward shore, and his crew was being slaughtered.

Quickly the 338 came charging up behind the 312 with its crew hammering away at the beach with the anti-tank gun. Before the 338 could reach the 312, a mortar round ripped through the bow decking, exploding against the inner hull. The front of the 312 was literately torn away right up to the cockpit. Flames roared through the crew quarters, heading straight for the fuel tanks.

Picking himself up off the deck, Lt. Keppner felt a tremendous pain in his right shoulder. Pulling himself over to the radio mast, he looked over to see part of one of his bow machine-gun supports sticking out of his shoulder. It had gone clear through his shoulder making the use of his arm impossible. As the flames began to consume the 312, it began listing harder and harder to starboard. Lieutenant Keppner quickly realized that his 20mm gunner and the mechanic that continued loading the hungry weapon were the only survivors left on board.

As the 338 came within just a few feet of the burning wreck, Lt. Keppner ordered his men to abandon the boat and jump over to the 338. By the time Lt. Keppner reached the aft of his sinking boat, he had lost so much blood that he no longer had the strength to make the jump. He motioned for Lt. Kirkland to back away and save his boat, but gunners mate Aldridge that had been operating the 20mm, jumped back to the 312. With the help of several men from the 338, they were able to remove Lt. Keppner before the 312 turned on its side and settled in the water.

Giving his engine full speed, Lt. Kirkland backed away from the shore as his crew continued firing the 37mm at anything they considered a target.

Over on the 323 Boat, Lt. Sterling had struck a small reef on the port side. As bullets tore into the boat all around him, he began rocking the boat trying to break free. Seeing two of his men killed in the first few minutes of the attack, the only thing he could think of was getting weight off the port side in a hurry. Yelling at his torpedo men, Lt. Sterling snarled, "Prepare to fire one."

As the bewildered crew followed orders, Lt. Sterling slammed his hand down on the firing button. As the torpedo jumped from the tube, Lt. Sterling slammed his engines into reverse and pushed the throttles forward. With a small crunching sound, the 323 lurched and jumped clear from the reef as a large explosion rocked the south side of the beach ending some of the firing. As Lt. Sterling swung his damaged boat to the north, he had to laugh, wondering what the Japanese thought when they saw that huge torpedo coming their way right up out of the water.

Chaplain Hammond ran past the cockpit as the 303 was backing away from shore at a rather brisk speed. As he reached Kowalski on the bow, still firing the .50 caliber, he lost his footing in the blood and nearly slid off the boat. Pulling himself back up, he pulled a prayer book and a small plastic bottle of holy water from his life vest. With the machine gun hammering overhead, and bullets from shore whizzing all around him, the chaplain went from body to body of the marines on the front of the 303 giving them all last rites, and blessing their bodies with the holy water. When he had finished, he noticed Kowalski was no longer firing as they had backed nearly half way out into the channel.

Standing up, the chaplain saw blood running down Kowalski's face. Reaching out his hand, he said, "Where are you hit, my son?"

Bringing up his hand, Kowalski wiped some of the blood from his forehead. "It's not mine Padre, It's Charlie Ansel's. The top of his head struck me in the face when he was hit. As tears ran down Kowalski's face, he dropped down to his knees and began to cry. Reaching over to the base of the machine gun mount, he picked up the piece of skull. "What do we do with it now, Padre. We can't put him back together again. Did you know his wife had a son about two months ago? Now, the poor little guy will never see his daddy. Looking down at the piece of skull in his hand he repeated, "What do we do with this now?"

Taking the bone from Kowalski's hand, the chaplain helped him back to his feet. "Come with me son, you can't stay on this deck, it's no longer fit for the living." He led Kowalski over to the roof above the crew quarters. "Lay down now and close your eyes. I'll be back in a while." Chaplain Hammond stated as he helped the very shaken sailor lay down.

Walking back to the cockpit, the chaplain looked down at Ed Yamry's body. Once again, he took out his prayer book and began to read the prayers for last rites. When finished, he helped Chief Petrovski carry him to the bow to be with the other casualties.

With the boats back out in the deep water near Dalupri Island, Buzz grabbed the mic for the TBS radio and began calling each boat for a report. When he was finished, he shook his head. Looking over at Lt. Hardy, Chief Petrovski and Chaplain Hammond, he said, "The 312 is gone along with eleven men, the 316 has heavy damage and four dead. The 323 took moderate damage and three killed, Kirkland on the 338 reports slight damage and one dead. Lieutenant Makely has slight damage with two dead. Add in our two men and that comes to twenty-three men killed and eighteen wounded."

As Buzz set course for Lingayan Gulf in the heavy fog, Chaplain Hammond walked up to the tired skipper. "What do we do about the bow, Skipper? We can't leave it that way, those poor boys deserve some dignity."

Without looking at the chaplain, Buzz replied. "It's dark, foggy, way too dangerous to work up there, Padre. We don't have bags for all of them, and right now I just don't know what damn difference it makes. I'll call ahead for a graves registration team when we get close and they'll deal with it. For now, go talk to the rest of my men. I have a boat to run for the last time."

Before the chaplain could say another word, the chief took him by the arm. "Come on, Padre, let's go talk to the men. Let the skipper be alone with his own thoughts tonight. He has a lot on his mind."

About halfway back to base, Buzz turned the wheel over to Lt. Hardy as he walked forward on the bow. Holding up the battle lantern they always kept in the cockpit, Buzz shined it over the bow and shook his head. The bow was littered with the bodies of eighteen marines, one Filipino freedom fighter that had made it off the island, and torpedo man Ansel and Yamry. Equipment was strewn everywhere, expended bullet casings from the .50 machine gun would fill six five-gallon buckets, and there didn't appear one place to walk that was not covered by blood.

Buzz knew this was his last mission, and last day as a PT skipper, but he wanted answers and he wasn't going to leave Lingayan Gulf until he got them, Capt. Robesky be damned.

Just before dawn, Buzz led his damaged flotilla back into Lingayan Gulf for the last time. As the saying goes, good news travels fast, but bad news faster. The pier was lined with nurses and doctors from the small hospital along with men from the graves registration team.

Mechanics, carpenters and ship fitters waited to see what repairs the boats required. Clerks, typists, cooks, marines and air crews from the nearby airfield stood silently, waiting to see what had happened to the battered PT crews they had come to know so well.

As the 303 docked, a hush fell over everyone. No one could believe the carnage they were seeing on the bow of the boat. Some men vomited, some cried, others just walked off hanging their heads. Slowly, the graves registration team went to work, logging the dead while placing their remains on stretchers.

The wounded were classified by the nurses before being loaded into ambulances for the short trip to the hospital.

Buzz leaned against the short wall on the back of the cockpit, feeling numb, as if he had just awoken from a bad dream, but with the carnage directly in front of him, he realized that no dream could be this horrific.

Slowly, Buzz walked from the cockpit and jumped down onto the pier where Chaplain Hammond waited for him. Stepping forward, the chaplain took Buzz by the arm, "Steady as you go there, my friend. I think you should check into the hospital for a rest, your nerves are shattered."

Looking over his shoulder to the aft deck where the crew was preparing to get off the boat, Buzz replied. "Look at them, Padre. They all went through the same thing I did last night. None of them are running off, none of them are complaining. How would it look if I caved in now. No, I'm not through yet, Padre, I still have some fight left in me." As if it didn't exist, nobody on the pier had paid any attention to a B-17 that had landed on the island as Buzz finished speaking.

Seconds later Capt. Robesky came storming onto the pier. "Maddox, do you have any idea of what you did last night? Do you know how many innocent people you killed, do you? Well, don't worry, it will all be spelled out in your court martial documents. I'm placing you under arrest for murder, and the shore patrol is on the way to take you into custody. This will save me the work of transferring you off my base."

Buzz looked over at the chaplain with a confused look on his face before turning back toward the captain. "What the hell are you talking about? I didn't see any innocent people last night. We were attacked from the moment the marines stepped foot in the water. Fire came from every inch of that beach, sir. I don't know where you received your information, but you had better double check it fast!"

Stepping directly in front of Buzz, the captain yelled, "You are responsible for the deaths of nearly one hundred and fifty Filipino freedom fighters. I dare say if I left you lose on this island, the local resistance would hang you from the highest palm tree and skin your sorry body for the buzzards to eat."

As the shore patrol officers arrived, the captain yelled, "Cuff him and take him to the brig!"

But before that was possible, the skippers from the rest of the boats and the crew of the 303, pushed Buzz away and surrounded him. Stepping forward, Lt. Sterling spoke up. "Captain, have you looked at these boats? Have you seen the dead and wounded? We were ambushed plain and simple by Japanese forces. We fought back, but we took horrible losses. I don't know what you were told or by who, but it's a damn lie!"

Capt. Robesky yelled out to the shore patrol, "Arrest this man for insubordination and mutiny. Does anyone else wish to say anything?"

Immediately, Chaplain Hammond stepped forward. Reaching into the pocket of his life preserver, he removed the top of Ansel's skull. Handing it to the captain he said. "This belonged to torpedo-man Ansel. He raced forward to the bow of the 303 in an attempt to pull the marines back on deck as they were being slaughtered in the water. He had pulled three men aboard when he was struck in the head. Luckily, that brave young man never suffered. I was going to give it to the graves registration team to put with his body, but maybe I should send it to his parents along with a letter telling them how their son died, and how the men that tried to save the marines were punished. I'm sorry, Captain, but you have no idea what happened last night. I do, I was there. These men never fired until they were fired upon. Someone fed you a line of crap, sir!"

Turning to the Chaplain, Capt. Robesky replied. "Well then, Padre, explain all the dead Filipinos. MacArthur wants to hang someone, and I have the culprits right here. So either you step back or I'll arrest you for mutiny as well!"

Not a word was said by anyone, and the shore patrol backed away as they waited to see what was going to happen next.

As Capt. Robesky reached for his sidearm, two jeeps came flying down the road that led to the pier. A deep voice called out, "Attention!"

With everyone standing at attention, Marine Col. Washburn and Admiral Denfield from New Caledonia walked onto the pier. Walking up to the bow of the 303, the admiral told the graves registration men to continue working. After looking at the stalemate on the pier, the admiral walked up to Capt. Robesky. "Hand me your service piece, Captain. There will be no shooting on this pier."

Reaching back, he gave the pistol to one of his aides. "The Colonel and I just arrived on that B-17 that landed a few minutes ago from

New Caledonia, after talking to Marine Lieutenant David Skripick who reported in from Calayan City. He told us that a large group of communist backed rebels numbering nearly three hundred, heard about the marine drop and were dead set against having any more Americans on the island. The lieutenant said a fight between the communist backed rebels and the American backed rebels broke out late yesterday afternoon near Bataraw Falls. The American backed rebels were over powered and nearly wiped out. A few were able to escape, but were not able to get away from the communist rebels until early evening. They didn't arrive at Calayan City to get help until midnight, when the battle with the boats was already under way. The marines on the northern part of the island had been attacked by some Japanese marines earlier in the day, and had their radio destroyed. They were waiting for the reinforcement team to bring them a new unit. Since the marines were waiting for a new radio, they had no way of contacting Lingayan to tell them not to land the marines. MacArthur's headquarters informed us this morning that the communist backed rebels in the Babuyan Islands have been a serious problem since before the war began. Lieutenant Skripick reported his combat team arrived at the beach around 0500hrs, and confirms they counted nearly one hundred and fifty communist backed rebel bodies and a radio in good condition."

Turning to Capt. Robesky. the admiral continued. "There were no friendlies or American casualties on the island. However, they were able to recover the bodies of the marines that were not able to make it back to the PT boats."

Walking over to Buzz the admiral held out his hand. "Are you Commander Maddox?"

Shaking the admiral's hand, Buzz replied, "Yes sir, I was skipper of the 303 boat, and was Commander of squadron seven until this morning. If there's any blame to be placed upon the squadron, it's my doing, sir."

"Why do you say you were commander until this morning? Are

you taking another job?" the admiral asked as he looked at Buzz's blood spattered tired face.

"Sir, I was relieved of command as of this morning by Capt. Robesky. He told me I was being reassigned to operate an ocean tug over at New Caledonia." Buzz replied, while glaring at the captain, not caring what happened at this point in time, to the captain or himself.

"Commander Maddox, you'll remain right where you're at. You brought five heavily damaged boats and their crews back to Lingayan under some pretty ugly conditions. Job well done," the admiral stated, as he patted a very tired commander Maddox on the shoulder.

Turning back toward Capt. Robesky the admiral shook his head. "Gilbert, I'm sorry but I'm relieving you of your command. I was not happy when they gave you the assignment in the first place. You were a hell of a boat skipper in your day, but I didn't feel you were cut out for this job. At the time of your promotion I was far to busy to get involved so I let it slide. However last night I promoted Commander Abergast from squadron three to captain to replace you. He's a hell of a PT man and I'll send him over tomorrow. You can pack your bags and return to New Caledonia with me this evening. Colonel Washburn will be in temporary command until Abergast arrives."

Looking at Chaplain Hammond, the admiral inquired. "Padre, where have our paths crossed? I am pretty sure I know you from somewhere."

Nodding his head, the chaplain replied. "I met you on Guadalcanal, sir."

"Ah yes, the canal. I don't even want to remember how many we buried that day. It was a damn awful place. So, tell me Padre, if I order a landing ship to be here by say 0700hrs. tomorrow, would you consider having a small service on the pier before we load the boxes on the ship?" the admiral asked as he looked at the chaplain's bloody uniform.

"It would be my honor, Admiral. I fought in my own way beside these men last night, it's the least I can do." Holding out the piece of Ansel's skull," the chaplain continued. "Sir, I blessed this skull last night along with all the bodies, can you have the shore patrol get it to the graves registration office so it can be buried with torpedo man Ansel."

Without a word being said, one of the shore patrol officers walked over and took it in his hand. Removing a bandanna from his pocket, he gently wrapped it and took a step back. He saluted the admiral and said, "Consider it done, sir."

Walking over to Col. Washburn, the admiral said. "Take charge of your men, Cal. They could use a shower, clean uniforms, hot food, and a long rest. Help the chaplain get the burial service lined up. Use some of the marines if need be."

After saluting, Col. Washburn nodded, "Good as done, sir."

At 0645hrs. the following morning, the pier was lined with men and women, sailors and marines alike, all in their dress uniforms. The ramp of the landing craft ship had already been dropped on the beach, right next to a long line of hastily built saw horses.

Exactly at 0700hrs, four trucks carrying wooden boxes covered with flags slowly made their way to the pier. Marines and sailors stood by, waiting to unload the boxes. Each box was placed on a set of saw horses, and two marines made sure the flags were adjusted properly as the make shift caskets were set down. With all twenty-three boxes resting quietly on the saw horses, Chaplain Hammond walked past them, sprinkling each box with holy water.

Returning to a small podium the carpenters had quickly assembled, he read off each man's name, the boats or units they were assigned to, and their home towns. After reading several passages of scripture, he opened his bible to St. Luke chapter twenty-three, verses thirty-three through forty-three. After reading it, he looked over the assembled crowd and reread the last lines. *'Jesus, remember me when you come into your kingdom, and Jesus replied, Truly I tell you, today you will be with me in paradise.'"*

Closing the bible, Chaplain Hammond began, "I can truly tell you that these twenty-three men are with Jesus in paradise today. For two nights they went out on an ocean so treacherous, I don't think even the apostles would have attempted it. They did not argue or complain, they thought it was a mission that would help bring this terrible war to an end. They fought gallantly, attempting to save the lives of the men around them, and the men on all the boats of squadron seven. Each of these men leave behind families that will grieve for them, while they deal with their own broken hearts and tremendous loss. Sometimes when I have completed a homily for a warrior, I wonder what their last minutes were like. In the case of these heroes, I know what it was like, because I was there. It was frightening, and incomprehensible to understand the amount of deadly fire they were enduring. They fought like the heroes they were, and made no attempt to quit, until God decided to bring them home. Some will ask, how did this man die? I will always answer, no matter the battle, each man dies alone, with his own thoughts, his own fears, his own faith, and with his last prayers."

Bowing his head, the chaplain ended the service with the Our Father Prayer. When he finished, from somewhere back at the edge of the jungle, a marine unit fired off a twenty-one-gun salute, followed by a marine bugler's solemn rendition of Taps.

As the crowd dispersed back to their assignments, Chaplain Hammond and Buzz watched the marines load the boxes onto the landing ship. When the last box was on board, the ramp went back up as the powerful diesel engine pulled the vessel back out into the gulf.

As the men walked past the 303, Buzz stopped for a moment to watch the repair crews begin working on the boat. Looking at the foredeck, Buzz shook his head. She looks a lot better than she did when we came in now that all the blood is washed off. But I don't think the 303 will ever be the same.

Chaplain Hammond placed his hand on Buzz's shoulder. "Will any of us ever be the same? I kind of doubt it, my friend."

Before Buzz could return to his hut to change uniforms, a runner from operations informed him that the captain wanted to see him right away. Buzz wasn't sure how this was going to play out, since Capt.

Robesky had cut orders before he was whisked off the island by the Admiral.

Entering the operations hut, Buzz snapped to attention and saluted as the colonel was sitting just inside the door reading reports. Colonel Washburn returned the salute as he stood up from behind the battered metal desk. Walking over to Buzz, he extended his hand. "From reading Capt. Robesky's notes and reports, you are the root of all evil on this island. Yet he never busted you or relieved you of command until the other night. Can you explain that, Skipper?"

Buzz just shook his head and said, "I hope my record speaks for itself, however, if the colonel prefers to send me to the tug boat at New Caledonia, I can still be ready within the hour."

Walking back to his desk, Col. Washburn picked up a file folder. "Maddox, in this folder are forms totally completed, sending you to Mindanao with a promotion to full commander, to take charge of the base there. The base has become increasingly smaller since the war moved on, but it still plays a vital part in our Philippine operations. Say the word and it's yours, because the admiral has already authorized it."

Buzz looked down at the floor for a moment before responding. "Sir, am I being kicked upstairs to get me out of a PT boat and hide me out until the end of the war?"

Tossing the file on the desk and taking a swallow of coffee, Col. Washburn shook his head. "No Commander, the 303 is still yours, and you will remain commander of squadron seven if that's what you prefer. You have done nothing wrong as far as we are concerned. There's no way you could have known what was coming down at Calayan. My opinion, and the admiral agrees, is that the raid should have been canceled until conditions improved. True, that was not good for the marines on the island, but they would have figured out a plan, they always do. So, which job do you want, Skipper?"

Smiling, Buzz pointed to his left. "The 303 is my home, sir. I'll turn down the promotion and stay put if you don't mind. And sorry for any inconvenience this causes you, sir."

Colonel Washburn smiled, "No inconvenience, Skipper. Go tend to your flock."

Walking back to his hut, Buzz felt relieved and somewhat happy. Now he had to find two men for his boat, and help look for enough crew members to fill out the rest of his squadron. Luckily, there were now quite a few new crew members, and old crew members returning from hospitals and rest periods he could choose from.

Over the next week, two veteran PT men were assigned to the 303. Dan Theisman, a veteran radioman and medic was returning from a leg wound, so he took over the job left by the loss of Ed Yamry. Darnell Patrick, another veteran returning from medical leave, was assigned as the new torpedo man. With Captain Abergast now in command, he was allowed to transfer PT 347 from New Guinea with a seasoned crew to fill out squadron seven. The skipper was Lt. Mark Jesop from Miami, Florida. Like Buzz, he had spent his entire life on the sea, operating charter fishing boats with his father around the Keys.

Crews, mechanics, carpenters and boat fitters worked day and night bringing the boats of squadron seven back to life. When all the repairs were completed, Buzz was extremely happy to take his small flotilla back out to sea, and get all the crews operating efficiently again. Lieutenant Jesop and his crew enjoyed being part of squadron seven. They were a well-seasoned crew that had spent time patrolling near the Panama Canal before entering the war at Rendova. The crew had stayed together after losing one boat in the Solomon's, and they were determined to end the war together.

After completing three days of training, the skippers were called to the operations hut at 0700hrs. on the fourth day.

Captain Abergast stood aside an Army Colonel by a huge map of the Philippine Islands. When the men were seated, the captain introduced Colonel Whitman from MacArthur's Headquarters Unit. "Good morning, men. As you are well aware, this war is coming to an end quickly, but we have some major problems here in the Philippines and the general wants them handled. The communist rebels are causing us tremendous problems in northern Luzon and the Babuyan Islands as you are already aware. We intend to land marines on Babuyan and Camiguin Islands tomorrow morning. We want squadron seven to cover the landings around Camiguin, squadron two will handle Babuyan. Support the landings with gun fire where needed, and stop the rebels from moving to other islands. You do not need to wait for orders to fire. We intend to clean out those islands in less than a week. It's that simple, gentlemen. We will see you on site at 0600hrs."

The men of squadron seven were happy to be of assistance, as they wanted to get some pay back for the damage inflicted on them during the operation at Calayan Island.

At 0430hrs. the following morning, squadron seven took to the open sea, charging through the four-foot swells at a steady 30 knots with their engines unmuffled. Chief Petrovski made Buzz nervous as he paced back and forth past the cockpit. Lt. Hardy finally told him to go below and look over the charts with the new radioman, so he had a good idea of where the reefs were located. Before going below, the chief looked at Buzz. "Guess I was getting on your nerves, huh Skipper?"

"Just a tad, Chief, just a tad. Get some coffee, check the charts, and breathe," Buzz replied with a smile, fully understanding the chiefs mindset.

As squadron seven passed Fuga Island, they could hear five-inch batteries on several destroyers already firing at targets on the island, being pointed out by aircraft overhead. Buzz allowed his skippers to scatter around the small fleet so they could move quickly where ever they were needed.

Lieutenant Jesop had barely slowed down to about five knots when his .20mm gunner pointed toward several small boats entering the channel between Camiguin and Fuga. Quickly, the 347 did a one hundred eighty degree turn and charged toward the boats at full speed. Within seconds, the 347 began taking light arms fire. The bow machine gun operator knocked out the engine of the first boat immediately, but the occupants refused to stop firing. Turning the boat to port, Lt. Jesop waved his arm in the air. Instantly, the bow gunner, the port dual fifty caliber machine gun, and the .20mm cannon opened fire. In seconds, the boats were sinking and there were no survivors, so Lt. Jesop returned to the fleet as landing craft were going ashore. The army landed about five hundred veteran jungle fighters on the island, along with five smaller Stuart tanks. Any shooting from the island toward the landing boats was quickly met with accurate devastating fire from the destroyers and PT boats. When that landing was completed, Buzz, along with the 323 and 316, escorted three landing crafts to the northern tip of the island where they went ashore.

With the small landing completed, Buzz took the 303 and 316 around the east side of the island to see what might be happening over there. Quickly, Lt. Hardy pointed out a Japanese landing barge sailing away from a small cove heading north toward Babuyan Island. Checking the barge with his binoculars, the lieutenant called out to Buzz. "They are not Japs, they're communist rebels!"

One of the rebels jumped up on the rear of the landing barge and began firing toward the PT boats with a Japanese type three heavy machine gun. Buzz brought the 303 around the starboard side of the craft, as Lt. Holbrook swung over to the port side. Immediately, every weapon on the two boats opened up on the slow barge. It only took a minute before smoke began to appear from the engine compartment. The men on the barge were a lot like many of the Japanese soldiers they had encountered. They fought to the bitter end, refusing to surrender. As Buzz closed in closer to the barge, a tall man jumped up from the bottom of the boat and ran to the type three machine gun. With his pistol already in his hand, the chief leaned against the radio mast for support and pulled the trigger twice. The heavy.45 round struck the man in the upper chest, lifting him off his feet throwing him overboard. Holstering his weapon, the chief nodded his head. "Nothing personal, but that's for Yamry you son-of-a-bitch."

Slowly, the barge rolled over on its starboard side and slid to the bottom of the bay. The two boats patrolled the east side of the island, giving fire support to marines most of the afternoon. By nightfall, the marines had wiped out any resistance on two thirds of the island. Squadron seven continued giving support where needed for several more days until the marines stated the islands were secured.

For the next three days a tropical storm roared over the Philippines, uprooting trees and smashing buildings. Every possible aircraft had been flown away to safety until the storm blew over. Luckily, the harbor where the PT boats were moored provided enough protection, so only three boats from squadron seven sustained some light damage.

As people assigned to island duty cleaned and repaired the base, Buzz took squadron seven out to sea around the northern coast of Luzon. They had barely begun running along the coast when they observed a band of about a hundred Japanese marines sitting on the shore waving a white flag. Several of the soldiers jumped into the water, attempting to swim toward the boats.

Buzz ordered the boats to move farther away from shore and not allow any Japanese to come close enough to toss a grenade at them. Quickly Theisman radioed back to base, asking what they were supposed to do.

Not wanting to have the Japanese soldiers walk back into the jungle and continue fighting, Capt. Abergast sent out a landing ship the marines had used on their mission in the Babuyan Islands. He also sent fifty marines to take control of the prisoners.

When the landing ship arrived, a marine translator jumped up on the side of the ship. He told them to strip off all their clothing, and leave everything they had on the beach, before walking over to the ship that would drop its ramp about fifty yards away.

Some of the Japanese immediately began to strip off their clothing, but about thirty of them walked off to the east, carrying their weapons while yelling at the translator. Realizing this could get out of control in a hurry, Buzz yelled to Kowalski on the bow machine gun. "Kowalski, give those palm trees a hair-cut!"

Kowalski sprayed the tops of the palm trees closest to the men. As branches rained down around the tired soldiers, they dropped to their knees, but did not drop their weapons or attempt to comply with the translator's orders. Buzz shook his head as he looked at the chief, "Guess we need to try something else." Leaning forward, Buzz called out to Kowalski. "Alright, kick up some sand on the beach around them, but for God's sake, don't hit anyone!"

Nodding his head, Kowalski once again cut lose with his machine gun, kicking up sand all around the angry Japanese. Slowly, the men dropped their weapons, took off their clothing, raised their hands and joined their fellow prisoners on the landing ship.

As the ramp went up and the boat backed away from shore, Ridman looked at Buzz. "What's to say they don't attempt to try and take over the landing ship before they get back to base."

The chief had to laugh, "When's the last time you decided to get into trouble bare ass naked, Ridman. Besides, they would have to run up the steps to the top deck and that .50 caliber machine gun near the bridge is a great deterrent. Naw, they're beat, all they want now is hot food, a dry place to sleep, and to get home alive. We may start seeing more of this."

Over the next several weeks, Squadron seven took several groups of surrendering Japanese soldiers from the island. However, the boat crews learned quickly that some of the Japanese wanted to die for the emperor and were not ready to be taken alive.

One Japanese soldier that had tossed his weapon and stripped off his clothing, walked toward the landing ship with his hands in the air. When he was about ten yards from the landing craft, he dove to the ground where a hand grenade was laying. Rolling across the sand he scooped it up, attempting to toss it into the well of the boat where other prisoners were seated. A marine standing alertly on the ramp, ran toward shore when he saw the man dive into the sand. He fired several rounds into the soldier's chest, just as he was releasing the grenade. Instead of getting the distance to hit the ship, it went straight up into the air. Returning to the ground, it exploded near five surrendering soldiers, killing all of them.

On another pick up mission, a soldier that was walking onto the landing ship with his hands up, jumped out of line, tackling a marine. Several more prisoners charged forward, attempting to pull the bayonet or rifle away from the downed marine. On the upper deck, the marine manning the heavy machine gun opened up on the ramp. As bullets ricocheted off the steel ramp, Japanese soldiers ran back toward the beach screaming. Some laid down in the sand, still hoping to surrender, while others ran for their weapons and began shooting at the marine manning the machine gun.

Buzz yelled at Wickman on the port machine gun to stop the situation. With a quick blast, the twin .50 caliber machine guns knocked down everyone that had picked up a weapon or was attempting to run back into the jungle. With the shooting over, three more marines charged down onto the loading ramp to aid their downed man. Miraculously, he only sustained several cuts from the bayonet, but he was completely shaken. He had just joined the marine detachment a few days earlier and had not seen any action yet.

Quickly, the balance of the marines on the landing ship charged down into the well of the vessel to regain control. With order restored, the marines directed the survivors to pick up the bodies of their comrades and load them on the ship, so they could be properly buried.

Sailing back to Lingayan Gulf, an old smoke belching Japanese float plane came flying from the north. All the prisoners began pointing toward the plane and yelling for the marines to shoot it down, as they were well aware that the pilot would attempt to crash his plane into the ship.

The PT crews were also well aware of the intention of the pilot, since he had a two-hundred-pound bomb lashed to the bottom of his aircraft. Immediately, every gunner on the landing ship and the six PT boats opened fire. Because of the slow speed of the aircraft, it was an excellent target as it hung low in the sky. Instantly, the lethal projectiles being thrown up by the small flotilla began to take a toll. The right pontoon fell from the plane, as did most of the canopy. Seconds later, half the horizontal stabilizer was torn from the aircraft, causing it to vibrate uncontrollably. Moments later the aircraft rolled over on its left side, spiraling into the ocean about fifty yards from the landing ship. For some reason the two-hundred-pound bomb never exploded on impact, and sunk harmlessly to the bottom of the South China Sea.

On August sixth, scuttlebutt circulated throughout the Philippines, that the United States had dropped a new type of bomb on a Japanese city, and that surrender was imminent, but nothing came of the rumor. Operations continued out of Lingayan Gulf, although most missions were returning without having any enemy contact, or observing any more soldiers willing to surrender.

Again on August ninth, scuttlebutt once more began rolling around the base that another one of those new bombs had been dropped on a second Japanese city. This time, everyone was sure the enemy would sur-render. However, midnight came and went without a word from either Washington or MacArthur's headquarters.

At 0600hrs. on August tenth, Buzz took the 303, 347 and 316 on a patrol north toward Laoag, where a small reconnaissance plane had reported seeing a dozen Japanese soldiers in a small fishing boat heading northwest at about fifteen knots. As the boats closed in on Laoag, they ran into a large rain squall that brought them to a crawl as they began searching for the fishing vessel. They had searched for half an hour when they received a call from Capt. Abergast, informing them the Japanese had surrendered and to return to base.

Picking up the mic, Buzz replied, "What about the fishing boat, Captain? The recon plane said it was in tough shape. The men on board may not survive this storm."

Instantly, Capt. Abergast came back. "The war is over Maddox, bring the boats home. Let God deal with those men."

About an hour later, all of squadron seven was tied up to the pier and the celebration was well underway. More bottles of liquor appeared than the shore patrol could ever confiscate. Capt. Abergast told the shore patrol to allow the men to celebrate, just don't let any of them do anything that might jeopardize themselves or others.

Staying away from all the drinking and horseplay, Buzz began walking over toward one of the landing strips the Seabees had carved out of the jungle. Sitting down on a log, he watched the marines packing equipment into transports. Several minutes later, Chaplain Hammond walked over, sitting down beside him.

"Surprised to find you here, Skipper. I like coming to this spot to watch planes and think. Something about it is kind of relaxing," the chaplain stated, as he watched a marine Corsair take to the heavy overcast sky.

Buzz shook his head, "I needed some peace and quiet. I can only take so many drunks, and there are way too many of them back there roaming around. Plus, I wanted to think about what I'm going to say to Connie the first time I see her. Damn, I can't wait to hold her in my arms again!"

Slapping Buzz on the back, Chaplain Hammond smiled. "I wish you the best, my friend. In whatever you and Connie decide to do with your lives. I know you'll do well, you're a great leader and a caring person. Actually, I wanted to find you to let you know I'm leaving on an air transport at 0800hrs. tomorrow, heading for New Caledonia. It's the first step on my own long road back home. I received a letter from my Bishop a couple days ago, stating that they need me back in Boston. Of course, when he mailed it, he could not have known the war would end two days after I received the letter, so it all worked out well. Buzz, it has been great getting to know you. I learned a lot about life from our time together that I can take back to my flock. Should make for some interesting sermons, if you know what I mean."

Buzz laughed heartily as he looked over at his good friend. "Padre, I'm going to miss you very much. I'm so glad we were able to get to know one another. Right now I'm not sure where Connie and I are going to end up, but it will likely be somewhere along the Atlantic coast for sure. I hope you won't mind getting a visit from an old war buddy from time to time."

As the two men stood up, Chaplain Hammond smiled. "I'm counting on it, Commander, and I hope to baptize your first baby."

Laughing, Buzz stated, "Remember now, Padre, I'm not catholic."

Nodding his head in agreement, Chaplain Hammond replied, "All things in good time, Skipper, all things in good time."

By midnight, most of the men at Lingayan Gulf had found a spot to sleep, or had passed out after a long day of celebrating.

Buzz was sitting quietly on the stern of the 303 looking up at the brilliant stars in the dark night sky, when Chief Petrovski walked up to him.

"So, this is where you disappeared to, Skipper. No one was sure what happened to you. Mind if I join you?"

Smiling at his chief, Buzz replied, "No Chief, have a seat. I came here a few hours ago to get away from the craziness so I could think. Somehow all the celebrating and merriment made me feel a bit sad. I started thinking about all the men we lost along the way since Tulagi. I thought about the two boats I lost, and all the other boats that were destroyed on our way here. The names and the faces of all those men will stick with me forever. They were good men, Chief."

Nodding his head, the chief looked up at the southern cross constellation. "I keep thinking of all the men that disappeared into the depths of that unforgiving ocean and were never heard from again. I guess burying the remains of a man is one thing, but having a man disappear into the depths and not being able to fully explain to their family members what happened is rather frightening. I always hoped if I died out there that my body could be buried on land somehow. It bothered me to think of my remains becoming part of the ocean. I guess dead is dead, but somehow a grave to me is a better ending."

Buzz nodded his head as he listened to the screech of some jungle bird not too far away. "Funny, I think I'm going to miss the screeching and howling of the jungle birds once I get home. There is something unique to all of it, even though the jungle is a deadly place to be."

Reaching into a bag he had carried with him, the chief took out a pint bottle of brandy and cracked the seal. "Skipper, the war is over, the killing has stopped, and those of us that survived are going home. How about a toast with me to all the men that will never return home, and those we'll never account for."

Reaching over, Buzz took the bottle and drank a long swig. After coughing, he laughed, "Yeah that's some really smooth stuff, Chief."

After the chief had taken a long drink, he poured the remaining brandy into the water and said, "Rest well, my brothers, rest well."

Looking back up at the southern cross, Buzz replied. "Chief, no matter where they are out there, God has supplied an outstanding grave marker for every single one of them, better than any man could ever make."

Nodding his head and removing his hat, the chief replied, "Amen, Skipper. Amen."

CHAPTER 24
ENDINGS AND BEGINNINGS

On August 19, 1945, four days after Japan surrendered in Tokyo Bay, ending World War Two, a flotilla of six scarred and weary veteran PT boats sailed past the island of Corregidor, entering Manila Bay in the Philippine Islands.

Buzz stood quietly in the cockpit of PT 303, as he and Chief Petrovski scanned all the damaged and half sunk Japanese combat and commerce ships littering the waters of the bay. Slowly, Buzz maneuvered his aging, battle worn boat around the wreckage that lined the once busy, prosperous commercial wharf, the envy of nearly every far east country before the war.

Here and there, small pockets of Japanese soldiers and sailors that were still coming down from the mountains, stood on the damaged piers, bowing in respect to the conquerors, as the flotilla of American victors passed them by. The once proud masters of the Japanese Far East Asia Co-Prosperity Sphere, now wore tattered, dirty, often blood-soaked uniforms. Some of them walked with canes or makeshift crutches, supporting legs or ankles that had been crudely amputated. Several high-ranking officers walked to the end of a large pier, placed pistols to their heads and fired, sending their bodies into the dark oil covered water below, choosing death over final surrender and personal humiliation when they returned home.

Sailing farther to the west, they observed what remained of the once proud city of Manila, known around the world as the Jewel of the Pacific. It now stood in absolute burned out ruin, as residents in tattered clothing roamed aimlessly through the rubble strewn streets, searching for any scrap of food to eat, or something of value they could sell for a few cents. The streets were clogged with burned out cars, buses and trucks, many still containing the charred remains of the people that rode in them. The stench of death and decay hung over the city, drifting slowly out over the ocean with the trade winds.

Women searched the streets with sharpened bamboo spears, looking for any remaining dogs or cats they could kill to feed their families. Due to the oil and other pollutants in the harbor, the shorelines were covered with the rotting remnants of fish, birds and blotted human bodies that added to the dreadful odor. Any sea life that did survive had long since moved out of the bay.

Buzz backed the 303 up against a former U.S. naval pier that already held fifteen other boats. Once the boat was secured, several Naval Security Officers stood by to lock down the boats once the crew disembarked with their belongings. The crews were taken by trucks to rather nice barracks built by the Japanese early on in the war.

The following morning, Buzz marched the crew of the 303 to an administrative building where everyone except Buzz and Ensign Hardy went through a quick processing procedure. When they had completed all the requirements, they were confined to the base until they could be shipped out to Hawaii on a destroyer that was already tied up at Corregidor.

That evening, as Buzz sat quietly drinking a beer outside a makeshift bar, Chief Petrovski approached him.

"Permission to speak freely, sir?" the always dependable petty officer inquired.

Buzz laughed, as he pointed to an empty stool beside him. He could tell the chief was having a very hard time saying goodbye to everyone.

Looking over at his skipper, the chief smiled. "Sir, I know we kind of covered some of this before, but I just need to explain myself one last time. I thought my naval days were over when I came to talk to you at Melville. But because of you, I've seen more action and covered more miles of ocean than I ever thought possible. I've seen many a good man die, made some great friends, and taught more men to stay alive than I could have imagined. Some days I wonder why I survived everything we went through and others did not. I was never so scared the day I asked you for a job, because I knew if you didn't give me a chance, no one would, and I would have been left out of this war. All I wanted to do was put the past behind me and prove myself capable of being a real team member in combat. Thanks to you, I accomplished that mission and I can hold my head high in a way that I thought I'd lost forever. Now here I am again, scared as hell, because I don't know what's going to become of me now that the war is over. Someday when the time is right, I want to meet my daughter and try to get to know her. I want her to learn that her daddy did amount to something when the chips were down. I owe that all to you, Skipper. But now I'm all too sure they're going to bust me out of this man's navy and send me packing. You wouldn't be in need of a tough sea going salt like me back on your fishing fleet, would you, sir?"

Buzz had to laugh as he set down his empty beer bottle. "Chief, I pretty much burned all those bridges when I left for Melville. I'm not at all sure the family will take me back into the business, and I'm not sure Connie wants to be the wife of a fisherman. Right now, my life is just as upside down as yours. However, I can put in a good word for you, my brother certainly owes me a big favor. And wherever I end up, if I'm in need of a man with your skills, I'll be sure to give you a call.

Smiling and nodding his head, he handed Buzz a piece of paper. "Here's my brother's address. He says I can stay with him as long as needed until I get myself settled in. If you need me, you know where to get a hold of me, and I'll come running as quick as I can."

After shaking hands once more, the chief saluted and walked away.

Before Buzz could get up, Gabe Ridman walked up to him. After saluting, he smiled. "Sir, no one ever stood up for me the way you did when we arrived on Rendova. I appreciated it then, and I still do. I've spoken with Captain Abergast about staying in the navy and going to

OTC. He said he thought the navy could use a man like me to keep things moving now that the war is over. He told me I needed two officers to recommend me. He said he would be one and you should be the second. Would you do that for me, Skipper?"

Buzz had to laugh, "You, an officer? Heaven help the navy! Hell yes, I'll sign for you, Ridman. Get me that paperwork and it's good as done. You'll make a fine officer and a great leader."

The last man that came looking for Buzz that evening was Kowalski. "Sir, you've been a great skipper to serve with. I always trusted your judgment and it always paid off. My parents were so angry when I wanted to be a PT sailor, but they came to accept it when I told them about you. My father just bought a ferry service that operates in and around Chesapeake Bay, and they have a job open for you if you're interested. But this time you might have to work for me, as Dad wants me to be a partner in the business with him."

Buzz laughed as he punched his forward deck machine gunner in the arm. "Joe, I need a job for sure, and I want to stay near or on the water. Let me think about it, and I'll get a hold of you down the road. Actually, I still have some naval time left to fulfill, and I'm not sure what they're going to do with me. Problem is, you might have to hire the chief as well if I take the job. Would that be a problem?"

Kowalski smiled. "I could do that, sir. We could use a man like him to keep the deck crews in line, as long as he leaves that damn .45 at home."

"I don't expect that will be a problem," Buzz replied.

The following afternoon a landing craft began taking PT boat crews over to Corregidor for their trip to Hawaii. Buzz was surprised at how much these tough combat veterans cried as they hugged each other and said their final goodbyes. Buzz stood on the pier in the middle of his crew, shaking hands and exchanging personal comments. He knew full well this was goodbye, and that he may never see most of them ever again. He had never done anything this hard in his entire life. After a second call from the boatswain, the crew of the 303 slowly walked up the ramp into the LCT. When they were all assembled inside the boat facing the pier, Joe Kowalski yelled out;

"Attention! Present arms!"

The men all stood like statues awaiting one last salute from their skipper. After nodding his head, Buzz returned the salute as a tear streamed down each cheek.

As the ramp went up on the LCT and it backed out into the bay, Buzz felt an emptiness in his stomach. He watched the LCT glide across the calm waters of the bay until it disappeared around the back side of the island.

Although the officer's quarters were neat and orderly, and the mess hall served decent food, there was not a lot for the men to do and they were strictly prohibited from leaving the base. The Sea Bees installed a rough basketball court and horse shoe pits, allowing the men to blow off some steam as they awaited their next orders.

About a week later, the men were returned to the pier where they had docked their boats. They were surprised to see the boats had been stripped of anything the navy found salvageable. A large hole had been cut in the rear deck of the boats, allowing salvage crews to remove all but the center engine.

When given the orders, Buzz fired up the single engine as Ensign Hardy released the mooring lines. Shortly, a caravan of ten boats idled back out into Manila Bay before turning south into the Pacific Ocean. They followed a large ocean tug that led them through hundreds of small islands before arriving at Samar Island.

The skippers of the boats stared in shock at the site that awaited them. All along the shore and out into the small bay were the burning remains of trusty PT boats. A crane sat on a pier waiting to pluck the last engine out of each boat before it was shoved by the tug boat out into the bay to be burned. As Buzz brought the 303 up to the pier, several workers jumped into the engine compartment with torches. In minutes, everything was cut lose, and the twelve-cylinder Packard engine was hoisted out of the boat and placed on a barge on the far side of the pier.

The skippers walked ashore and stood near several buildings as they watched high grade aviation fuel being dumped on their boats. Moments later several torches were tossed into the pitiful looking green combat vessels that had done so much to keep the Japanese at bay before the navy could rebuild. A large whoosh filled the air as the fuel ignited the dry wood. Large orange flames leaped skyward as clouds of black smoke rode the winds out across the bay and dispersed over the ocean.

Several officers, including Buzz, wiped tears from their faces as they watched their trusty boats turned into a funeral pyre. The first thing to collapse on most of the boats was the roof over the crew quarters. Once that caved in, the fire swept quickly throughout the interior, sending showers of sparks and cinders skyward. Buzz shook his head as he watched the foredeck of the 303 cave in, as the hull begin to burn. One by one the boats were shoved out into deeper water by the tug, where they would unceremoniously sink, as the flames broke open the hulls.

Buzz and Ensign Hardy were glad to see the landing craft arrive to take them back to Manila. They didn't want to watch the 303 sink out of sight forever.

The next day most of the officers climbed aboard a heavy cruiser for the trip back to Pearl Harbor, Buzz and Ensign Hardy among them. After spending so much time on a wooden boat that bounced like a cork at times, Buzz was impressed with the ride and comfort of such a large modern fighting ship. The food was always hot and on schedule, the bunking areas were dry, and the wind didn't blow the damp night air in until your blanket was soaked. This may be a Cadillac of ships, but in the final tally, it had none of the charm, the excitement or the crew closeness of a small eighty-foot PT boat.

Five days later as the cruiser entered Pearl Harbor, the officers stood at attention on the port side and saluted, as the ship passed what remained of the U.S.S. Arizona. It had been just a few months short of four years since Japan had bombed the harbor to begin the war. It was hard to believe the base could have been rebuilt and expanded at such a rapid rate, while continuing to build and repair the weapons of war.

After the ship was secured at the ten-ten dock, the officers were taken to temporary quarters near Hickam Field where they would be processed and sent home for leave or discharged.

That evening, Buzz picked up a ride to the hospital, hoping to surprise Connie. He had not given her any idea in his last letter when he would be returning to Pearl. Walking into the surgical ward, he spotted Connie at the nurse's desk writing notes in a file. He placed his index finger over his lips, signaling the other nurses that were smiling to keep quiet.

Walking up behind Connie, Buzz bent over slightly and whispered. "I'm in pain, I need a nurse, but not just any nurse, I need really pretty nurse!"

Letting out a scream that he was sure could be heard all the way to Diamond Head, Connie jumped from her chair, throwing her arms around Buzz as she wept. All the nurses clapped and cheered as Buzz swung Connie around in a circle, before placing her back on her feet and kissing her.

It was several minutes before she was finally able to speak. After regaining her composure, she smiled. "You survived, we survived, let's get married! I'm not letting you out of my sight ever again, sailor!"

Buzz kissed Connie again before replying. "Meet me at the main gate when your shift is over. I'll take you out for the best steak in Honolulu and we'll talk about everything."

After a marvelous dinner in one of the hotels near Waikiki, Buzz and Connie walked along the beach as the stars twinkled overhead and the moon illuminated the palm tree lined beach.

Reaching into his jacket pocket, Buzz pulled out a small box containing an engagement ring. Kneeling down in the warm sand, Buzz looked up into Connie's green eyes. "I have been waiting a long time for this, and there were times I never thought we would get here. I have forty days of leave to take right now, and then they want me to teach gunnery school at Annapolis for the next six months before I'm discharged. I have a job offer to operate ferry boats in Chesapeake Bay, or I can beg forgiveness and get back into the family business, or we can stay in the navy. No matter which way we go, I want you as my wife. Connie, will you do the honor of marrying me?"

Pulling Buzz up from the sand, Connie threw her arms around his neck as she kissed him. "Yes, yes, a thousand times yes," she whispered, as she held Buzz tightly. "I don't know what you have in mind, but there's a small wedding chapel a few blocks from here. We could get married there tomorrow, so when they ship you home for leave, they'll have to let me to go with you. I already checked into it, as I was hoping you would ask me to marry you right away."

Buzz laughed, as he nodded his head. "Yes, tomorrow sounds great. I can get permission to be off base for three days for a quick honeymoon before beginning my processing."

The next afternoon, with Ensign Hardy and one of Connie's friends as witnesses, Buzz and Connie were married in the chapel on Waikiki Beach.

Being able to secure a cabin at a discounted rate on the S.S. Lurline, the happy couple settled in for a relaxing five-day cruise from Honolulu to San Diego. On the third day of the trans-pacific cruise, a man approached Buzz and Connie in the dining room.

"I hope you don't see this as an intrusion into your privacy, but I couldn't help over hearing your conversation this morning with the other naval couple. My name is Marvin Crittendon, and I have owned Blue Seas Boat Works in Newport for the last twenty-five years. Before the war we made the Montague line of yachts. Well, the navy took over my business in 1942, and had us build several types of landing vessels. Now that the war is over, we're going back to building yachts, and a new line of small fast boats. I heard you skippered PT boats, and I thought you just might be the man to take charge of our test pilot operation. My son just purchased two of the last PT boats coming off the assembly line since the war ended. We would like to use that design to construct our fast boats. We've purchased sixteen Packard V-12 engines that were surplus, and twenty large diesel engines that were going to be placed in landing craft, so we have a good supply of engines to start with. You told that other couple this morning that your family ran fishing boats up at Kennebunkport before the war. It sounds to me like you are very well suited for my operation. I'll pay you well if you'll help us put the Montague name back out on the high seas with good quality vessels. Are you interested?"

Buzz looked over at Connie who appeared to be about ready to explode. Nodding his head, Buzz replied "That sounds like the type of job I would love to have, but I have one problem. I still owe the navy six months before I can take the position."

Mr. Crittendon nodded his head. "That's fine. It's going to take at least that long to change over the shop to build yachts again, so when the navy cuts you lose, come and see us. Is there anything else we can do for you, Mr. Maddox."

"Well, actually there is. If you hire me, I was wondering if you might possibly consider hiring a former naval chief named Walter Petrovski. He knows how to shake down a boat, how to diagnose engine problems, and how to manage a crew better than anyone I know," Buzz replied.

Mr. Crittendon laughed heartily. "Commander, my son and I are practically starting over from scratch, so I'll take anyone you recommend. Get a hold of the chief and tell him he has a job and I can find him a cheap place to live not far from our boat works."

After shaking hands, Buzz smiled. "Sir, we'll make some great boats, you can count on it."

Arriving in San Diego, the happy couple flew cross country to Kennebunkport, making several stops along the way. Buzz wasn't entirely sure what kind of reception he was going to receive, so he attempted to prepare Connie for the worst.

For a short while after landing in Maine, Buzz was thinking they weren't going to get any type of reception at the airport, as not one family member came to greet them. After collecting their luggage, Buzz pointed to a sign that explained where the taxicabs were located. It would be a costly ride to Kennebunkport, but there really were no other options available.

Suddenly, Jolene burst through the crowd, yelling for her brother. As she threw her arms around him, she said. "I'm so sorry, I got caught up in traffic and couldn't find a place to park, then when I—"

Buzz placed his finger over her lips and said, "Shhh, Jolene, it's fine. Now, I would like to introduce you to my wife, Connie."

Turning very red, Jolene hugged Connie and said, "I kind of lose it when I get excited and this trip to the airport scared the heck out of me!"

Connie laughed as she kissed Jolene on the cheek. "Sweetheart, I think we'll get along just fine. You have no idea how excited I can get at times."

With the luggage in the trunk, Jolene handed the keys to the 1941 Cadillac to Buzz. "You can drive home, I've had enough driving for one day."

Turning onto the highway, Buzz looked in the rearview mirror at Jolene. "So, what can we expect from Mom and Dad when we get home? I'm not sure coming home was the right thing to do."

Jolene looked out the window for a moment before clearing her throat. "Your brothers are fine and are looking forward to seeing you. Of course Josh now worships the ground you walk on after seeing firsthand what you were doing out there in the Pacific. Mom was glad to get Josh home of course, but she and Dad are still somewhat upset as to how you dealt with Angeline before you left. They felt you placed a very black mark on the Maddox name within the local society."

After a moment of silence, Jolene continued, "Now there are investigations as to how much Angeline's father really knew about what was going on, and if he financed any part of Swenson's operation. Things in Kennebunkport have not been the same since that story first broke, especially with Josh being involved right up to Swenson's capture. I'm sure it will take a while for Kennebunkport to settle down."

Buzz took a deep breath as he drove the long black Cadillac into the driveway, parking near the front door.

Paul, the long-time butler employed by the family, quickly removed the luggage from the trunk and placed it in their bedroom. After congratulating the couple on their wedding, he turned to Buzz. "Dinner will be served in about an hour if you wish to freshen up. Josh will have his fiancée Anna Marie Borgland here as well. She's always been a very nice girl, and she stuck by Josh the entire time he was missing in action. I'm sure you remember the Borgland's, they owned the lumber mills in Vermont and Connecticut your father did business with for quite a while."

Buzz nodded his head. "Yes, I remember. It sounds like an action-packed dinner coming up. Is Carl seeing any one special that you know of?"

Paul smiled as he patted Buzz on the shoulder. "I don't think there is a girl in Kennebunkport that will ever tie that boy down. He's been going down to Boston whenever he gets a chance, so there may be somebody in the wings we're not aware of yet." After both men laughed, Paul shook Buzz's hand one more time saying, "So glad you came back in one piece, Commander. Nice to have you home for a while."

The dinner went over very well, although Mrs. Maddox made several excuses for not being able to offer her guests certain foods, since rationing was still in effect on certain items.

During dessert, Buzz and Connie explained the job Buzz was offered during their cruise on the Lurline.

Josh looked intently at his brother. "So, you're not coming back to the fishing fleet then. To be honest, I had that feeling the day you left for the Naval Academy. Dad has turned day to day operations over to Carl, and I'm handling the fleet. If you ever change your mind, there will always be a job open for you."

Buzz nodded his head after taking a sip of coffee. "I appreciate that brother. But Connie and I are going to start a new life around Newport, and raise our family there. I think the deal Mr. Crittendon offered us will pay dividends in the future."

After dinner, as the men sipped brandy in the den, Josh looked at his younger brother. "I suppose you heard that Swenson Bellington was killed in jail while he awaited sentencing. After his father was released for lack of evidence, the family moved out of Kennebunkport, and sold off all their business holdings in the state. Rumors are that they moved to Canada."

Buzz nodded his head. "Yes, I did hear that. Say what you want, but Swenson would have swung at the end of a rope one way or the other. He would never have walked free ever again. He was a traitor pure and simple, and I don't care where the family went. Sad to say there's little doubt they made a fortune with their ties to the Axis powers, and I'm certain much of it was hidden away. No matter where the family went, I'm damn sure they're still living the life of luxury and it makes me sick."

After listening to what had been said, Alfred stood up and looked out the window for a moment before turning to face Buzz. "You know, it's only right that you speak with Angeline now that you are home. You owe her that much, son."

Shaking his head, Buzz stood up. "Men died because of her boyfriend, and you'll never convince me the Stevenson family was not aware of it, or made money because of it. I'm sorry, but I owe her nothing, not now, not ever. I made my position clear to her from the start. Once we leave here, I never want to hear anything about her ever again. I'm sorry if all that messed up your plans, father. But a Maddox, Stevenson marriage was never going to happen. Money is a fine thing, but don't put more on it than it can carry, Father."

After purchasing a 1940 Oldsmobile a week later, Buzz and Connie drove down to Annapolis where they found a nice apartment. Buzz was putting in long hours at the academy teaching gunnery tactics, while Connie found a part time nursing job at a local hospital. After six months, Buzz was given his separation papers from the navy. With everything they owned packed in a small rental trailer, Buzz and his now pregnant wife made the short drive to Newport, Rhode Island, where the Crittendon boat works was waiting for their arrival.

After spending a week getting acquainted with the engineers and the Crittendon family, Buzz strolled down to the pier to take a look at PT 711. The boat no longer had the same appearance as the trusty PT boats Buzz was used to. There had been many design changes since the 120 and 303 had rolled off the production line, but it still contained three thirsty Packard engines, and the cockpit was about the same, except for the place for a real functional radar screen. As Buzz walked up onto the foredeck, he heard a familiar voice behind him.

"Well Skipper, are you just looking, or are you thinking about taking her out for a spin? You should never buy a boat like this without a test drive. Permission to come aboard, sir?"

Turning around, Buzz saw Walter Petrovski and Albert Stockey standing on the pier. "Permission granted!" Buzz called out, as he walked over and hugged the two men.

Stockey walked around the boat for several minutes before returning to Buzz. "This gal is really different from the 303, you can hardly tell she's a PT boat." Turning back toward Buzz, Stockey continued. "So, the chief called me and told me about the jobs here. I needed the work so I drove down here with him. I understand there aren't any machine guns or torpedo tubes for me to use on the yachts we're going to build, but Crittendon's son said he could use me in the assembly shop since I had so much experience on a PT boat. I never even gave it much of a thought, I just snatched up the job."

Buzz smiled, feeling very happy having two of his crew members near him again.

After shaking hands once more with Buzz, Stockey said. "The chief is right skipper. If you're interested, you really need to give her a test drive. I can cast off and the chief can handle the engines. What do you say, Skipper? Let's show the Crittendon's how a real PT boat can be handled."

Nodding his head, Buzz yelled, "What the hell are you standing there for?"

With the huge Packard engines warmed up and the exhaust ports open, Stockey and the chief threw the mooring lines on the deck as Buzz idled the 711 away from the pier. After several circles of the Bay, Buzz pointed the bow out into the North Atlantic as he shoved the throttles all the way forward. The bow rode up over the first wave before crashing headlong into the next, sending a shower of water fifteen feet into the air. Spinning the wheel hard to starboard, the boat skipped along the water just like the 303. After making several wide turns at nearly full speed, Buzz pointed the bow straight for the side of a Portuguese oil tanker about a mile away.

With a broad smile on his face, Buzz called out, "Prepare for torpedo attack, man your battle stations!"

For a moment, Buzz could feel the tension in the air, as he watched the ghost crew of the 303 prepare for the attack as the chief called out, "1500 hundred yards and closing, Skipper."

Although there were no tubes to check on, Stockey stood behind the cockpit, holding onto the mast as he quickly responded with a broad smile, "Tubes one and two ready to go, sir!"

Buzz might have been operating the new 711 boat, but the ghosts of the 303 were still alive at sea with him, avenging the flames of Samar.

Buzz held his arm in the air for several seconds before dropping it back down to the wheel, "Fire one and two!"

Over the sound of the roaring engines, Stockey yelled out, "One and two away, Skipper!"

With tears shining in his eye Chief Petrovski called out, "Running true and hot, Skipper!"

As Buzz spun the wheel hard to port, in his mind he could hear the chatter of the machine guns and the twenty-millimeter cannon firing at the ship as the torpedoes slammed into the side of the hapless vessel. As Buzz spun the wheel back to starboard, bringing the boat on a heading back to the boat factory, he could see crew members and officers on the tanker standing by the rail shaking their fists, and most likely calling out insults to him in Portuguese.

Idling up to the pier, several workers from the boat works helped secure the mooring lines as Buzz shut down the new Packard engines, still enjoying the beautiful sound.

Marvin Crittendon came walking down the pier, clapping his hands as he shook his head. I have never seen a PT boat handled with such flare, and I went over to Melville many times during the war. Tomorrow morning we'll begin working on the blue prints for our first new yacht now that we have been released by the War Materials Commission. Mr. Maddox, I want you and the chief in the board room at 9:00am. Mr. Stockey, you can report to my son, he'll begin setting up a new production quay in building seven.

As Buzz began to walk off the boat, he looked over to see Connie standing at the top of the pier. Cautiously, she made her way down to the 711 and looked it over. "This boat is a lot different than the ones you operated. She is very nice, but it doesn't have the tough looking appearance of the 120 or the 303. They'll always be my favorites." After giving Buzz a kiss, she continued. "I came over here to see if you wanted to go out for lunch after your meeting. I'd barely arrived when I saw you leaving with the boat, so I went up to Mr. Crittendon's office and he let me watch you with binoculars. Buzz, you scared me like nothing has ever scared me before. I know you have done things like that, and probably worse hundreds of times during the war, but our baby needs a father not a statistic. You're all done playing war. Being my husband and the father to our baby should give you enough challenges."

Buzz smiled as he took Connie into his arms. "Sweet lady, you are so right, the war is over. But I think the old saying is accurate. You can take Buzz out of a PT boat, but you'll never take the PT boat out of Buzz Maddox."

As Connie and Buzz walked up the pier to get lunch, he looked back over his shoulder at the 711. Smiling, he saw his veteran 303 boat tied up against the pier, as the crew smiled and waved at him. With a tear in his eye, Buzz knew the legacy of the crews and the fighting PT boats the Pacific would forever be solidly etched in the naval history of World War Two.

*Bodies of PT boat crews that were killed in action and were recoverable, were very often buried in temporary cemeteries on the island where they were based. After the war, the bodies were repatriated and buried in the Punch Bowl in Hawaii.

*Torpedoman Dan Greenman lost his lower leg at Tulagi. He returned home to Detroit, Michigan, married his high school sweetheart, and went to work for the Ford Motor Company building aircraft engines. After the war, he continued working for Ford building automobiles. He died in 1999.

*The body of Torpedoman Jeff Anderson was never recovered from Ranongga Island during the rescue of the Beckwith family. He is listed as missing in action.

*20mm gunner Carl Zumwaldt, returned to Louisville, Kentucky where he went to college on the G.I. Bill and became a dentist. He died 2000.

*Motor Machinist Darwin Crowder, went to work building engines for General Motors in Detroit. He died 2003.

*Chief Walter Petrovski took a job with Crittendon boat works in Newport, Rhode Island. He retired in 1980. He spent his retirement years traveling and building model boats. He was united with his daughter and became an active part of her family. The chief died in 1999. His prized .45 pistol was donated by his family to the Wyatt Earp Museum.

*Machine gunner Albert Stockey worked for Crittendon boat works until 1987. After retiring, he taught sailing for many years. He died in 2002.

*Bow Gunner Joe Kowalski Worked in his father's ferry operation the rest of his life. He and his wife Stella moved to Honolulu when they retired. Joe died in 2000

* 20mm gunner Gabe Ridman completed the Naval Officer Candidate school. He served during the Korean war aboard the battleship New Jersey. He retired from the Navy in 1975 after 33 years of service at the rank of Captain. He and his wife had three children. He died from cancer in 1998.

*Machine gunner Dick Wickman stayed in the navy, working his way up to Senior Chief Petty Officer. He and his wife retired in Honolulu, Hawaii after thirty-two years in the navy. He volunteered at the Arizona Memorial site until his death in 1998.

*Captain Nate Reddings retired from the navy after 30 years. He and his wife lived in Seattle, Washington where he worked part time for the Seattle ferry system. He died in 1990.

*Captain Abergast retired from the navy after 31 years, reaching the rank of Rear Admiral. He and his wife lived in Los Angeles, California, where he spent his retirement years writing books, as well as appearing in several minor roles in World War Two Movies. He died in 1975.

*Captain Robesky spent several months in the hospital in Hawaii recuperating from combat fatigue. After being discharged from the navy, he was unable to hold down a steady job. He died in 1953 from acute alcohol poisoning.

*Ensign Will Gruenke's body was never recovered.

*Ensign Stu Kirkman stayed with the navy for thirty years, retiring in 1971 at the rank of captain. He married his high school sweetheart in 1946, and they eventually retired to Mackinaw City, Michigan, where they had grown up. He passed away in 2003.

*Lt. jg John Kennedy became the 35th President of the United States. He was assassinated by Lee Harvey Oswald on Nov. 22, 1963 in Dallas, Texas.

*Japanese Sgt. Kokawa committed suicide in a prisoner of war stockade in the Philippines in 1945.

*Japanese Captain Numura was captured in Manila in 1945. He was repatriated to Tokyo, Japan in 1946. He died in 1968.

*Chaplain Hammond returned to Boston's Basilica of our Lady of Perpetual Help Diocese, where he served for the next eight years. He served in several other Parishes in the diocese over the next twenty years, before once again returning to the Basilica. He retired from the priesthood in 1985. After retiring, he spent several years studying in Rome, while writing a book about his war time experiences. Buzz and Connie visited him many times after returning home, regardless of where Fr. Hammond was serving. Since Connie was already a Catholic, Buzz decided to join the church. Fr. Hammond baptized Buzz, and all three of the couple's children. Chaplain Hammond passed away in 20001.

*Angeline Stevenson left Kennebunkport in 1947 after the investigation into the Stevenson's ties with Swenson Bellington ended. She moved to New York City where she found a job in the fashion industry. In 1949, she married a Congressman from the Manhattan Congressional District. She passed away in 2005, insisting to the end that she knew nothing of her former fiancés dealings with Japan.

*Oscar Bellington, Swenson's father, was found not guilty for any dealings Swenson had with the Japanese and Germans. After selling off all their holdings in Kennebunkport, the family moved to Montreal, Canada, giving up their American citizenship. After Oscar died in 1982, the family found a notebook under his mattress containing the names of fifteen well known wealthy American's, including the Stevenson's, that were involved with supplying war materials to the Japanese. None of them were ever charged.

*Josh Maddox took over full control of the fishing business when his father died. He and Anna Marie had four children and seven grandchildren. Josh passed away in 2002 from cancer.

*Anna Marie (Borgland) Maddox helped Josh with the financial parts of the fishing business throughout their entire marriage. She sold the fishing business in 2003 after Josh passed away. Anna Marie died in Boston in 2012.

*Carl Maddox married Lucinda Craymore from New York City in 1949. After their marriage, Carl left the fishing business to became partners with Lucinda's father in a wholesale car distribution network in New York. Carl and Lucinda had two children and three grandchildren. Carl passed away in 1998.

*Lucinda (Craymore) Maddox worked as an executive secretary in the New York Mayor's office for twenty-five years. After Carl's death, she moved closer to their daughter in Buffalo, New York, where she enjoyed spending time with her grandchildren, and doing volunteer work. Lucinda passed away in 2005.

*Jolene (Maddox) Rentmeir, married Charles M. Rentmeir, an executive with Germany's Lufthansa Airlines in 1951. They had two children and lived all over the world. The couple was killed in a train accident in Spain in 1993.

*Buzz Maddox retired from Crittendon boat works in 1978 after a heart attack. He and Connie had three children and five grandchildren. They loved traveling and sailing on Chesapeake Bay on their twenty-seven-foot sailboat. Buzz died in 1999, several days after returning from a Cross Atlantic cruise on the Queen Elizabeth Two.

*Connie (Russell) Maddox wrote two children's books and loved spoiling her grandchildren. She passed away in 2005.

*Ramos disappeared during an attack on Mindoro Island six weeks after the rescue mission.

*Aquino was captured by the Japanese and tortured to death a month after the rescue mission.

*Ernesto became the leader of Aquino's guerrilla force after he was captured. Ernesto fought to the end of the war and helped liberate Manila. He was decorated for valor by General MacArthur. Ernesto became a popular senator in the new Marcos government. He and his family were murdered by a car bomb in 1958.

Pearl Harbor

The account of the U.S.S. Monaghan sinking the midget Japanese submarine in Pearl Harbor during the Dec. 7 attack is accurate. What remained of the submarine was raised by engineers and buried along the sea wall. During renovations to the docks in 1952, the sub was dug up and reburied farther from the water front.

The story of the body parts hanging from the Banyan trees on Ford Island after the Arizona explosion is factual. It has been published in many books.

The story of the PT boat attack in Blackett Straits where they expended thirty torpedoes without one exploding is factual.

The sinking of John Kennedy's PT 109 by a Japanese destroyer, and after-action reports filed by other PT boat commanders is accurate.

The story of the destruction of the PT boat fleet on the island of Samar in the Philippines is accurate. Most of the boats were in such tough shape, the navy decided it was easier to destroy them in the Pacific than to pay the enormous price to bring them back to the states. Many of the last boats coming out of the construction yards were sold to other navies around the world. As the design and concept of the PT boats served well in World War Two, many of the small naval attack boats used in Vietnam were based on the design and armament requirements of the original PT fleet.

DIAGRAMS AND MAPS

DECK LAYOUT ELCO 80 FOOT FOOT PT BOAT

1 TORPEDO TUBES (4)
2 DUAL .50 CALIBER MACHINE GUNS (2)
3 .20MM CANNON
4 BOW .50 CALIBER MACHINE GUN
5 AMMO READY BOX
6 SMOKE GENERATOR
7 LIFE RAFT
8 HATCH TO FOREPEAK
9 HATCH TO GALLEY
10 HATCH TO DAYROOM
11 RADIO MAST
12 SPOT LIGHT
13 ANTENNA
14 COCK PIT
15 STAIRS TO RADIO/CHART ROOM
16 DAYROOM CANOPY
17 CHART HOUSE
18 WINDSHIELD
19 .20MM AMMO READY BOXES
20 ENGINE ROOM HATCH
21 LAZARETTE HATCH
22 SAMPSON POST

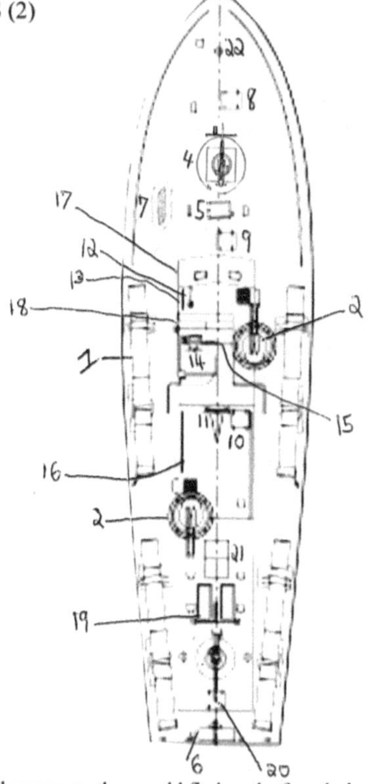

Skippers of PT Boats were allowed place any usable weapons they could find on the fore deck. Most often it was a .50 caliber machine gun as this boat is configured. Often times .20mm cannons such as the aft gun, or .37mm anti-tank guns were creatively installed as did John Kennedy on PT-109. The problem with the .37mm was that it could not be easily swiveled if at all.

A. Water tight doors.
B. Ladders to below decks.
1 Forepeak, rope locker, anchor.
2 Crew's head.
3 Storage.
4 Crew's quarters.
5 Exec. Officer.
6 Galley.
7 Ward Room.
8 Officer's head.
9 Fresh water (200gals.)
10 Radio/radar equip.
11 Desk.
12 Captain.
13 Ammo, weapons locker.
14 Fuel tanks (3000 gals.)
15 Heat exchanger.
16 Vee drive.
17 Auxiliary generator.
18 Engines Three (1250 h.p. Each)
19 Seat for engineer.
20 Lazarette.
21 Work bench.
22 Mufflers.

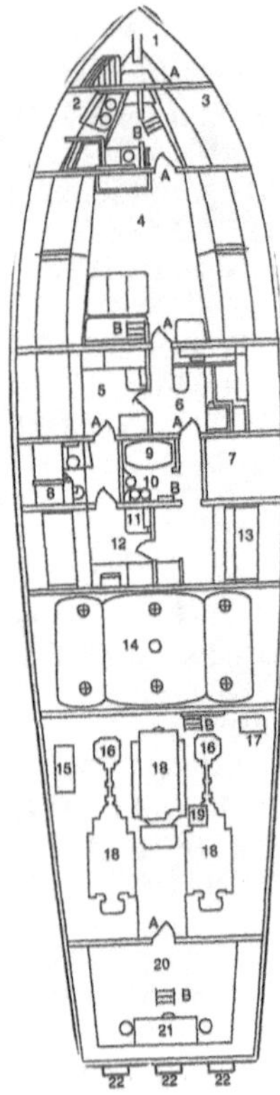

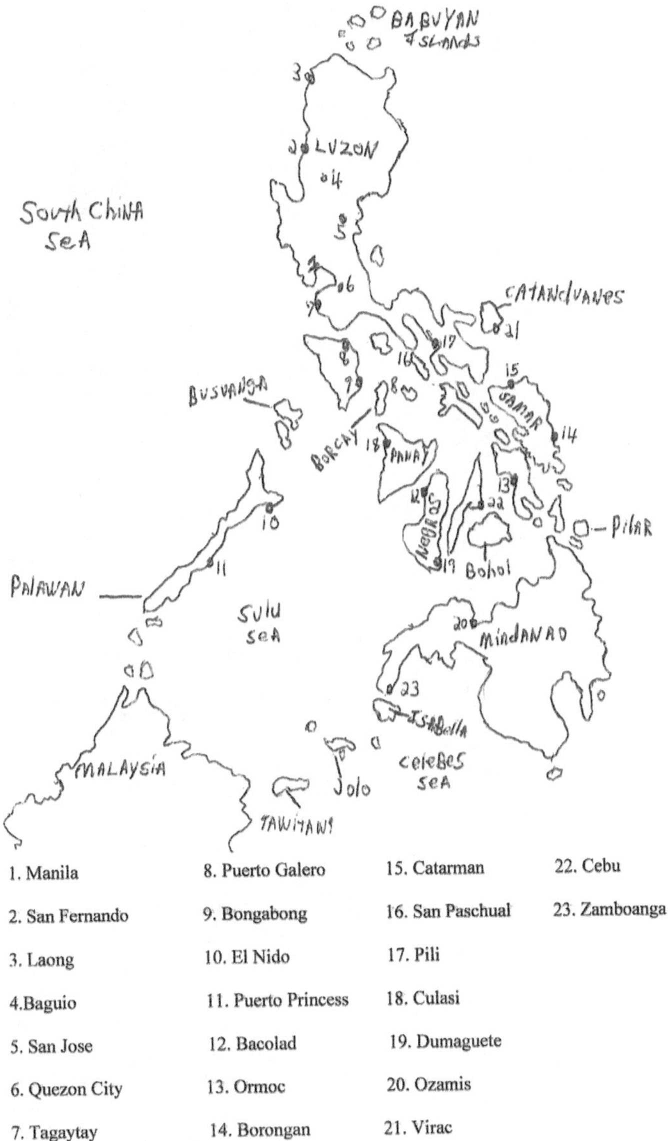

1. Manila	8. Puerto Galero	15. Catarman	22. Cebu
2. San Fernando	9. Bongabong	16. San Paschual	23. Zamboanga
3. Laong	10. El Nido	17. Pili	
4. Baguio	11. Puerto Princess	18. Culasi	
5. San Jose	12. Bacolad	19. Dumaguete	
6. Quezon City	13. Ormoc	20. Ozamis	
7. Tagaytay	14. Borongan	21. Virac	

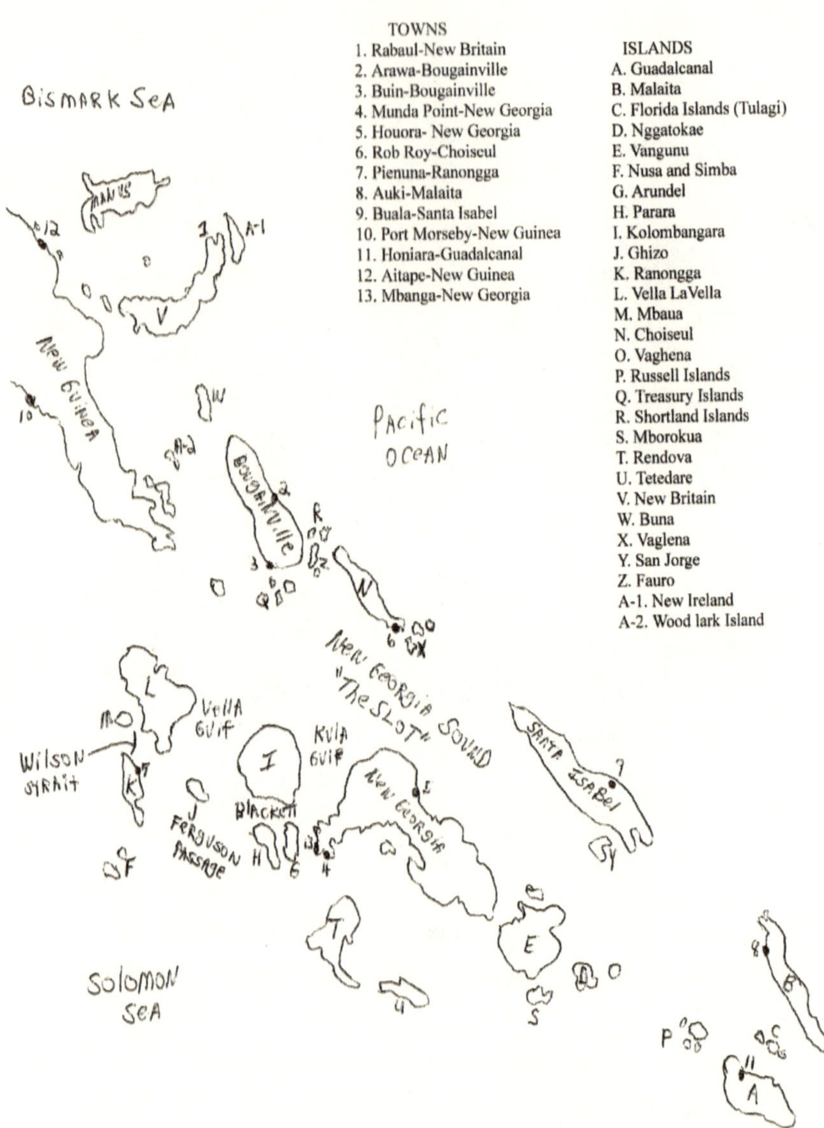

TOWNS
1. Rabaul-New Britain
2. Arawa-Bougainville
3. Buin-Bougainville
4. Munda Point-New Georgia
5. Houora- New Georgia
6. Rob Roy-Choiseul
7. Pienuna-Ranongga
8. Auki-Malaita
9. Buala-Santa Isabel
10. Port Morseby-New Guinea
11. Honiara-Guadalcanal
12. Aitape-New Guinea
13. Mbanga-New Georgia

ISLANDS
A. Guadalcanal
B. Malaita
C. Florida Islands (Tulagi)
D. Nggatokae
E. Vangunu
F. Nusa and Simba
G. Arundel
H. Parara
I. Kolombangara
J. Ghizo
K. Ranongga
L. Vella LaVella
M. Mbaua
N. Choiseul
O. Vaghena
P. Russell Islands
Q. Treasury Islands
R. Shortland Islands
S. Mborokua
T. Rendova
U. Tetedare
V. New Britain
W. Buna
X. Vaglena
Y. San Jorge
Z. Fauro
A-1. New Ireland
A-2. Wood lark Island